SIST

D0562768

Also by Charlotte Watson Sherman

One Dark Body
Killing Color

SISTERFIRE

BLACK WOMANIST FICTION AND POETRY

Edited by

Charlotte Watson Sherman

▲▲▲▲▲▲▲▲▲

HarperPerennial

A Division of HarperCollinsPublishers

HarperCollins books may be purchased for educational, business, or sales promotional use. For information please write: Special Markets Department, HarperCollins Publishers, Inc., 10 East 53rd Street, New York, NY 10022.

FIRST EDITION

Designed by Alma Hochhauser Orenstein

Library of Congress Cataloging-in-Publication Data

Sisterfire : Black womanist fiction and poetry / edited by Charlotte Watson
    Sherman.
        p.   cm.
    Includes index.
    ISBN 0-06-055351-0 (cloth)—ISBN 0-06-095018-8 (pbk.)
    1. American literature—Afro-American authors. 2. Feminism—United
States—Literary collections. 3. Afro-American women—Literary collections. 4. American literature—Women authors. 5. American literature—
20th century. I. Sherman, Charlotte Watson, 1958–   .
PS508.N3S54   1994
810.8'09287'08996073—dc20   94-795

94 95 96 97 98 RRD(H) 10 9 8 7 6 5 4 3 2
94 95 96 97 98 RRD(H) 10 9 8 7 6 5 4 3 2   (pbk.)

95262

For my mother, Dorothy Ray Glass, and the line running from her, and into my daughters, Aisha and Zahida

NYENGA YOBE MULANDA

Kaonde proverb that means "A sister is a friend."

Contents

PART THREE
Prelude to an Endnote: The Body's Health

PART FOUR
An Anointing: Sisterfriends

PART FIVE
Is It True What They Say About Colored Pussy?: Sex

PART SIX
Eclipse: Black Women in Love with Men

PART SEVEN
Visitations: Aging

Acknowledgments

I would gratefully like to acknowledge the tireless efforts of my editor, Stephanie Gunning, whose sharp eye helped shape a wild idea into a concrete reality. Special thanks also to my agent Beth Vesel.

I'd also like to thank the women who offered words of encouragement along the way—Marsha Leslie, Marilyn Fullen-Collins, Brenda Peterson, Raina Shield, Colleen McElroy—and especially my sisterfriends Julia Boyd, Barbara Henderson, Carletta Wilson, Faith Davis, Jody Kim, Lenore Norgaard, and JoAnn Moton who offer continuous support no matter what I may dream up.

Finally, I would like to thank the women of Calyx Books and Seal Press for leading me to several of the *Sisterfire* contributors, and to acknowledge the multitalented writers who shared their work and sent ongoing notes of encouragement.

Introduction

Fire. Smoke. Ashes. The bones of a city laid bare. Black bodies twisting in flames of rage.

Shortly after the Rodney King uprising, I woke from a dream with a voice telling me to "do the anthology." I never questioned that voice or the need for an anthology like this one. I had been waiting to hold it in my hands for years.

I waited. And waited. Still no anthology such as this. Not since *Home Girls: A Black Feminist Anthology* (Kitchen Table: Women of Color Press), edited by Barbara Smith, 1983. Ten years is a long time to wait to hear how African-American women are interpreting contemporary events through their fiction and poetry, to see what Black women are writing about the experience of being Black and female in the nineties.

I live to read the works of other Black women writers. Once, at a privileged midwestern college, an older European-American woman asked me why the writing of African-American women touched her in such deep and intimate ways, ways in which the work of other writers did not.

I could not answer for her, but I nodded my head in agreement. I knew what she meant.

The testimony of African-American women writers touches me in my "inside place and call[s] my name," to paraphrase Toni Morrison. This sense of affirmation of our most intimate truths, our joys and sorrows, our ways of knowing, is a source of inner strength I draw on. This strength allows me to continue on with the challenges of my little life.

The revelations of "this too shall pass" and "everything's gonna be alright" found in the words of African-American women writers allows us all to continue on, the "brave, bruised" women that we are. Realizing that larger, but no less human, footsteps have gone this way before, I call on their words of guidance, illumination, and transformation to sustain me on my journey through life. I know I am not alone.

A lot has happened since 1983. Over 50 percent of the women with AIDS in the United States today are Black and Hispanic. The crack epidemic and Black on Black crime has hit our community with a type of devastation not experienced since slavery. One in eight women will develop breast cancer. Some say the percentages are higher for lesbians. We have already lost Pat Parker, Audre Lorde, and countless unnamed others. June Jordan is now fighting this deadly disease.

Battering, rape, and incest have not been eliminated; the struggle against the rights of women to control their bodies intensifies.

The divisions within the African-American community over the Anita Hill controversy and the Mike Tyson rape trial illuminate the ongoing need for African-American women to continue to fight against sexist oppression in all its forms. No matter the color of the oppressor.

We continue to fight "the good fight" against racism where we find it and have at last reached a point in history where Black lesbians and straight women recognize the similarities they share in terms of their independence, self-reliance, and unwillingness to have their lives revolve around men.

As we reach the gate of the twenty-first century, we know in the deepest place inside us that we have no room for hatred and fear of difference. We know we must leave anything that will keep us entrenched inside the insanity of the twentieth century behind.

Our community is being devastated on many levels; we have lost too many people to AIDS and crack and drive-by shootings and domestic violence and all manner of desolation. Our children look at us with odd expressions on their faces, their entire world now, too often a sphere of despair.

And yet. And yet. There is always hope, as the old folks say, though now they say it behind quadruple-locked doors and barred windows, many of them frightened of this new generation.

Combined with the hope of the old folks is the faith that we as Black women have in ourselves, our sense of humor that cushions us as we face the many challenges of life, the new knowledge about loving and taking care of ourselves that we add to the lessons of survival our mothers taught us, and the comforting, welcoming arms of our sisterfriends.

Nothing will allow us to give up the struggle. Though we may mourn, we also rejoice as we learn to heal our wounds. Though the reality of AIDS causes us to change the way we love, we still know how to love ourselves and our lovers well, as we recognize our right to experience the ecstasy of good safe sex alone or with a partner. We continue to revel in our sensuality and our glorious Black bodies.

With the wisdom of age, our vulnerability, sassiness, and the courage we possess, whether choosing life or learning to face death, we are able to find our way out of depression to fight injustice against all people, again, another day.

As we face these challenges, we call upon the strength of the women we have come from and add it to the self-confidence and resilience we need as warrior women in the twenty-first century.

We know we can do no less than our mothers to raise children who love themselves and create solutions for the problems of the coming generations.

We all know we have to leave tracks. A way for the ones coming after us to make it through the maze of this world.

Where do African-American women fit in this landscape of changing American culture? Where do we go from here?

African-American women remain marginalized and invisible, "backdrops on the landscape of American society." Though we are affected at disproportionate rates by every ill impacting contemporary society—AIDS, teenage pregnancy, domestic violence, drugs, and so on—our experiences continue to be marginalized, our womanhood devalued.

There is a belief that you can change your present circumstances if your history is told, if your story is given recognition and legitimacy. In the past, when access to psychiatrists and psychotherapists was limited for communities of color, people were able to heal each other by talking about the things that hurt them, concerned them, and brought joy into their lives.

The words of these griots-historians-shamans-seers—wise women encompass the Black female experience from a womanist perspective. They speak to the lives of contemporary Black women, raise our voices, and help make us visible.

I hope this anthology duplicates the healing energies of the traditional African women's hut, where women gathered around the fire to share their joy and sorrow, to affirm their lives, and plan for their futures.

The ashes we rise from. Our words, the flame. With our sisters we make fire, we dance in the glow.

Sisterfire.

I am glad I did not think about how difficult the process of compiling this collection was going to be before I decided to do it.

I wanted to include everyone.

But I faced the reality of living in a world with limits.

It was the content of the submissions received that determined the structure of the anthology. I had several contemporary issues I felt needed to be addressed in poetry or fiction, otherwise, whatever the sisterwriters thought to be the issues of the day is represented.

As Bernice Reagon, of the a cappella singing group, Sweet Honey in the Rock, said in describing the tradition of congregational singing, "Singers create as they go along. Although a leader introduces the song, there is no solo tradition. Once the song is raised, the group joins and the creation becomes collaborative. You must be open to what will happen to the song and you in performance."

Each individual voice added to the collective song of this anthology. I have included a range of styles and voices, a myriad of new voices many of us have not heard from before, linear narrative as well as abstract, fragmental, nonlinear narrative.

Audre Lorde, in explaining that poetry is not a luxury for women, stated, "As we come more into touch with our own ancient, noneuropean consciousness of living as a situation to be experienced and interacted with (as opposed to viewing living as a problem to be solved), we learn more and more to cherish our feelings, and to respect those hidden sources of our power from where true knowledge and, therefore, lasting action comes."

Our poetry is the naming of our feelings, our experiences. According to bell hooks, "Literary work captures life's and sexuality's complexities in the subtle, yet piercing ways, that theory never can."

I hope these stories and poems, these tracks, these singular and yet collective voices, resonate within your deepest darkest places for years to come.

chant to the ancestors . . .
for ida and zora

karsonya e. wise

be still my ancestors
and rest
for in me
your spirit
shall be revived

my ancestors rest
and be still
your spirit in me
shall be revived

revived in me
your spirit shall be
so rest
my ancestors

in me
shall your spirit
be revived
so dear sweet ancestors
rest

revive,
my ancestors,
your spirit
in me
and rest

rest my ancestors
and know
that in me
your spirit
shall be revived

be still
my restless ancestors
for in me
through me
in spite of me
your spirit
will be revived

▼▼▼▼▼▼▼▼

PART ONE

Becoming Fluent: Mothers, Daughters, and Other Family

Once, while sitting on a pew in a storefront church in Harlem, I listened to a recovering crack addict sing, "Sometimes I feel like a motherless child." As I listened to the woman's pure, earnest voice, tears pooled in my eyes. I was not motherless, but I was in a large city and felt terribly alone. As I sat listening to the song and silently weeping, I thought about the complex relationships we have with our mothers, the push-pull nature of that love.

We have been told that Black mothers love their sons and raise their daughters, with the unspoken insinuation being that our mothers do not love us. But the reality is that many of us spend a good portion of our lives trying to learn how to live as independent-spirited grown women in spite of struggling with the fierce controlling love of our mothers.

If we are lucky, our mothers gave us the tools that allow us to function as emotionally healthy and whole women in the world. Or, perhaps, we gained our living skills and strengths from a beloved grandmother, sister, or other relative. In any event, as we become mothers, we pass the lessons we learned about living as an African-American in this world on to our children, and oftentimes, in loving our own daughters, we learn to love ourselves.

After Reading *Mickey in the Night Kitchen*
for the Third Time Before Bed

RITA DOVE

I'm in the milk and the milk's in me! . . . I'm Mickey!

My daughter spreads her legs
to find her vagina:
hairless, this mistaken
bit of nomenclature
is what a stranger cannot touch
without her yelling. She demands
to see mine and momentarily
we're a lopsided star
among the spilled toys,
my prodigious scallops
exposed to her neat cameo.

And yet the same glazed
tunnel, layered sequences.
She is three; that makes this
innocent. *We're pink!*
she shrieks, and bounds off.

Every month she wants
to know where it hurts
and what the wrinkled string means
between my legs. *This is good blood*
I say, but that's wrong, too.
How to tell her that it's what makes us—
black mother, cream child.
That we're in the pink
and the pink's in us.

[1989]

Becoming Fluent

LILLIEN WALLER

for Cathy Cohen

one

When we are new,
the world comes to us
in syllables:

Mama says, in words sliced
small enough to swallow,
Eat every thing on your plate.

This is good advice
for the young and hungry, suckling
a strong mother, afraid
of big words and the world.
This is protection.

two

It's in the frame,
what the bones tell us,
written in the body:
the way you hold things, cupped
and hunger to know, to tell,
remember.

three

Gather your stories like earth—
salt, sweet—
return to them, return.
Learn to grow old, retrace

a visceral memory,
feed yourself.

Daughter says, in words sliced
small enough to swallow,
Eat every thing on your plate.

Mama

MARILYN FULLEN-COLLINS

"Mama, hi." "Come in, Child, I've been waiting for you." She stands on the old wooden landing that leads to the tattered screen door. She urges me to watch my step saying, "Mr. Jackson keep sayin' he gonna fix them steps. Shoot, he been saying that since Methuselah was a boy." She grins, big and safe. I reach for the splintered banister, lose my footing and stumble into Mama's arms. Powerful, henna-colored arms that held me even before my mother did. My eyes catch the never changing entirety of her life. Who my grandmother is is drawn in the vitality of her living room.

A makeshift altar rests near the entrance to her kitchen. She uses her best Christmas linen as altar cloths. White, starched creases that are ironed so sharp they could make you bleed. A three-foot-tall statue of Jesus stands guard over her apartment and her life. His sacred heart is swallowed by flames, His feet balance on top of a weary world. She keeps a white votive candle steadily burning in perpetual adoration of her Savior. A scarred, silver crucifix rests nearby, along with a copy of this month's *Catholic Digest,* her well-used indigo rosary is nestled in a saffron receptacle that contains Pope-blessed holy water, a dun-colored palm from last Palm Sunday, and a tiny splinter of wood said to be from the cross on Calvary. On the opposite wall is a grand portrait of Marcus Garvey in full military complement. Underneath, she keeps a small photo of the Black Star Shipping Lines masthead as a reminder of her desire to go home to Africa.

Heading for the kitchen, my hand brushes against the back of her maroon horsehair sofa. I always thought I could fly when I jumped on it. Mama used to encourage me to jump for the stars. She always believed I'd make it. Even when I didn't. Pushing past the weighty kitchen door I am bombarded with a thousand smells coming from her old O'Keefe and Merritt stove.

"Sit down, Girl, your dinner be ready soon enough." I do as I'm told, and she places a cup of coffee before me strong with cinnamon and chicory. Grabbing a cup for herself she settles down in the chair facing me. "You know, Honey, we never had much, always a struggle just to keep food on the table." She laughs, deep in her throat, her intonations as sensual and sexy as a teenager's. "Your granddaddy always say I was too young and fine when he met me. Guess I was too, but times change and people change. Life puts lines in your face. Plugs up your ears, sometimes makes you feel like you all used up."

She rises from the table, tying her favorite apron around her abundant waist, the one she embroidered with the farmer's wife scattering grain to the chickens. She lifts the silver top off the big pot and steam rises up to blush her well-lived face. The hairs tucked into her bun break free and crinkle around her forehead and ears. She talks as she stirs teeny tabasco peppers in with the ham hocks and collards. "Yes, Child, people say, menfolks specially, that a woman's no good after twenty-five. Don't you believe it! Hell, I done my best living after fifty! Outlived your granddaddy didn't I?" She snickers as she dices onions, celery and baby bay shrimp that will make up her secret potato salad recipe. Mama brushes a thatch of gray hair out of her way with the back of her wrist. "Good God Almighty, old ain't no disease. It's proof you alive! I get so made when I go into the Safeway and see these women buyin' hair dye." She measures her eyes on mine until I squirm in my seat. "Yes, I know you been thinkin' on buying some of that mess too cause you got a couple of strands of white hair. Shoot, Girl, if you didn't have that how you gonna prove you been alive? Each one of them hairs signifies somethin' important!"

After rinsing the shrimp smell from her hands she reaches for my hair. Gently she peels a strand away from the rest and pulls my head under the table lamp. "Now, lookee here. I can tell you when you got each one of these."

I look up. "Mama, you good, I'll admit, but not even you can tell me where I got this mess of gray on my head."

Her leathery hand chucks me easily under my chin. Cloudless eyes stare me down. "Girl, why I always got to prove you wrong, uh?" She laughs that laugh again and continues pulling threads of hair from my head. "You got this one when that boy, Tyrone Hicks, done stood you up for the St. Mary's prom. This one over here you got when your cat Bubba got runned over by a car on New Year's Eve. Sure was a sour year too. Now lookee here, see this cluster right here? All of it come up soon after you had that abortion." Tears bite my eyes. She sees them.

Rocking me against that perfect breast, she says, "Oh Babygirl, I ain't namin' off no sin. It just be life that's all. Ain't nothin' happened to you, ain't happened to most women whether they care to admit it or not. You strong, Babygirl. You a woman. You gotta be."

That was eleven years ago. Yesterday we buried my Mama. Just the way she wanted too. Had the service over at Our Lady of Perpetual Sorrows, right there on Central Avenue. The church was packed with flowers, and resting at the foot of her bronze casket was the grandest spray of lavender African violets this town has ever seen. And poised against the pulpit was the picture of Marcus Garvey in full military complement. The Reverend Father Julian Mansfield pontificated about Bertha Lee's life as a living saint. Talked about all the good she'd done, the homeless she'd housed, the starving she'd fed, the forgotten children she'd loved. The congregation "uhhed" and "amenned" her right into heaven. There I sat, alone in the front pew, feeling like a motherless child until I looked up at the massive mahogany cross spotlighted in the sanctuary, and I saw her smile. Smile and nod and whisper, "Remember, Grand Babygirl, you strong, you a woman, you gotta be." And I finally under- stood.

Daughters

JACKIE WARREN-MOORE

for Andrea

Red tipped triangle of the Ancestors.

I find myself there. Waiting and laughing. Holding hands
with my daughter. Loving her as I never loved myself.
Little girl laughter in threes.
Old self,
New self,
Daughter.

We are three.
We are one.
Splashing water that falls in triangles against soft brown
skin.
Shadows form as I prepare to leave.
I am reluctant to leave them there.
We join hands—old self, new self, daughter.
Skipping home.

Water Bears No Scars

AKUA LEZLI HOPE

The poor mother gave her daughter a best to Sunday in
The poor mother gave her daughter rags to glad in
The poor mother gave her daughter thought for food

The poor mother gave her daughter a can of tuna fish and said
necessity is my name, out of one thing make many

The poor mother showed her daughter the difference between
    cotton and polyester
    sweet and sour
    cheap and inexpensive
    casual and sloppy
    cutting on the bias and the crooked

The poor mother gave her daughter special occasions
The poor mother gave her daughter spankings
The poor mother gave her daughter museums
The poor mother gave her daughter duty and discipline
The poor mother gave her daughter libraries
The poor mother gave her daughter songs
The poor mother gave her daughter neat hair
The poor mother gave her daughter a guitar
The poor mother gave her daughter a way to flow
The poor mother told her daughter water bears no scars

A Thin Neck to Snap

KIM JENICE DILLON

I sat on the edge of my sister's bed and watched her packing clothes in such a hurry that she wasn't even folding them. Andrie was just jamming them into a Samsonite duffel bag. I couldn't believe she was gonna do it, but I was glad she was leaving. I'd offered to help her pack, but she just rolled her eyes at me. She hadn't said much, ignoring me as usual, but at least she hadn't told me to get off her bed or get out the room.

My sister couldn't be doing anything better for me than to leave like she was. She'd been messing up my life ever since she'd started living with us. I tried not to grin too hard at her in case she figured out how happy I was to see her go. She might stay out of sheer meanness.

"Kendra, get me my jewelry out the bathroom." My sister's request was an order, as usual, but I didn't mind this time.

"Sure." I ran out of our room and couldn't help but be excited at the prospect of it being only mine again.

As I was getting her blue Oriental cloth jewelry box, I opened it and looked closely at what was usually off limits. Andrie was always telling me not to touch her jewelry, which consisted of various brightly colored plastic hoops, turquoise rings, and pukka shell necklaces that her boyfriend had brought back from Hawaii on his last tour of duty. I wondered what made her think I would want this junk anyway. I was just getting ready to close the box and bring it to Andrie when I noticed a pair of familiar earrings. Before I could think about it, I was running back to our room with only them in my hand.

"Why are *my* earrings with *your* jewelry? You trying to steal 'em?" As I yelled at her, I held out my hand with the tiny pearl earrings in the palm. I stared at her with my eyes wide, waiting for her to lie as usual.

"What you talking about? Them's my earrings. Linda said they was mine." She looked at me with her what-you-gonna-do-about-it-anyway? look, and she snatched them from my hands.

"Mom would never give you my birthday present, Andrie." But my retort was unsure, and I didn't attempt to get them back from her.

Andrie just smiled at me and said, "Look. You know you can get another pair. You always be getting everything, anyway. Don't be a baby about some earrings you know your parents will replace."

All I could say was "Well, I'm telling." I tried to give her a defiant look, but she wasn't even looking at me nomore—she'd gone back to ignoring me. I sat back on her bed and, not to be defeated, I tried to burn a hole into the back of her nappy head with a hot stare. She refused to let Mom press her hair, and she never oiled it, so I thought for sure if I allowed all the heat inside of me to pour out at her through my evil eye look, her dry hair would ignite. But it didn't, and I gave up trying cause I was getting a headache.

Andrie stuffed as much as she was gonna into her worn suitcase and struggled to close it. After she sat on it and managed to get it shut, she set it near the door next to her duffel bag. Then she finished putting clothes into the same trunk she'd brought all of her things in when she'd first arrived to live with the family.

When she finally looked up at me, she had a smirk on her face. She always smirked at me when she thought she'd just gotten to me.

"Well, I hardly think your mother really got much to say to me now. Especially about no earrings. Anyway, I'll be gone before she get home. Terrence gonna be here any minute now."

Hearing this cheered me up, and I momentarily forgot about the earrings.

"Where you two going?" We'd never shared much in the ways sisters will, but today it seemed okay to ask about her plans. Personally, I felt almost too excited to be sitting there calmly asking her questions, but I knew how quickly she could clam up. She'd been that way ever since I'd met her.

"I don't know, but we never coming back here." She said the last words with an anger I didn't understand, but I couldn't help feeling relieved at her promise not to return.

I didn't hate Andrie, but she'd been hard to get along with ever since she'd arrived here from living with Aunt Addie. My parents told me that she'd wanted to stay in New Orleans when we moved to California five years earlier, even though they had asked her to come with us. But for some reason, unfortunately, she'd changed her mind about coming here. So, all of the sudden I had a sister, and I had to share my room and bathroom with her. Nobody explained why she came, and I figured she was adopted like me, even though I used to think she was my cousin or something cause I'd seen her at family gatherings when we lived in New Orleans. My parents told me and my brother Michael that she was family, and that was that. But she always got treated different, and I didn't think it was fair, though I wasn't going to say nothing to my dad or my mom about the fact that she never got yelled at for doing stuff that I would certainly be punished for doing. I mean, if I left my clothes lying around like she did or didn't make my bed every day with them hospital bed corners, I'd get my butt whipped. But my father always let her alone, never coming in to inspect any chore she did. She always seemed nervous around my dad, but I didn't think it was because she was afraid he'd yell at her or take the strap to her butt. He never hit her. Andrie and Pop, as she called him, never seemed to talk really, and my mother only suggested to her once in a while that she really oughta learn how to be a better housekeeper if she was ever gonna get married.

"Y'all getting married? Or you just gonna shack up like Mom thinks you are?" The question popped out of my mouth, and I could hardly wait for her answer. I really hoped she would tell me something kind of nasty, like they were gonna have sex out of wedlock.

"Not that it's your business, but we getting married as soon as possible. Terrence'll have orders to leave San Diego soon, and I'm going with him."

She got a real goo-goo look on her face. I never could understand why she loved that boy so much. Terrence Black sure wasn't fine or anything. He was real big, taller than my father, who's over six feet, and he didn't have a neck. Seriously, he had no neck. His small, round head looked like it grew right out of his broad shoulders. He was supposed to play football at some college, but for some reason joined the Army instead. My parents couldn't stand him cause he was twenty-five, and they said he was a "dufus boy." My dad said he wasn't wrapped too tight, and that they wouldn't have taken him in the Navy. I remember one time, Terrence locked himself up in the bathroom and threatened to kill himself if Andrie didn't stay being his girlfriend. My mother told my sister then that she should lose that boy quick, but he was still around. My parents never spoke to him when he came around the house, so my sister was always sneaking out to see him. Sometimes I covered for her, but not cause I was trying to help keep her out of trouble. No, actually, I got a little excited thinking that somebody was pulling something over on my mom. She thought she knew everything about everyone in this house. Sometimes she would tell me what I was thinking, whether or not she was right. So, if my sister could lead a secret life now, maybe one day I'd be able to do it too, if I watched how she did it. It wouldn't do me no good to get her busted and have my mother find out our sneaky ways before I could try them out.

When it looked like Andrie was ready to leave the room, I stood in front of her. I pursed my lips out and put my hand out for hers and said in my best rich white folks way, "Well, my dear, I hope you'll be happy, and perhaps I'll see you at the holidays." I tried to keep the glee from coming out in my voice, but my sister picked up on it.

"Well, you get to be Princess again. With Michael in the service now and me married, you'll be the only child." She batted her lashes for effect. I just ignored her. Her words didn't affect me cause I knew she was leaving. I just batted my eyes back at her in response and smiled.

"You better hurry, or Mom'll be here before you can get away." I hoped I didn't sound too pushy.

"I'm waiting on Terrence," she said with importance.

The two of us looked at each other and then away. We didn't have much to say. As I glanced around the room, trying to avoid looking at my sister, I heard a car pull up in the driveway. She threw a quick half smile at me and strained to pick up the trunk. It appeared to be very heavy, but she declined my offer to help her with it.

"Bring my suitcase if it ain't too much for you." She somehow managed to make it sound like a challenge. One she knew I'd rise to.

I got up and tried not to look as if I were struggling with it, even though the bag was trying to pull me to the ground. I followed her into the hallway, determined not to let the suitcase slow me down. I wanted very much to see the couple leaving. I even tried to practice looking a little remorseful when I'd wave a final goodbye to my sister. By the time we got into the living room, Terrence was already knocking on the door.

When Andrie opened the door, I felt a little let down at their ordinariness. I don't know exactly what I thought would happen, but I guess I'd sort of thought a bit romantically about their running away together. I imagined them kissing passionately, forgetting about everyone except each other. But once again, my sister managed to cheat me out of one of my imagined scenarios by replacing it with her dull reality. My scenario of the two faded even further when they began to speak.

"So, you ready to go?" The words were uttered in the same voice Terrence used whenever he picked her up for a show or something.

My sister's "I got another bag in the back room" only solidified the event as average, and I couldn't wait to help them load up the car and see them go. I felt I must be imagining the tension that accompanied us to the black Trans Am, where Terrence put Andrie's belongings into the trunk. My sister didn't seem as excited about running off with her lover as I'd assumed she would be. I passed it off to my presence. Maybe they simply weren't mushy in front of other people.

Perhaps it was the tension which kept us so engrossed in our loading that we never noticed my mother, who managed to surprise us by appearing quite suddenly, home a little earlier than usual from work.

"What you think you doing?" she snapped, looking straight at my sister. She glanced quickly from Andrie to Terrence, and I knew she couldn't help but notice all of Andrie's bags in the back of the car. She fixed an even stare on my sister's face that suggested backing down was out of the question.

"I'm leaving, Linda. I'm sure the news makes you happy." Andrie's voice didn't sound as bold as her words, but she did keep her eyes steady with my mother's, refusing to drop hers first.

"You what?" My mother looked away first, but only to give Terrence an if-looks-could-kill glance. He refused to meet her obvious challenge and got into the car to seek shelter from whatever storm was about to tear through the driveway.

"Kendra, get your butt in the house," my mother snapped at me.

"What'd I do? Why you mad at me?" I couldn't believe she was sending me away. I wasn't the wrongdoer in this drama.

When my mother looked at me as if she'd take her handbag to my head at any minute, I ran into the house. Instead of going to my room, however, I ran to my brother Michael's old room, which had a good viewing and hearing advantage cause it was in the front part of the house where I could see the driveway pretty good. Unfortunately, my mother must have, once again, guessed my intentions. She spoke in such low tones that I couldn't hear a thing, no matter how close I got to sticking my ear through the screen on the window. I stared really hard at my sister and mother arguing in the driveway, thinking I could read lips or something, but it wasn't happening. The only thing I was certain of was that my mom was real pissed. Her big eyes bugged out even harder than usual, and her dark full lips were pursed together very tight while she was listening to whatever Andrie was saying. When she spoke to Andrie, she spoke with her lips still pressed together all tight, and I knew she was tearing her up cause Andrie was blinking her eyes quickly while she spoke. At least, I thought, if the neighbors were lookie-looking, they wouldn't be able to hear any nasty words being said. Although, if my mother hit my sister, Old Man Doberman next door would be the first to call the police, talking about gang violence or something. I was surprised his stupid dogs weren't barking their heads off with so many black people out in the open.

When my sister abruptly turned away from my mother to get into the car, my mother's right hand shot out quickly and grabbed Andrie by the hair. Oh no, I thought, getting excited. Here we go. Doberman's probably calling the police right now! I was fascinated at the possible drama that could result if the police came to smooth out some domestic violence in this usually boring neighborhood. But my fantasy didn't even get as far as a scream of pain, for my mother let go of my sister's hair almost as quickly as she'd snatched it. She said something to my sister while she was still up in her face. Finally, she dismissed my sister with a quick wave of her hand which came close to slapping her. My mother didn't hang around to wave goodbye or nothing as my sister closed the car trunk and got into the car. Terrence started the engine and tore out the driveway like he couldn't get away fast enough. When my mother headed for the front door, she took the time to stoop down and grab the afternoon paper off the front lawn. If I'd just arrived to the window at that moment, I would've thought her coming into the house was just the routine return from work. I was dying to know what had passed between them.

I quickly went into my room, as though I'd been there the whole time, instead of trying to eavesdrop. I waited a few minutes for my mother to make it into the house and into her bedroom. She always went straight there when she came home to make her daily visit to her own private bathroom. My mother didn't trust the cleanliness of those people she worked with at the Navy PX and refused to use the workers' washroom. After a few minutes, I heard the toilet flush, and I knew it would be all right if I went in. Maybe she would tell me about what had passed between her and my sister.

Coming into my parents' bedroom, I said, "Mom, you finished?" When I didn't get a response, I moved all the way into the room and sat on the big king-sized bed. The pale blue sateen cover always made me slide down, and I tried not to let it do so this time. My father hated messed up beds, and sometimes my mother would forget to smooth out the covers after I was on the bed, and he'd be yelling about how the house wasn't in order or something. My mother never told on me, though, so he always thought she hadn't made the bed good enough and yelled at her. But I didn't want my mother to get annoyed with me and then not tell me what happened, so I was careful. My mother still hadn't come out the bathroom, so I looked in the mirror squares which covered my parents' closet doors. It was always kind of fun to move my head around because each square changed the shape of my face. Some squares made me look like I had a really long, thin face. I liked these because my eyes didn't seem as squinted in the reflection. I tried to avoid those squares which made my face look rounder and my eyes more slanted. I thought about how funny it was that most people just thought I was my father's child from another marriage. But when I was with my mother only, people seemed to act funny at her introducing me as her daughter. It was as though a black woman marrying an Asian man was something so out of the believable, that it was downright scandalous. A Navy man and an Asian woman, though, wasn't nothing unusual. Everyone thought I was half Filipina.

"What you doing in here messing up my bed?" My mother's words brought me out of my world of reflections. I wasn't afraid of her words, though, cause I could always tell if she was mad at me. No, she was definitely thinking about something else, and her words of reprimand were more out of habit than anything else.

"You gonna tell me what you said to her?" ı couldn't wait for the juicy tidbits.

My mother just looked at me for a moment without saying anything. Then she just shook her head slowly.

"I don't know what that girl's problem is. We give her a good home and a chance to get out the gutter, and what do she do? She try to take the first ride back. Well, your father gonna be pretty pissed. I wouldn't be surprised if he go after her, kick her butt, and bring her back to her senses."

"But she loves Terrence. They getting married and starting a life together." I said this quickly, so that my mother would know that what my sister was doing would be best, not only for her, but for all of us.

"Girl, please. Don't take your sister's silly words as truth. That girl don't even know how to clean her butt good, and she think she can be married? Well, I say 'go on' to her, but your father gonna sure enough be pissed." My mother's words, while interesting to hear, were not exactly telling me what had passed between them in the driveway. My mother took off her work clothes and changed into the pink running suit she always wore around the house.

"All I can say is, don't you be following her actions. You stay your butt in school, go to college, and get you some education. There ain't gonna be nothing in this world for you but some aching, without those papers."

"Don't you want me to get married?" I was surprised to hear my mother speaking like a women's libber or something. She was always saying in front of my dad how she couldn't wait till some men took us girls off their hands.

"You can get married after you get to be who you gonna be. Don't be a Mrs. Somebody. You know what I mean?" She looked at me, and I could tell she didn't really want an answer. She was telling me as usual.

"Are they going to New Orleans?" I was anxious for my mother to really tell me something.

"N'Orleans? Is that what she told you? I can't believe she'd want to go back there, after all what happened to her. Just like a colored girl, running back to what she said she don't want." My mother grew quiet and didn't say anything for a while.

I didn't know if I should keep pressing her for information on the driveway incident cause she was on the verge of talking about stuff I'd never heard before. I didn't know why Andrie had come to live with us. My parents just told me I was supposed to be sisters with her, and I never felt I had a right to ask why and what for. My parents were like that. They just told me what I should believe and expected not to be questioned about it. I'd gotten pretty good at just nodding and agreeing. After all, I wasn't grown.

"Your sister was abused in N'Orleans. I ain't gonna tell you no details, but your Aunt Addie was not a good mother to Andrea. You understand?" My mother gave me a direct look which took my understanding for granted, though I was more than a little confused.

"Did Aunt Addie beat Andrie?" I couldn't believe it.

My mother stopped speaking, and I could pretty much tell that the conversation for now had come to a close. The only action I could hope for was when my father came home and heard the news. And, even then, I knew I'd be trying to hear everything through some devious method from my bedroom or in the hallway near, but out of sight, to my parents when they discussed the whole thing.

I followed my mother down the hall and into the kitchen, where I knew she would start making dinner. I liked helping her by chopping things up or stirring something. She always made me feel helpful, even though she ended up pretty much redoing whatever I'd helped her with. When I did the dishes, she always came behind me, cleaning things over to get missed food or rinsing glasses that still had dishwater soap in them. If my father looked at dishes I'd cleaned before my mom did, I would usually get yelled at. "Girl, what you trying to do? Kill people with this filth?" He made me nervous, so I was happy when it was only me and my mom in the kitchen. Plus, it was during this time that my mother talked to me about things that were going on. This evening, however, silence worked alongside us in the kitchen. It prevented my mother from telling me any other secrets about my sister. Maybe she thought my father would be home at any minute, and he might not like hearing us talking about Andrie like that.

When I heard my father's key in the door lock, I looked at my mother. She didn't say nothing or even look up from the carrots she was chopping. My father, like my mother, always headed for the bedroom first. I never followed him in there. I couldn't hang around him, like I could my mother. He always thought I should be doing something useful, not just hanging about wasting time. After a few minutes, my mother finished chopping the carrots, rinsed off her hands, and dried them with deliberately slow motions. Then, as if she could no longer put it off, she walked down the hall to their bedroom.

I couldn't hear anything from the kitchen, so I began cautiously working my way down the hall to get close enough to their door and hear something. At first, I couldn't hear anything, but then my father started yelling, and it wouldn't have mattered where in the house I was. I got a little scared and thought maybe I should go in my bedroom and close the door. I did go in my room, but I kept my door open, and I couldn't help but hear my father's words clearly.

"What you mean she done left? What you say to her?" My father was struggling to keep himself in control. I'd heard him this angry before, and I could imagine him breathing heavily through his nostrils in an attempt to calm himself down. The doctor had told him that in order to avoid another heart attack, he'd really have to keep his blood pressure down. My father took several kinds of medication a day because of hypertension. I wondered if his fists were clenched like they got sometimes when he was really mad.

"I ain't said nothing to that girl. I told you, she was already leaving when I come home from work. If I'd been a few minutes more, she would've been gone without me talking to her. Her mind was set." My mother's voice had a hint of anger in it, but she kept a tighter control on herself than my father was able to.

"Where she go? Did she at least tell you that?" I could hear the beginnings of defeat in my father's questions.

"She said something about going up to your uncle's in L.A. till she and Terrence can get married."

There was no response, and I wondered what my father was thinking. I began to imagine him driving up there and beating my sister up. He'd never hit her before, but he seemed angry enough to beat her butt this time. She really had screwed up. Then I regretted my pleasure at such thoughts. If he went up there, he'd bring her back here, and things would be even worse than before. She really wouldn't want to be here then, even more than before, and she'd be unbearable.

"Who you calling?" My mother's voice brought me back to the immediate situation, and I listened closely for the answer.

"Who you think I'm calling, woman? I got to stop this girl from her own stupid self." He stopped talking, and I supposed he was waiting for whoever he was calling to pick up the phone.

"Uncle Willie? Yeah, this Marcus. Umhmm. Just fine. Listen, you seen Andrea?" My father was silent for a few moments, and I could only imagine the rattlings on of my father's great-uncle. The man stayed in a constant Colt 45 frame of mind. He was very difficult to follow, in whatever he said or did, and his breath was best avoided. He weighed about ninety-six pounds because he only drank his food, being on a self-imposed alcohol diet and all. I did love the old man, though. Unc, as I called him, was the only grandfather I'd ever known.

"Well, she done run off with that boy of hers and about to do something crazy. Look, Unc. If she show up there, just tell her to call me or she'll have to answer to the police. Umhmm. The girl only seventeen. Nothing but a runaway."

A runaway! The police! This was getting better than I'd ever dreamed. Maybe she'd go to the Juvie or something. I could see my parents doing that, just to teach her a lesson. Ooooh, ooh, ooh. I was about to wet myself from excitement. I thought up a scenario where I would come and visit my sister in jail with nothing but sympathy in my face, as I waved at her through the bars. I smiled and almost started chuckling out loud, when I heard my mother calling me.

"Kendra! Where you at? Come help me finish up dinner." She didn't need to say it twice.

Later, at the dinner table, everyone was quiet. My father never usually said much, but once in a while, he'd make me squirm, asking me questions about school and stuff. But tonight, even my mother was silent, only asking us if we wanted some more pork chops or corn bread. I was very disappointed that nobody was saying anything about the absence of Andrie. When we were almost finished with dinner, the telephone rang. Again, I was disappointed with the lack of drama as my mother went to answer it as though we weren't waiting for an important call.

"Hello? Hold on for Marcus." She held the phone out for my father with a certain look, and I prepared myself to be sent to my room. But my father just got up and took the phone. I could see that he was struggling to keep himself calm. He licked his lips a couple of times. His almond-shaped eyes narrowed, and his nostrils flared slightly as he took a deep breath before speaking into the phone.

"Yeah? She there? Tell her I wants to speak to her." He was quiet for a moment. "Well, she can speak to me or the police." Again he was quiet, waiting for Andrie to make the next move, I assumed.

"You tell that boy to get you back to this house tonight, or you both going to jail. Don't give me no flap. He over twenty-one, and you still a child. You know what that mean in California law? Jail. Now, what it gonna be?" The vein on the left side of his face could be seen pushing against his dark brown skin, and he was perspiring as if he'd just come back from running. He wiped at the sweat on his forehead and his closely cropped afro with the back of his free hand. With an "all right now," he put the phone on the receiver with too much force, and my mother went over to put it back correctly.

She raised her eyebrows in a silent question, but he just ignored her. He went into the TV room, which was actually the old patio that my father and brother had converted into a den, lit up his pipe, turned on the television, and started watching the news. Without even one glance at me, my mother started clearing away the table. I got up to help her. I thought that maybe, while cleaning the dishes, she might confide in me a bit, like she did sometimes after dinner. My father usually went to his room to shine his shoes and get his Navy uniform ready for duty. He did this without fail, even if he wasn't on duty that week.

"You got some homework?" My mother's question startled me, and I just shook my head.

"Well, I think you better go to your room for the rest of the evening, cause your father ain't in too good a mood." She raised her eyebrows at me in her okay? look. She never really wanted me to say anything because okay? for her wasn't an inquiry. I looked at my mother for a moment and wondered what she was thinking. However, her face didn't reveal any particular expression, and I knew she was probably waiting for me to respond somehow. I took my time scraping the leftovers from the plate in my hand so I could see if my mother would reveal anything, but her face was turned away from me. I could only see her profile. Her shoulder-length dark brown hair needed a color touch-up with Ms. Clairol, as my mother referred to the product. She'd just pressed it, and it was pretty straight, so the gray hairs showed clearly. I was thinking maybe a comic reference to her needing to wash that gray right outta her hair might break some ice, but when she turned suddenly, her impatient rise of the eyebrows sent me out of the kitchen pretty quick.

Without a word, I went into my room and lay on the bed, staring up at the ceiling. I didn't have a clock cause my mother said I didn't need to learn to rely on such things yet. I'd asked for a clock radio for my birthday last year, but my mom had said that eleven was still too young to be jarred out my sleep. My mother woke me up every morning, since she thought that was the most gentle way for me to face the new day. My father told her it was stupid, and that I should get used to being up early and getting things done before I went to school. Yet, for some reason, my mother had won out on this issue. So, I lay there for a long time with no idea of what time it might be. I hoped for a while that my mom would come and talk to me like she did sometimes. She would ask me about books I was reading in school, and we'd laugh sometimes about how stupid some of the white people in the books were. I liked listening to her talk about growing up in Mississippi, the oldest of eleven children. Once she told me that she'd wanted to have at least five kids, but that after Michael was born, the doctor had said no more children. And that's why they adopted me when they were stationed in Japan several years later. She'd been a volunteer with the Protestant Women's Guild on the Naval air base station in Atsugi, and they helped various orphanages by collecting clothes, raising money, and trying to place orphans with military families. She'd chosen me from the photos of all the little girls who were up for adoption from a Korean Christian orphanage in Seoul. I smiled thinking about how she said she "didn't want no baby-baby cause that'd be too many dirty diapers to change," and how "the seven-year-old was too old to really be her little girl." So, she chose me, "the three-year-old with no teeth, grinning all hard anyway." After a while, I knew she wasn't coming to my room for one of our visits. She was probably watching my father, making sure he wasn't getting too worked up or something.

I began to wonder why my father seemed calm about this whole business. I'd really expected him to do something more exciting, like drive up to L.A. and take out Terrence. It wasn't as if my father was a truly violent man. I mean, he'd never hit my mother, and he only beat my butt when I was real bad, the kind of bad that my mom wouldn't deal with. Yet there was something about him that made me think of him as a kind of violent man. There seemed to be something in the way his face tensed up and all the muscles worked hard against the control he imposed on himself that was threatening. I wouldn't want to be in Andrie's shoes right now.

I must've fallen asleep cause loud voices surprised me into a vague awareness of my surroundings. I had to reach back in my memory to figure out why I was on top of the bedspread in clothes instead of my pajamas. My first thought was that my mother would be pretty mad if she saw me now. Then I recognized one of the voices as hers, and I knew I was safe for the moment. Just to be sure, I changed into the yellow flannel pajamas I'd gotten at Christmas, instead of the "impractical" silk ones I'd asked for.

I opened the door slowly to hear where the voices were coming from. I wondered who was fighting. My mother and father? Or had Andrie come back, and my parents were wailing on her now? This last possibility propelled me to creep quietly into the hallway. I could make out Mom's and Andrie's voices, and I wondered where my father was. I guessed he couldn't be in there cause he'd never let my mother do all the talking.

"Let go of my arm! Where Marcus at?" I recognized Andrie asking for my father, and I wondered again where he was.

"He got called to duty again. You gonna talk to me first. You should be glad you don't have to face him." There was control in my mother's voice, as if she'd triumphed over Andrie.

"Why you care about what I do? You never wanted me here noway." Andrie was struggling to keep her angry voice down.

"No, I didn't want you here, for exactly what happened today. You just like your sister Addie. A whore running around with any man. Sure, it's Terrence today, but it'll be some other man if he don't do what you want him to. I didn't want you here, cause Marcus done too much for his sisters already. I was willing to be a mother to you, cause your sister been doing you wrong your whole life. I don't beat you. But what do I get from you? Nothing but a heartache. You so selfish, you don't ever think about how much your brother done for you. You lucky he ain't called the police on your crazy ass."

I didn't understand what my mother was saying. How could Andrie be my father's sister? She called him Pop. I started remembering all those times Andrie had said "your parents" to me, and I'd always thought she was trying to be grown. Some of my friends called their parents by their first names when they weren't around. I'd thought that Andrie had been attempting the same kind of disrespect. This started to make sense. She came to live with us when she was already twelve years old, and I always guessed she was a cousin. Well, if she wasn't a cousin, then I guess she was kind of an aunt to me, and I really disliked the idea. I mean, an aunt was someone higher up on the respect ladder. I had to be nice to my other aunts and uncles. Did this mean I had to be polite to Andrie? In my confusion, I missed some of the conversation going on, but the mention of my name grabbed my attention.

"What you gonna tell Kendra about who she really is?" Andrie's question had a kind of triumphant tone I didn't understand.

"What you talking about now? What Kendra got to do with you?" My mother wasn't going to be easily goaded.

"You know what Addie and them saying? Kendra really Marcus's daughter. He got some Oriental woman pregnant when he was stationed in Korea, before y'all went to Japan."

I couldn't believe my ears. I sat down quickly, so as not to faint from confusion. Andrie was lying. I knew my parents would tell me something like this! I willed myself not to run into the other room and tear her lying head from her shoulders. I wiped at the tears rolling down my face with the backs of my hands and tried to remember that she would say anything to hurt my mother. I knew she had to be lying.

I didn't know if my mother'd said anything to Andrie in response while I'd been digesting the latest turn in the conversation. In fact, there seemed to be an awfully long silence, until I heard some strange noises, as if someone was having a hard time breathing. I got up from where I was and tried to see into the darkness of the room. Around the corner from the dining room, I could barely make out my mother's figure. She was bending over Andrie on the couch, but I couldn't tell what she was doing. As I got closer, I could see Andrie's hands shoving at my mother in the chest. My first reaction was to run over and stop her from hitting Mom, but then I noticed that my mother actually had her hands around Andrie's neck. I thought, Oh my God! She's choking her! I stood there, unable to move. I screamed.

My mother jerked her head in my direction. I couldn't tell if she really saw me or not. Her eyes looked as if they belonged on another face. A crazy person's face.

"Momma. What're you doing?" I managed to whisper. I took a step closer, and she seemed to recognize me.

"Go back to bed. This ain't your concern." Her voice snapped out of her, as if it took all her strength to utter the words. Andrie was making horrible, gasping noises. I ran over and tried to pry my mother's hands loose.

"Momma, let go. You'll kill her. Let go, please!" It must have been the urgency in my voice, cause she snatched her hands back, as if they'd been in boiling water.

She rubbed them together like she was rubbing hand lotion over them after having washed the dishes. I looked at my mother, and though she was looking at me, I didn't think she really knew I was there.

Andrie was taking in deep breaths of air, and she was sobbing, so she sounded like a five-year-old who'd just had a tantrum and was trying to stop her hysterical crying under the threat of getting a whipping.

"You okay?" I was scared she was going to do something, though I wasn't exactly sure what that would be. Maybe she would rise up and grab my mother by her neck, and I'd have a horror movie on my hands. But Andrie just sat up and looked at my mother with an expressionless stare on her face. It was strange, but for some reason, I didn't feel she meant to do any harm against my mother.

Andrie turned and looked at me. Taking a deep breath, she smiled a shaky smile at me. She said, "You go to bed, before you get in trouble. We almost finished here. Okay?"

I thought she must have lost too much airflow to her brain. Here she'd almost been choked to death, and she was trying to send me off to bed, as if nothing had happened. I didn't get it, and my head was really starting to hurt. I was confused and still a little scared, and I rubbed my eyes as if I could wipe away everything I'd seen. I didn't want to go to bed, but then suddenly, I didn't want to be in that room anymore either. There were too many weird things going on, and I wished I hadn't been so nosy. I thought about just going back to bed, like Andrie said to. Maybe I didn't really have any business being here.

"You're not my sister, are you?" I asked the question abruptly, surprising myself since it popped into my memory like a bad dream.

Andrie looked at my mother, who was now sitting in my father's La-Z-Boy, just staring out into the darkness, with tears streaming down her face. Looking back at me, she shook her head.

"No. I'm really your father's youngest sister. You know that your grandparents died before you got here from Japan, right?" She didn't wait for my response and continued, "Well, I lived with your Aunt Addie, my sister really, until I come here to live with y'all. Your father the only father I know. That's why I calls him Pop."

I stood there thinking that this was about the only time I could remember talking to Andrie without being angry with her. Or jealous of whatever attention my father gave her. I couldn't believe that no one had told me any of this before. I mean, this was very serious information, and I didn't know if I should ask about what she'd said earlier about me. I looked at her neck, and I could see faint hints of bruises.

"You gonna tell Dad about tonight?" Now I was really scared, because I thought this would be the time my father went off on my mother. He might beat her up, leave or something else awful, and what would become of us then?

"No. Ain't nothing happened here tonight. Right?" She looked at me very seriously, and I found myself nodding my head.

"What about what you said about me?" My voice trembled a little, and Andrie looked at me for a moment before saying anything.

Andrie looked over at my mother, who was now looking at us— well, really at Andrie. She looked like she was pretty much herself, and she was also waiting for the answer to my question.

"I was just angry. I made it up, cause I knew it would hurt Linda. You don't even look nothing like your father, do you?" Though Andrie was speaking to me, she never took her eyes off my mother's face.

I couldn't tell whether my mother believed Andrie or not. It was difficult to see because she wore no particular expression that would give me an answer. Looking back at Andrie, I could see her resemblance to my father, and I couldn't believe I hadn't seen it before. I didn't know what to think anymore. There was something going on between my mother and Andrie that didn't seem to include me, and I felt like crying for some silly reason. All of a sudden, I didn't think I knew anything about myself and wondered if I should care. The only important thing seemed to be getting things back to order around the house before my father came home unexpectedly or something. I walked over to my mother and gave her a hug, as though she were a five-year-old.

"I guess we better get to bed." I tried to make my voice sound matter-of-fact, and I wondered at my control. My mother didn't say anything, and I had to tug at her arm to get her up. I looked at Andrie, who just stared at the two of us.

"Well, you better get to bed before Dad gets home, Andrie."

She looked as if she was going to challenge my suggestion, but then she just nodded, as if she knew there was no better way.

I led my mother past Andrie, down the hall, and into her bedroom.

During this whole time, my mother never said a word. She didn't protest against my leading, and it was almost as though she were actually leaning on me. After I helped her to get in bed, I leaned over, pulled the blankets up around her neck, and kissed her good night. Tears had rolled slowly from her eyes, and I whispered, "I love you." I turned off the light, closed the door, and listened for a moment outside in the hall. I didn't hear her crying out loud or anything, and I knew she'd be okay.

I went into my bedroom and sat on the edge of my bed. I could barely see myself in the mirror over the dresser because of the darkness, so I got up and turned on the little lamp that sat on the dresser. I looked closely into the mirror. I studied my small, almond-shaped eyes and my light brown skin. I felt the one thick braid my mother had plaited earlier, and I touched my thin lips. I thought I saw a lot of things, but I didn't think I could see my father. In fact, I knew he wasn't there. I didn't want him to be. I loved my parents as much as I thought they loved me, but I didn't want to be blood-related to my father. Would my mother really love me if I belonged to some other woman Dad had gotten pregnant? I knew my mother loved first and thought second, but I didn't think she could treat me so much like her own, like she had for as long as I could remember, if I was my father's and someone else's. I started to cry a little, and I wondered why I had to hear what Andrie had said to my mother. If I went to sleep, maybe the next day would make everything normal. Tonight would never have happened.

With an uncertain feeling about the lie Andrie had tossed out so viciously, I got under the covers of my twin bed and fell asleep out of exhaustion. I didn't wake up again until my mother came in to get me for breakfast. It was Saturday, so I had been allowed to sleep in. Sometime during the night Andrie had come to bed cause her bed was unmade.

"Kendra. You better come eat your breakfast, before it get cold." My mother came all the way into my room and pulled the curtains back to let the sun in. Until the memory of the night before popped back into my mind, I could almost imagine like it was any other Saturday morning from the tone of my mother's voice. I looked at her for any traces of the disturbing events, but she just lifted her eyebrows at me in that same old okay? look of hers. She looked at me real hard and then smiled. She only smiled like that when she wanted to say a lot of things without any words. I smiled back, though I still felt a little uncertain. I didn't know what would happen next.

My father and Andrie were already sitting at the dinner table when I joined them. There was enough food to feed the whole neighborhood, and I imagined my mother had been cooking for quite some time. I looked at my father's face and tried to place a recognition there. But the only familiarity lay in the way he chewed his food loudly and slurped his orange juice. I was glad to know this about him. He looked at me, and I imagined I saw the usual look he'd always given me. It was the same look he gave my brother and Andrie. But I must have looked at him a little too long because he raised his eyebrows, like he did when I had to ask him for money for the show or some other important business. I looked away cause I knew there was no point in letting any doubts mean anything. Especially with my father.

"Kendra, your sister getting married this summer after she out of school." My father's words only surprised me a little.

"You want to be a bridesmaid and wear a pretty dress?" Andrie's question teased, but didn't anger me.

I just looked at her and tried not to voice any of the questions I had inside. How had she managed this? Why was everyone acting like nothing important had happened recently?

"I don't know. What do you think, Mom?" My mother had just sat down and started eating.

"Well, this what your sister want, and she gonna finish school first. So, I think she making an okay choice." There was nothing in her voice that indicated her true feelings.

I had no trouble guessing how my sister had gotten my mother to support her wishes after the previous night's events. The only way my father would've gone for this was if my mother had somehow managed to convince him it was the best thing to do. I wondered how my mother really felt about Andrie, who'd still be seventeen in the summer, getting married so young, like she had. I supposed it was the best thing for everyone. Andrie got what she wanted, and I got rid of her, I guess. My father wouldn't have to care for her anymore, as a daughter or a sister, because it would be Terrence's responsibility. And I didn't really think my mother had a choice.

My mother noticed I wasn't eating and said, "You better eat something before the food get cold." She nodded in her go-ahead way, and I had to swallow the sudden feeling of nausea threatening to ruin breakfast. I put a spoonful of grits on my plate and picked at it with my fork, avoiding my mother's look.

"So, Kendra, you gonna be Princess again when I leave. Your whole world can be just like it was before I came here." She smiled that annoying smile of hers.

I looked at my father, but he seemed oblivious and got second helpings of everything. I wondered if he had any idea of what'd happened this morning. I didn't think things could seem so normal around the house if he did know something. For a flash, I wanted to bring up what Andrie had said about me to my mother and force everyone to stop pretending everything was okay. I wanted my father to talk to me for once, and tell me something that wasn't an order or a scold or a get lost. I knew I was going to cry, so I started coughing really loud.

My mother asked, concerned, "Are you feeling okay?"

I shook my head no and asked to be excused.

My father looked at me, and I stared at him for a moment, until tears started running down my face.

"Girl, what's wrong with you? You got something on your mind? You ain't feeling well?" He looked from me to my mother, as if to say "Do something here," cause he couldn't stand it when I blubbered in front of him.

"Kendra, you okay?" Andrie's concerned voice surprised me a little, I just nodded my head a little in confusion, but I couldn't speak.

"You better go to your room," my mother said gently. "You want me to come with you?"

I shook my head slowly and got up from the table. I was walking out of the dining room trying not to look at anyone, not my father or my mother, when Andrie put her arm around my waist. I hadn't even noticed her getting up from the table.

When we got to our room, Andrie sat me on my bed and was quiet for a few minutes. Then she began to speak. "You want to go shopping with me for my wedding dress?"

I just stared at her. I couldn't believe what I was hearing. Why was everyone acting so normal? Didn't anyone remember last night? I looked away from her and started crying again.

"Why are you pretending like everything is all right?"

"Last night was a mistake for everyone. You shouldn't let what's said in anger decide what's true. I told you that Linda pissed me off, and I just wanted to be mean to her." Andrie shrugged her shoulders as if to imply that it was that simple, but she kept her look even with mine to see how I was reacting to what she said.

"I don't believe you," I whispered.

"It don't matter what you believe, Kendra. Don't you know by now things are gonna be what they are, how Marcus, your father, say they are? You ain't going nowhere, so ain't no use in your working yourself up to some trauma case needing a head doctor or something. What does it matter anyway? You got a home, and Linda and Marcus love you. They ain't never done you no kinda wrong, so what you want now? What you think you need to know besides that?" Andrie's tone wasn't angry, and this was the only time I could remember us talking without fighting.

"Do you hate my mother?" My question took her by surprise, and she was silent for a moment.

"No. I don't hate nobody. Hate don't change nothing; it just keeps you angry, and you don't ever do nothing with your life. You know what I mean? I think Linda and I just have to remember who we are and that I ain't never gonna be a daughter to her. But I think that'll work itself out, just like things do." She stopped talking, and I began to understand some of what Andrie was saying.

When my mother knocked on the door, I looked at Andrie, and she said, "Come in."

My mother poked her head through the door opening and raised her eyebrow in that inquiring way of hers. She looked at my face and came all the way into the room, stopping at the foot of my bed.

I looked at her and then at Andrie and said, "Can I pick out my own dress for the wedding? Andrie has bad taste, and I don't want to be looking all stupid at my sister's wedding." I rolled my eyes Andrie's way, and she threw a pillow at my head.

"Well, if that's what you want, and you get a color that matches what Andrea wants, we can get it when we go shopping for the wedding dress." Mom looked at Andrie, and I wondered if last night was still too fresh to have been gotten over like this.

But Andrie's response, "That's fine," seemed to let the matter rest.

Riding the Wheel of Fortune

VIKI RADDEN

I never told my brother about it. I figured, why should I? I just said to my homegirls, since we took care of the situation, why not just leave it the way that it is, and then act all mysterious and innocent like?

See, the thing with James is that he thinks he's the only one who helps anybody, since he's the big brother and all. I have to admit that sometimes he really does take care of me, like that time when Joe Prowell, that big nasty bully in the eighth grade, called me a nigger right out loud, in front of my whole science class. Actually, see, I thought I took care of it myself, since I did end up beating him to a pulp at the front of the room. And then *he* got suspended. But James, when he found out about it—and believe me, I didn't even tell him, somebody else did—James got some of his friends together and they all rode their bikes over to Joe's house, see? And then James, he says to him, "When you see my sister walking down the hall, you cross over to the other side, OK?" I always wondered why he never bothered me again for the whole school year.

Anyway, that was way back in eighth grade and now James and me have got high school to deal with, and as anybody with a head sitting on their shoulders should know, high school is not the same game as junior high. Not at all. High school—that's where the Big Boys play. But what people don't seem to know is that sometimes the Big Girls, the Big Mamas, we got to get in there, too.

See, we girls got ourselves a club. Called the A.L.B.G. It's small. Only four members. And the only reason we got that many people is cause that's how many black girls we got at Littleton High. I know it's a shame, but it's all we got and we got to stick together. Oh, I almost forgot: A.L.B.G. stands for The Association of Lonely Black Girls, cause straight up, that's who we are. We're lonely cause none of us got a boyfriend, but give us time. We're not even sixteen yet. I'm the leader, cause Keisha and them say I got charisma, but we still have to agree on everything we do, all four of us.

Sometimes we do graffiti up on Broadway, but mostly we do little quiet, undercover things. We figure we have to be kind of a little secret society, you know, a Girl's Club. So when I told my girls what happened to me and my brother last Friday, that's when me and my homies, we walked to the 7-Eleven on Littleton Boulevard, got us some Jolt cola and chips, and got down to some serious discussion.

It was a topic that had come up before: the Holliman family. Actually, I don't know if the whole family's messed up; I just know those two boys at our school can't seem to leave my brother alone. See, I know what it is, they're just jealous cause they can't stand to see a black boy being the class valedictorian and publishing haiku poetry and all that. Those Holliman boys, see, they don't have nothing going for themselves, and even though their parents were stupid enough to buy a car for that oldest one, Brad, with his hair the color of dirty dishwater and his pointy little head—they bought him a '63 Volvo, just like the one James has—those boys still ain't got nothing going for them. All they know how to do is turn wheelies on the corner and speed past our house, looking for James to come out so they can hassle him and call the two of us names.

So anyway last Friday, we're riding to school in James's car, right, like we usually do, and since James is the class val, he gets to have his own private parking space with his name on it, just like all the other student government kids. So we're riding to school, then we whip into James's space, but instead of his name on his parking space, somebody had spray painted over it in black and then they wrote something else, in big white letters: JIGABOO. Me and James, when we saw it, we knew right away who it was. We just sat there and stared at it for a while, but then James, he just went to King Soopers and got a few spray cans and some stencils and redid his name with even more flash than it was before. I think he just swallowed his pride, considering he was almost getting ready to graduate. But me, well I got two more years at Littleton High School, and that Holliman boy, him and me and the girls, we got some tangling to do. But, see, we going to tangle so quiet like, that lame boy ain't even going to know he's doing the dance.

That day at lunch we homegirls had to go into emergency session. We figured we had to do something but that it had to be strictly on the sly. Keisha came up with the master plan and we all loved it because we got our revenge as black people and as girls, too. See, I can't stand those Holliman boys, but especially that older one, Brad. Soon as I got to high school, I seen him looking at me sometimes, looking at me like he's licking his chops or something, and then one day when I wore shorts and a T-shirt to school, he got the nerve to come up to me and say something about my butt. White boys like him make me sick—he says he can't stand black people, then all he does is hassle my brother, but me, since I'm cute, he's just the kind who wants to have sex with me, but then he'd be too embarrassed to let any of his friends see me and him together. See what I'm saying?

So what we did is, we decided to do something to that '63 Volvo he loved so much. That's another thing that used to just get on his nerves—he couldn't stand that James had such a posh car. It used to be Dad's, but when James got his license, Dad gave the Volvo to James and got a new car. So of course Brad just had to go out and get all that fancy new work on his car, the new upholstery and lamb wool seat covers and the shiny metallic red paint job and all that. He just had to do James one better.

So anyway, those old cars, they're easy to mess with. I know that, cause you can open up the hood without having to get in the car. And like I said, the A.L.B.G., we're secret agents extraordinaire, so we do things on the sly, and we do things that people think girls aren't supposed to know how to do. And since we're not even all the way grown up yet, we still know all those tricks from our kid days, like blowing up watermelons and stuff. I knew that if you put sugar or salt in a car radiator, it would wreck the engine. So that's what we decided to do.

That morning at school I walked over to King Soopers and bought one of those one-pound boxes of sugar. Around eleven that night I snuck out of the house and walked over to the Hollimans' house. I was wearing black and carrying the box of sugar under my jacket. It was scary walking over there, even though it's only two or three blocks, but then later it felt so good, just standing there under the stars by myself, pouring that C & H sugar in Mr. Loser's radiator, a few grains for each time he's called us niggers, but most of all, the sugar was for the spray paint on my brother's parking space. It's like Mom says to us all the time, what comes around goes around.

Life is like that, I guess, kind of like a Wheel of Fortune. Sometimes you're up and riding high, but then you've got to start your way down. Like Brad Holliman.

But on graduation day, me and my brother, we were riding right on top of the crest. James gave his speech up there on that stage and everyone was screaming and throwing their caps in the air, especially me and Mom and Dad and the few other black faces in the gym. Me and my brother left the gym together. We headed down Broadway, then turned west onto Littleton Boulevard. The sun was setting behind the Rockies; it was blazing red, and James and me, we headed straight toward those fiery mountains, riding high in our white '63 Volvo, the only one like it in town.

vvvvvvv

PART TWO

Night Vision:
Crack and Violence
Against Black Women

This woman is Black
so her blood is shed into silence
this woman is Black
so her death falls to earth
like the drippings of birds
to be washed away with silence and rain.

FROM *OF NEED: A CHORALE OF BLACK WOMAN'S VOICES*
BY AUDRE LORDE

Byllye Avery, founder of the National Black Women's Health Project, once stated that violence is the number-one health issue facing Black women. Violence in the form of battering, emotional and verbal abuse, sexual harassment, lesbian bashing, incest, molestation, rape, and murder affects the lives of all Black women, regardless of age, class, or sexual orientation.

Black women are especially vulnerable to these and other forms of violence because of the prevalence of negative stereotypes and myths

▼▼▼▼▼▼▼▼

about us that are a part of what feminist scholar, bell hooks, calls the "institutionalized devaluation of Black womanhood." We see this devaluation in the images of us that appear on television, in movies, and in music videos; we hear the insults in the lyrics of misogynist rap songs.

Often a woman intuitively senses this devaluation and that sense, compounded with actual personal experiences of depreciation of her worth, accumulates into an overwhelming sense of sadness and pain. She may choose to pursue solace in the netherworld of alcohol and/or drugs like crack.

Other women find different ways to battle the devaluation, by fighting to improve the status of Black women, of all women, in the world, and also changing our personal relationships by instilling the words of Audre Lorde's pronouncement into our deepest consciousness: *"I am wary of need that tastes like destruction."*

▲▲▲▲▲▲▲▲

the woman's mourning song

bell hooks

i cry
i cry high
this mourning song
my heart rises
sun in hand
to make the bread
i rise
my heavy work hand
needs
the voice of many singers
alone
the warmth of many ovens comfort
the warrior in me returns
to slay sorrow
to make the bread
to sing the mourning song
i cry high
i cry high
i cry
the mourning song
go away death
go from love's house
go make your empty bed

Gospel

PATRICIA SPEARS JONES

for my mother

She's been crying now
for hours
singing old songs
She is a blues song
8 bar   12 bar
blues song
long
long
past the last chorus
and it is midnight
or later
and there's a whiskey
or maybe just a beer
and it's quiet
so quiet
except for the music
of her tears

The sounds in her
throat
start waves of memories
suddenly
there is an echo
of a chorus
of a gospel pearl
about returning
to the temple
to be cleansed
to be cleansed

White uniformed sisters
stand guard 'round their
weeping comrade
and all the pain
goes away
in the shout
in the holding on of hands
in the sweat
sweet water
scent of cheap cologne
and talcum powder
returning to the temple
to be cleansed
to be cleansed

There are stars in her tears
Light-years have crossed her brow
She has traveled with this knowledge
of pain
of rape
of pain
for too long

and that gospel song
comes like a blessing
beautiful
black
loving
returning to the place
of mercy
of mercy on me/ she
stops her weeping
stops her dreaming
stops this silence
with the clenching
of her fist

with the opening
of her heart
much like a rose
under Arkansas sun

She has made her blues song
gospel
She has made her gospel
real
She claims all her powers
perhaps curses the darkness
and waits to generate new heavens
in her eyes.

Busted

JOY GRAY

We be after a good feeling, that's all. Don't everybody be after a good feeling? We jest go after ours in a different way. And everybody be on our case sayin' we ain't nothin' but junkies and crack whores. Well, everybody's a whore for somethin', you know.

I goes ovuh to Hunting Park to find my shit. Use to go to West Philly, but that played out real quick. You got to find somebody with a car to take you ovuh there or be spendin' your money on subway tokens, when you could spend it on butter.

So I keeps my ass in the neighborhood, somewheres I can walk to. My sister tag along most o' the time. That's what I called her when we was comin' up, Tag-a-long. Where I go, she gotta go, too.

Mainly, we be at Sylvester's house. It be ovuh by Eighth and Butler. It useta be a bad ass crib 'fore the Jamaicans took it ovuh.

They came blowin' into Philly and nearly drove the homeboys, the Junior Black Mafia, outta business in they own hometown. And them goddamn Jamaicans crazier than the JBMs, too. When they take over a house they block in the windows and put all this metal shit behind the door to make it harder to break down if the cops come. So it be real dark in this place I'm talkin' about. But that don't matter. What we does can be did in the dark.

That day, me and Sylvester was tryin' to raise enough money to buy a dime bag. And Mookie was there, messin' around. Some mens come by looking for Rits and Tees. Sylvester knows one of 'em, so he let 'em in. Turns out that nigguh has jest hit the number for a cool three hundred dollars, chile. Real paper, you know. They had stopped at the state store and copped a fifth of Bacardi and a fifth of vodka. The one with the money, him named Chris, he looks me up and down and acks how much. You know how a nigguh is. Give him some paper and he wants some liquor, some dope and some pussy.

I say that depends.

"Depends on what?" he acks.

"On what you want," I say.

I look at him closer. He don't look half bad. Jest a skinny dude with a little mustache and a goatee. And his clothes be pretty clean, not like some down-and-out piper that ain't got a place to lay his nappy head at night.

"I wants me some pussy," he say.

"Five dollars."

He nod.

"Where?"

I done started leadin' Chris ovuh to a mattress on the floor in the corner of what used to be a bedroom when Mookie come swishin' up to put his two cents worth in.

"Hey, baby, anything she can do, I can do better," he say.

Next thing I know he got ahold of Chris's other arm and is brushin' up against him like a goddamn cat.

"Bullshit," I say. "Ain't no man a woman. You might think your asshole is a pussy, but it ain't."

"Bitch, I got somethin' better than some ole stretched out pussy," Mookie say.

I'm jest about ready to go up side his head. Five bucks will buy my share of that dime bag me and Sylvester after and here come Mookie gon' mess everything up.

"I got enough for both of you. When I hits, I hits big," Chris say.

I be some kinda surprised 'cause he don't look like he go both ways. I thought I could tell them AC-DCs from reg'lar peoples. But I ain't about to look no gift horse in the mouth. So we goes on ovuh to that ole funky mattress. Soon as Chris lay down, Mookie unzip Chris's pants and take his thing out. Soon Mookie got Chris's dick in his mouth, suckin' on it fit to kill. Well, a man got a mouth just like a woman do, but he ain't got some other things. I take my shirt off and give Chris a mouthful of titties and put his hand on what he after.

We had done fucked plenty and was smokin' our dime bag of gray tape before it happen. Us was all gathered 'round the table in the kitchen. Me, Sylvester, Mookie and Chris and his two friends was hittin' and passin'. We had done drunk most of the Bacardi and was startin' on the vodka. Sylvester had the pipe and was suckin' it in when the doorbell ring.

"Get the door, Annette," he say.

I turn to Mookie and tell him to answer the door.

"Not right now," he say.

I didn't want to go up front 'cause my hit was next, as soon as Sylvester was done.

"Hey man, get the door," I told one of Chris's friends.

My eyes was closed when they come in. I always close my eyes when I'm smokin' dope. Makes it feel better and last longer, like when you fuckin', you know? I was drawin' real hard on the pipe when somebody knocked it smack out of my hand. The pipe went a skiddin' off the table. It fell on the floor and cracked, wastin' good dope. I was down on my hands and knees tryin' to pick up some crumbs when it hit me. I seen the guy's shoes. They weren't no sneaks or work shoes. They was big and black and shined. Cop shoes. I looked up.

"You can stand up," the plainclothes one said. He was a brother. There was two white guys in uniforms standin' behind him.

I scrambled up to my feet. I didn't say nothin'. Wasn't nobody else saying nothin' neither. They had done caught us red-handed.

They took me and Sylvester down to the roundhouse in the same cop car. He was on my case all the way ovuh there.

"Damn it, bitch. If you had gone to the door like I acks, we wouldn't be busted. Don't no hard head like the one you sent to the door know how to check peoples out 'fore he lets 'em in," he say.

I didn't say nothin' back. I knew that the Jamaicans would bail Sylvester out. They need him to sell their dope for 'em. But don't nobody need me for nothin'. I knew that my ass was busted good.

Like I said, we do it for a feeling. And if you ain't never had the good feeling cocaine give a person, you ain't had shit!

crack annie

ntozake shange

i caint say how it come to me/ shit
somehow/ it just come over me/ & i
heard the lord sayin how beautiful/ &
pure waz this child of mine/ & when i
looked at her i knew the Lord waz
right/ & she waz innocent/ ya know/
free of sin/ & that's how come i
gave her up to cadillac lee/ well/ how
else can i explain it/

who do ya love i wanna know i wanna know
who do ya love i wanna know i wanna know

what mo could i say

who do ya love i wanna know i wanna know
who do ya love i wanna know i wanna know

it's not like she had hair round her
pussy or nothin/ she aint old enough
anyway for that/ & we sho know/ she
aint on the rag or nothin/ but a real
good friend of mine from round 28th
street/ he tol me point-blank
wazn't nothin in the whole world smell
like virgin pussy/ & wazn't nothin in the
universe/ taste like new pussy/ now this
is my friend talkin/ & ya know how
hard it is to keep a good man fo yo self
these days/ even though i know i got
somethin sweet & hot to offer/ even

then/ i wanted to give my man cadillac
lee/ somethin i jus don't have no mo/
new pussy/ i mean it aint dried up or
nothin/ & i still know what muscles i
cd get to work in my pussy/ this-a-way
& that but what i really wanted/ my
man/ cadillac to have for his self/ waz some
new pussy/ & berneatha waz so
pretty & sweet smellin/ even after
she be out there running wit the boys/
my berneatha *vida*/ waz sweet & fine
remember that song "so fine"
so fine my baby's so doggone fine
sends them thrills up & down my spine
whoah-oh-oh-yeah-yeaeaeah-so-fine

well/ that's my child/ *fine*/ & well
cadillac always come thru for me/ ya
know wit my crack/ oh honey/ lemme tell
ya how close to jesus i get thanks
to my cadillac/ lemme say now/ witout
that man i'd been gone on to
worms & my grave/ but see i had me
some new pussy/ waz my daughter/ lemme
take that back/ i didn't have none/
any new pussy/ so i took me some/ & it
jus happened to be berneatha/ my
daughter/ & he swore he'd give me twenty-five
dollars & a whole fifty cent of crack/
whenever/ i wanted/ but you know/ i'm on the pipe/
& i don't have no new pussy/ & what difference/
could it
make/ i mean shit/ she caint get pregnant/
shit/ she only seven years old
& these scratches/ heah/ by my fingers
that's/ where my child held onto

me/ when the bastard/ cadillac/ took
her like she wazn't even new pussy at
all/ she kept lookin at me &
screamin/ "mommy/ mommy help me/ help
me"/ & all i did waz hold her
tighter/ like if i could stop her
blood from circulation/ if i could stop
her from hurtin/ but no/ that aint how
it went down at all/ nothin like that/
trust me/ i got scars where my
daughter's fingernails broke my skin
& then/ when he waz finished wit my
child/ cadillac/ he jump up & tell me
to cover my child's pussy/ wit some
cocaine/ so she wdn't feel nothin no
mo/ i say/ why ya aint done
that befo/ why ya wait til ya done/
to protect her/ he say/ befo i lay
you down & give ya some of the same/
dontcha know/ ya haveta hear
em scream befo ya give em any
candy/ & my lil girl heard all
this/ my child bled alla this/ & all i
could do waz to look for some more crack
wit the fifty cadillac done give
me/ but/ i wazn't lookin for it for
me/ jesus knows/ i wanted it for
berneatha/ so she wouldn't haveta
remember/ she wouldn't have to
remember/ nothin at all/ but i saw dark purple
colored marks
by her shoulder/ where i held her down for
cadillac/ i'm her mother & i held her
& if ya kill me/ i'll always know/
i'm gonna roam round hell talkin
bout new pussy/ & see my child's

blood caked bout her thighs/ my child's
shoulders purple wit her mother's
love/ jesus save me/ come get me
jesus/ now/ lord take my soul & do
wit it what ya will/ lord have
mercy/ i thought berneatha waz like
me/ that she could take anythin/ ya
know/ caint nothin kill the will of the
colored folks/ but lord i waz
wrong/ them marks on my child/ no/
not the marks/ from cadillac/ the scars
from my fingers/ purple & blue
blotches/ midnight all ruby on lenox
avenue at 7:30 on sundays/ that heavy
quiet/ that cruelty/ i caint take
no mo/ so lord throw me into hell befo
berneatha is so growed/ she do it
herself/ all by herself/ laughin
& shovin me/ & prowlin &
teasin/ sayin/ you a mother/ what
kinda mother are you/ bitch/ tell me/
now/ mommy what kinda mother/ are you/ mommy/
mommy/

i say/ i heard etta james in her eyes/ i
know/ i heard the blues in her eyes/ an
unknown/ virulent blues/ a stalkin
takin no answer but yes to me
blues/ a song of a etta james/ a
cantankerous blues/ a blues born of
wantin & longin/ wantin & longin for
you/ mama/ or etta mae/
song of a ol hand me down blues
hangin by its breath/ alone
a fragile new blues
hardly close to nowhere/ cept them eyes

& i say/ i heard a heap of etta james
in them eyes/ all over them eyes/
so come on Annie

so tell mama all about it

tell mama all about it
all about it
all about it

tell mama

night vision

LUCILLE CLIFTON

the girl fits her body in
to the space between the bed
and the wall. she is a stalk,
exhausted. she will do some
thing with this. she will
surround these bones with flesh.
she will cultivate night vision.
she will train her tongue
to lie still in her mouth and listen.
the girl slips into sleep.
her dream is red and raging.
she will remember
to build something human with it.

Child Molestation Is a National Affair

MICHELLE T. CLINTON

In elementary school, the worn places
in my underwear were dirty secrets
under my skirt. But junior high issued me
a gym locker, a line to stand in, & a bench
cold & public where other girls
got their chance to snicker at my drawers.

The steam from the showers fogged my eyes
so I squinted at the pubic hairs of older girls,
I watched for their breasts, who knew
what a woman would grow to be, me in my
bra-less sore lumps, a bald vagina,
I seen my best friend Sheila bouncing
in the nude, I smelled her & saw
kotex underneath panty hose.

Sheila had matching pastel slips & clean brassieres.
Sheila had a father that bought her family money,
a brick house, a daily change of panties. Sheila could
curse, & she was moody, & wouldn't let her father
kiss her in the morning. At night he snuck in
her bed, wanted to get her ready for breaking
in, so he fingered her more & more.

Sheila could string together nasty words
like a ugly wino, a crazed washer woman sick
of her kids. Sheila showed me how to make
my fingers like a dick & balls that mean
          fuck you mother sucker
& Sheila pointed out the purple marks on girls'
thighs, the welts swollen in the steam,

exposed in hot water, with pointed breasts
& boxes of menstrual pads for feminine
protection, I didn't want no daddy,
would keep flat & dry forever
without a period of physical education:

keep tight my legs from sprouting
something a man might wanna touch
& keep my nasty panties, the holes
in my drawers, a private dirty secret.

Peace Be Still

A. YEMISI JIMOH

Lord, things ain't been the same since I lost my baby. Sometimes I regret that Cindra was my only child. I loved her more than I loved my own life. Like to killed me when she left. Twenty-four ain't nothing but a baby. She had her whole life ahead of her; now she's been taken on away from me. . . . Better comb my hair now and get on out of here. Where did I put that old coat of mine? Probably should get a new one, but Cindra really liked this one on me.

. . . Never hardly even gave that child a aspirin. How could she be taking drugs? Surely she didn't know. Something or somebody must've told her it was okay. . . . I watched her and that James Earl grow up side by side. Cindra's little skinny legs and plaits changed so fast. . . . Suddenly she was a little woman—miniature version of myself not so long ago.

"Now where's my pocketbook? Can't go nowhere without my little change."

. . . And that James Earl, yeah a kinda studying-type boy; a little on the mean side though. . . . Called himself Sizwe. He say, "We all Africans, but we been ripped off and taken from our home." Suppose I never did feel too welcome here.

. . . I didn't mind when James Earl and my baby got together. He was a pretty good boy; had him a few years of college too. Naw, I don't blame him for those drugs. . . . I don't understand it though. Me and that boy's mama thought things would be different for our children. Huh, things are different, but we still got problems. Both our babies dead. Cindra from drugs and James Earl . . . Well, the Deputy Chief of Corrections says that boy hanged himself up in that jail; just like the rest, just hang themselves up there, but I ain't sure. . . . His mama say he just asked for death to come after what happened to Cindra.

"Oh mercy, what's this—all watered-up in the eyes? No time for sitting-down sorrow. I better get on out of here. Time is moving on."

Been almost two years that all this trouble began and six months under that was when James Earl was found in that jail. They say his mama is a bit touched. But those two girls of hers are taking good care of her. Me, I got to get some work. This looking for jobs takes so much out of me. Actually though, I been blessed with steady work with the Davisons this last year. And I'm pretty good at what I do . . .

"Here's my pocketbook; Hmm, yes, and my letter's right there inside."

This letter I got from Dr. Davison's wife should get me work real fast. She says how good and dependable I am and gives me high regards as a respectful and diligent worker. Seems Mrs. Davison was glad to know that I wanted to take on weekend work. She even tried to tell me she knows how hard times is now. She say that there was a time when her and the doctor had a cook and a housekeeper five days a week, and a yardman on weekends. Times is hard all right, but I know, as God is my witness, that woman don't know any more about hard times than a horse know about birthing chickens.

"I better hurry; it's 6:00. My bus will be here in fifteen minutes."

. . . Did pretty good getting out of here today. After all this rush, I still got enough time to pick up a newspaper from old John on the corner. I like the empty sound early in the morning before the traffic and noise bring the city alive. It feels like God done spoke the word and commanded "Peace Be Still" with such power and force that nothing and nobody dare disobey. . . . Oooh, the wind is cutting straight through me. . . . Good it's not raining, but the air is mighty cold. Suppose complaining ain't going to do me no good, because this little string of a belt is doing the best job it can of holding this coat. I enjoy this early morning time, though; it gives me a chance to think. It's this looking for work that has my spirits down just now. . . . Hope I don't catch my death of cold. Walking this block and a half to the bus stop seems like an eternity. There's John, as faithful as ever with the morning paper. I have to get one.

"Hello, John, give me one of those *Morning Heralds;* let me see what's going on around this place."

"Hello, Bett, how ya be this morning?"

"Fine."

"Look here, they got a big article about that doctor and his wife that died over in Luxury Greens."

"Yeah, it's a shame, ain't it?"

"Didn't you used to work for them?"

"Uhm huh, worked for them until they died, and it's tiresome this looking for work again. I was real lucky to get that job right after my

Cindra passed on. . . . But let me tell you something, John; them folks and the way they live. . . . They got so much money that real life don't mean nothing to them no more."

"How you getting on, with all that's happened? Well, you know, with Cindra's passing on and all? Has keeping busy with work helped ease the lonely times?"

"The truth is, I been barely keeping life and limb together, but I know the Lord won't stop this old bus we call life to let me off before my work is done. Anyway, tell me where's that article about the Davisons."

"Here it is at the bottom of the front page. Listen, let me read it:

Prominent area physician Dr. William A. Davison and his wife, Jane C. Crighton Davison, were found dead in their Luxury Greens home last weekend. Recent reports from the medical examiner's office have been sketchy. She reports that initial toxicological tests have not shown any abnormalities, but further tests have been ordered. Green County's Chief Investigator, Robert Heath, has called their deaths "a mystery" because there were no signs of forced entry at their home and no visible causes of death. Both the doctor, who was 59, and his wife, who was 52, were in excellent health.

Officials still are concerned about the possibility of foul play, because of old drug charges against the doctor. Three years ago Dr. Davison was linked to an illegal drug ring. The doctor was eventually cleared of charges that he had sold drugs out of one of his medical offices.

Chief Investigator Heath has launched a full investigation.

"Something else, ain't it, Bett?"

"Yep, sure is. Well, here's my bus and your quarter for the paper. See ya later."

"Bett, you're full of strange habits. Truly strange habits."

. . . Seems like a nice driver today. He's pulling right up to the stop, not too far in front and not too far behind it. As usual I got just about the whole bus to myself this time in the morning. . . . Here's a good seat right by the window. Might as well get comfortable and relax for the next two hours . . .

No doubt about it, I hate looking for work. But there's surely work that needs to get done. . . . Wonder if that Deputy Chief of Corrections needs a housekeeper-cook . . .

On the Turning Up of Unidentified Black Female Corpses

TOI DERRICOTTE

Mowing his three acres with a tractor,
a man notices something ahead—a mannequin—
he thinks someone threw it from a car. Closer
he sees it is the body of a black woman.

The medics come and turn her with pitchforks.
Her gaze shoots past him to nothing. Nothing
is explained. How many black women
have been turned up to stare at us blankly,

in weedy fields, off highways,
pushed out in plastic bags,
shot, knifed, unclothed partially, raped,
their wounds sealed with a powdery crust.

Last week on TV, a gruesome face, eyes bloated shut.
No one will say, "She looks like she's sleeping," ropes
of blue-black slashes at the mouth. Does anybody
know this woman? Will anyone come forth? Silence

like a backwave rushes into that field
where, just the week before, four other black girls
had been found. The gritty image hangs in the air
just a few seconds, but it strikes me,

a black woman, there is a question being asked
about my life. How can I
protect myself? Even if I lock my doors,
walk only in the light, someone wants me dead.

Am I wrong to think
if five white women had been stripped,
broken, the sirens would wail until
someone was named?

Is it any wonder I walk over these bodies
pretending they are not mine, that I do not know
the killer, that I am just like any woman—
if not wanted, at least tolerated.

Part of me wants to disappear, to pull
the earth on top of me. Then there is this part
that digs me up with this pen
and turns my sad black face to the light.

Finished

AI

You force me to touch
the black, rubber flaps
of the garbage disposal
that is open like a mouth saying, ah.
You tell me it's the last thing I'll feel
before I go numb.
Is it my screaming that finally stops you,
or is it the fear
that even you are too near the edge
of this Niagara to come back from?
You jerk my hand out
and give me just enough room
to stagger around you.
I lean against the refrigerator,
not looking at you, or anything,
just staring at a space which you no longer inhabit,
that you've abandoned completely now
to footsteps receding
to the next feeding station,
where a woman will be eaten alive
after cocktails at five.
The flowers and chocolates, the kisses,
the swings and near misses of new love
will confuse her,
until you start to abuse her,
verbally at first.
As if trying to quench a thirst,
you'll drink her
in small outbursts of rage
then you'll whip out your semiautomatic,
make her undress, or to listen to hours

of radio static as torture
for being amazed that the man of her dreams
is a nightmare, who only seems happy
when he's making her suffer.

The first time you hit me,
I left you, remember?
It was December. An icy rain was falling
and it froze on the roads,
so that driving was unsafe, but not as unsafe
as staying with you.
I ran outside in my nightgown,
while you yelled at me to come back.
When you came after me,
I was locked in the car.
You smashed the window with a crowbar,
but I drove off anyway.
I was back the next day
and we were on the bare mattress,
because you'd ripped up the sheets,
saying you'd teach me a lesson.
You wouldn't speak except
to tell me I needed discipline,
needed training in the fine art
of remaining still
when your fist slammed into my jaw.
You taught me how ropes could be tied
so I'd strangle myself,
how pressure could be applied to old wounds
until I cried for mercy,
until tonight, when those years
of our double exposure end
with shot after shot.

How strange it is to be unafraid.
When the police come,

I'm sitting at the table,
the cup of coffee
that I am unable to drink
as cold as your body.
I shot him, I say, he beat me.
I do not tell them how the emancipation from pain
leaves nothing in its place.

It Must Be Her Heartbreak Talking

PATRICIA SPEARS JONES

She says
It's a war zone out here
Every woman I know is being battered
Malevolence rules the city like a scarred Emperor
outraged at physical perfection.
Just yesterday a friend of the family was robbed
and raped in her own home—a woman in her fifties!
What more do they want?
What more can they take?

She says
In clear light I see escalating indifference
suspicion, fear.
The Jewish woman on the subway
holding her pocketbook tightly
against the brown of my skin. She seems
full of weapons and this bitterness between us
competes with the August heat for our anxious attention.
How much longer can we not see each other?
How much longer can we survive this way?

She says
This is insane
to feel so desperate
when there is enough to eat.
To feel angry all of the time.
All the time.

She says
I must get away from here. There is too little space
and there is even less for me.

Where is it better than this?
She gives no answer.

Vanity

J. CALIFORNIA COOPER

I'm sittin here thinking, ponderin, over life. I hear my radio playin music softly round me. Beautiful full religious music bout God and what he does. I am listenin . . . and I am thinkin . . . about this life. Even death.

Sometimes you get something in life and you don't know you got it, so you don't do nothin with it. Then sometime you get something and you know you got it and you want everybody else to know it too. You be just done got lucky, even got something you can share, like beauty. But some people turn a gift into a weapon and use it on everybody. Sometimes, they think they be goin up, up . . . but they ain't. They be goin down, down . . . and taking people with em! Two fools. Fool for doin it, and a fool for goin down with it. One thing I do know, life is like a bank sometime. You ain't gonna get no more out of it than you put in it! Tho it do look like some people do . . . in the end, they don't.

Some people say everybody got a Guardian Angel looks over you. I ain't sure God got that kind of labor to waste on some people, but if he do, I don't envy the one was watchin over Vanity.

My mind is turned to these thoughts by death. A strange death, ugh!, of a woman I knew. A friend? I don't know was she a friend or not. She might'a tried, I don't know. I was her friend tho. I do know that. Vanity. Vanity is her name.

I knew her well. Very well. I am a little older than she was. I used to keep her, sit with her for her mama when Vanity was little. She was grown then, in a little way. She talk to me all her life. She thought I was her friend . . . well I was, but I was a little scared of her. I was. She didn't seem to have nothin in her heart for nobody but herself. I watched her think, listened to her talk.

Just listen what she said to me a year or so ago, when her trouble started. Another kind of trouble she didn't understand. See, she didn't have no women friends for too long. They didn't like her for long. But she never cared noway. She get lonely she just come find me. I knew all her secrets. I think. Just listen what she said to me when we be sittin on the front porch, laughin, talkin softly. She be drinkin champagne. She drink enough to keep even a Guardian Angel high.

She say, "I was always very beautiful. You may not believe that, but it's true. I know. I am still beautiful.

"I knew I was beautiful the day I was born. You may not believe that either, that a newborn could know that, but I did. The doctor did not want to slap me, the nurses looked at me with envy and hate. My mother was elated. She was . . . uncomely. But I let that pass. ME. I was the important one . . . and . . . as I said I was beautiful. But bored . . . from birth.

"Bored! Do you know how long I had to wait to walk? To speak? To buy things, beautiful clothes, to enhance my beauty? Several years. But I used the time well.

"I studied my father. I wrapped his heart around all my fingers. Many times he slept, holding me, instead of my mother. That became a problem, but I don't wish to talk about that now. But . . . I was practicing, yes, practicing for my future. When I spoke, I spoke in question marks. 'Will you buy that for me? May I have that? Do you think this is right for me? Don't you want me to have that? Does this look good on me, compliment me?' Oh yes, I knew what to do with me, my beauty.

"I wanted to goooo somewhere. Beeee somebody. Doooo something with what I had. I was born decided not to be a victim. Determined. And I had the greatest tool I know in life. Beauty.

"At five, ten, twelve, fifteen years of age, I knew, I knew, just by looking at people looking at me. I knew I was superb . . . that I could acquire things and people in proportion to my beauty. The world lets you know they are fools because they love beauty no matter how empty it is. However, I was not empty. I was full of thoughts. Of myself. Well . . . what better? Who should you be thinking of? See?" She said and laughed, "I'm still into question marks?

"Reasons, causes and effects, results . . . that's what I studied on. Hard. But not too hard . . . it wasn't necessary . . . for all. Boys and then men became monotonous, always telling me of their love. What did they think I thought? Didn't I know they would love me? Want me? I was delicious to look upon. Ask my father. He gave me everything! He loved to touch me, assure himself I was his. My mother had very little, she didn't need it anyway. She had her chosen man . . . who really belonged to me after I was born. She had us. She had him anyway. I was there I guess. But only I had me.

"Many, many hours were spent, me with myself, alone. The sun rose and shone on ME, sent its warmth into my soul. Flowers bent when I passed, God knew. Everyone, anyone, who looked on me, their heart beat and throbbed with the thoughts of love and possession. Men and some women too. Desire . . . ahhhh, desire, the crux of the whole life matter.

"I was young . . . innocent, in a way, in my body, not my mind. I was sad because I had to wait for life, get older. Wait for the joy of being a woman. A beautiful woman. To get my due. I said prayers. After all, God was, is, greater than I, at least." (I know her Guardian Angel almost choked!)

"So many loves came into my life, before my eyes. I was always smiling, happy. At peace with my self and my glory. I cared, oh!, I cared for myself because when I first looked at me, I loved, loved me.

"At twelve years old, I washed, creamed and smoothed my body. I brushed, combed my luxuriant hair that it might nestle on my lovely soft shoulders and be a cape of beauty for others to enjoy. Yes, I thought of others, sometime. I loved my arms, my waist, my legs, so full and smooth, beautiful . . . and mine.

"You know I loved clothes! To sheath my body! Let them be expensive! Let my father struggle to do what he had to do to afford them for me. Wasn't I his child? Wasn't he supposed to do for me? Getting anything I needed? I needed beauty. As I grew older, I HAD to have lovely, beautiful, costly things. Wasn't I ME!? Mama had had her time and got him . . . and me . . . now it was my turn. Practicing, practicing. My hands, my nails, my shoulders, my breast, beautiful. My legs, my thighs, my feet . . . all of me, I oiled, creamed, smoothed and loved. And I felt joy. Anything that made me look like me . . . beautiful . . . I loved. Not people . . . just things.

"The only thing that bothered me was time. TIME. Always moving, passing, getting away. But too slow for me. I had to wait, wait and waste those early years I needed, to be admired and loved. I got up early, mornings, to have more time to be admired. I have sat looking out my windows, hours and hours, weeks and weeks, just waiting for someone new to come along, pass by, to look upon me and know . . . I was beautiful. I watched their eyes.

"Seasons meant nothing to me. All were mine. Except, I learned I must stay out of the sun. Ahhh, and it was such a spotlight.

"One day after school graduation, after all the shit I had to go through to get to my life, my freedom, I said to myself, 'I'm not beautiful enough.' You see, I had seen others then, that might come close to me. And I wished, tho I looked better than all others, that all, ALL pretty women, even cute women, would die, DIE. And leave me to have all the men, all the adulation, my choice, anybody I wanted . . . to love me.

"Somebody special to love me. It was now at the time when loving myself was not enough . . . not enough. I began to know fear. Fear is a low, low, sad feeling. But it was into me. I couldn't help it. Of course, I should have known better. What had fear to do with me? YET . . . I feared. Somehow I knew . . . I might not . . . might not . . . have everything. Oh! my lord, ME!?

"Now! It was now time. I was eighteen. Through with high school. My parents could not afford college where I might have found my true future, my love to love me as I should be loved. Riches, position, everything! No . . . I had to work with what I had. Well, it was quite a bit. But, still, all by myself. Only, only?, my beauty to help me. And it did. Don't you make the mistake that men will not let anything go for a beautiful thing to look at. In the morning, the evening, especially the night. Men are fools. Good grand fools. Don't let me mislead you, they are alright. Are they not rich sometimes? I still believe the world belongs to a woman, but only because it belongs to men and they give it to her! Just fools for beauty. Is it beauty? Or is it body? Hmmmm. But . . . I was always just like a lady, a real lady. A beautiful, beautiful Lady."

Yessss, chile! All those things Vanity said to me . . . and more. I can't remember everything now, my mind is mixed up with death . . . and life.

I'ma tell you something, bout this life I done found out. Sometimes from the birthstone to the tombstone ain't nothing but a few steps. High ones, low ones. Don't matter. And sometime you don't even know you been walking on the road of time, think you been standin still and you been flyin with your feet. Laughin, having a good time, even cryin, having a bad time. Then, one day, you look up and you way, way up the road. One day you twenty, overnight, you thirty, one movin year . . . forty, one afternoon . . . fifty. After that, it pass by like hours, minutes! All the time you thought you was spending only money, you been spending time. TIME. Chile, time. The most valuable thing you got! Or ever gonna have!

Now, if you ain't there where you think you ought to be when you think you oughta be THERE, and you done spent time til you broke and you ain't even enjoyed gettin to where you are! If you don't understand what I'm sayin, I do, I just maybe ain't sayin it right for you to understand. Try.

There was no lie about it! Vanity was a beautiful thing, a beautiful woman to see. Not to know. Just to see. Her Guardian Angel had a JOB!

But, back to her family, her dear mother saw the love transferred away from her. She wasn't no longer the center of the home. She just waned and drifted to the background with the second daughter she had, Mega. The father often slept with Vanity cause she said she had bad dreams, holdin her, pettin her, kissin her. As she grew older, them kisses grew lower and lower until she was kissed by father all over her body. It was like a form of worship to her. If it is true some men had their own daughters way, way back there in them cavemen days without feelin shame nor fear, that is still in some men. I don't blive he went that far with her tho. Just fondles, touches. But she grew to expect, and get, the same thing from most all her men the rest of her life. Her Guardian Angel musta shuddered.

Then, when Mega was born the father expected to have another great beauty to show off. He smiled and waited. But, as she grew, her beauty was neat, plain, sweet. He might could'a grew to understand those was also wonderful things to love, but Vanity always movin between them, pullin on his arms when he played with Mega, wrappin herself round his head to shield his eyes from Mega. In time, he centered on Vanity again. The mother cried awhile, then smiled thru her tears and took Mega to herself. Mega grew up affectionate, patient, sweet and, I guess, just normally normal. The mother refused to have any more children. So they each had one!

But these things tells on a woman who loves her husband. She loved her husband, had dreamed of the perfect home. Her love grieved, her spirit grieved. She was alone in her home, in her marriage, in her life. She was a sad, sad heartbroken woman, whose daughter had stolen her husband, with a smile. A beautiful smile. A Guardian Angel grieved, I know.

In time, when Vanity was seventeen, Mega fifteen, the parents divorced. The mother could take no more, could not watch Mega's confusion no more. The family had been divided too often and too long by

Vanity's demands on her father. The mother took Mega, naturally, and because I don't have time to tell just everything, I'll just tell you they did well. Mega had a normal life, I guess. She wondered, from time to time, about the family ways. She loved them all. She was patient with them all. Just like a real little lady. Her time passed that way, and she grew up strong in spite of all of them.

All this time Vanity was runnin after hearts . . . anybody's. Had great pleasure in takin the heart of a boy, or man, who seemed to love another girl, or woman. Even her closest friends' beaus. Of course she ended up with no friends! But Vanity didn't care, she was havin a good time. Just like a lady (she thought). And time passed. Don't it always.

Her father bought her everything. Sometime being late, very late, with payments for Mega. Vanity explained that away to him by saying she gave Mega all her cast-off clothing and things, that Mega didn't need as much right at that time of her life.

Also, at that time of Vanity's life, she was twenty or twenty-one then, dancin, laughin, always goin out, riding, playin. Life was gettin dull to her. Same old crowd, growing smaller. Some gettin married. Women shyin away from her. Men already been burnt by her, keepin a distance. No magic around for her to play with. She turned her lofty head to look over the horizon for fresh life and dreams. Her Guardian Angel was in dread.

Vanity loved picture shows. Lookin at one, one day, she decided she had always wanted to be a movie star. She knew she looked as good as those up on that screen. She prepared her father a good meal (in her gloves). Set a beautiful table, candles and all, just for her father and her. His eyes just sparkled, he was so proud of his daughter and happy she had decided to stay home with him an evenin. Vanity didn't waste no time tho, she just came right out and told him almost soon as he sat down to eat.

"Daddy, I need some money. I've made up my mind what I want to be, at last. I'm going to Los Angeles to seek my fame . . . and my fortune. I know I will be successful. All they want is beauty! So . . . I am prepared." She laughed, he frowned, started to say something. She thought she anticipated him. "You always wanted me to be serious about something. Now, I'm ready."

He sighed. They argued awhile. He lost, again.

He said, as he sighed, "Well . . . if that's what you really want. I'll transfer my job . . . and we'll move."

She pursed her beautiful lips. "Noooo. I want to . . . I need to go alone. I'm over twenty-one now. I want to be on my own. Just send me some money. But I want to be alone." She thought of all the men there. And Dad was gettin old and showing it. Ugly comin. She didn't like ugly.

He was hurt . . . and feared loneliness. "You'd leave me? You'd go alone? So far from me?"

She turned her beautiful lips down, and snapped, "What do you expect me to do? Be here under . . . with you the rest of my life?"

He stammered, "No . . . no . . . I . . . I thought . . . "

She stopped his thought. "Well, I am grown. I will go alone. You can't be with me forever! I have to have my own life! I am your daughter . . . NOT your wife." He groaned and twisted in his seat, dinner, candles forgotten. She continued. "You'll . . . you'll still have Mega . . . and Mama, if you can get her to leave her new husband and come back to you! But I . . . "

He bent his dumb head. "Your mother will never leave that man. He loves her . . . and Mega." He looked up suddenly, angry. "He better not be doing anything to my child!" He looked sad again. "Let me get a house there and we . . . "

She threw him a disdainful look. "Dad. I . . . am . . . grown. I have to go alone." Her tone softened, "I have to see if I can make it on my own. So you will be proud of me. Just a little money to help me til I am rich and can make it on my own." She smiled brightly, beautifully. "Then I will send for you to come . . . visit me sometime."

Anyway . . . she got her way. Her Guardian Angel shook its head . . . and waited.

Vanity went to Los Angeles expecting to have heads and hearts rolling in the streets. Instead she found so many beautiful women everywhere she went to seek a job. Everywhere she walked, ate, sat, looked. She got nervous and was throwing up every night. Got sick even, but didn't get a job in films. Men had so much pretty to look upon. She was just one of them. Beauty was five feet deep in Los Angeles. Talent wasn't. Vanity didn't have much talent. In two months she called home for a ticket back. Back to safety and some kind of throne. In Los Angeles they didn't even know she was gone, cause they hardly knew she was there.

Her daddy smiled sadly, gladly sent the money, borrowed money. He had been sending her so much to keep her in the style she thought she had to have, to keep her happy, he was most broke. But he was happy he was gonna have his "baby" back! Her Guardian Angel must have smiled with relief cause a whole lotta things wait for pretty girls in them big busy cities.

She returned to her little three-legged throne. Told everybody she didn't like it in L.A. because the people had no class. But she read that writin on the back of that throne, looked at the horizon again, saw "marriage."

Now ... one man, Robert, really worshipped Vanity. You know right there he was a lightweight fool. He had done gone to college and had a future, but the future wasn't there yet, so he was still in the strugglin stage. He sure knew how to talk tho. And he could kiss her from the feet up ... she had to have that! He wrote her poems. Sent her flowers. Kissed her feet. Used his eyes as mirrors for her. Since she saw herself so much in his eyes, and thought he had a future, she married him. Her daddy surely did go into BIG debt for that weddin. I blive he still owe some on it and he dead and gone now!

The mother and Mega came. The mother lookin sad, Mega smiling with joy for her sister. She wasn't asked to be in the weddin. She was married now, with one child. Vanity said she needed a pretty matron of honor with some money so she could get a better present from her. She seemed to understand Vanity, didn't seem to mind, but I knew she was hurt cause she was a family person. She cared. She knew how to love people for real reasons.

Anyway, the Guardian Angel must have held its breath, but the marriage lasted only three years. Til Vanity was twenty-five. Turned out Robert's struggle was lastin too long ... and the kisses didn't last long enough, cause they got borin and all tied up with cookin (in gloves) and eatin, going to the bathroom and snorin, his dirty clothes, underwear and all, and blowin noses and payin bills (she made). He be tired and she need another dose of worship. She took to leavin him snorin and going out to get what worship she needed, in them expensive clothes she charged on him. Her daddy was still payin for some of her clothes too, she sure could spend money on herself. He was still livin then, poor fool. She never did buy nobody else nothin!

Now, Vanity didn't go too far out. Not very much adultry, cause that wasn't what she was after. Just more love and worship. The few times she did commit adultry was cause her worship bank was low and she couldn't get that worship no other way. She ended up having two abortions for two reasons. One, she didn't quite know whose baby it was. Two, she was never gonna mess her body up with nothin! Her husband never knew. Her daddy never knew. Even her hairdresser never knew. Just her and the one who gave her the pills and things, and me, cause I had to help her, care for her.

Now that took a little toll on her looks, but it didn't show right then at the time. That little bit of drinkin, she loved champagne, didn't do much harm, but it did some. She liked to smoke cause it made her look classy, she thought. That took a toll, too. But you couldn't see it cause she made-up and dressed-up so good. But . . . she still got bored after awhile. Her Guardian Angel used to whisper things to her conscience to make her life fuller, more satisfying to all. But it found nothin there to listen to it.

She got divorced. She didn't get no job tho. She lived off the money from her father and what she could get out of her ex-husband. She could work with that money. Somebody else's! Cause she wouldn't work FOR it.

Then she made friends with a wealthy older woman, Snity. Snity spelled her name "$nity." Her new friend was almost just like her, so $nity didn't let Vanity round her husband too much. $nity did go all the way with her admirers. She was growin old and losin her beauty from livin so hard and much. She did introduce her to other wealthy men tho.

Vanity was a good catcher for $nity and was used as such for a long time, til she was thirty or thirty-one. She got to travel, go places she never could have gone before. She was lonely, so she was sleepin around a bit. But you had to give her some money then, cause she needed clothes to keep up with $nity. Her Guardian Angel weeped.

Finally a older man came along who $nity didn't want. Name Edward. The man had some little sense cause he had made a lotta money. But, between $nity talkin him into it and Vanity bein so beautiful (still), he asked Vanity to be his wife. Vanity opened her arms wide, showin all her beauty at once, and flew to his side like a Condor jet! Guardian Angel held its breath again.

As life would have it, Edward got bored early with the kissin from the feet up. Wanted hisself kissed from the feet up. But mostly he wanted someone to share his mind with. He took a clear, longer look inside his beautiful wife and . . . HE got bored!

The man still had some sense, so he took the good from the marriage. Vanity was a good hostess, handled his business meetings at home well. Could socialize successfully. He kept her. And she kept him. In time, tho, she became bored, less men paid attention to her. She became lonely. Edward wasn't often interested in makin love and worship to her. He became lonely. No one to really talk to in his home. She didn't care for his grown children. They were uncomfortable, so they just gradually stayed away. He had to visit them. He was welcome, but it wasn't like bein at his own home. Guardian Angel shook its head in sorrow.

Edward liked Mega, even did some business with her husband who was moving right along with his business, using elbow grease and brains. But even Mega didn't come round much cause she had three children that Vanity didn't like.

No, Vanity didn't seem to like children at all. Edward didn't know it, but Vanity had already had one abortion with him. It was his child and he sure would have loved it. The child would have tied them closer, into a family. Guardian Angel wept again.

Another thing Edward didn't know, Vanity was workin with a doctor to plan an appendix operation which was really goin to be a historectory. She told me she could not keep up them abortions. She had got real sick from the last time and thought Edward might find out why, for real, if it happened again.

She looked over at me, over that glass of champagne she had brought over to my house and said, "I simply cannot afford to ruin my body. Not for any baby, nor any man! My body is all I have, and I am not sharing it! The baby will end up with all my looks and all I will have is a 'baby.'"

The woman was a lonely woman, very lonely inside all her beauty and didn't know how much a baby, her own child, could mean. But the baby might have been lucky not to have been born, after all. I don't know, cause I don't know everything. So, historectory it was.

When Vanity got to be round thirty-five she was runnin round like she was crazy. Going to every party, every show, every nightclub, about every night. Driven dissipation. She was desperately trying to be rich and happy. Sometimes her despondence and dissipation was pitiful. She cried. But not too long, cause it made you ugly. Her tears musta been champagne cause she drank it all the time. Carried a bottle in her car. Opened. Guardian Angel asked to be relieved of its duty. Devil grinned cause he likes destruction and confusion.

She kept that up til she was round thirty-eight years old. Beauty goin cause beauty ain't somethin you can beat to death every night. Edward was so bored, disgusted, tired of everything so empty, he was in pain. When I say, "bored," don't take that word lightly. "Bored" can be miserable, miserable. That is what he was, miserable. And each month the bills were higher. He was payin plenty to be miserable. Divorce came on his mind, naturally, cause he never was a real stone-fool.

Mega's husband died round that time, too. She was broken nearly to pieces by his death. She truly loved him. Theirs was a good marriage. She had the children tho, and he left her pretty well fixed. Edward, of course, went to console her. In her innocence, he was consoled. She looked healthy and warm, too. And her house had lots of love in it.

Vanity's and Mega's father died round bout then. Death comes like that sometime. In threes, people say. His heart was probly broken, cause it sure was starved. Vanity didn't never have no time for him in her fast life. He was like some child she didn't want to be bothered with. She was in New York partyin at the time. Called and told Mega to decide everything and take care everything, see bout the insurance money. That she would TRY to get back in time for the funeral. Guardian Angel tried to quit.

I was her friend, but I got mad at her then, and didn't know whether I'd keep on bein her friend or not! I could see how she might do me one day! Or anybody! Her father did everything she ever wanted! She never paid no time to her mother either, but that old woman made it so she didn't need Vanity. She had her Mega and grandchildren. I know she would have loved to be closer to her daughter Vanity tho. You know mothers.

She did make it to the funeral . . . late. Mega did all the work need to be done. Mega cried the most. The mother too. Vanity cried, with a glass of champagne in her hands all through the funeral, what was left when she got there. Edward was disgusted . . . again. He had his arms round Mega, consoling her, more than he had em round Vanity.

Well, now . . . Vanity had all the money she needed, but them admirers was fadin away. Edward was fadin away. Vanity was lonely, unhappy. Her beauty was really fadin away too. She decided to go in for all that plastic surgery stuff. Edward put his foot down, then he put his marriage down. They got a divorce. Now, she really was alone. Lotsa friends don't last long sometime. Vanity was very, very lonely with only herself. But that was the main person she had loved.

Everything happened so fast. Edward and Vanity divorced and we looked up and Edward was marryin Mega, who probably saw in him the father she never had. He was good to the children too! Neither one was marryin for money cause they both had some. He older, but they still together and it look like they happy to me. That whole family! His kids is welcome now to his home.

Vanity like to died, sure nuff! when they got married. She said Mega had always tried to take everything from her she ever wanted. Lied. She consoled herself by trying to take every dime she could from him. She told everybody her sister had broken up her happy home. Lied. Friends (?) smiled and turned away. Guardian Angel had a sore neck from shaking it.

Vanity was thirty-nine years old then. She spent plenty money on that face surgery. It did some good. Then her mother died. She said she couldn't let herself cry like she felt, cause her operation was too new, it would ruin it. But even with them operations, she was beginnin to look like her mother. She had mirrors all over her house. She would see herself all day, wherever she moved. Sometimes she just scream, break out in tears and run jump in the middle of her sumptuous bed and cry, tryin to hold her face straight.

Vanity went into retreat. Wouldn't come out for nothin. Ordered everything brought in. Chile, the woman was somethin! Layin out there in that big ole house with all the rich stuff in it. Lonely and unhappy . . . and scared. She had never lived like that before, and she didn't know what to do. Everybody who would help her was gone . . . or dead. She was alone. No mama, no daddy, no close sister, no child. Alone, chile.

Mega who was nowhere near her in looks had her husband. Vanity knew something was wrong. The men were gone. She was free, divorced, and the men weren't rushing in. It must be her beauty. She really stayed out of the sun. Spent hundreds of dollars on lotions and creams, magic formulas. Like a lady, she thought. Her Guardian Angel looked over the world, saw the starving, the sick, and cried. That was the saddest angel!

So . . . she lived her life alone. Retreated from all her "friends" and "admirers" for, to her, the reason for their admiration was fadin away.

She wanted to be remembered as the most beautiful. The most beautiful lady ever in their world. Yea . . . so she retreated from the world. Like a lady. Her Guardian Angel took a deep breath, sighed and rested in defeat, but hope.

But . . . no matter what you do or how you hide, this world, life, is not going to let you get away without livin. Long as you breathin, something is going to happen to you!

Her life proceeded in a quiet way. All her days was spent alone. She might talk on the phone just to keep up with what was goin on in her old world. She didn't want any company. Maybe $nity, but $nity didn't want to come nowhere dark and quiet. She was old, but she thought she was still goin strong, tho now, she was givin the men her money.

Vanity told $nity, "You are a fool! Givin somebody all that money you have worked hard lyin, layin and marrying for! A man wouldn't know how to fix his lips to ask me for any of my money! I'll never get that old and need any loving from anybody who expects something for it other than my time and my beautiful body!" She laughed. "I don't need anybody, or anything that bad! A man coming into my life better bring something with him!"

After long days, bathing, drinkin, creaming her body, wearin her lovely delicate negligies, drinkin, eating, lookin at TV, staring out in space through the curtains of her huge windows, drinkin, listenin to records, starin into mirrors, drinkin again, she was bored and restless, but did not want to go out where people were. She actually thought she was gettin ugly, but she really wasn't ugly. Older, naturally, but, she didn't look bad as she seem to think.

She lay in bed at night, lonely, longing. Staring at the mirror over her bed. Wishing for someone. Her first husband . . . no. Her second husband . . . maybe. Rainy nights were the hardest. She played blues records and, yes, sometimes she cried. She felt sorry for herself that everyone had left behind, somehow. They say the blues ain't nothin but a woman cryin for her man. Well, she just didn't exactly know who her man was. He had to be in her past. Sure didn't look like he was in her future.

Sometimes . . . she felt just like the dogs she could hear howling at night. Oh! Lord! They sure must have the blues, to sound so, so sad. So blue. Even lost, deserted. So lonely . . . in the darkness of the night . . . in the rain . . . in the quiet. Sometime she would cut off all sound, music and TV, in the house and lay and listen to the sound of dogs callin to each other. Mating calls. Sad longing songs that sounded full of need and painful feelings. Alone. In need. Alone.

Her life was so quiet, she began to look forward to orderin things somebody had to bring. The groceries was the most likely thing, cause she did like to eat good food. The liquor store, too, was the most regular delivery.

The man who delivered the liquor was very mannerable, respectful, quiet, youngish . . . bout thirty-eight or thirty-nine years old. Always smiling. Gentle, smooth, smart. Knew how to do a million things around the house that always need doing and always did a few before he left. Hang a plant different, move a table, a large chair. Fix a small pipe, see why a light didn't work. All those kinds of things. You know. All the things some women wish a man was around the house for.

He never touched her. Even accidently. No, no. He remained mannerable, never familiar, never out of line. Didn't even curse a little bit. Just never did anything wrong. You know. Like I say, the kind some women wish was around the house. He was good-lookin too. Bright, youngish face. Hell, he wasn't old anyway.

He liked good music. It got to where she always searched for something new to play for him . . . to hold him a little longer. Then it got to where she had something fixed for him, something he had said he liked to eat. He drank very little. She ordered so much liquor to get him over there, she could have stocked a speakeasy. She liked to see him. He was just about perfect. Her Guardian Angel became alarmed. Because, you see, the angel knew.

Yes, he was almost perfect. He had practiced a long time. He had several older women he always delivered to. A few with money, they had to have money, had even become what they thought was "his woman." He made love to them. Good love. He was gentle sometimes, rough sometimes, but always only just enough. He never did anything too much. With them.

He had a nice life. Just deliver liquor. His customers bought so much, the owner let him handle just the ones he wanted to deliver to. He could do something extra if he wanted to. He had wanted to deliver to Vanity. He had watched her for several years. She hadn't seen him. Until she was alone.

He wouldn't live with any woman. Wanted to be alone, free. Wanted everything he wanted and all he could get of it. He really didn't want for nothin, not with them ladies he had. He dressed, always in good taste, very expensively. He liked hats and he sure looked good in em!

He knew when not to see someone. He was a bit cruel. He could ignore either one of his "women" for a week or two. Send someone else with the order. Not call for two or three days. You know. They always end up givin him what he wanted. He never asked, just mentioned. And he only mentioned once. So you better remember what he said and hurry up and get it if you wanted him comin back.

Vanity came to expect him. To count on him. Even to love him . . . a little, and he had never touched her. Yet. Her Guardian Angel whispered to her, but she really couldn't hear the angel I guess.

His name was Jody. Jody was born, I think, with something left out of his soul. The ability to love somebody, anybody, but himself.

Yea, he came into her life. Yes, chile. Ain't it the way life is? Just keep foolin round with it . . . it will fool back with you!

Jody had all the charm, all the manners, all the look-like concern and care for the female race they needed. He was warm and affectionate with his voice. Color of a sunny Hershey bar, lookin just as rich and sweet. Warm, admiring eyes and a gentleman to the hundredth degree. Six feet tall, large shoulders, played football and basketball in school and college. Yes, he went to college and still just a delivery boy. He wore bikini underwear. Don't ask me how I know! He, also, had five children he claimed were all not his.

In two months, they were close, old friends. Watchin the results of all they had done in the garden at night. Vanity would only come out at night. He smiled that warm, sweet smile and started workin with her. He had to build some new shelves on his day off, for all the liquor she had bought. He never asked for a dime. Never accepted a dime. Anyway, that started him spendin most his days off with her. One of em anyway, she didn't know he had all of em off if he wanted to.

Then, his television broke. He could fix everything, but he couldn't fix his own stuff. Naturally they spent several evenings, just friends, lookin at TV. Somehow Vanity mentioned, in a laughin voice of confidence between friends, how she loved to make love in the mornings, and when it rained, when it stormed, when it thundered. You know?

One day, when the weather report said "rain, storm," he came by that night, to check on her, of course. She sat down and lay back, in one of them flimsy rich gowns and looked at him. He was quiet, but he knew how to look back. He looked so good, so big, so strong. Vanity squirmed, crossed her legs back and forth, all them things we do. She finally jumped up when the programs was finished, news, weather and all. Jumped up and said, "Go! Please go! I . . . I . . . I don't know what's wrong with me! Please go."

He smiled a warm intimate smile, said, "Talk to me. Tell me what the matter is."

She couldn't.

He said, "Am I your friend? I guess I'm not. And I . . . I feel so much for you. I want you to like me. But . . . I know you can't." He looked down into his drink, then back at her, deeply. "You are so beautiful. So beautiful. You could talk to, or have anyone you want in the world." He stood, as if to go. Vanity raised from her seat, but she didn't stand, just sat up. He went on talkin, "I am only me. So . . . I understand. I'm not . . . something enough for you."

Vanity slowly got to her feet, reached one hand out to him. "Oh!" Her other hand touched her throat. "Oh, you are everything wonderful to me. You are my friend. The only one I have. Do I really look beautiful to you?"

Jody reached out to her slowly, with that warm hand. Took her arm that had brushed against him so regularly lately, pulled her to his side. She buried her face in his shoulder. He used his chin to nudge her head around til their lips met . . . then he kissed the shit out of that woman.

Moments later, with heavy breathin from both of them, he said, "I better go . . . I'm only a man . . . and you are a beautiful woman. I won't be able to control myself." And he left, even tho she was holdin him and pullin on that man for all she was worth. He left. And she longed.

Vanity went to the phone, ordered more liquor. A big order. Then she went to her dressin table, made up her face. Perfumed her body. Soon the delivery came, Jody brought it. Not long after, she came. Jody brought it.

His time had come. The next time she saw him he said, "I am ashamed to have taken such a liberty with such a beautiful woman of whom I am not worthy." You ever seen or listened to a woman convince a man he is worthy of her? Well, all I can say is her Guardian Angel wept for her.

Vanity told him he was worthy of her when she came again . . . and he went away, satisfied. She came . . . he went . . . and that ain't the same thing. You know it! But Vanity fell asleep, satisfied. Like a lady?

When she woke up the next day, everything else did too. Passion, love, need. All for a man whose address and telephone number she didn't even know. A man she didn't even know what his dreams was. A smiling man she didn't know, who brought her liquor when she ordered and paid for it. A stranger. Maybe we are all strangers, but, Lord help a woman at such a time in life where she will put her heart in strange hands full of blood and tears. Lord help the men, too, cause it's all kinds of strangers out here.

Jody didn't come back with the next order . . . nor the next. A young, young boy did. Vanity like to died. All her morning had been about getting ready for him. She called the store and asked for him . . . he was not there. She had no-where else to call and the store owner could not give her his number, he didn't know it. Finally, in a few days, he just dropped in about 11:00 at night. Her heart bloomed, opened, screamed out at the sight of him. He had come again! And so did she. But this time there was fear in the coming and she did not sleep so soundly satisfied when he left at 1:00 in the morning. The heart that had blossomed, had wilted with a little hurt pain. He gave her no number, no address. Said he had no phone and was never hardly home anyway. Always lookin for a job to do. He had huge bills to pay. "But, no, don't worry, I will make it." He said, "I don't want your money." She had offered, of course. She loved him and his painful beauty.

The next week passed. No call. No visit. When, finally, he did come, all the anger she had planned, vanished. She loved him who loved her beauty. For the first time, he had brought her something . . . a lovely golden mirror. "A magic mirror," he said. "So you can see your beauty framed by me." Vanity looked into that mirror all the time. All the time. Like a fairy princess . . . preparing for her prince.

In the following months they kinda had a relationship, least a year and a half. He still came to her at his will. She was always ready because he took so long. Sometime, when he and his regular girl were on the outs, yea, you know he had one, he would stay a day or two. Til he and his regular girl were together again. The regular girl woulda missed him for the two days and be eager to mend things. He would have lain around, eaten, watched TV, made love once, slept . . . and thought. He would then have to go see about his other regular old ladies, also.

Sometimes he would come to Vanity and sleep only on top of the covers, while she lay beneath them, body smoldering, longing for him to enter her. But he would not get into bed . . . let lone into her, tho she begged.

Jody did not kiss her from the feet up. For the first time she longed to kiss him from the feet up, but was afraid her beauty would not look good from that distance. He kissed her lips . . . when she asked him, or when she seemed to be gettin tired of longing for him, ready to quit her grief. He would not see her for five, six, seven, eight days at a time. Let her suffer.

He made dates with her. Then she would do a lot of cleaning. Herself! Cooking, setting the table, puttin out flowers, all of it. Then, looking out the window, sittin, waitin for him. . . . He did not come. Then . . . she looking into that magic mirror . . . to see what was wrong. She saw lines, wrinkles that were not there. In that mirror, when he did not come, and she could not . . . her beauty faded, faded.

She began to buy him clothes, lay them all out on the bed. If he didn't come . . . she would want to throw them all away, give them away. But, she never did, because she had the good sense to know she really wanted this man and would need something to lure him. She "forced" money on him, which he never asked for, just needed, but he took. He folded away, smiling, hundreds of dollars that disappeared deep into his pockets, never to be seen again.

Valentine's Day. No card. He didn't call.

Birthday. No card first year. Only a card the next year . . . late.

Christmas. The second time. A handkerchief. Not wrapped.

Easter. No card. No eggs. Not even his.

Thanksgiving. Said he had to work, needed the money. She cried, again, for she had cooked a full, good meal . . . for him. She couldn't eat.

All the time, he was having a good time witn the money from his other little old ladies and his woman. Yet . . . he really was with nobody in his heart. Nobody at all. Vanity spent so much money on him to ease the worry he said was on his mind, made me sick! I mean, really sick, I got ill.

Vanity asked that man to marry her. Marry her! She wanted a lifetime of all that pain. That's what she was askin for! He said he had never planned to marry. He didn't trust women to be true to him. Now! She tried to convince him of her love and faithfulness. He thought about that, a long, long time. Sometimes, he looked into that golden mirror he had given Vanity. Looking at his own beauty. Thinking of marryin Vanity. Of livin in the dark, cause Vanity kept her house darkened. She thought she looked better that way.

Once or twice, when he had come to Vanity, he had been a little sick. She cared for him better than anyone else he knew. Vanity! Caring for somebody else! In a day or so, he always felt better and left with some money.

When she spoke to him of marriage again, he thought a moment, then asked for the use of the little roomette she had in her yard in the back. She gladly gave it to him, tho she said he could stay in the house with her til he decided. Til HE decided. Her Guardian Angel just stayed quiet and grieved all the time now.

He took the roomette, but did not LIVE in it. He used it a lot. He liked to be alone, he said, so she often just looked out at the little house, glad he was out there, close. She would cook and take him food. Sometimes he didn't let her in, said he would be on in her house, later.

Often, when he did come in later, he would be so shinin and sweet to her. He kissed a lot and spoke much of her beauty. But he didn't make love much. He sure talk to her tho!

"My lord! You are so beautiful! So beautiful to me! How do I deserve you? You could have anyone in the world you want you are so beautiful."

Vanity's answer, always, was "But I only want you."

She began to pester him about lettin her come visit him in the little house. "What did he do there? Couldn't she be with him? She would be quiet, not bother him. He wouldn't have to make love to her. She wouldn't ask him or touch him." Can you magin a woman sayin that to her man?

She told him one day, "I always look so beautiful to you when you come out of your hideaway. If I was in there with you, and I was quiet, I could look beautiful to you longer. In there."

He said no, and no, and no, no, so many times. Til he looked at her one night, thoughtfully. She was sittin there with little tears in her still lovely eyes, waiting, waiting for any little sign he loved her. I hate to think she was such a fool!, but I don't know bout this kinda love!

He answered, touching her cheek, "Soon."

"Soon" came one night when he needed some money and asked for it for the first time. She hesitated, cause she thought that would help him leave. He read her mind, said, "I will let you come with me to my hideaway." She gave him the money. He left. He was back soon this time.

He looked at her another long time. Then sighed, and said, "Give me one half hour, then come."

She did. Her Guardian Angel cried aloud, screamed to her, "Beware!" then wept again.

The little hideaway was darkened. Persian type blankets and carpets covered everything. A small, low table on the floor was draped, covered with little saucers and things. He sat her down beside it, smiled down at her, warily. He then picked up a pipe. A pipe he used for free-basing cocaine.

The Guardian Angel could not come in, but it pounded at the door and screamed for Vanity to hear. She did not hear. She was looking at the man she loved, smiling. Just like a lady.

Jody fixed the pipe. Used a lighter to heat the stem til he reached the rock inside and melted it. Drew the first breath, blew it out. Took another breath, closed his eyes and held it in. Opened his eyes, smiled, and handed the pipe to her. Said, "Do what I do."

His hand reached out, slowly. His beautiful, powerful, strong hand that had held her, stroked her, seemed to love her. He held that hand out to her with the cocaine-rock, crack, in the pipe. She already loved that hand. She remembered only the pleasure it had held for her. Her eyes, lovely tho wrinkled around, misted, then clung to his smiling face.

She took the hand, that then gently removed itself from the pipe, leaving it in her once lovelier hand, then gently raising it to her once lovelier lips. Her eyes held to his own. Just like a lady.

Then? Then . . . she slowly finished lifting the pipe to her lips, closed her eyes with the imprint of his smiling face in them, pursed her lips and drew her first breath from the pipe. The magic pipe. She opened her eyes, the smoke wafting slowly through her body, inundating her brain, while looking at this gorgeous man. Then she smiled, raised her beautiful head, parted her lips . . . and blew . . . her . . . life . . . and all her beauty . . . away. Forever.

Just like a fool.

The devil slapped his knee, leaned back and laughed.

The Guardian Angel gave up. On its knees, beside the garden house door, it wept. The angel's voice was silenced by the golden pipe, the golden man. The golden pipe had a new voice to whisper in her ears. The Guardian Angel could only come back if she sought it. It will wait, even for nothing.

So . . . I'm just sittin here, lookin into this magic golden mirror Vanity has gave me because she could not bear to look into it anymore. She could not see the self she sought. The golden pipe has lied.

PLUS, I know she needed the money I pressed into her thin little hands. Almost all her beautiful things are gone . . . sold for that wisp of smoke. And that man she can never have for her own.

I am ponderin . . . ahhh, ponderin . . . thinkin about life . . . and death. Love.

Ahhhh, but so much happened. So much I didn't know about til way much later. My heart aches for her, but . . . it was HER choice, HER life.

In tryin to understand what had happened to my friend's mind, her life, I searched, asked questions of them people who knew her then, were her friends. Friends? I will tell you what I found out. It was pitiful. And if you got youngsters, you better listen to this first, then decide do you want them to hear this truth. This is just one day in the later life of Vanity, just fore she died from a heart attack, a broken, busted-heart attack.

Early one wintry morning after bein out all night til bout 5:00 A.M. . . . Vanity went inside the shell of her large, once beautiful house, empty now. Everything being sold, piece by piece. First, by Jody, then, at last, when her need was great and she started doin crack without Jody, she sold her own things, her own self. So the house was empty now.

The house note hadn't been paid in thirteen months and was soon to be foreclosed on. Gone. All her usta-be dreams. Gone.

The lectric company had turned off the lights. The gas company had done turned off the gas . . . and it was cold, cold, cold in that house. The water was the only thing on cause Jody knew how to turn it back on after the water company turned it off. So Vanity could drink water out a paper cup or a leftover tin can. Didn't need no water for cookin cause wasn't nothing to cook. She didn't have no appetite anyway for nothin but more crack . . . them bumps, them hits of rock. She was thin, thin, thin. Skin and bones. Somehow, she managed to keep her phone workin, cause she had to be able to get them calls from them fellows who might give her a bump. A Bump!

This particular night, and I know now there were lots of these kinda nights, she had been workin for that crack. She didn't call it "workin," but I do.

Jody was no longer the only man in her life. Now, she had had all kinds of men. All kinds. Kinds she wouldn't even use to spit on! Them "Bumps" had sucked and bumped all her pride out of her brain. That shit must be some powerful, cause you remember how full of pride she was!

Now . . . from the lowest person in a garbage can, man or woman, to the crack dealer who was the highest she could get, even they only wanted to use her for a half-hour or hour. Not even them so much anymore cause they had all already tore her down, stripped whatever little dignity she mighta had left. Yes, the bottom was as high as Vanity could go now. Them old days was gone. Like her beauty. Like her health. Like her life. Gone. No future to it. Nothin meant nothin to her now but that next bump, that next rock. Low-life crack users called her a "Rock Star," laughin and graspin their crotches. I heard about em!

See, she had a big reputation, well deserved, they say. She was known, far and wide, as the best "head" in the city . . . and anything else you wanted you could get from her if she needed that crack! Her! Can you magin?! Her?

Anyway, she had come into that empty house that dark wintry morning. She closed the door, leanin back against it. Tired. Worn. She looked at the phone tho. It wasn't ringin. Then she felt her hunger. She hadn't eaten in bout five days. She didn't have no energy. Her mouth tasted like sex from goin down on eight men in the last ten hours. Two others had refused her head, preferred anal sex. So, besides her mouth feeling used, stretched and bad, her rectum was bleedin a little.

Little pains shot through it now and again, cause of the huge . . . organ . . . one man had smashed into her, hard. She had cried out, but he laughed and stuck his chest out in front of the other men (yes, chile, they do it in front of everybody!) and thrust harder. She wanted to scream and tell him to stop!, BUT she wanted that rock he had promised her. That crack. If this is what it cost, well, she didn't have no money, so . . . this is what it cost!

When he, finally, finished and it was time to give her her reward, her bump, he decided to tease her . . . and degrade her even more. He melted the crack on a pipe, took him a big deep puff of it, blew the smoke at her to make her want it more. He was smart, he knew what he was doin. He leaned toward her, offering the pipe with the crack to her then, pullin back when she reached for it. She looooooooonnnggggeeed for that pipe.

Involuntary, she snarled and lunged to snatch the pipe. He saw her comin . . . He caught her in the top of her long, used-to-be-pretty, hair and pulled her face down to his penis what was still coated from that anal sex they had just finished.

He told her, "Lick it clean."

That stopped her a moment, brought her back to some ooold reality, the times before she ever thought about crack. When she was beautiful and only dealt with the best of people. She felt disgust. She started to say "No!" and shake his hand from her head. BUT . . . then . . . her eyes fell upon that pipe in his hand. As he knew they would. She remembered that big rock he had just melted in that pipe. All thoughts of disgust just flew away. She closed her eyes . . . leaned over into the man's lap . . . and cleaned him with her tongue . . . her mouth that sits right in her face.

When he had had another orgasm, this time in her mouth making her swallow it, he let go her hair he had been pullin. She raised her head, lookin down at the large, limp penis . . . for the rough spots that felt like sores to her tongue. They were there. She wiped the back of her hand across her mouth and almost gagged. But didn't. She wouldn't allow herself to think about the sores now. She needed that pipe now.

She sat up, didn't even pull her clothes straight fore she asked, "Give me my hit now?"

He, that piece of cancer sore, looked down at her with contempt, looked at the other fellows with laughter. He sank back comfortably, flicked his bic and heated his pipe stem, moving the fire to the end where the cocaine-rock was, then he took a pull, a hit. He thought it was a real good one, so he kicked back and let the death hidden inside the good feeling reach into his body and brain, chippin away at what was left of his sanity. He did not know that in six months he would be dyin from just what he was doin now . . . and from them sores. He would be slave to the King Crack then. He was already, just didn't blive it, but he would do anything for it too!

But, now, he just laughed, and thought how he had got over on her. Humped her from the behind and then stuck it in her mouth to clean it! All them users had the same aim, like he did. They was so low they just wanted to degrade, humiliate other people, specially women. Then, too, it was because she was so beautiful once, it still showed. He had never ever even talked to anyone who had been so pretty and almost rich. He knew she would never have even looked his way, if she had not become this . . . thing . . . called a rock star. They would do the same thing to a ugly woman, but they wouldn't enjoy it so much, or gone so far . . . maybe.

He looked down into Vanity's pleading eyes, waved the pipe in front of her face and said, "Bitch, I ain't givin you nothin! The best thing you can do is get your funky, dirty ass out of here!"

She cried out, "You promised me!" Wiped her mouth again with the back of her hand, "Give me my bump!?"

He looked at the other fellows, laughed, said, "You just got your bumpin! Get the fuck out of my face, ho!" (That's short for whore.)

Another fellow there felt a little sorry for her. He didn't really like to see people dogged, til it was his turn. He wanted to speak up, but he owed the crack dealer some money and he wanted some more crack hisself, so he didn't want to mess up his own game. So he sat back and let it all happen. He laughed a little too. He thought to himself, since he felt sorry for her and knew she was walkin, that he would give her a ride home. Then she could clean herself up. Maybe . . . even give him a little head fore he went home. He didn't want nothin else from her cause he knew how many men she had to go through to get some crack and he didn't want no disease to take home to his wife and kids. He musta not known you can catch a disease from a mouth too!

Vanity never did get her bump, her hit. They put her out instead. The man hurried and begged up on his rock then rushed out to catch up with Vanity fore she found somewhere else to go beggin for crack and he lost her. He wanted that head! He drove and caught up with her, offerin her a ride home. Fore he got her to her house he told her they would look for some crack. He got his head. But he pulled to the curb front of her house and put her out, sayin, "Let's try later, baby. I'll try to get hold of some money. You try to get hold of some too. I'll call you." Then . . . he drove off with his crack deep down in his pocket. His own wife didn't know he was a user. Or that he already had that bug in his blood that would kill both of them . . . just from makin love. That's all his wife did to get it, make love to him, her husband. Chile, chile.

Anyway . . . Vanity was home. Home? Her back against her door. Hungry, wet, cold, dirty, stinkin and sick. She never had got that bump. They had just used her, again.

Her body wanted to sleep, but she couldn't get that bump, that feeling she wanted, out of her mind. Her brain raced, trying to think of somewhere, someone, she could get some money from. Sell some head to. She thought briefly of Mega, but Mega had loaned her so much in the beginning, never gettin it back. Now Mega watched her so carefully when Vanity was in her house because she had lost so many small valuable things that Vanity could put in her brassiere or under her dress. Couldn't go there. The early mornin time never entered her mind cause when she wanted some dope, she didn't care bout no inconvenience to nobody else.

Sellin some of her head came back into her mind. Vanity's mind snapped back to the man who had had anal sex with her then made her clean him with her mouth. She remembered the sores on his penis. She worried: AIDS? Syphilis? Gonorrhea? Herpes? What? She pulled her tired back away from the door, went to wash her mouth out with the peroxide Jody kept there for when she made oral sex to him. After she did other people in front of him sometimes to get both of them a bump, he didn't like her to do him without washing her mouth out. Jody never wanted her body anymore. That is, when she did get to see him. She couldn't see him noway less she had some crack to share.

She rinsed her mouth. She didn't think of the fact she had swallowed everything and that peroxide couldn't reach it. Then she lay her tired, abused body across the old, dirty quilt thrown on her bedroom floor. She fell asleep . . . for a while.

The phone rang! She jumped awake to answer it. It was a fellow saying he had a rock he would share with her . . . for a little fun. She told him to come on over.

He said, "No, we . . . I rather ride awhile."

She quickly answered, "Okey, I'll be outside waitin."

They came. There was two of them, fellows. One got out to let her get in the middle and they drove off, sayin they was going to some-body's house. They had the rock.

She asked, "How we all gonna use one rock?"

They laughed, answered, "Ahhh, we share all things all the time."

But they drove too long, too far. She became afraid. The feelin in the car was not good. The men were groping over her legs, her breast. She kept pushin their hands away.

She asked, "Where we goin? Where is the rock?"

They laughed and turned off the highway. Who needs to tell it all?

They finally stopped. Pale, early mornin. Deserted woods. They made her get out, go down, lay down, then go down again. She cried all through everything. Mad cause they had fooled her and there was no rock. Then they talked awhile to decide should they take her home or not.

One, the "nice" one, said, "It's kinda dark, man, and cold. Let's take her back into town anyway." So they did that. But they never did give her a bump or puff from their pipe. Why should they? They had had all the fun they wanted anyway. Well, at least they didn't beat her too. Yes, they did that to her sometimes.

Vanity still ain't had no food.

She didn't have enough clothes on, she was frozen almost.

She ain't had no real sleep for almost four, five days.

Her body is stinkin and dirty, again.

But her brain still wouldn't think of nothin but that dope. That bump. That puff from a pipe. What kind of stuff must that be that can strip you, make you do ANYTHING to get it? Take everything away from you? House, furniture, automobile, bank account, clothes; yours and everybody else's you can get your hands on!? Takes your honor, your dignity, your pride in yourself. Your very life! I wouldn't even want to SEE it, much less use it! It scares me to death!

Well, she came to my house. She looked so bad, so sad, my heart broke for her. She wanted to "borrow" some of my little, hard-earned money. She already owed me plenty fore I got wise that she wasn't gonna buy food or nothin she needed. Just dope.

I fed her. Ran bath water, gave her some clean clothes. All mine was better than all hers now, and I really didn't have nothin special. She lay down and slept. I took advantage of that to wash her clothes and run to the store to get somethin better for her to eat and to cash a small check to give her a few dollars of my small money.

When I came back . . . she was gone. So was my watch I was stupid enough to leave layin on my dresser. My only watch what had belonged to my mother. I loved that watch! I cried. I know that crack took my watch, not her, but it was gone right on.

Vanity didn't stop to pawn my watch, I mighta got it back if she did. She took it straight to the crack dealer and got her three rocks for my beautiful watch. Then she went home and blew my watch away . . . in a hour and a half. Just like that!

At last, her body just dragged her down to sleep. And even while sleep she waited for that phone to ring. When it did ring, she went out again . . . and everything started all over again.

All over again. All her whole life now, given up for a bump, a hit, a puff, a feeling. A little piece of death . . . that had such a hold on her mind that only a full death is stronger. Or God. But she wasn't likely to run into Him. Her Guardian Angel wasn't allowed to go into the places she went into. Her Guardian Angel just sat over her and wept sometimes when she was home waitin for a call. It did that til she died, then they parted forever, and it went to its home, sadly sayin, "I hope I never have to go to Earth again."

Five years is all it took. Five years of days just like the one I'm tellin you about. She lived all that, every day, over and over and over again. And, surely, some worse ones I don't know about.

I couldn't do it, couldn't take it. I don't want nothin that strong to kill my life and me! Do you? Would you?

So . . . I am sittin here ponderin . . . ahhh, ponderin . . . thinkin about life . . . and death.

Love.

And Vanity.

Lord, Lord.

▼▼▼▼▼▼▼▼

PART THREE

Prelude to
an Endnote:
The Body's Health

There are folk who are concerned about what happens to a Black woman's body—those who wish to restrict our access to abortions, for example, and yet do not support the necessity of access to affordable health care for all of us.

And then, there are folk who could care less what happens to a Black woman's body—those who for so long refused to include specific women's illnesses related to HIV infection and AIDS in the Centers for Disease Control's definition of AIDS, which caused HIV positive women and women with AIDS not to be able to qualify for much-needed financial assistance. Over 50 percent of the women with AIDS in the United States are Black or Latina.

One in eight women will develop breast cancer in this country. Poets Pat Parker and Audre Lorde died of breast cancer. Now June Jordan and countless others struggle against this lethal disease.

For some of us, it may seem as if we cannot fight against yet another difficulty, in addition to fighting oppression in all its forms. But we must take our health and therefore our lives more seriously, because we are the only ones with the true best interests of Black women at heart.

The Right to Life
What Can the White Man Say to
the Black Woman?

ALICE WALKER

Pro-Choice/Keep Abortion Legal Rally
The Mayflower Hotel, Washington D.C.
April 8, 1989

What is of use in these words I offer in memory and recognition of our common mother. And to my daughter.

What can the white man say to the black woman?

For four hundred years he ruled over the black woman's womb.

Let us be clear. In the barracoons and along the slave shipping coasts of Africa, for more than twenty generations, it was he who dashed our babies' brains out against the rocks.

What can the white man say to the black woman?

For four hundred years he determined which black woman's children would live or die.

Let it be remembered. It was he who placed our children on the auction block in cities all across the Eastern half of what is now the United States, and listened to and watched them beg for their mothers' arms, before being sold to the highest bidder and dragged away.

What can the white man say to the black woman?

We remember that Fannie Lou Hamer, a poor sharecropper on a Mississippi plantation, was one of twenty-one children; and that on plantations across the South black women often had twelve, fifteen, twenty children. Like their enslaved mothers and grandmothers before them, these black women were sacrificed to the profit the white man could make from harnessing their bodies and their children's bodies to the cotton gin.

What can the white man say to the black woman?

We see him lined up, on Saturday nights, century after century, to make the black mother, who must sell her body to feed her children, go down on her knees to him.

Let us take note:

He has not cared for a single one of the dark children in his midst, over hundreds of years.

Where are the children of the Cherokee, my great-grandmother's people?
Gone.
Where are the children of the Blackfoot?
Gone.
Where are the children of the Lakota?
Gone.

Of the Cheyenne?
Of the Chippewa?
Of the Iroquois?
Of the Sioux?
Of the Akan?
Of the Ibo?
Of the Ashanti?
Of the Maori and the Aborigine?*

*Tribal, indigenous children destroyed during the white "settlement" of the West.

Where are the children of "the slave coast" and Wounded Knee?

We do not forget the forced sterilizations and forced starvations on the reservations, here as in South Africa. Nor do we forget the small-pox-infested blankets Indian children were given by the Great White Fathers of the United States Government.

What has the white man to say to the black woman?

When we have children you do everything in your power to make them feel unwanted from the moment they are born. You send them to fight and kill other dark mothers' children around the world. You shove them onto public highways into the path of oncoming cars. You shove their heads through plate glass windows. You string them up and you string them out.

What has the white man to say to the black woman?

From the beginning, you have treated all dark children with absolute hatred.

30,000,000 African children died on the way to the Americas, where nothing awaited them but endless toil and the crack of a bullwhip. They died of a lack of food, of lack of movement in the holds of ships. Of lack of friends and relatives. They died of depression, bewilderment and fear.

What has the white man to say to the black woman?

Let us look around us: Let us look at the world the white man has made for the black woman and her children.

It is a world in which the black woman is still forced to provide cheap labor, in the form of children, for the factory farms and on the assembly lines of the white man.

It is a world into which the white man dumps every foul, person-annulling drug he smuggles into Creation.

It is a world where many of our babies die at birth, or later of mal-nutrition, and where many more grow up to live lives of such misery they are forced to choose death by their own hands.

What has the white man to say to the black woman, and to all women and children everywhere?

Let us consider the depletion of the ozone; let us consider home-lessness and the nuclear peril; let us consider the destruction of the rainforests—in the name of the almighty hamburger. Let us consider the poisoned apples and the poisoned water and the poisoned air, and the poisoned earth.

And that all of our children, because of the white man's assault on the planet, have a possibility of death by cancer in their almost imme-diate future.

What has the white male lawgiver to say to any of us? Those of us who love life too much to willingly bring more children into a world saturated with death.

Abortion, for many women, is more than an experience of suffer-ing beyond anything most men will ever know, it is an act of mercy, and an act of self-defense.

To make abortion illegal, again, is to sentence millions of women and children to miserable lives and even more miserable deaths.

Given his history, in relation to us, I think the white man should be ashamed to attempt to speak for the unborn children of the black woman. To force us to have children for him to ridicule, drug, turn into killers and homeless wanderers is a testament to his hypocrisy.

What can the white man say to the black woman?

Only one thing that the black woman might hear.

Yes, indeed, the white man can say, your children have the right to life. Therefore I will call back from the dead those 30,000,000 who were tossed overboard during the centuries of the slave trade. And the other millions who died in my cotton fields and hanging from my trees.

I will recall all those who died of broken hearts and broken spirits, under the insult of segregation.

I will raise up all the mothers who died exhausted after birthing twenty-one children to work sunup to sundown on my plantation. I will restore to full health all those who perished for lack of food, shelter, sunlight, and love; and from my inability to recognize them as human beings.

But I will go even further:

I will tell you, black woman, that I wish to be forgiven the sins I commit daily against you and your children. For I know that until I treat your children with love, I can never be trusted by my own. Nor can I respect myself.

And I will free your children from insultingly high infant mortality rates, short life spans, horrible housing, lack of food, rampant ill health. I will liberate them from the ghetto. I will open wide the doors of all the schools and the hospitals and businesses of society to your children. I will look at your children and see, not a threat, but a joy.

I will remove myself as an obstacle in the path that your children, against all odds, are making toward the light. I will not assassinate them for dreaming dreams and offering new visions of how to live. I

will cease trying to lead your children, for I can see I have never understood where I was going. I will agree to sit quietly for a century or so,
and mediate on this.

That is what the white man can say to the black woman.

We are listening.

Disappearing Acts

TERRY McMILLAN

My period is late.

It was due two weeks ago. I wanted to tell Franklin, but I couldn't. The last thing we needed right now was a baby. And besides, I'm not even his wife. I just imagined what he would say if I told him, "Franklin, guess what? We're having a baby." He'd probably look at me and say, "A what?" It wouldn't be like it is on TV, that's for damn sure. He probably wouldn't throw his arms up in the air and say, "I'm gonna be a Daddy? Hot damn!" No. He probably wouldn't be all that thrilled.

He's been going through a lot of changes as it is, trying to keep Pam at bay, and last month, when Derek turned fourteen, Franklin didn't have any money to buy him a birthday present. I asked him what did he think Derek would want? "Nikes," he said. "What size?" I asked. He told me elevens. I spent thirty-nine dollars on a pair of high-tops— since Derek plays basketball—and gave them to Franklin. "Take these over to him," I said. "Baby, you didn't have to do this. He ain't even your kid." My kid. "I know he's not *my* kid," I said, "but he's *your* kid, and I want him to know that his father didn't forget his birthday. Can't you forget your stupid pride for once? Don't disappoint him, Franklin." Derek never has had too much to say to me, but the last time he came over, he was smiling and wearing those sneakers. I felt like we were finally making progress. All I wanted to do was get to know Franklin's kids.

My Daddy would have a fit if he found out about *this*—him being in the church and all. And Marguerite is so old-fashioned, she'd probably persuade Daddy into talking me into coming home and having it anyway. I'd have to listen to them condemning me for getting involved with a married man—which is what it boils down to—so I can't tell them either.

I swear, I don't want to have another abortion—really I don't. But what other choice do I have? Franklin's job situation is so iffy, I'd probably end up taking care of all three of us. I couldn't handle that. Lots of women are having babies these days without being married, but I never imagined myself giving birth without having a husband to go along with it. I can take feminism only so far. We've never even talked about having kids. What if he *doesn't* want any more? But what if he does?

Any way I look at it, I'm still scared.

I'm also starting to feel like shit. When I wake up, Franklin's cigarette smoke—especially those disgusting ashes—makes me feel like I want to throw up. The other day, I was cleaning out the bathtub, and the Comet made me feel the same way. It seems like I smell everything twice as much now, and the scents pass through my nostrils, land in the pit of my stomach, then work their way back up inside my throat and stay there. I should've known something was up—the way I've been eating these past few weeks—but with all the other things I've got on my mind, I haven't slowed down long enough to think about it. This morning, the scale told the truth—I'd gained six pounds. I looked at the calendar on the bathroom wall, then stuck my finger between my legs. I was hoping to see red. My fingers came back the same color, and I panicked. I knew it wasn't coming, because every twenty-eight days it arrives like clockwork. Shit.

Ironically enough, Claudette's on her way over here with the baby. Why does she have to be six months pregnant? I know it was stupid of me to invite Portia and Marie too, but I wanted them all here. I had to tell *somebody*. And I can't keep this to myself. Not this time.

Franklin was at the gym and was spending the day with his kids. His kids. When I heard the buzzer, I started to run down the stairs like I always do, but something rushed to my head and made me feel dizzy, so I walked. Portia and Claudette were standing there together.

"Hurry up, girl. It's cold as hell out here," Portia said through the door.

"Where's Chanelle?" I asked Claudette.

"Home with her father. She's got a little cold, but I felt like getting out of the house. So can we come in, or what?"

I unlocked the door, and we went upstairs.

"So, girlfriend, what you gon' do?" Portia asked.

I walked over to the sink and got out the coffee cups. I took the croissants from the refrigerator and slid 'em into the oven. For some reason, I wasn't hungry. "I really don't know," I said.

I heard the door buzz. "Claudette, would you let Marie in, please?"

When Claudette got up, the only thing I noticed was her big belly. I put my hands over mine and rubbed it. Why now, God? I wondered. And why me? It wasn't as if I didn't use anything. Should I be reading this differently—that I'm *supposed* to go through with it? That things happen for a reason? This would make three abortions. Three times that I stopped a life. But having it would be stupid. Where would it sleep? We'd have to get a bigger place, which would mean more rent; pay a baby-sitter—*everything* would change. I'd probably have to stop my voice lessons, and how would I learn to juggle my time so I wouldn't have to give up singing altogether? What if my seizures flared back up and I'd have to get back on phenobarb? I'd be taking a chance that my baby could be born with something besides ten fingers and ten toes. I don't want to take that chance. Not right now. Not until I can trust science more. You're just being selfish, Zora. All you're thinking about is yourself. No, I'm not. Yes, you are. If *I* don't, *who* will? Of course I've read about women whose seizures had long since stopped, and they had perfectly normal pregnancies and healthy babies. But it'd be just my luck to have fits for the next nine months. And Franklin would find out before I had a chance to tell him. Maybe he'd feel deceived and leave me. I do not want to be a single mother, that much I do know.

"Hi, girl," Marie said, as she kissed me on the cheek. "Are you okay?"

"I'm trying to be," I said. "The cups are right here; half-and-half, sugar; the croissants should be warm enough. Help yourselves."

"Let me ask you a question, Zora," Claudette said. "What exactly were you using? You *were* using something, I hope?"

"The jelly that goes into my diaphragm."

"And that shit didn't work?" Marie asked.

"Obviously not," I said.

"Why didn't you use the damn diaphragm too?" Portia asked.

"Because Franklin's too big. In the beginning we tried it that way, but it felt like it was moving up into my damn chest."

"Niggahs and their big dicks, I swear," Portia said, and took a sip from her coffee. "Why don't you just take the pill?"

"Because I can't," I said.

"What do you mean, you can't?" Marie asked.

"I've tried about five different kinds, and each one gave me a different side effect. I got white splotches all over my face. My breasts got even bigger and were so tender I couldn't stand to touch 'em myself. I never wanted to make love—"

"Well, that ain't the end of the world, you know," Marie said.

"Well, maybe not. I was on one kind for about two months, and I put on fifteen pounds. I just gave up." The truth of the matter was, back then the phenobarb screwed up my metabolism so much that it broke down the hormone in the pill. I'd have gotten pregnant anyway.

"You should get yourself an IUD," Claudette said. "They work— believe me. Before Chanelle was born, I had one for five years, and it never gave me any trouble."

"You don't want no IUD, girl," Portia said. "Those things are gonna be taken off the damn market. Hell, ain't you heard about those women who been hemorrhaging and dying from them things? Some of 'em are sterile, *and* some have gotten pregnant with them things still up inside 'em. You don't even wanna think about getting one of those."

"Right now I'm not worrying about what to use in the future. I'm worried about what I'm going to do about *this*." I had put my hand over my stomach, which was throbbing. It felt like my period was coming, but I didn't feel a thing sliding out.

"Have you told Franklin?" Marie asked.

"No."

"Why not?"

"Because he'd probably want me to go through with it."

"How do you know that?" Claudette asked.

"It's just a feeling, but the bottom line is that I want this decision to be mine. Franklin has a way of talking me into things that I sometimes regret later. I don't want this to be one of 'em."

"Well, I don't know what the big deal is, really. Why don't you just go on and have it? You love the man, don't you?"

"Yes, I love him. But it's more complicated than that, Claudette. We're not in any position to get married right now."

"What exactly do you mean by 'not in any position'?" Marie asked. "This guy isn't married, is he?"

All three of them turned their eyes toward me. They wouldn't understand if I told them that Franklin's been separated for over six years. They wouldn't understand that the reason he hasn't gotten his divorce yet is because he hasn't been able to afford it. They just wouldn't understand.

"No. He's not married," I said. "But he's laid off work right now. We've got bills coming out of our asses, and my voice lessons aren't exactly free. I don't know what I would do with a baby right now."

"Zora, it's nine whole months away," Claudette said.

"I wouldn't have nobody's baby without a diamond on my finger," Portia said.

"Would you marry him if he asked you?" Claudette asked.

"I don't know, to tell you the truth. I love him, but we've got our share of problems."

"Who doesn't?" she said.

"We're constantly broke. Franklin wants to go back to school this winter. He wants to learn how to start his own business."

"What's his B.A. in?" Marie asked.

Damn. Why do they have to ask so many questions? "He doesn't have a B.A.," I said.

"Well, where'd he go to college?" Claudette asked.

"He didn't finish" was all I said. I had to defend him. They wouldn't understand if I told them he never finished high school. They wouldn't understand that Franklin's brilliant on his own terms, that college doesn't automatically make you smart. They just wouldn't understand. "By trade, he's a carpenter. You see that cabinet my stereo's on?"

They all turned to look at it.

"Franklin made that," I said.

Marie and Claudette looked impressed, but Portia said, "Right now the question is, Is the man really trying to find work, or is he just laying up on his black ass, daydreaming?"

"He's trying, believe me, and the saddest thing in the world is to see your man out of work."

"Well," Claudette said, "if he can build furniture like this and he's trying to get back into school, I'd hang in there. It'd be different if he wasn't trying."

"I'm not thinking about giving up—yet. But how do you know when you've hung too long?"

"When you get tired," she said, eating her third croissant. "Or when you feel you're running in place."

"Personally, I wouldn't wait that long," Portia said.

"Hell, when Allen and I got married, I was in law school and he was only in his third year of medical school. Talk about hard times. Sometimes I was ready to fly out the door. After I passed the bar, I was making all the money, paying all the bills—while he studied. But he had asked me if I really thought I could handle it, and I said yes. It's called commitment, honey.

"And don't be so naive as to think that Allen and I are always lovey-dovey. Honey, we argue, scream, slam doors. Once in a while I break a dish. I even pulled the phone out of the wall once. But this is all par for the course. You've got to take the bitter with the sweet. Just as long as you're not the only one doing all the struggling, I'd stick with the man."

"I plan to, Claudette," I said, "unless I run out of gas."

"All this Ann Landers shit sounds good," Portia said, "but we supposed to be trying to help the girl decide what's best for *her* right now—not *him.*"

"I say get rid of it," Marie said.

"How late are you?" Claudette asked.

"Two weeks."

"Well, that's good," Portia said. "There's lots of places in Manhattan where you can get it done early. Have you ever had one before, Zora?"

At first I thought about lying, but then I realized we were all women, so why should I? "I've had two."

"Shit, I've had three or four of 'em myself. It ain't no picnic, is it? I swear, if men only knew what we had to go through just to get a damn nut—this kind of bullshit," she said.

"Well," Marie said, "when they finally come up with birth control for *their* asses, I bet they won't be so quick to unzip their pants. The burden of responsibility's been on us for too damn long, if you ask me."

"What kind of birth control do you use?" Portia asked her.

Marie got the strangest look on her face, then blurted out, "Foam." Something, I don't know why, told me she was lying. I've never heard her mention any particular man before, but I've never had the impression that she was gay either.

"Well, the last one I had was a bitch," Portia said. "They gave me a damn Valium, and that shit didn't do nothing, girl. It felt like somebody was pulling dry, brittle branches out my pussy."

"All right, Portia, spare us the details," Claudette said.

"I was knocked out both times," I said. "How much does it cost now?"

"Your insurance should cover it, won't it?" Marie asked.

"I can't let the school find out about this."

"Well, fuck it," Marie said. "You got any money?"

"Not really," I said, embarrassed.

"Well, all you gotta do is look in *The Voice*—there's a whole page of ads for 'em," Portia said. "They compete with each other, girl. You wanna get knocked out again, don't you?"

"I have to. I couldn't take being awake, watching it, knowing what they're doing. I swear I couldn't."

"Then it's probably gonna cost you about three hundred."

"Three hundred?"

"Look, I can lend you about a hundred," Marie said.

"Where are you getting money from?" I asked.

"I got a gig."

"Well, why didn't you tell me?"

"Shit, since you've been in love, you've been so busy. Who can catch up with you? Whenever I call, you're either playing the piano and singing, or wrapped up in Franklin's arms, or some shit like that."

"I can lend you a hundred too," Claudette said. "More if you need it."

"I'm good for fifty," Portia said.

"Thanks, you guys. I don't know what I'd do without you—really I don't."

"Well, I'll go with you, 'cause you're gon' need somebody," Portia said. "It don't matter if you're wide awake or knocked out. When it's over, you damn sure ain't gon' wanna be alone."

I heard the key in the door, and saw Franklin and Derek.

"Hi," I said. "What are you doing back so soon?"

"I didn't mean to interrupt anything," he said.

"You're not interrupting anything," I said. "I just didn't expect you, that's all."

"Hello, ladies," he said.

Everybody blushed, then said hello. Boy, did the room get quiet all of a sudden.

"Hi, Derek," I said. I introduced everybody, and then the silence grew even more obvious.

"Where's Miles?" I asked.

"He's got the chicken pox," Derek said.

"Oh" was all I said. I knew Franklin could tell we'd been talking girl talk, and I prayed that he wouldn't suspect anything other than that.

"Well, I'd better be getting back to check on Chanelle," Claudette said, getting up.

"Can I get a ride to the train station?" Portia asked.

"Look, ladies, you don't have to leave on my account. I just came to get my racquetballs, that's all."

"We were about to leave anyway," Marie said. "Let me just get my coat."

Franklin looked at me apologetically, then went to get the balls. He gave me a kiss on the cheek, and everybody left at the same time.

I sat down on the couch and felt so light-headed that the room started to spin. "No," I said out loud, and got up. I walked up and down the hallway until I felt stationary. I forced the room to stop turning.

Portia met me in front of the place. I'd been throwing up all morning, until I'd gotten the dry heaves. Now there was nothing left in my belly but the baby. I kept getting hot and cold chills, and felt so weak that I had to take a cab. Franklin had left at his usual time and wouldn't be back until after three. I'd been told that I'd be home in less than three hours and feeling pretty much back to normal by afternoon.

"How you feeling?" Portia asked. She didn't give me a chance to answer. "You don't look so hot. But don't worry, girlfriend. It'll be over before you know it."

When we got inside, the large white room was full of women. Some of them looked miserable, some just looked scared. I knew I felt both. I signed in and walked back over to Portia.

"Just try to relax a minute, Zora. Now sit down," she said.

"Portia, God is going to punish me one day for doing this, I know it. Just watch: When and if I ever decide to have a baby, it'll probably come out retarded or deformed or an epileptic. I can't keep doing this, I just can't."

"Don't even talk no stupid shit like that around me. This is damn near nineteen-fuckin'-eighty-three, girl. Women got a right to decide whether or not they wanna have a goddamn baby. Shit, just because the fucking birth control didn't work, why should we have to suffer? You know how many of our lives are fucked up 'cause we got kids we can't afford, didn't plan, or didn't want? And with no help? You don't wanna be one of those statistics, honey, so sit your ass down and be quiet."

I waited for them to call my name, and when I finally heard it, I was scared to move. The room suddenly felt like it was full of women who weren't moving.

"It'll be okay," Portia said, and ushered me to the door. I couldn't even turn back to look at her.

My head is falling off my shoulders as they wheel me into a light blue room. They stick a plastic needle into my vein. I feel the walls of my mouth expanding. It tastes like gasoline. But I don't have a car. Someone in a white mask tells me to start counting backward from a hundred. Why one hundred? One hundred. *Baby number three. Gone. Down the drain. Make it quick, would you? I've got a voice class. What voice? You've taken my voice? It's gone? I can't sing, anything, ever again? Is this how much a baby cost?* Ninety-nine. *I promised Dillon or Percy or Franklin—one of them—something. What was it? Dinner. Oh, shit. All we've got in the house is baby food.* Ninety-eight. *No. There's steak in the freezer. But it's frozen. Stiff as a stick.* Ninety-seven. *Steak. Stick. Who, me? No, I didn't. Go ahead, stick me. I dare you to stick me.* Ninety-six. *Go ahead, step across that line. I'll hit you back, I swear it. I warned your ass!* Ninety-five. *Cheater.*

When I woke up, I was lying on a table in a different room. There was a beautiful dark-skinned girl in a burgundy recliner. She couldn't have been more than eighteen. She looked African—Senegalese, maybe? What was *she* doing here? Another woman, who looked about my age, was in a black recliner. Both of their legs were propped up.

"How do you feel?" the doctor asked me.

"Okay, I guess." I didn't feel any pain, anywhere.

"Then why don't you sit up and come over and rest like these young ladies over here," he said. I got up with relative ease and sat down beside the dark-skinned girl. There was a square white pad on the empty seat. I eased into the chair, and the doctor pushed on the back of it. My feet went up into the air. They were on the same level as the girl's. The doctor left the room.

I couldn't think of anything to say to her, so I just stared at my feet. I put my hands on my belly. It was empty now. Tears started rolling down my cheeks, but I didn't feel like wiping them. The girl handed me a Kleenex, and I nodded thank you. Why couldn't Franklin and I have just fallen in love and gotten married? Why couldn't he have a regular job? Why couldn't I have a recording contract? Why . . .

"Where are you from?" I asked her.

"Senegal," she said.

Why I felt relieved, I don't know.

"What were you using?" I asked her.

"Nothing," she said.

"Oh."

The doctor came back into the room, and without even realizing it, I heard myself ask him, "What was it?"

He just looked at me. "I'm not at liberty to say. Don't you worry yourself about that now," he said, and walked over to another woman, who was now on the recovery table. She was lying on her stomach. Her hair was thick, black, and matted. She looked around the room until she spotted the three of us.

"Where am I?" she asked.

None of us said a word.

"This is so silly," she said. Then she turned her head sideways and closed her eyes.

Portia was reading *Cosmopolitan* when I came out. She threw it on an empty chair and rushed over to me.

"So you feeling okay?"

"Yeah. Just a little tired is all."

"I told you it was nothin' to it, didn't I?"

After convincing Portia that I'd be fine, I took a cab home. Franklin wasn't there yet—thank God—so I lay down. When I heard the door slam, I sprang up in bed. He came into the bedroom and stood in the doorway.

"What's wrong with you?" he asked.

"I've got a yeast infection, that's all."

"Oh, yeah?"

"Yeah."

"How'd you get it?"

"Women just get 'em every now and then. It's a buildup of bacteria, and I have to use these suppositories to get rid of the infection."

"But I need some pussy, baby."

"You'll just have to wait, Franklin."

"You mean you can't make love?"

"No."

"Why not?"

"Because I could give this to you, and you'd be itching and everything, and then you'd have to take antibiotics. You wouldn't want to go through that, would you?"

"I can use a rubber."

"No, you can't. I'm not supposed to have anything inside me until the infection's gone."

"Well, just how long will that be?"

"Two weeks."

"Women," he said. "I'm glad I ain't one. Y'all get more shit wrong with your bodies than any other species on earth."

"Yeah, but what would you do without us?"

"What's that supposed to mean?"

"Just what I said: what would you do without us?"

"Action speaks louder than words," he said, and walked back out the front door.

What did I say?

Just Becuz U Believe in Abortion Doesnt Mean U're Not Pro-Life

LAINI MATAKA

recently i read a medical report that claimed
women who had abortions were not traumatized.
the person who said that, shld have been aborted.

it was probably some right-to-lifer
who believes that all pregnant women shld be made
to have babies even if they've been raped, even if
it was incest, even if it means their sanity, even
if they cant take care of a baby.

that same right-to-lifer
wants children to have the right to be born in dire
poverty, to have the right to live with rats and roaches
to have the right to have a number instead of a name,
to have the right to be born into a situation they
cant possibly live thru.

just let the babies come; it doesnt matter what they're
coming into; it doesnt matter whether they're wanted
or not; it doesnt matter whether they'll be welcomed
by crack-heads, alcoholics, pimps or molesters.
lifers believe in quantity not quality, and they almost
never volunteer to take care of some of these babies
they want to force to be born. yet, when it comes to
killin babies in somalia, uganda or yugoslavia:
no problem. no demonstrations. no blocking the entrance
of invading armies. no protests against dropped bombs.
they only understand the concept of life within the
context of amerika, which everybody knows is the center
of dead meat.

to hear the lifers tell it, it's a pleasure for a woman
to lay up on a table and have her insides sucked out by
a human-eater-vacuum-cleaner. they think all u have to
do is blink yr eyes and u're thru and ready to go
to the club later, and meet mr. destiny. yet some
lifers are women who wear make-up which they're too
stupid to kno was made from the dead fetuses.

lifers wanna tell u it's murder to abort a fetus.
and i say, if it must be done, its better to abort at
3 weeks than at 13 yrs of age. look at our city streets
and there are unwanted children walkin, beggin, sellin
rippin, killin: becuz nobody wanted them, and they kno it.

lifers claim they've got the church on their side
(hell, the church started chattel slavery) but
we wont talk about the baby bones that have so often
been found when convents are torn down.
they say the wrath of God will visit anyone who has
an abortion/but i got news for them—most women
punish themselves more severely than God ever cld
or wld. and any God that cant forgive, needs to
be replaced.

nobody really wants to get up on that table!
nobody really wants to kill a part of themselves.
nobody wants to meet their ancestors with blood on
their hands/but when a woman knows she CANT
handle bringing a new life into fullness/she *more than*
has the right, to beg that life's forgiveness
and send it back to the spirit world.

there are women who say they dont believe in abortion
and they have baby after baby by man after man
and their children suckle themselves on empty tits
and later kill somebody over a pair of tennis shoes.

there are men who say they dont believe in abortion
and finesse their way into the front door to knock
somebody up before they slide out the back door.
and like bees they go from flower to flower
flying forever away from tiny faces that look
just like them.

i hate this society for creating an atmosphere so terrible
that good, clean women feel compelled to stop life
from coming fully into being/and yet
i thank the Mother-God for the technology
that allows a woman to free herself from the possibility
of becoming a horrible mother.

An Elegy for Jade

TIYE MILAN SELAH

Hold a true friend with both thy hands.

—Kanuri Proverb

Before retrieving the morning paper, I put on a kettle of water for the herbal tea mixture that I blended for the day. The plants in the greenhouse looked unusually upbeat. I checked the thermo-hygrometer, which showed that the climate control system was doing a proper job. Tribal masks I'd collected from around the world, an empty antique bird cage, and a jukebox completed the ambience in the greenhouse. A few clouds in the sky, but I surmised no real threat of rain. An ordinary day.

An Express Mail carrier arrived with an envelope in her hand. She smiled as she greeted me. Minneapolis? Inside I found a green piece of paper, neatly folded in two, and a bundle of stamped envelopes, each tied in green ribbon; all addressed to strangers. I opened the note. It read:

Dearest Leilani,

Just so you will know the contents of these envelopes, the message reads:

THREE FRIENDS

I had three friends.
One asked me to sleep on the mat.
One asked me to sleep on the ground.
One asked me to sleep on his breast.
I decided to sleep on his breast.
I saw myself carried on a river.
I saw the king of the river and the king of the sun.
There in that country I saw palm trees,
so weighted down with fruit,

that the trees bent under the fruit,
and the fruit killed it.
—*Yoruba poem*

The effects of being HIV positive have become very real to me. As your friend, I would like to encourage you to get tested.

Leilani, I really feel that this is the best way to handle warning my past lovers. Anonymously. I thank you in advance for your help.

Eternally, Jade

Five years ago Jade had asked me to be the executor of her living will; I naively felt a sense of honor. "You are the only person I feel comfortable with, that I feel would be able to handle the task. The women in my family have spent so much time consoling others, being brave, neglecting their own needs, being *strong black women*. I cannot allow myself to be a burden to them. I should be there to care for them," she explained to me.

As I entered the kitchen now to quiet the screaming kettle, I understood what I held in my hands. Jade was private and responsible regarding her illness. There was still a lot of shame surrounding her condition, the fear of not knowing the facts on how the disease was transmitted kept her from seeking support from family. When she was admitted to the hospital, the doctor had told her she'd contracted tuberculosis. She didn't realize until later that the doctors assumed that the drug-resistant strain of tuberculosis she was battling was a strain linked to AIDS. Jade felt it was her obligation to respond as though she was living with the HIV virus. But she did not want to bring the pain to her family that she knew others who had died from AIDS had suffered. Services addressing the needs of American women of African descent were not offered in her area. Jade was proud. It was going to take a lot of work for her to find treatment possibilities. She needed to get over the TB first. Since the TB was not responding to any drug therapy, a month ago she was ordered to take complete bed rest as an alternative to chemotherapy.

In my capacity as the executor of her living will, she wanted me to mail the letters that would inform her former lovers of the past four years that they may have come in contact with the HIV virus and should seek testing.

Jade once told me that she prayed every day for the Creator of life and all ancestors of the celestial entourage to give her strength to help her get through this time—of exile from her family, periods of loneliness, isolation, fear, and contrition, and to help support her spirit in her pursuit of health. I don't think she was playing the martyr, it was shame that consumed her and fueled her commitment to go it alone. I also prayed for her.

As I drank the tea, I found myself reminiscing about our last conversation. After years of hitting the glass ceiling with our heads, we wanted to quit our jobs. Jade wanted to own a transcontinental venture. She had undergraduate degrees in chemistry and marketing, and advanced degrees in chemistry and international marketing. She believed education, hard work, a good plan, and faith were major keys to success. She'd worked for the past fifteen years, as a perfume chemist with extensive travel experiences to different laboratories in Paris, Cairo, and China. Her plan was to cultivate a perfume line, using the exotic scents of indigenous flowers from regions all over the world.

I wanted to open a jewelry store featuring exclusive ethnically crafted fine jewelry. I am a master gemologist skilled at cutting, grading, and evaluating stones. Becoming entrepreneurs made sense to both of us, and it became part of our dream. As Enriquita Longeaux y Vasquez once said, "A woman who has no way of expressing herself as a full human has nothing else to turn to but the owning of material things." Jade and I were preparing for a new type of self-expression.

I tied the usual double knot in the laces of my Nikes and prepared for my morning meditation/power walk. Then I grabbed the letters and put them in my Kente cloth fanny pouch and commenced my five miles. First stop, the U.S. Post Office.

Going yourself is better than sending someone on an errand.

—Hausa Proverb

When Miss Ginger Rose asked me to take her to Jade's house I knew that she sensed that something was wrong, I just did not know how. Miss Ginger Rose would not fly so we had quite a drive from Philadelphia to the Twin Cities. I was glad she wanted to go, because I

▼ 115 ▼

felt Jade had given up on this life when she sent the letters to me. Telling Jade that we were coming would not help matters either, so I decided that our visit to see her would be a surprise.

Miss Ginger Rose had prepared quite a feast (like grandmeres are famous for) to bring with us. She made some of Jade's favorites: plenty of fresh vegetables and choice herbs; jars of canned Macintosh applesauce; stewed peaches; figs in brandy sauce; several bottles of special cooking oils with exposed green and red chili peppers and off-white garlic cloves bobbing beneath the corked glass; parched corn soup; golden hominy; crawfish; corn bread; and naturally, some red beans.

I loaded the car, and we started out on our trip. I felt like we were duplicating the opening scene of *The Beverly Hillbillies*.

"My grandmother died of tuberculosis. Not long after that, some people came around asking questions to the union about workers getting sick at the factory. Now you know that they wouldn't let colored people into the union, they claimed that there weren't enough of us to be represented. Most of us worked cleaning and glazing the tiles and pots. I remember it being hot and dusty. Once one of us got sick, we all seemed to get sick."

You got sick, Miss Ginger Rose?

"Oh yes! I came down with such a cough and fever, and night sweats. It was so hard for me to swallow I lost interest in food. I had chest pains so strong that I thought that I was going to have heart failure. I couldn't eat, or get a restful sleep. I was always tired and looked like a close relative of a skeleton."

Well, what did the doctor say?

"We were all afraid to go to the doctor because you might lose your job or they might try to take your family away. Finally, my auntie suggested that I go up to Philadelphia to a place called the Henry Phipps Institute's Negro Clinic that had a highly regarded colored doctor named Dr. Henry Minton and a staff that worked to help colored people with tuberculosis. All of the doctors and nurses were colored people. I had never seen so many colored people in one place in my life. They told me that I got TB from working in the pottery factory. I figured out then that this was probably how my mother and grandmother had died also. We all had symptoms of the same illness."

I never heard of the Henry Phipps Institute's Negro Clinic or Dr. Henry Minton. I thought Mercy and Frederick Douglass Memorial hospitals were the main health centers for African-Americans in Philadelphia back then.

"Yes, but the Phipps Negro Clinic was something special too. Dr. Minton was from South Carolina. He was a well-respected doctor among whites and colored folks in those days. He wanted to make sure that all of the colored people in the community were educated about TB so that everyone would know how to take care of themselves and their families. Educating folks was part of the way he practiced medicine. I was in such awful shape when I arrived that I didn't know whether I was coming or going so they sent me to Philadelphia General because they let colored people with bad cases of TB get treatment there. The major colored hospitals just couldn't keep TB patients for months at a time. They really didn't have any drugs to treat TB in those days, but they would send people off to a sanatorium in the mountains for fresh air. Since I came there from West Virginia, and my condition was so bad, they decided to use a treatment where they collapsed my lung and removed a part of my rib cage. That sure was a tough way to stop smoking!"

Dites moi qui vous aimez, et je vous dirai qui vous etes.
(Tell me whom you love, and I'll tell you who you are.)

—LOUISIANA CREOLE PROVERB

The yellow glow of the morning sun, shining brightly behind us, prepared the way for our journey. We both felt refreshed after a brief, yet deep sleep. As I became more comfortable with Miss Ginger Rose, I let my curiosity get the better of me and I began to ask more personal questions.

"Miss Ginger Rose, Jade lived with you for most of her life?"

"Yes, my granddaughter lived with me for more than half of her life," she answered proudly.

"I don't mean to pry, but I never knew what happened to Jade's mother, all Jade said was that she died in childbirth," I said.

"Jade's mama, Eva, became very interested in nursing, and decided to go to nursing school on her twenty-second birthday. Part of the reason was the success of my treatment at the Phipps Negro Clinic. She wanted to be involved in an organization like that. She ended up in a general teaching hospital during her training, giving primary care to TB patients. They assigned her to the colored wing. At this time, most of the white nurses did not get this training because they claimed they were afraid of catching TB. Eva had a good relationship with the patients and their families. She knew that she had a responsibility to the patients but also to the community. She often went to churches to try to convince people to get tested so they could get treatment. People were very scared to let anyone know that they had it because of the policy of quarantining whole families.

"Eva used to tell us how there were times when colored people would be on the waiting list to get treatment but no beds were available, while in the annex where white people convalesced there were empty beds.

"Eva was monitored throughout her studies to make sure that she did not contract the TB. But when Eva was three months along with her second baby, she had a positive test. That was the danger of working in those treatment centers. TB moves through the air like the wind. The very next day, the police came to our house to escort Eva, Clay (Jade's daddy), Jade, and myself to have further testing. As we were driving away they were posting a QUARANTINE sign across our door. Everyone in the area could see that we supposedly were sick.

"After our neighbors in South Philly saw the sign, we had to move. There was such a stigma with TB, such shame and embarrassment at the time. People reacted this way because of fear and ignorance. Lots of people did not realize that you did not have to do anything wrong or immoral to contract the disease. It was like having the plague. None of the neighbors would let Jade play with their children, we would not get visitors, and I lost all of my sewing clients. They eventually burned down several houses in that neighborhood that had been "labeled" and abandoned by families like ours.

"Eva received all kinds of treatments. She had a miscarriage. They preserved the child and hoped that she would agree to donate his body and organs to medical research, but she did not want to have experiments done on him, she felt his body should be at peace with his soul.

"That night, Eva took her son and performed a rite of passage in which she cremated him. She took the ashes out into the yard area amongst the trees and flowers. She took a third of the ashes and sprinkled them over the foot of the strongest tree. She left an offering of a flower that she had picked by the garden. She dug a hole and poured some of the ashes inside, then she consumed the rest. That way he would always remain a part of her and a part of nature.

"Eva would never tell them what happened to her son, so they sent her to another sanatorium, this time for the insane. Eva was given electroshock treatments, and high doses of drugs. Because of her resistance she received a chemical lobotomy.

"During this time Jade's daddy died in the Korean War."

> When an elephant is being killed no one notices the death of a monkey.
>
> —HAUSA PROVERB

I spent most of the night finishing some hand sewing on the comforter I was making for Jade. By the way Miss Ginger Rose was calling hogs, I knew she found her hotel room bed quite comfortable.

I reached into my overnight case, and got a thimble, some scissors, and beads. I filled selected patches in the comforter with beads and gems to simulate the sensation of touch when placed on the skin. There were old pictures of us woven into the fabric; old sorority clothes; silk stockings and black lace; FREE ANGELA and FREE MANDELA buttons; messages from fortune cookies; a worn candy cane shoestring from a roller skate; dried flowers from my wedding bouquet; and a mandala as the base.

I thought about the "village" support Jade was receiving. Anger began to consume me because I knew the group therapy program she was involved in was not working for her. Although the programs in her health center are highly regarded, they were not designed with an African-American woman in mind. Jade was receiving counseling services from an organization whose main clientele was gay, Caucasian, and male. Organizational funding was received from celebrity-sponsored benefits. Wealthy benefactors within the gay community, and affluent people regardless of racial background or sexual preference, bequeath their lucre to demonstrate solidarity and support for this organization. Jade told me that she was grateful for it because she needs treatment and they have the most up-to-date information on the disease, a whole network of services including legal and financial advisers, counseling for partners, shopping and home management services to help clients live day to day.

Jade realized that TB can be associated with AIDS in this era and feared if she didn't participate in this program it may have a negative effect on future support services for African-American women. Funders may look at statistics on clients served by this program and assume African-American women are unresponsive to support groups set up for this disease. Would they attribute this to cultural denial? I told Jade that I felt African-American women don't have support groups of our own because we feel that *someone else* will organize it for us, *or* as a community of women we do not celebrate our uniqueness through supporting and empowering each other, *or* we do not have a vision quest for our own health agenda.

I have read that the experiences of a woman with AIDS can be entirely different than those of a man with AIDS, including previously uncategorized types of vaginal yeast infections that repeated use of *over-the-counter products* cannot cure. More and more women, African-American and Latina, are becoming the fastest-growing AIDS statistics in this country.

In seeking treatment from an African-American community-based AIDS health care provider Jade found they were geared more toward intravenous drug users, or programs for mothers and children with HIV because *someone* has determined that is where the problem lies and that is where the funding goes. She did not fit into those categories either. She also encountered overworked physicians and health care workers because facilities were understaffed. "I feel for them," she told me. They all must undergo an incredible amount of stress, especially when so many people are desperate for a cure and the grapevine insists a cure exists; one developed in Africa.

I held back the tears as I completed the final stitching on the comforter. I thought, Where is the village? What if Jade loses her employer-based health benefits? What will happen to other people like Jade if we continue to segregate our community-based assistance in helping people with AIDS?

I've read articles about Cuba and how they have compulsory mass testing for HIV, and a required quarantine for all persons who test HIV positive. Once people are quarantined, all their medical expenses are paid for, residential parks are sites for housing, patients have access to nutritional counseling and exercise facilities, patients are paid their salary or given a stipend if they were unemployed. Health reports from

Cuba describe low HIV transmission rates in the general population. I looked at Miss Ginger Rose and thought about Jade's mother. I realized, maybe the quarantine approach is not the best *option* for people here in the United States, but a lesson can still be learned from it.

I looked at the finished quilt. The word LOVE glowed and shimmered in the dim light from the center of the mandala. At that moment I wondered what Dr. Minton would do.

If you know the beginning the end will not trouble you.

—KANURI PROVERB

When we arrived in Minneapolis, we discovered that Jade had been in the hospital for three weeks and in intensive care in a coma for the past three days. Miss Ginger Rose sat and waited at Jade's bedside for her to awaken, constantly massaging her, trying to let her know through touch that she was there. Jade was attached to a respirator.

I went over to Jade's house. It was so neat, I felt that if I cleaned, I would mess it up! Jade lived by the motto: a place for everything and everything has a place. Her closets were organized, medicine cabinets, her shelf paper in the kitchen even matched the kitchen floor tiles. I watered her plants and I turned on the stereo to find some music to lift my spirits. I turned up the bass, put in a CD, and pressed play. The Four Tops; "I'll be there . . . Reach out!"

With a duster in my hand I sang my heart out, mixing up all the words. During the middle of the song, with tears streaming down my face I collapsed on the couch overcome with emotion. But there was something magic in the music. Then I heard the selection change and the groove for "Proud Mary" begin. Tina Turner's voice with her introductory mellow rap made me smile. Something in it made me believe that everything was going to be all right. I remembered the dance steps that Jade and I used to do imitating Tina when we were younger. Jade could always outdance me then, but this time, during the climax of the song, you could not tell me that Tina and I were not one. By the end I was out of breath and fell back onto the couch. I had to laugh at myself.

After I composed myself I entered Jade's library. I could clearly hear Diana Ross singing "Ain't no mountain high enough" in the background as I dusted books all along the shelves. I opened the rolltop desk and found a wooden box. Inside were two prototypes of perfumes, one bottle labeled Ginger Rose, and the other Leilani. There were illustration boards of the bottle designs and ad campaign concepts. I sniffed both fragrances and they were beautiful. Next to the box was a manila envelope which contained Jade's living will, complete with power of attorney instructions for me, and directives for her physicians. When I returned to the hospital, I knew that Miss Ginger Rose and I would have to discuss Jade's wishes and make a decision.

different ones #6—Future Possibilities
(An AIDS Soliloquy)

VIKI AKIWUMI

it is a puzzle for the insane
this disease that has
carved itself like a slavers
lash into our minds.
we are walking timebombs
of sexual awareness
a sterile madness
afraid has become a synonym
for life
and our pockets are brimming with rubbers
for the moment when we fall into
the arms of lovers whose hands
are full of questions.
will we bend in this assault
will we feel tongues and lips
receding into white gloves
which take the place of moments
where we once breathed deeply
into each others mouths
trying to understand what
our mothers and fathers tried
to prepare us for
can we say that they have failed
as the reality of our lives comes
to dance under the gaze of truth
as we look at our brothers/lovers/
sisters/daughters open to eyes
that wonder and hands that offer
no assistance
as their bodies twitch in pain

rolling in spasms
wracking bodies already limping
from the respiratory disorders
of toxic racism in Harlem
and Chicago
mercury poisoning causing
the Zulu people to drop
like fallen warriors.
and meanwhile
we try to dodge
the bullets
aimed at communities
whose skin color caused them to
die
on this day
before they had their daily bread.
and we hit the dirt
like a jackhammer on concrete
we people of colors and sounds and smells
must raise our faces to look
at the dying
because their televisions
and radios
only spoke of hair relaxers
and skin lighteners
there were no public service announcements
to teach the young ones.
now we must rise
a collective union
with the hammers of our voices
and our hearts
we must break the glass windows
puncture the rubber gloves
so we can massage
the backs that yearn
for our touch.

2
when it was just beginning
rumours of a plague setting us up
for madness
moving us into delirium
international borders closing
master lists of people infected
men/women/children/babies being
led to prisons disguised as hospitals
led like the prisoners at Auschwitz
or the long lines of human flesh
walking onto the planks
at Gorée Island.
it is possible for this madness
to come to reality
to flourish
like the skunk cabbage
under our feet
this disease in its beginning
we turned our eyes
whispered softly
and twisted our mouths
at this "gay disease"
we lived as we have always lived
and yet
when Uncle Henry and Auntie Rhonda
and Sister Maybelle from round the
corner
stopped going to the store
stopped going to the fish market
stopped going to pick up the mail
stopped going to get hair done
and nails fixed
we whispered but nobody really wondered
nobody really saw their bodies lying
covered with sores

coughing and wondering how to endure
pain that cripples.
let us lift our eyes
out of illusion
so that we may see
our brown faces
our red faces
our white faces
dying of this disease
killing so swiftly
so many
we must light the candles as
knowledge descends like lightning
we must light the candles
for the IV drug users
and pass them a needle they
can call their own.
we must light the candles for the gay
and bisexual man whose choice
of difference is not the problem now
the problem is when he is treated like a beast
made to lie down until bedsores
become gaping holes
bleeding.
light the candles for the babies
crying in their own urine
in a dark ward as people pass
with earplugs that keep out the
sound of their own pain
light the candles for the Latina woman
hiding in a small room under a blanket
of fear
machismo keeps her tears quiet like
the morning dew that settles in El Barrio
light the candles for the bodies being
lowered in the earth

our eyes must be clear
our hearts strong
as we seek to know this disease
as we realize
that our babies will soon become
museum pieces to gaze upon
when we wish to remember their smiles.
we must use the light
as we seek to understand the movements
of our arms
our legs
our eyes
we must know this disease
so that once again
we can reach out to
our lovers/mothers/fathers/babies
smiling
into a hologram of future possibilities

touch

CHARLOTTE WATSON SHERMAN

C'Anne hadn't lied when she told Raina the man she wanted Raina to meet had nice hands.

"Those long sensitive-looking fingers like you like. If the man wasn't an X-ray technician, I'd swear he was a masseuse," C'Anne had told Raina.

Raina had to force herself not to stare at those hands as she gazed into the amused eyes of Theodore Massey, who sat across from her at the small table inside The Dilettante, where he sipped a passion fruit Italian soda as she nursed a double latte.

Theodore was trying to explain the significance of Michael Jordan retiring from basketball to Raina, a woman who secretly believed most athletes were Neanderthals.

Raina watched Theodore's lips move as sounds fell from his mouth like melodic bouncing balls. She wondered if she could paint his hands so the light hit them just so, so the brown in his skin would be orange with flecks of green beneath. She puzzled over whether or not she could capture the way the skin on his hands almost gleamed like snakeskin, as she painted those slim fingers caressing a masked woman's face.

"So I think it's going to teach the media a lesson. They can't treat those men like slaves. They make 'em too much money. I know they were sick in Chicago to see Michael retire, they're probably still sick. Athletes have a right to their own private lives."

"Private lies?" Raina slowly brought herself back into Theodore's monologue.

"Lives. Private lives," he said agitatedly.

"Oh, right. Well, they sign their lives away for all that money. I think they're all just high-priced slaves."

"But who working today isn't a high-priced slave? No. That's what they thought Michael was, but he showed them. . . ."

Raina's skin was hungry. It had been over eighteen months, almost two years since her limbs were entwined with another's between soft sheets. Now the thought of having her naked legs caressed by Theodore and his delicate hands running over her body made her eyelids twitch.

She liked the smell of Theodore, his Lagerfeld cologne mixed with a deep muscular man smell. She liked the shape his compact body made as he sat in the chair opposite her.

They had been meeting for almost one month in coffee shops and restaurants trying to get some sense of each other. Normally, Raina would have had The Talk with Theodore by now, but the sight of his hands and the pressure of her relentless celibacy distracted her.

Seven months ago, she had stopped seeing a man who had failed The Talk.

"I don't make love anymore without a condom," Raina had told him.

"I don't like using rubbers," he had said.

"You know, there's all kinds of condoms—lubricated, flavored, ribbed or smooth. You can even get some that glow in the dark. I'm willing to go shopping with you to help you find a kind you like," she had offered.

"Where's the romance in putting on a rubber?" he had asked.

"We could make it a part of foreplay," she had responded.

"I take good care of myself and I know I don't have AIDS," he had said.

"Have you been tested?"

"I don't need no test to tell me what I already know. I don't have it."

"But I know we've both had sex with other people, unless you're telling me that at thirty-eight years old, this would be your first time having sex?" Raina had asked unbelievingly.

"I haven't been intimate with that many people, have you?" he had asked, defensively.

"It doesn't matter how many people we've been intimate with. When we sleep with each other, it's like we're sleeping with all of the people we've both gone to bed with. I can't enjoy sex when I'm worrying about a virus running wild in my body."

"Well, I can't feel anything with a rubber on. I don't want to use 'em."

"Well, you can't feel anything when you're dead either," Raina had told him as she finished her double latte and exited the café.

Now it was time to have The Talk with Theodore. But she couldn't bring herself to say the words. His hands and the light. His lips soft on her skin. His hands on her body in the light, stroking, easing into that soft core where she had been happily alone but waiting still for a touch as gentle, as light-filled as Theodore's was bound to be.

And he looked so clean. Plus C'Anne had introduced them. C'Anne, her best friend. He had to be safe. How could a deadly virus enter a body with hands so filled with light?

That evening in Raina's apartment, Theodore and Raina ate salmon pasta and sautéed asparagus tips from the extra-large indigo plates she had recently purchased at The Chicken Soup Brigade's thrift shop. Theodore brought the wine.

"How long have you been painting?" Theodore asked as he surveyed several of Raina's walls.

"Well, I've always dibble-dabbled with it. I decided to start taking myself seriously five years ago."

"Have you been in any shows?"

"I've had a few pieces in group shows, nothing solo yet."

"I like the way you use color. There's a lot of passion in these women's faces."

"I'm glad you can see that. Most men react to the nudes' bodies; they don't even see the intensity of emotion in the faces."

"To be honest, I am having a reaction to the tension in those bodies," Theodore said and laughed. "It's good to see a Black woman working in the arts. Do a lot of us support your work?"

Raina took a long sip of wine from her skinny wineglass.

"I get some support from people. Some people say my art isn't Black art."

"This isn't Black art?"

"The skins are blue and green and purple. These women could be any race. Plus, they're not singing. I guess that's the reason it's not Black art."

"Ah, if it's Black art, then the people have to *really* be black."

"Whatever that means," Raina said, and they both laughed.

Theodore insisted on washing dishes after they finished dinner.

"It's the least I can do," he said, smiling.

"Oh, I plan on getting paid for my services," Raina said, and Theodore burst out laughing. His laughter came from a deep place inside him, and Raina had always admired a man with depth.

While Theodore washed dishes, Raina let down the foldout bed and lit the row of multicolored candles on the low table near the bed.

She loaded the CD player with the Sade, Anita Baker, Luther Vandross, and Toni Braxton CDs C'Anne had given her.

"These tunes make my legs open up like I'm being hypnotized. Ask Mr. P," C'Anne had said. "This music will have both of you good to go. And, Raina, don't play any of that weird shit you like to listen to. You want the man to make love to you, you don't want him to start chanting and meditating."

Raina stood beside the window that overlooked the street slowly awakening to the coming night. She knew that some of the dark spots moving down the street had pink and green hair, that the larger shapes were lovers strolling, that the erratic movements of some of the shapes were the motions of college boys jostling each other.

She didn't startle when Theodore eased behind her at the window. He traced the outline of her lips lightly with those fingers before he curved his body into hers as he bent to kiss her neck. They stood fastened at the window for some time.

Then Raina turned to kiss him. As she closed her eyes, the color she saw was sapphire livid blue, then lavender-blue, then fuchsia.

She tried to kiss him deeply enough to see the color of his soul. But she would not see that until they had stripped and lay exposed inside the Egyptian cotton sheets, until they each had opened the closed doors inside of themselves, until they reached that naked place outside the body where the act of making love, the sex of the sex, had taken them on and off through the night, and only then did Raina catch a glimpse of the vermilion of Theodore's soul.

Three weeks later, while Theodore gave Raina a full body massage, he found swollen lymph glands in her neck. A few days later, she came down with the flu for the second time in six months. She didn't think this illness was anything serious, though she usually went years between colds.

Theodore brought flowers to her apartment each day of her illness, but Raina soon grew to realize she better get tested.

As Raina sat in the smooth-backed chair with her right arm resting lightly on the small school desk–like platform before her, she began silently to recite her litany of fears:

The fear of air, the fear of bacteria, the fear of beards and beds, the fear of being afraid, the fear of being alone, the fear of being bound, the fear of being beaten, the fear of being buried alive

Thank God the smiling woman coming towards her with rubber gloves and a needle didn't have a beard, though she did have a long strip of rubber to bind Raina's upper arm.

The fear of being dirty, of being egotistical, the fear of being scratched, being stared at, the fear of birds, the fear of blood

Raina watched the tip of the needle pierce her skin, she marveled at the dark tears running from the green vein in her arm. She wondered what the smiling woman wondered as Raina's blood filled the crystalline vial. Did she think Raina was promiscuous? Did she think Raina used to do drugs?

The fear of cancer and cats, the fear of certain names, of childbirth and children, the fear of churches

In churches Raina had learned to fear certain names—blasphemer fornicator demon unholy one—and books that named names. Her little black book. So hot and heavy in her hands now. A finger pointing. A book of testimony. A book of crimes. The book of naming names. Raina's book of desire.

The fear of being confined in a house, the fear of corpses, the fear of crossing a bridge

When you came to it, right down to it, Raina almost couldn't enter the hospital waiting room door. Almost couldn't lift her feet to mount the stairs because she didn't want to ride the elevator, didn't want to chance seeing anyone she knew in the elevator. This was her second test in six months. The first had been positive. She was hoping there had been a mistake. That someone had made a terrible mistake.

The fear of crowds, the fear of dead bodies, the fear of deformity, of
demons, of depths and dirt, the fear of disease

Raina tried to pinpoint when this could have gotten into her body, invaded her blood and cells and tissue. She must be able to recollect the precise moment of entry, when something so evil, when something as pernicious as this, had found a home inside her. She knew she hadn't been infected by Theodore, the onset of her symptoms had begun too soon after they had made love. But who? She had only slipped once or maybe twice before. She didn't know what she would do if she had now infected Theodore.

The fear of disorder, of doctors and dogs, and dreams, the fear of
drugs, the fear of duration

Raina could not even begin to imagine enduring this invasion of her body for the duration. She had seen the ravaged bodies of the men they showed on TV. Those dark spots that tattooed their faces and limbs. That slow-motion wasting away of your very self.

The fear of elevated places, and empty rooms, the fear of enclosed
space, the fear of everything, the fear of eyes

What would become of Raina's eyes? She, a painter, must have them to see. What would she see with her eyes now? What would she be seeing? What would there be to see now that this was inside her? Would it get inside her eyes?

The fear of failure, fatigue, feces, and fire, the fear of fish and
floods

Raina's body was awash now, her body has been flooded now, her body has betrayed her now, her body is not her body now, her body, her body, Raina started to beat her body, started to pound her breast with her bandaged arm, she did not cry out, she was not loud, she would not become an enraged black woman in need of security to escort her out of the building. She stayed in her place in the school desk–like chair. She beat her breast until the Band-Aid loosened its hold on her skin and fell to the ground. Raina fell to the ground. Though enraged she was not loud. The nurse on duty was alarmed. "Do not call security. I repeat, do not call security," the doctor said.

The fear of flying and fog, the fear of germs, the fear of ghosts, the fear of glass, the fear of God

Inside the black hole where Raina disappeared after having her blood drawn for her second positive HIV test, there was no God. Though she heard whispers about God, no one ever said that word aloud when she was near. It was the devastation seen when one looked inside Raina's eyes that silenced any talk of God or tomorrow or promise: visions of Bantustans, infants with swollen bellies, cities where flies covered fresh meat and raw sewage spilled forth like copper geysers of repressed hope.

Raina's co-workers at the law firm where she worked her day job as a word processor grew increasingly disturbed. They were used to her laughing and cracking jokes; this new Raina was moody, distant, dangerous.

At a staff meeting Raina did not attend because she had told them to leave her the hell alone and let her do her job, they decided Bev Turner, the only Black attorney at the firm, would talk to Raina and *make* her do something to get back to her old self. Otherwise, Raina was going to be out of a job.

She still had not told Theodore.

Raina listened to the monotoned voice at the other end of the telephone. She willed herself to keep the great beast of rage at bay.

Name?

Raina Belle Sargent.

DOB?

10/14/58.

That makes you uh, thirty-five.

I'm glad you're good at math. It makes me feel like I'm in good hands.

Huh?

Never mind.

Oh, OK. Let's see. Address?

▼ 134 ▼

635 Broadway Ave. E. #8.

Are you single, married, divorced?

Single.

Any children?

Raina was silent a long while.

Hello?

No.

No?

No children.

Are you taking any medication?

Not since I stopped taking birth control pills.

Oh, why did you stop taking them?

Raina did not respond.

OK, I'll leave that blank. Maybe you'll trust your therapist with that information.

Raina snorted.

Any problems with alcohol or drug abuse?

No.

Have you ever had suicidal thoughts or attempted suicide?

No, what do you think I am, crazy?

Have you ever had any previous counseling?

No.

Why are you calling for counseling today?

So I can go back to my job tomorrow.

Raina had braced herself for the intrusive questions she knew they would ask. Still, the beast shifted in the pit of her stomach once she hung up the telephone with an appointment the following afternoon to see Southshore Mental Health Clinic's only Black female therapist.

The telephone rang, but Raina let the answering machine pick up the call. She had been allowing the machine to take all of her calls this past week. She knew who was calling before she heard C'Anne's pleading voice on the other end of the telephone line.

"Raina would you please pick up the damn phone. I know you're there. I need to talk to you and we've been friends too long for you to keep doing me like this."

Beep.

Thankfully, Raina's machine only allowed callers to leave a thirty-second message. Raina didn't like to talk on the telephone in even the most ideal circumstances and those who talked on and on on the machine really worked her nerves, even her best friend, C'Anne.

Theodore had stopped calling months ago, after Raina had insisted that he leave her alone.

Raina would talk to C'Anne when she was ready. Probably in about one hundred years. For the rest of her life, Raina would remember every detail of their last conversation, when Raina had tried to gather the courage to tell C'Anne she had found out she was HIV positive.

"I found someone new to read my tarot cards. Wanna come?"

Raina listened to the eager sound of C'Anne's cool-toned voice on the other end of the telephone. Practical, rational C'Anne talking about going to have her tarot cards read. The same C'Anne who faithfully watched CNN and believed that if Bernard Shaw's finely tuned mouth didn't comment or report on a happening, then it simply hadn't happened.

"I love you and all of your contradictions," Raina said. "I guess this means Mr. P isn't upset anymore about those two hundred dollars worth of phone calls to the Psychic Hotline?"

"All water under the bridge. I'll be over to pick you up in twenty minutes. Mr. P is at work, so I've got the whole day free."

"Take your time. I just started a new painting."

"Still working on the masked women?"

"Yeah. And it's taking me a while to get into this latest one, so I'll be ready for a break by the time you get here."

"Mr. P asked if this masked woman thing you're working on is some kind of S & M thing, but I just told him to get a life."

Raina started to laugh, then stopped. It would be nice if things were as easy as telling someone to get a life and they could. Should she tell C'Anne now?

"See ya."

"Yeah," Raina said as she slowly hung up the telephone without saying a word about the HIV. Maybe it would be easier to tell C'Anne face to face.

Ever since she found out she had tested positive it seemed as if she were living in a dream. Each step, each breath, each sweep of her arms through the air felt accentuated and unreal. Her sharp dark eyes, usually able to focus on detail, were glazed. Her lips, unsensuously languid. The bustling sounds of the street outside her studio apartment in one of the most vibrant neighborhoods in the city were muted. She no longer smiled when she heard the sounds of throngs of friends and lovers walking briskly down the avenue, cracking jokes or singing as if their lungs might burst.

Raina no longer felt safe inside the haven of her brick building with the ivy that climbed up the sides and protected the structure inside its slender green fingers.

If Raina hadn't been able to keep this deadly virus out of her own body, what did it matter whether the building she lived in was safe?

At one time, she had enjoyed the northern light that made the austere apartment radiant. She had once loved the way the sunlight caused the wood to gleam on the old oak floors and her spindly antique desk. She had loved to see the shine on the gold-framed portraits of her mother, Circe, and father, Amilcar, that sat proudly on the desk.

Now when she looked at the floor-to-ceiling bookshelves that lined an entire wall of the apartment, she felt nothing. What use would the library she was trying to create have for her in the grave?

Raina stood near the easel which held the latest canvas she had been working on. The lines weren't right, the shape of the face was wrong, the eyes . . .

Raina picked up an unopened tube of chartreuse acrylic paint and poured a small dab into a compartment in the egg carton she used for mixing her paints.

She used her fan brush to lightly spread the chartreuse over the woman's face.

There was no way on earth she was going to be able to tell anyone about this. Not Theodore. Not even C'Anne. Though they had been friends since third grade and had stayed best friends even after C'Anne's folks moved C'Anne and her two brothers to Baltimore because C'Anne's father was an engineer for the government and got a promotion, Raina still did not know how she could even fix her lips to tell C'Anne.

Cool C'Anne. Married for thirteen years to the same man C'Anne. C'Anne who had only slept with one man in her thirty-five years and then married him. C'Anne the optometrist, the only black woman Raina knew who had two graduate degrees in science. The only black woman Raina knew who had two graduate degrees period. And Raina had completed her four years of college as if they had been a prison sentence and, once released, she had never looked back.

No. She could never tell C'Anne this. She had heard the way the people she knew talked about AIDS. Like it was something none of them could ever get.

How could she tell them she might soon have it?

As Raina sat in the waiting room, waiting patiently for her therapist to come for her, she wondered how she was going to be able to keep putting C'Anne and Theodore off.

She was growing weary of the lies she was telling, tired of feeling as if she were some kind of criminal because she had a disease. Automatically, she began her litany:

The fear of going to bed, the fear of graves and hair, the fear of heaven and heights, the fear of heredity, the fear of home

Her home was beginning to feel like a grave. She wouldn't let anyone come over and she didn't dare go anywhere. She hadn't picked up a paintbrush in weeks. The canvas sprinkled with layers of green covering a woman's face still stood on her easel.

The fear of horses, the fear of illness, of imperfection, of infection, the fear of infinity and inoculation and injections, the fear of insanity

Raina was beginning to believe she was going insane. She was so afraid of people now, of people knowing her secret, of them knowing how this illness would infuse her blood and cells and tissue until her body was illuminated with disease.

She refused to sleep at night. Sleeping now reminded her of death. The thought of closing her eyes without consciousness terrified her. She stayed up nights watching black and white reruns on television and listening to her meditation tapes.

The fear of insects and itching, the fear of jealousy and justice, the fear of lakes, the fear of leprosy, the fear of light

There was no justice in this. She had railed against the God of her mother and father, railed against the Goddess of her friends. On her knees, with the night entering her apartment like an evil thing, she had railed against what would become of her body, too weary to curse the gods for what would become of her soul.

The fear of lightning, machinery, and making decisions, the fear of making false statements, the fear of many things, the fear of marriage, meat, and men

She could not continue making false statements. She would have to make the decision to tell the truth, to everyone. C'Anne, Theodore, the people at work. All of them would have to be told. She hoped this therapist would help her find the words to tell them.

Shadows over Shadows

KESHO SCOTT

Anti-communists would sleep tight tonight if they knew what we do in the dark corners of our lives that abort revolutions before the crack of dawn. Rebels come in all breeds. They live and die for the smell of fresh inked leaflets, paper illusions. Ginger is a part-time file clerk and rebel and her spice has a fuse.

I first met her at the Free Medical Clinic downtown in Main and Middle Urban America. The town was in its winter clothes, and we waddled in thick blue parka coats, underneath a mountainous regime of bulk. There we were—rows and rows of women—clutching empty prescription bottles and holding empty gazes, eyes lost in the details of indoor-outdoor carpet and shit-brown paneling. Clinics, like bus lines, collect those who miss the mainstreet of life. Women swinging passively between illusions and dying and staying sick to live.

Ginger straggled into the clinic with the other regulars I knew and took a number. The nurse gave her that kind of don't-ask-me-no-questions look and directed her to take a seat. She hesitated for a moment before seating herself next to me. Her hesitation drew our eyes to read the story on her face. I tensed up. I flinched, recoiled and readjusted my attention to the floor. This goddamn blood pressure medicine has me seeing double, I thought, to resynchronize my insides to the routine sniffles, sighs and sterile silence.

I dropped my prescription bottle underneath the chair. As I weaved in and out of chairs to regain it, eyes met mine, sympathetic and annoyed. Kelly stood up and moved her chair. Our previous conversations flashed through my head. . . .

Girl, my husband wants to fuck all the time. Lord, the man done started coming home for lunch and pussy. What am I gonna do? Doctor say I should take something for my nerves and calm down. My man say, "Woman, you don't give me enough!" I feel like I'm losing my mind. I'm tired all the time. Ain't got no children. Ain't got no energy to have none either! I'm so tired.

Her mouth, now decorated with a pile of fever blisters and her legs sprouting hair, made the perfect picture. I nodded so she could set her chair down.

Doreen asked, "Did you find it?"

"Yes, thank you."

"Give me your coat. I'll hang it up," she said. "That way we can get a little more room in here."

As it was, we were strangers sitting back to back on cold, hard, caramel-colored, cast iron chairs. I felt grateful as I had when she lent me the cab fare home two weeks earlier. The woman barely knew me, but she knew the bus ride would kill me. "Oh, by the way, I've got your fare to return to you."

"Keep it!" she said abruptly. "I might not need it. Doctor said I might be dead by next week." I had heard that "What the fuck!" tone weeks ago, when her baby son of sixteen was shot in a stick-up and a month before anticipating something would go wrong with her daughter's graduation from high school. Doreen talked real fast, as though afraid she wasn't gonna be able to get it all out before the nurse called her number. And when called, she always jumped up like an attentive five-year-old, smiling tightly and marching—knees high, step one, two, three—in line to the doctor's inner office.

My eyes surveyed the room checking all the debutantes from the end of the bus line. There was Vida, the swinger who lived downtown— and uptown on something. She was twenty-four and drunk on daylight. Vida was always talking in a kinda in-between rhythm: "Yeah . . . baby . . . honey . . . darling, and what's it to you, sugar?"

She alternated between filing her long purple fingernails and fits of chipping the paint from the chairs.

Willie Mae sat two seats away dressed in her starched white uniform, clutching her pocketbook with cash register fingers. She didn't like Vida.

"She's a hood!" she'd say under her breath. "She don't need no doctor. She need to go somewhere and get straight."

"I don't know, Willie Mae. You're being kind of hard, don't you think?" I asked.

"So what! She'll knock you in the head like anyone else." Vida could make Willie Mae close her legs tight and turn her nose toward other irregular body smells. Willie Mae just didn't like undefined things going in the body because, as it was, she couldn't keep her own IUD in place or in peace.

Mrs. Shelton, with the bleeding skin rashes that came from eating colored folks' food, said very little most of the time. But twelve noon would signal daytime soaps in her head and the entertainment would begin: "Erica is sick. The boy done gave her a house, a car and a bunch of clothes, and she just can't be satisfied. Now she's chasing Antoinette's husband, Arthur, who they think gots something going with Michael. Erica is about to give me a heart attack. I just wish I could tell her. . . ," she'd say. And on and on and on.

I asked her once how she was coming along with the treatments.

"They cost too much. The doctor suggested that I eat supermarket baby food. I've been trying it a month now, and I really can't feel no change."

And, of course, there was Crystal and Sue. Crystal had the voice of an angel and 300 pounds to keep her falling from the clouds. She always gave me and Sue her church programs with her name in bold caps: CRYSTALLE and no last name. Sue, we called her Lady, sat in the corner and ran dialogue with herself in full verse. Her lips moved to the caricatures of Al Jolson and, without paying admission, we got our money's worth of showtime. Lady Sue, often tripping over her dough-nut roll stockings that hung over combat boots, sat with a three-inch smile, drumming her foot.

Ginger spoke first, not to me but to Lady Sue. "Lady, you all right?"

Lady Sue turned away and increased her own silent volume.

"Uhn! I've been here at least a hour and a half," Ginger snapped, attacking the silence.

I peeped my head around my huge school-diaper-grocery-bag purse and said, "The doctor won't be in until after one."

"What do they think we are, a motherfuckin' herd of cattle? It's a goddamned shame there's only one doctor for all of us. We pay taxes! If this office was down on East Lafayette, we'd have a red carpet and lunch by now, ain't that right? One o'clock, my ass! Do they think all we have to do is wait around all day? We should all just get up and leave. Uhn! How would that son of a bitch make his money then?"

Our eyelids caught themselves in their sockets as we heard famil-iar words. Light bulbs went off in our heads—she was right of course—and to her sermon, in order of succession, we splattered upon the silence a series of "yes, Lords;" "A-mens;" and "well, well, well's." Lady

Sue shifted her seat toward the center. I stopped fiddling in my bag and turned off my reoccurring nightmare. She stood up and asked one of those politician questions, the kind people asked after Bobby Kennedy's death. "Well, what's it gonna be, people? Liberty or death?"

Back then I was saying goodbye to my childhood and running smack dead into waxed living, an American skateboard to slip and slide beyond one's resources and below one's potential. The 60's turned out the 50's and turned on my agenda: BURN, BABY BURN! Everything was in full color: Afros and red-necks, po-lice and su-burbs, Mal-colm X and John-son, Viet-nam and De-troit. Street people were claiming major victories. Afros had replaced tulips and cussing brought forth detente. Kelly, Doreen, Vida and Willie Mae were on the front lines then. Crystal was directing them in a chorus of Curtis Mayfield's song, "We're a win-ner . . . and never let anybody say . . . you can't make it cause an evil mind's in your way." Mrs. Shelton didn't have no skin rash then, cause her and Miss Rosa Parks were churchgoing friends. And now Ginger had just lit the pilot and boiled our memories of talking back to white folks, to men, to the FBI, and protecting our sister, Angela.

The nurse, caught between her color and calling, rang her desk bell and broke our collective déjà vu. The sound lured us back from the hills where rebels hide out. Ginger, seeing the group in danger, made her move toward the nurse, hollering: "Enough of this shit! We want that motherfucker, right now! You know where he is. Ya'll always know where he is. . . !"

My soul stepped completely out of its container, and I watched a part of me drop to the floor like an old coat. Startled, I looked around, and we were all standing, right behind Ginger. ". . . I bet he's been eat-ing his lunch all the goddamn time!"

"He's finished. Ginger, you may go in now."

Ginger slipped through the door. Poof!

Silence filled all the spaces between us. I found myself another spot on the dirty indoor-outdoor carpet to plant my gaze and drew a big fat blank. I was a walking, talking time bomb firing blanks, anyway. Free clinics give permanent residency to my kind.

"Somebody's in there whimpering," Lady Sue said, putting sounds to her words for the first time. I turned to Kelly with the hairy legs, dropped my prescription bottle on purpose this time to get everybody's attention.

"It sounds like someone is crying to me," I said.

Vida, nodding out, said, "Yeah . . . it's the one . . . with the big mouth . . . shi-i-i-i-it! They must be whipping her ass."

"No way! It must be somebody else in the doctor's office," Willie Mae said, straightening her collar.

Doreen, thinking they had called her number, jumped up, stopped, then sat down again. "I didn't see nobody else."

"Neither did I," Mrs. Shelton said dabbing her oozing skin rash with her Sunday hankie. "But I think it's her. She's been crying since she went in there."

We all looked over to the other side of the room where Crystal had begun humming "Precious Lord" as Ginger's whimpers turned to screams. Our ah's and ooh's and shifting body sighs commenced when the screaming settled down and the door opened. Ginger walked out and placed her chart in the rack and left. Looking for the smoke to appear, I responded to the nurse's "Next," and moved toward the inner door. I paused for a moment to catch the silence in the room, and my eyes locked onto the words on the doctor's chart. *Diagnosis:* Ginger is sick. *Prescription:* She needed to cry.

and do remember me

MARITA GOLDEN

The house loomed around her, reeking of loneliness and neglect. Entering the foyer, Macon set her briefcase and several envelopes from her mailbox on a table in the hallway. Shadows from the sudden arrival of evening filtered in through the sheer curtains at the front door window and intensified the momentary hesitance that frequently gripped her when she entered her house. At times like these, she had an eerie, fleeting desire to go no further. This was the house where she had fought the possibility of death. This was where she had begun to heal, only to find the process more daunting than she had ever imagined. In the living room Macon turned on the light and gazed at the newspapers strewn on the floor beside the sofa, the stacks of videos atop the television set, the yellow legal pads, the books on the coffee table and the coffee mugs on the side tables, as though assessing the handiwork of a stranger.

Once she had been almost fanatically neat. Now she had grown used to the disheveled atmosphere that prevailed in nearly every room of the house. The disorder that once could threaten a headache, now soothed her, took on a presence of its own that she respected. It was merely an extension of her life.

Sitting on the sofa, Macon reached for the remote control and turned on the television, which she kept on now virtually all the time. The face of one of the city's most popular black anchormen sprang into view. Gazing at the screen with the sound off, Macon realized that she was hungry, but the thought of trying to decide what to eat sent waves of fatigue through her. Instead she removed her jacket, tossing it into a nearby chair, and stretched out on the sofa. She would rest a few minutes, she told herself, instantly falling asleep.

Three months after her forty-fourth birthday, Macon discovered the cancer while examining herself after a shower. The hard tiny lump felt like a bullet lodged beneath her skin. A biopsy of the lump revealed that the cancer had spread so rapidly that a modified radical mastectomy was immediately performed followed by chemotherapy. Within a month of discovering the lump, she had only one remaining breast. How, she often wondered, could her body have been plotting to kill her without her knowledge? Except for the tiny lump, she had no other signs of the illness.

Two weeks after the surgery, Macon attended an American Cancer Society seminar on breast prostheses. Entering the room, she saw five tables lined with thirty different types of prostheses on display. There were breasts made of silicone gel, cloth and plastic. There were breasts the color of deep chocolate, breasts with brand names like Bosom Buddy and Nearly Me. How suitable, Macon thought, when she picked up several prostheses shaped like teardrops. The hour spent looking at these prostheses had depressed her so much that she had considered not wearing one at all. Her doctor had not been able to give her a medical argument for its necessity.

She had challenged the conventional wisdom in the classroom and in her life, but, even after a long talk with a friend who had chosen not to wear a prosthesis, Macon had decided to wear one. It changed nothing. She remained a one-breasted woman living with cancer. Yet how important it had become to fool the world, if not herself. Her hair had begun to grow back and she had symbolically burned the wig she'd had to wear during the chemotherapy treatments. She was determined not to have to wear one again.

Pearl stayed with her for a time during the worst of the ordeal, which Macon now recalled as the entire time. Macon, so independent, so self-sufficient, had subtly tried to resist Pearl's competent, nurturing hand. But after a while, her protests that she was fine had exhausted her. During the chemotherapy treatments after the operation, she was home for three months.

While watching a movie on TV one night, Pearl turned to look at Macon during a commercial and said, "It's only a tittie. That's all they took. A tittie."

"But it was *my* tittie, mine," Macon said, feeling the inevitable, hot tears well quickly in her eyes. Pearl hugged her gently and Macon thought, It wouldn't be just a tittie to you.

As an actress Pearl valued her body, her looks; she cherished her physique, her attractive face. How she depended on it, even as she had sought to destroy it over the years with alcohol and men.

"I wasn't making light of what's happened," Pearl apologized, turning off the television and huddling at the foot of Macon's bed. "I was just trying to put it in perspective."

"I know, I know," Macon said.

"At AA," Pearl began carefully, "they told me I'd have to learn to love what I'd been through—waking up with a head the size of this room, the crow's-feet around my eyes from the alcohol fucking with my veins—I'd have to learn to look back on all that as just *stuff* that had my name on it, that belonged to me and my past but that couldn't claim me now. You'll have to learn to love that empty spot on your chest. Besides, you've been more scared than you are now, I know. Tell me something that scared you as much as what you're facing now."

"It's not just having one breast, it's the cancer, it could come back."

"Tell me," Pearl insisted. Macon stared at the walls, her lips pursed tight, as though reining in a potential explosion, and refused to speak.

Pearl said, "When I had my second abortion a couple of years ago, I thought if I have to go through this again I will die. The anesthesia always took me out. I felt like I was having DT's. And with this last abortion, it took me a long time to come out from under the drugs. I felt like I was stuck inside this dark horrible tunnel."

"When that dog bit me outside the courthouse in Greenwood," Macon said slowly. She coughed and wiped her eyes with a tissue. Sinking back against the pillows, she said, "Believe me, girl, I was scared. That business about your life passing before your eyes is true. I was only what, twenty? There wasn't much life to recall but it zipped by when that dog's teeth sank into my right arm. I'd never felt such terror."

"Terror, my dear," Pearl pronounced solemnly, "is also the first day of sobriety, the longest most gruesome day of your life."

They sat up the remainder of that night, trading horror stories, sharing near misses. The retelling of stories they both already knew—old miseries, old defeats, redefined that which made them friends.

Pearl had helped Macon pick out a wig when her hair began to fall out because of the chemo, turning the wig-hunting expedition into a farce, prancing around the shop in a suburban mall, assuming a different identity to match each wig. It was Pearl who was there when

Macon was sick to her stomach from the chemo, holding her head while she wretched in the bathroom and it was Pearl who cleaned up after her as if she were a baby.

Macon woke up still tired, still hungry. When she turned on her answering machine, there was a message from Courtland. He was coming to Washington next week, and wanted to drop by to see her, he said. She had finally reached a point where she could be in the same room with Courtland and not feel herself drenched in regret. It had taken a long time but she liked to think they'd backtracked to the beginning and were friends as at the start. The last year of their marriage had been a protracted stalemate that neither possessed the courage or good will to break. Macon had wanted to adopt a child and shape a marriage that included greater intimacy, the possibility for surprise. Courtland insisted that he could only father his own child and that his political work was still paramount. The divorce was the only thing they were able to agree on in the end. After it was over, Courtland returned to Mississippi, where he had been marshaling support for a run for Congress.

For several years after the divorce she had thought about adopting a child. She had gone so far as to make inquiries with public and private agencies. But the depth, the weight of the need of the children she saw overwhelmed her. They had been battered, beaten, born to drug-addicted mothers, shunted from one often abusive foster home to another. Their need for love and stability struck Macon as bottomless. She gave nearly a dozen lectures during the school year at colleges around the country. Her research required frequent travel, sometimes abroad. The world had become her village. What would she alone, with no partner to lean on for help, be able to give to a child who needed someone who could always be there? If she were married, if her life were more predictable, if she could afford and live with the decision to hire live-in help—the ifs piled up around her desire to adopt and soon left it quietly buried under a blanket of doubt.

There was also a message on her machine from Noble Carson. He was at a meeting he said but wanted to stop by to see her that evening. He would call back later to see if she was in.

*   *   *

They had gone out for dinner twice in the last month. The sound of Noble's voice on the machine filled Macon with a familiar mixture of fear and desire. It had been a long time since she was involved with a man.

Around the time she discovered the lump, there had been the beginnings of an affair with a black dean at Jefferson College. When she found out about the cancer she simply told him that everything had changed; she could no longer see him. She had not even given him a decent explanation; she had felt that her disease allowed her to be thoughtless and rude. She did not care about his feelings or his sincere hurt when she hung up abruptly during a call to see how she was.

During the actual battle against cancer, her body had been poked and probed so much that the thought of a man's touch had totally dismayed her. But since the doctor had confirmed that she was in remission, she had continued to live a life of celibacy. First, she had not wanted to be touched, then when Macon realized she was out of harm's way, she wanted to avoid the emotional disarray and confusion that love always seemed to bring. But in the wake of Noble's promise to call her tonight, she felt desire stir in the pit of her groin, unmistakable and full-fledged.

Noble Carson was one of the first people Macon met when she moved to Washington. She knew him before his divorce, before his fall from grace, before his time in prison. An aide to a senior black congressman, Joshua Fairbanks, Noble was a member of a group Macon worked with mobilizing against investments in South Africa, demonstrating in front of the South African embassy against apartheid. Their arrest during a demonstration sealed their friendship.

A compact, whirling dervish of a man, Noble was prematurely gray and glided across a room like a panther. As the oldest son of one of Washington's most respected black preachers, Noble had inherited his father's eloquence and genius for rallying others to action. Often after long meetings plotting the defeat of apartheid, Noble asked Macon to join him for a drink or a late night snack. Noble Carson talked the way James Brown moved his feet. His conversation was incisive quick-witted poetry. He told her all the dirt about congressmen and senators on the Hill and viewed his job with a pragmatism that sometimes disheartened Macon.

One evening Macon met him in his office on the Hill. As they strolled down the halls of the Longworth Building, he said with a sweep of his arms, "Just look around, Macon, this is why blacks get elected and are never heard from again. This is Disneyland," he said, a wicked, raucous laugh echoing gently down the hall. "This is a place so comfortable, so nice, you never want to go home, and some of these guys never do." He told her about the Capitol gym, the bank, the medical services and the myriad perks that ensured congressional privilege and encouraged abuse of power. "What's a black politician gonna say when he gets stationed here except Thank you, boss?" he'd asked, squeezing her tight for emphasis and kissing her cheek playfully.

"Oh, Noble," she'd protested.

"Come on, Macon," he'd said as they left the building and headed for her car, "when was the last time you heard a member of the Black Caucus criticize Israel? Say anything about a subject that doesn't have to do with race? Rock the boat? Just like the white boys, they're bought and paid for. After a while you could do this blindfolded."

She loved to listen to him talk, savored the sound of his laughter. She had been falling for him even then. Macon just hadn't known it.

Nonetheless, she was really not surprised when he was arrested for stealing three hundred thousand dollars from the campaign chest of Joshua Fairbanks. She had heard rumors about his weakness for gambling. Macon had seen him in the eight-hundred-dollar suits he wore in the "glory days" as he called the period when he talked easily and casually with Senator Kennedy when he ran into him in the halls of the Rayburn Building. Those were the days when he twisted arms and made promises, all to raise money for Fairbanks. He had answered virtually to no one then, not even Fairbanks himself, so much was he trusted by his boss. The world, to Noble Carson, was an orchard and he entered it every day with an appetite and two skillful, fast-moving hands.

Sentenced to five years in prison, Noble served two and had been out on probation for the last year and a half. When Macon went to visit him at the federal penitentiary in Lewisburg, Pennsylvania, she asked him why he stole the money. As she sat waiting for his answer, she wondered if his was a political mistake or a personal tragedy?

"It was so easy," he told her. "So easy. It was there. I could do it. And I did. Lots of times the contributions came in the form of cash. Sometimes checks were made out to me, since I was the main fund-raiser. Josh trusted me. I cashed them."

Even in his prison uniform, Noble Carson looked suave, fashionable. Staring at him across the wooden picnic table in the visiting area, Macon thought that he looked better than she had seen him look in years. The haunted, hunted look of the weeks preceding his sentencing had given way to an unperturbed mellowness.

Yet beneath his calm exterior a furtive combustibility still lurked, a warm, radiant heat that Macon knew had fired both his political commitment and his greed. But it was this contradiction, this studied conflagration of cross purposes that defined Noble. Even sitting across from him in Lewisburg, Macon battled with the passion that shot across her heart like a meteor. Noble's arrogance and pride offended and seduced her. He would not admit to a moment of remorse; his only regret, he said, was that he had betrayed Fairbanks, who had been a mentor and friend. In the clubby, familial atmosphere of Capitol Hill, Fairbanks had relied so much on Noble's expertise and political skills that Fairbanks had vainly tried to cover up the theft. But a congressional committee got wind of the crime and forced Fairbanks to press charges.

When Noble revealed during Macon's visit that his wife, Angela, had filed for a divorce, Macon was surprised at the relief she felt. For, she had assured herself, no, she did not want Noble Carson. Never in a million years.

Macon erased the messages on the answering machine and recalled that when she and Noble had gone out the previous week she had told him about the cancer, about how afraid she had been, how much she had wanted to live.

He told her about prison, saying, "There was a period, around the middle of my sentence, when being there was a relief. My creditors couldn't get to me. There were almost no decisions that I had to make for myself. I didn't have to try to impress anybody. Everybody there had fucked up. Nobody was pointing a finger."

"Are you saying you experienced a spiritual awakening in prison?" Macon asked.

"I wish I had," he said slowly. "I know this has been hard on our friendship, your view of me. You must think I let you down, that I sullied the reputation of the race, and affirmed everything white folks think about niggers with power." A brittle edge frosted his words.

"Noble, I don't give a damn what white folks think. But I was afraid for you."

"I don't want to tell you how many times I was afraid for me too."

"Are you seeing anyone?" he asked.

"Why do you want to know?"

"I have my reasons."

"Since the operation I've kind of avoided relationships."

"Oh, damn, Macon, I don't believe this, not you, in emotional retreat?"

"It takes time," she protested.

"I want to see you sometimes," he said, the request a soft kiss on her cheek. In response to her silence, he said, "Macon, I want to bring you flowers."

"Noble, I don't know," she said, wanting to run, wondering how he would feel if he saw her chest.

"I do," he insisted, his voice brisk with impatience, with the stubborn, take-charge force that she loved and hated at the same time.

"But we're friends. I don't want to lose that."

"How do you know we won't remain friends?"

"Lately, my track record hasn't been so great."

"Macon, I'm lonely. You don't have to say you are too. Just tell me I can take you out. That I can kiss you. Bring you flowers. Why can't you just say yes? I've been before one judge and jury. I don't need another one. Will you be my court of appeals?"

Noble had called again, sounding happy to find her at home, and told Macon he would see her around eight-thirty. The house was a mess. Macon made a turkey sandwich and gobbled it down. She changed into jeans and a tee shirt and cleaned up the kitchen and the living room, deliberately, carefully, even vacuuming the floors and dusting the massive bookshelves. She cleaned the house in a frenzy of dedication and when she was done she fell on the sofa, her body moist with sweat, fatigue and exhilaration. But the desire was still there. She had not extinguished it as she had hoped. After a quick shower, she dried herself in front of the full-length mirror in her bedroom. Her doctor had proudly called the incision a clean cut. The skin where the cut was made had folded over into a soft flap. Macon stood before the mirror and caressed her breast and rubbed the skin over her chest. No man had seen her like this. For all the courage she liked to think she possessed, the thought of Noble seeing this terrified her. A week ago she had had a checkup—the blood test, the bone and liver scan—to see if the cancer had returned. The tests were all negative. But she would never again be able to take her life for granted.

When Noble arrived, he kissed Macon gently, holding her close in the hallway before entering the living room. To her surprise, she did not resist him, but felt oddly relieved by the assertiveness of his touch.

She told him about the ransacking of the BSU offices, saying, "You know what frightens me most? Young people did this. Kids. I think I could handle it better if I knew adult Klansmen had done it. But if kids did this, what happens to the idea of each generation being an improvement over the one that preceded it? What am I doing in the classroom? What are any of us doing there?"

"Racism is a virus," Noble told her with a weary shake of his head. "And since nobody's really looking too hard for a cure it reproduces itself over and over again."

Noble was working as a consultant at a black think tank in downtown Washington, conducting research on shifts in black voting patterns in the last decade. He'd had a particularly rough day, he told her. "I'm not a desk man, somebody to sit in front of a computer and punch in statistics, graphs and all that. With Josh, I was his front man, the arm twister, the person who rallied the troops to reach into their pockets and pull out their checkbooks. I'm restless and bored doing research. And they know it."

Macon made Noble a rum and Coke and fixed herself a mug of herbal tea. They watched the late news. When Macon turned the television off, Noble told her, "You know my parole ends soon."

"If I didn't know better, I'd say you almost sound sad."

"In a way I am."

"You'll miss being on parole?"

"I'll miss my parole officer."

"You're kidding!" Macon exclaimed.

"No, I'm serious," Noble said, folding his hands behind his head, stretching his legs out before him. "He's a righteous dude. Righteous. Remember when we used to say that?" Noble winked at Macon. "He never made me feel like shit because I blew it. He just faced me man to man. Something my dad never did."

"Your father's a minister, what do you expect?"

"Yeah, it's been rough all these years mainly because he's never been my father, he's always been my minister," Noble said bitterly.

"And your parole officer?"

"I guess what I mean is—" Noble began.

"He forgave you."

"Yeah."

"The way your father hasn't."

"The way I'm scared he never will."

"You're his son. He knows that."

"Hell, I learned how to raise money, grease palms, how to soak the rich and the poor watching my daddy pastor a church." The words were vintage Noble—easy, enticing, only half true.

"Are you saying there's no difference between what you did for Fairbanks and what your father did in the name of God?"

"I wish I could, Macon. But even I'm not that bold," he admitted.

"Of course you are," Macon said.

"Can I be that bold tonight? Will you let me?" Noble asked softly, reaching across the length of the sofa, pulling her close to him. "I don't feel like being a gentleman," he whispered in her ear. "And, Macon, I don't want you to be a lady."

As soon as they walked into her bedroom, Macon turned off the lights, but Noble quickly turned on the lamp beside her bed. He unbuttoned her blouse, his fingers nimble and quick, as Macon stared at a corner of the room, afraid to look at his eyes when he saw her chest. He gently pushed the blouse over her shoulders and kissed her on her neck, whispering, "Relax, please, don't fight me, not now."

His plea was so deep, so real, that Macon gave in. She rested her arms on his shoulders as he unfastened her bra in the back. The prosthesis came off easily, and Noble laid it on the bed beside them. He kissed her there, kissed her there first, on the place where she had thought for so long that she was empty. Dead. Noble made tiny circles of kisses around the place where her breast had been and then gazed up at Macon and kissed her eyes, stalling the onslaught of tears. They lay in her bed for a long time Noble simply running his hands over her body, caressing her. When Macon reached for him, Noble said, "No, wait, let me make love to you."

Beneath his touch she was renewed, her body a continent he joyously discovered. Later, lying in his arms, Macon asked quietly, "Does it matter to you?"

"Not one bit," he said, letting his hand again rest there and gently fondle her. "One day it won't matter to you either," he assured her.

"Noble, I want to live," she sighed. "I want to live a long time."

"So do I, Macon, so do I."

Prelude to an Endnote
(or why no chemo/no mastectomy)

FATISHA

for Dr. H. Freeman
Harlem Hospital, N.Y.

I

Presupposing there is a karmic match
yield to the Healer
submit to scalpel/lay under the
knife/fill up any blood bags presented
let tissue be sampled by experts
from all over the world

now is not the moment
to cease being generous

forgo the compulsion
to describe the life
of the Ego before
desire became distracted
by dis-ease/don't
make a scene—
tears cause the Healer
to waste power

don't let self-pity fake itself
into sentiment/don't try
to squirm from under doubt
(which is the last horror
and the last temptation)

dogging your wit day & night
whispering: *"what if this is
all there is. . . ?"*

the Healer
bone-tired/is needed at the micro-
microscope and the computer
even with glory/even with
the crown/even stationed
at the Heart's door & praised
for well-done deliveries the
Healer is weary/like the Sun
bored with light & still intent
on life/the Healer merely cuts out
the toxin to dissuade the body from
resorting to imperfection in any
future life.

II

Healer
listen to what I see
as I dematerialize

i see
knifelessness
no blood to be shed
no bodies to purify
hand held to the breast
but only to receive
and give comfort
no more decayingness
no not knowing
no tongues rolled back
and hidden in the kidney
causing thirsts for

dope and alcohol
no denial of Truth
no humiliation

there is light
enough to see through
to the Soul without
any kind of tool or nuclear
machinery

there is no fury & no
gross shedding of tears
no wicked passion/no
hidden & persistent enemies
no dreams to distract
karma from destiny
no bewilderment
no bogus mystery

there is no nostalgia
there is no haunted
past/no undisclosed
future/there is the
knowing of what
eternalness is
& why now is as it
should be.

III

Healer
be advised
the non-English
speaking have
scanned my bones

charted my blood
& put my tissue
in a jar for future
reference

& I decide I cannot
let you slice me
even if curettage
would prolong breathing/
it would not save or
give me life.

As a part of
eternalness
I happened to Earth
when rhythm became
quirked/in response
to earthquake or turmoil
a misfiled seed/from a
cry of pain/not from
the shout of passion
I have been damned
here/doomed in/I have
been taught as well as
enlightened/I have embarked
and I have failed/I weakened
& rotted my own organs before
I knew what a body is worth
my grief is a songdom
my voice a gush of human anguish

and now
Healer/at the last gate
I feel giddy with delight
like Jonah out of the whale
like Job restored
like the woman who bled

all those years & quite divinely
bleeding stopped

in Reality & in Truth
Healer
Death is the cure—
the only way out of
Hell!

▼▼▼▼▼▼▼▼

PART FOUR

An Anointing: Sisterfriends

My mother always says that if you have one good friend you can trust, you are lucky.

Too often we have been told that women cannot get along with each other, that we cannot trust each other, that we do not like each other.

But if you have someone in your life who jealously guards your secrets, someone you can tell the truth to, someone who's "got your back," you immediately recognize the fallacy and self-hatred involved in perpetuating these obsolete notions.

How can we not love the image of ourselves reflected in the beauty and strength of another Black woman?

When the forces of racism and sexism and classism and homophobia align themselves against our spirits, it is often to another Black woman that we turn for comfort and reassurance that we are OK. The love and wisdom of our Black women friends revitalizes us as we support each other so that no more of us need fall from the weight of fighting oppression as we try to live our lives.

Despite differences in class, skin color, hairstyle, educational background, sexual orientation, and other things that can divide us, Black women will continue to provide sanctuary for each other. What would we do without our sisterfriends?

An Anointing

THYLIAS MOSS

Boys have to slash their fingers to become brothers. Girls trade their
 Kotex, me and Molly do in the mall's public facility.

Me and Molly never remember each other's birthdays. On purpose. We
 don't like scores of any kind. We don't wear watches or weigh ourselves.

Me and Molly have tasted beer. We drank our shampoo. We went to the
 doctor together and lifted our specimen cups in a toast. We didn't
 drink that stuff. We just gargled.

When me and Molly get the urge, we are careful to put it back exactly
 as we found it. It looks untouched.

Between the two of us, me and Molly have 20/20 vision.

Me and Molly are in eighth grade for good. We like it there. We adore
 the view. We looked both ways and decided not to cross the street.
 Others who'd been to the other side didn't return. It was a trap.

Me and Molly don't double date. We don't multiply anything. We don't
 know our multiplication tables from a coffee table. We'll never be
 decent waitresses, indecent ones maybe.

Me and Molly do not believe in going ape or going bananas or going
 Dutch. We go as who we are. We go as what we are.

Me and Molly have wiped each other's asses with ferns. Made emergency tampons of our fingers. Me and Molly made do with what we
 have.

Me and Molly are in love with wiping the blackboard with each other's hair. The chalk gives me and Molly an idea of what old age is like; it is dusty and makes us sneeze. We are allergic to it.

Me and Molly, that's M and M, melt in your mouth.

What are we doing in your mouth? Me and Molly bet you'll never guess. Not in a million years. We plan to be around that long. Together that long. Even if we must freeze the moment and treat the photograph like the real thing.

Me and Molly don't care what people think. We're just glad that they do.

Me and Molly lick the dew off the morning grasses but taste no honey till we lick each other's tongues.

We wear full maternity sails. We boat upon my broken water. The katabatic action begins, Molly down my canal binnacle first, her water breaking in me like an anointing.

Hummers

DEB PARKS-SATTERFIELD

Thanks to Carol B.

SIDE A

because we're black, because we're women
because you're beautiful and so am i
we don't speak
we
hum

hands on cats-in-a-bag hips, necks on ball bearings
lips curled back in derision
acknowledgment loaded with contempt . . . yo' hair, yo' clothes
yo' everything
stripped mashed onto a slide shoved under a microscope thick
with who the fuck do you think you are or could be?

i won't tell you yo' slip's showin' or there's lipstick on yo'
teeth or even that yo' woman is sleepin' with me
no
i won't tell you you 'bout to lose yo' job or yo' boy is sellin'
crack at school
no
i'll just hum

SIDE B

black women's eyes
molten chocolate eyes unite with mine

submerging
we nod smile

that deep secret smile we know something you don't
we know how we came to be in this moment
our contact speaks worlds centuries of understanding cuts
through class and the darkness or lightness of skin
i know you know no matter what facade i've chosen to
help me survive this day
and the days to come that we are exactly the same
when we stop to talk our voices slide into a familiar silky
rollercoaster cadence. "girrrl puhleeze no you didn't!"
we surface
too brief, not enough
black women's eyes

The Tree-Line

SHERLEY ANNE WILLIAMS

from Meanwhile in Another Part of the City

When I first came to Mission University as a graduate student in the sixties, I hung out with some of the other single students, one of whom had been in residence during a recent renaissance of the English Department. If I mentioned the names, you'd know them, a Pulitzer Prize–winning novelist, a Tony Award–winning playwright had recently been on the faculty in English. Neither had won those awards then and though the stories were amusing—"Consider the Lilies," another young prof had replied haughtily in a honeyed southern drawl when asked if she'd made the dress she wore, "neither do they toil and neither do they spin; Solomon in *all* his glory was not arrayed as I am." Then, brayed and drawn out, "Chiiil'," a dramatic pause, "my eye is on the cosmos!" I'm sure they told some stories about old characters, but it was the stories of the "young profs" that got my attention. All had been fired, their contracts "not renewed" on various and bogus charges, mostly, to hear the graduate students tell it, because the brightest young faculty always wanted to bring the College of Liberal Arts into the twentieth century. Oh, some departments were all right but English wasn't one of them. Really, this was not what I'd come to the District to hear. People were saying things about the white man that could not be taken back; negroes were messing with history. The English graduate students spent their time talking about how good Mission wasn't or reminding each other where Toomer had walked and tracking down Georgia Douglas Johnson's address.

I started going to events advertised on flyers and hand-lettered signs: rallies, lectures, exhibits. I found the cultural nationalists at the New School like that; through them I met a nationalist couple from Indiana who leased a row house on Third Street near the campus. Turned out, the husband's brother knew the brother I'd dated in high school. The Student Nonviolent Coordinating Committee radicals found me a rally. They were plotting a coup against the integrationists in Atlanta—you know, to get enough people in key positions to change the direction of the organization. Weekends we'd drive to Philly, sometimes New York. I slept while the men planned direct actions and propaganda campaigns. The only one I remember is Black Women Enraged—over black men fighting in Vietnam for what they didn't have at home; I was to coordinate the women in the District. In those days my politics were pretty much defined by the men I slept with and, though I didn't know it then, this made my name known in some pretty radical places. I hadn't had many lovers, and those two were poles apart politically. But I was marked in certain circles because of them. Instead of coming to the big city, as I thought I was doing, I had, in many ways, moved from one small town to another—but, like, I've been told me, that's the nature of the black middle class.

The nationalists invited me to move in with them shortly after Christmas. By then the couple had expanded to include two co-wives. They, along with their new baby, had the first two floors of the row house. A sister named Nell rented the top floor, though I seldom saw her that winter; I took the basement room next to the furnace. The heat that was supposed to radiate from the hot water pipes that crisscrossed the basement ceiling never materialized and whenever I plugged in the hot plate they had given me to cook on, it blew all the fuses on the first floor. I didn't exactly *complain* about these conditions; I sort of muttered about the heat because I wasn't quite sure who to confront. The "harem" seemed to have turned into a group marriage, at least there was another brother there some mornings when I went up to make coffee in the kitchen and another of the co-wives looked like she was going to make another "contribution to the black Nation." That wasn't my business of course, but I sometimes had the feeling that this was how they thought everyone should be black. Embarrassment kept me quiet, and after a while all I ever seemed to say to them was "How you doing?" managing to walk on by before anyone answered.

Actually I spent as little time there as possible. I had become interested in the Harlem Renaissance, or at least the music. What time I didn't spend at the Library of Congress, in the Archive of Folk Song, I spent camped out on someone's couch, as long as their place was warm. I sometimes dressed in the basement but when I slept there, I always did so ready-rolled.

The separate entry under the broad front steps, in the daylight, that had been a selling point for the room was damp, cobwebby, and dark at night; the light fixture was shot. The sister told me to see the brother; the brother said he'd get to it as soon as he finished a paper, took a test. I used the front door; but after a while, the first floor people began some muttering of their own about my using their entrance and stomping through the halls late at night. I wasn't stomping, of course, but it seemed like you could hear every step anybody took on the hardwood floors all through the house. I guess it really made a difference at ten or eleven o'clock at night when their baby was sleep. Certainly everyone could hear him crying all through the house at all hours, but, as one of the wives told me when I mentioned this, I "*knew*" they had a baby when *I* moved in. Anyway, I finally got up the nerve to use my entry one night; when I turned the key in the door, the lock fell out in my hand and the door came unhinged when I pulled on the knob. I had propped my steamer trunk against the door, slept ready-rolled, determined I wouldn't spend another night like that.

When she came down the back stairway the next morning, Nell found me in the kitchen, huddled over my third cup of coffee, wrapped in all my coats, muttering over who to make my complaint to. She had a kind of brown baby beauty, skin the color of toast, unruly black hair; men were always trying to care for her, though it was me they fed. On dates, I would pick dutifully at the steak or lobster, then ask to have it wrapped up; Nell was especially partial to vegetables and fish, but I thought we needed more meat protein. Quite naturally, when she asked me, I told her what I was muttering about and, of course, she had her own list—chief among which was that crying baby. She invited me up to her room for herb tea and music.

Nell was so deep into blues I couldn't believe she was from California: wailing mouth organs and throbbing basses. It was the kind of gut bucket, back-in-the-alley blues the aunt who raised me had despised—I think because it made her friend Miss Ima Jean grind her hips in lewd circles after a few glasses of the sherry which all my aunt's frowning didn't discourage her from drinking. I admit the music was pretty meaningless to me, but by then I thought anything my aunt hated must be pretty hip. By afternoon Nell and I were fast friends.

Nell had worked for a couple of years out of high school to save tuition and was then what she called a mature undergraduate in "Vis Art." Art wasn't just painting and sculpture; it was process and performance. A good artist didn't just use media, she created it. Nell really talked like that, which was part of what drew me to her.

See, I worked at I.U. one summer—a whole nother story—but the brothers my boyfriend there hung with were grad students, older, sometimes just out of the service. They argued about Baudelaire and Padmore, Kant and Coltrane, Garvey, Malcolm, drank Beaujolais and Heineken, and went careening through late night streets howling defiance at shuttered storefronts in white neighborhoods. This was during that brief lull some places had in the sixties when the enforcers of white power and black men could still sometimes deal with each other like everyone involved was human. So, as long as the brothers stayed near the campus, they were treated like college students, just told to keep it quiet, if the police stopped them at all. I'd read enough to recognize the names the brothers dropped, to know their conversation was heavy, to want company like this for myself.

I was mostly homeboy's girl and never aspired to be much more. I thought nationalism, at least that heavy, fist-waving, political kind, was a stage we were all going through and, as a topic of conversation, that it was far more interesting than bid whist or that other pass-the-time shit the negroes at my undergrad school were into. I couldn't have said what I wanted, but I knew I wasn't going to find it being one of the few colored students at my local state college.

And Mission did satisfy my craving for *talk;* I told you, I knew some sharp sisters in the District: Chocolate to the bone Paulette, who worked in the Summer School Office with me, was in first-year law. Her friend, Gina, was a caramel-colored pocket venus who talked stuff and took none—and so slickly you didn't know you'd been handed your hat until you felt it in your hand—was first year in architecture. Charlane was nut brown, big boned, and so wholesome you smiled when you saw her, a sister who knew early childhood education—what black children needed in preschool in order to get a decent start in life. I met her through Nell.

Nell was into museum pieces then and took me to art shows with huge ugly paintings I would be afraid to hang in my house. She involved me in discussions of scale and value and "public" art. And she fucked just because she liked it—that was her word; I was still calling sex "it." I was tickled she was so bodacious, and deceptively so. She had a fey look about her and seemed too out there to be so bold. And, wouldn't you know, we had a lover in common? One of those exiled easterners, who, it turns out, really was from Harlem. They'd "fucked around" one summer when she was up there visiting relatives. Nell rated our mutual lover a lot lower than I did, but then she'd had more experience with men. She'd also been arrested for sitting in on the steps of the White House a couple of years before we met. The picture of her slung between two policemen had been front-page news across the country, and the specter of jail hung over her the whole of that spring and summer. And neither her painting, nor the music we both loved, nor the men she insisted on laying, could keep that terror fully at bay.

The sisters were my friends, not a "posse"; we met on the fly and compared notes, too busy for "hen parties" and "sisterfests." But none of us pretended we had more than a clue to how you hold the future; all of us out there scuffling, trying to be what the future said we could be: beautiful, successful, secure. We would be loved and valued as the brothers said our mothers had not been. But nothing had been promised to us and we didn't even have that to lose.

The nationalists kicked Nell and me out of the house in the spring. I think she'd threatened to throw one of the wives down the stairs— probably about that crying baby, which by then Nell swore must be abused. I refused to pay my rent: the door, the lock, the lack of heat. This was all about some money, but I think, really, didn't any of us want to be nationalists anymore, at least not all up in that one little house. Nell and I were one step ahead of being put out in the streets when I spotted the For Rent sign in the second-floor bow window of an apartment on a quiet street, just below the tree line, not far from the park. Nell spotted the name of Mr. L, a sculptor whose name we both remembered from the Renaissance. The rent was more than we could afford, but Nell exaggerated her savings, my stipend, and the pittance I earned typing copy for the Summer School Office and talked us into a six-month lease. This was the District—Mission—in the sixties. We knew we stepped, if not into history, then at least into fiction, and Nell and I were determined to live our dreams. We both would have done more than a little lightweight lying to be near a living black artist.

I thought I'd missed the spring in the District, it had rained so much. But the blossoms the rain had washed away were only the beginning of the season in the city. The weather seemed to hover in that just-right warmth you sometimes get at the tail end of spring. Some nights Nell and I sat out on the fire escape outside our bedroom window and watched the traffic, big cars heading toward the safety beyond the tree line, the occasional pedestrian. If you looked in just the right direction, you could see the hooded spire of the Washington Monument, its single red eye glaring down on the inner city that was then both shabby and black.

Mr. L, the sculptor, had the big, top-floor studio with a ceiling that was mostly skylight. A sister lived beneath him on the third floor. For a long time, she was just an elegant figure, shadowy, seen from a distance—who drove a bad car. Later, I found out she was working on her Ph.D. at A.U. there in the District. A Latvian refugee named Billie lived on the first floor. Nell and I speculated that she'd been involved with the CIA, though nothing she said had a thing to do with politics or espionage. We created wild adventures for her as we sat on the fire escape talking late at night, and stopped speaking of her completely after Nell saw the numbers tattooed on her wrist. Nell put me in the way of knowing them all; she was like that, refusing to be stranger to the people she lived among.

Celeste, the elegant sister, had once taught at Mission, was then on the faculty of a small private college in Maryland while she finished her dissertation on some obscure metaphysical poet. She could quote him at will, ending with "that line, chiiil', he *worked* that line!" I thought I'd die of delight the first time I heard her say "child" and realized she had to be the legendary figure of "Consider the Lilies." It always tickled me to hear her speak of some dead Englishman in that raucous tone of voice. Oh, I wasn't tight with her; she was our senior and moved in circles far removed from ours, but, every now and then, she invited us up for coffee. She made that rich, creole coffee her mamma sent from down home—strong, sweet, so brown it was black, the roasted whole bean that Celeste ground fresh herself. And she was almost that color, a rich black-brown that hinted gold when you expect red or even blue—and had a profile the government should have coined. Tall and slim with what they called when I was coming up ass for days. But it wasn't just that Celeste was always togged; Mission was known for its dressers, its raconteurs and characters, and Celeste had achieved legendary status among them.

I saw in Celeste what Nell saw in Mr. L: myself, down the road. You know; if I worked hard and did—. What? I wasn't sure. I had read my future in the present of Mission's female victorianist, a big, paper-bag colored woman, who worshiped at the shrines of dead white men, wore tweeds and oxfords, and hadn't married until her midforties. So I guess I admired Celeste for all the things we weren't supposed to back then: a mustard-colored Jag sedan, not quite old enough to be classic, elegant clothes that didn't come off any rack, a coolly minimalist apartment, almost Zen in its sparseness, except for the small collection of black art covering the walls and a wooden tub full of old *New Yorkers* in the bathroom. Once, she talked me through the bronze miniatures and assemblages, and the postcard-size oils by Mr. L that she owned, pointing to the gaping knees of the stick figures, a blue the color of bronze patina daubed between them, and the snakelike lines I hadn't even recognized as genitalia. In his most recent work, the figures were drawn in no recognizably human posture; the space between their thighs was filled only by that streaky green-blue. When she finished, I felt like I'd invaded his privacy, she suggested his secret war with his sexuality so vividly. But I'd have given a lot to read a surface that deeply.

I knew by then English wasn't for me, but I liked following a trail of ideas, piecing together stories from bits and hints, the way one thing can suggest ten or twenty others. I could have stayed in Founders Library for days at a time, just riffling through pages and papers, sampling sentences, paragraphs. Our people had left us a rich record; we didn't have to rely on the white man's mouth to verify ourselves, not if we took the time to reconstruct our own records and force a re-reading of others. It seemed to me a worthwhile endeavor to help recover those records, for the revolution, for the greater good; because I liked the cool dark depths of Founders and the worlds I discovered there. I wanted to "be" a historian; I didn't too much know how one "did" History, but I knew I wasn't going to "do" History by organizing enraged black women.

I had another radical boyfriend—not that I was so radical; I wasn't. Hair was very political then; I'd cut the perm out of mine the night I got my B.A.—and been told by my aunt not to darken her door till I looked decent about the head again. Took years for my hair to grow back. I didn't know it then, but men were my politics. My short crop seemed like a political statement to the radical nationalists or at least it had enough potential for them to take me up. I let them, though no one I knew thought much of the radical nationalists. The arts people Nell hung with thought the radicals were fascist—though they'd never say this where it would be heard.

The government's "poverty money" was starting to trickle down and the nationalists at least paid lip service to the need for black art and black artists. The integrationists still didn't want to hear anything about "black." My friend was to the extreme right of the NUART crowd—"Art that doesn't make the Black Man mad ain't worth shit to the revolution." Nell wouldn't even mention his name after he said that. He traveled a lot—organizing, rabble-rousing—so it wasn't all that awkward. I don't think Celeste ever met him. I know I never mentioned her to him more than two or three times. She was too sharp, too down for him to write off as merely bourgeois. She scoffed at Martin, the "Moses," scoffed at the whole notion of a "Mes-si-ah"; just the way she said it reduced even the idea to the ridiculous. Any fool could see Joseph and his brothers had to be the new negro text. I thought her analysis was pretty hip, but when I told my boyfriend, he dismissed it. Chick, meaning Celeste, was obviously steeped in the slave master's religion; and wasn't she the one who drove that showy Jag and permed her hair?

Celeste had a Jackie Kennedy cut and looked good in it, too, but Nell and I had tried to talk her down about this. The sister could have rivaled Nefertiti if she'd let go that "straight to the bone" look. No kidding. We were baffled that she couldn't see this. "Nefertiti's been dead for three thousand years," she reminded us and didn't have to add that Jackie was still kicking. As far as Celeste was concerned, that closed the subject.

I knew a lot of the stuff Brother Man talked was silly—there'd be no "world revolution" by 1970 when "the BlackMan" would take over the earth, not even in the white man's dying cities. But the nationalists were also dreamers, weird visionaries who, it seemed to me then, just might make some of their shit work, which kind of awed me. I mean, what would it be like if black people ruled the earth, maybe not in 1970, but what about 2010 or 2020? Surely, no worse than what white men had put us through and maybe, given what we knew, a good deal better. Except when it came to that killing shit—and that got to be a very big "except"—what the nationalists said made a kind of crazy sense to me. It put me on a tantalizing edge to contemplate their success, gave me a giddiness that was part fear, part joy. I couldn't name this then; I handled most of my differences with others by not speaking of them.

The brother had been on me about organizing some women. This day we were up at the New School; the nationalist storefront on Georgia Avenue. I got so tickled thinking about Paulette and Nell out there marching—they would be enraged all right—that I slipped and told him I was a scholar not an organizer, that I wanted to teach at Mission or some other major black college. He walked over to the three-shelf library and pulled down a book called *The Black Historians,* published in the late fifties. He opened it up to the table of contents, held the book so I could see it, and ran his finger down the page, all the while looking at me. He turned the page and ran his finger down that leaf. He stopped halfway down the next page. There was only one woman in the entire book; she was listed under "Lay People." He turned to the entry, which filled less than a third of the page. Laura Eliza Wilkes. His finger underlined "teacher in the public schools of the District," or words to that effect. Neither of us had said a word through all of this. When I finally looked at him, he snapped the book closed. "Better go on and get you that teaching credential, Earth Woman. Our young people need strong sistas in the classroom." I didn't say anything. After a while, I got my books and left.

It was the middle of the day, but I walked from Georgia Avenue damn near to Connecticut and arrived at the apartment, sweaty and tired as well as mad. Celeste was just coming in, impeccable, incredibly cool, not even a shine in all that heat; she looked at me, and looked at me again, then invited me up for coffee.

Celeste kicked off her shoes at the door and put on some music that made you think of smoke and dark places, Sonny Rollins maybe or Dexter Gordon, anyway, somebody playing a horn. I had a seat on one of the cushions surrounding the round cocktail table in the middle of her parlor while she put on the coffee. The table, the stereo, an antique rug were the only furnishings; the shades were pulled against the afternoon's heat. Celeste had on a colorful caftan when she returned, carrying the coffee service on a tray along with a small bottle of Jack Daniel's Black. She did some fancy things with sugar, the liquor, and whipped cream and served this with the coffee in real china cups, all the while keeping up a running stream of tales about Charleston and the negro middle class. She seemed to have pulled all the light in the room into her face and dress; I couldn't take my eyes off her. Guess that was as much the fault of that lethal coffee as anything she said. All homeboy's mess seemed just that, reactionary claptrap I didn't need to concern myself about.

But, much as I admired Celeste, I knew I didn't want to be part of her scene; color still seemed too much a part of it. I mean Celeste had been the first dark-skin homecoming queen at Tubman Institute, *the* bastion of blue-veined black women. Celeste turned her head when she said this as though it were something to be ashamed of. I never quite caught whether she was embarrassed for herself or for the people. I didn't ask, of course; talking about color was even touchier than talking about hair and I wasn't about to get into that, not as ripped as I was. But I thought Celeste had to know she was what brothers in *Ebony* and on the block said they wanted, and couldn't find, a beautiful, intellectual sister, who could get down, without getting dirty, who knew how to use the right fork, when to play Mozart *and* Monk. Brothers were going to build a world around us where dark was beautiful and she, black as espresso beans, hair nappy as steel wool under that perm, would be royalty, and even someone brown as me might be pretty.

I thought we had changed our tune forever. Except I kept flashing back on Ms. Wilkes, the final line in her entry: She complained bitterly to Woodson because he wouldn't review her work in the *Journal of Negro History*. I wouldn't let myself really *read* that entry that afternoon with Celeste; but Ms. Wilkes's complaint stuck in my mind. By this time, Celeste and I were into what she called a very soft something or other, almost like a German October wine, but drier. It looked like sunshine in a glass. We were both smashed. Why had the English Department dogged her? I asked Celeste. Surely not for being black? But I kept that last question to myself. She had been dogged, as it turned out, not for color, not for skin, but for the politics, baby.

English at Mission was like English at every other university in the country then, dedicated to celebration of dead white men. And Celeste didn't mind that; her dissertation was on a dead white man. But she also wanted to celebrate black men and women. Mission didn't have one course on black writers at the time she taught there; far as Mission's senior English faculty was concerned there was no one to teach. Young people didn't question senior profs at Mission, especially if, like Celeste, you had gone to a black college. Now, Celeste had also done M.A. work in Italy, even published a little note on a previously unremarked exchange of letters between Amy Lowell and Jean Toomer she'd found in Founders Library. Students fought to get into her class. The English Department didn't renew her contract after the second year and didn't give any reason. Not that Celeste said anything like this straight up. She looked you in the eye, smiling as she told little vignettes so you almost had to put her answer together like you do the meaning of a poem: a department willfully veiling itself in awful imitations of white people and self-satisfied mediocrity, too real to be funny. This was what the nationalists had been telling me all along; the negroes at Mission were not ready.

Celeste wobbled a little when she got up to change the record—Dinah Washington. Not the later, crossover stuff but something grittier. "Long John," I think. Like I said, we were both smashed. But Celeste didn't miss a beat when she said her husband had left her for some white woman, and I didn't even blink. I mean, I thought it was—what? Sad and regrettable. But Celeste was always with some suave brother. And sometimes you had to look very close to see the brother on them, and even then couldn't be sure. I thought it uncouth to ask, though, again, Nell and I sat on the fire escape and speculated, scandalized and intrigued, about the white men who must be dying to get into Celeste's drawers. Fine as she was I knew she wouldn't be alone forever or even for long.

"Go on and get your degree," Celeste told me that day and raised her glass in salute; "you've put in too much time to quit over some little boy." I hadn't said a word about the conversation with my radical friend, but after this, I figured I wouldn't try anymore to hold on to things I just liked. Since grief was inevitable, I would only be shot through the grease for things I craved or loved.

Daughters

PAULE MARSHALL

The evening she met him in Viney's apartment on Ninety-third Street, he had his large black-leather portfolio spread open on the coffee table in the living room and he was showing her and Viney sketches for a book jacket he hoped to do for Macmillan. Everything had been cleared off the table and it had been moved a little away from the couch to make room for the portfolio. In fact, she had the impression that everything in the room—all the furniture, books, the prints and paintings on the walls—had been shifted around, rearranged to accommodate not only the oversize leather case but Willis Jenkins as well—his long legs, his long narrow feet, his shoes that came she could tell from one of those men's stores where there are no prices in the window, his close-cropped beard, his voice like Ron Carter's singing double bass, and the elephant-hair bracelet in gold around his wrist. Gold against his blackness. A man all black and gold.

She was happy for Viney, but envious. Envy for a moment soured on her tongue the wine she was drinking with them. Because those were the years—years that felt like an entire lifetime—when there wasn't even a Lowell. An inventory of her life then would have turned up only NCRC—the job morning, noon and the better part of her evenings—the pool at the Parkview Health Club on West End Avenue twice a week, a night out with Viney on the weekends—a club, a concert or a party. Viney and her parties! And the occasional date that was seldom repeated. And there were the faithful visits to Triunion. She spent the holidays and every one of her vacations there, up-country, in the old Mackenzie house up-country. Sometimes, on the spur of the moment, she even took the plane and flew down for a long weekend. And she never missed an election.

"How do you expect to meet anybody running down to that island every minute? You tell me there're no men there to speak of. You need to stay on the scene more." Viney, acting the part of her RA in the dorm again, would lecture her. "All right, so it's rough out here. But you need to do like me. I refuse to think about all the things ag'in' us. The black men–black women ratio thing to begin with, more of us than them. That's a downer right there. And these fancy-sounding job titles a few of us have—assistant vice president this, associate director that—that scare the brothers away, and the little white girls out here eyeing what we eyeing, and the brothers who only have eyes for them. And not to mention, not to mention *pu'leeze* those among the brothers who have eyes only for each other, or for themselves—you know, the me-me-mes; or the ones who believe, really and truly believe, that things go better with coke, and love that more than they can ever love you. And you know I know of what I speak. I've been there and oh, that can be some heavy competition. But I refuse to let my mind dwell on any of it. And that's what you need to do. Don't think about all that mess. Don't let it get to you. Just hang in there. You got to hang in there! You get discouraged too easily."

For years Viney zealously followed her own advice. There wasn't an opening at the Studio Museum uptown or the Cinque Gallery downtown she didn't attend. She was at every exhibit, screening, symposium and panel discussion, every book signing and poetry reading held at the Schomburg Center for Research in Black Culture on Lenox Avenue. At every concert of the Uptown Chamber Society and nearly every jazz concert, dance recital (Alvin Ailey, the Dance Theatre of Harlem) and cultural festival. Viney on the scene at every major Black History Month event in February and at the round of African receptions at the U.N. in the fall. "Looking for an ambassador. Won't settle for anything less than an ambassador." And there were the parties, those she gave, those she was always being invited to, and the ones she ferreted out and appeared at uninvited.

"Party!"—said like a battle cry over the phone when she called to get Ursa to come along. "I feel tonight's our lucky night. Put on something outrageous and come."

"I don't have anything outrageous."

"Well, put on one of those mumu dresses of yours and come anyway. You need to get out."

"I was out until six in the morning with you last Saturday, remember? Nina, crazy Nina, at the Village Gate, remember? The woman kept us waiting two hours before she even showed up and then another hour before she decided to sing. Then you just *had* to go to that after-hours club after that, and when that closed you just *had* to have breakfast at the Empire. It was dawn's early light before I saw my bed. No, thanks. Not tonight. I can't keep up with you and the marathon, Viney."

"Please, Ursa. I really feel lucky tonight. Please."

A long silence during which she saw her friend's face over the phone, the strain and pleading there. . .

"All right."

For a time she put her faith in something called Black Professional Selective Introductions—"It's all done by computer, Ursa. You should try it."/"No, thanks."/—and the Black Singles Vacation Club. Later on, in the desperate years just before Willis Jenkins, there had been the Friday and Saturday night take-home men from the bar for the Beautiful People on Columbus Avenue not far from her apartment. "It clears the tubes, Ursa. You think and feel better the next day. You need to get out here and get you some." A Viney who didn't even sound like herself anymore. And for a long frightening year, when she was involved with an account executive at Merrill Lynch, she became a fixture along with him at the other, more notorious bar for the BPs that was even closer to where she lived on West Ninety-third, the one nicknamed "The Pharmacy." Every and any remedy could be purchased there.

Ursa rarely saw her then.

Viney. She partied hearty, always looking with her long, lean, angular frame and the flawless clothes she wore as if she were about to step onto the runway at the annual Ebony Fair Fashion Show, a hand at her hip, her body at a model's slant, and the red hibiscus mouth in bloom under the icon of a nose.

"You got to hang in there!" She had taken her own counsel, had hung in there, had refused to think of all the things ag'in' her, and had finally met Willis Jenkins, who not only drew beautiful illustrations and talked of book jackets, art editors and the publishing business, but whose daddy longlegs outstripped her own.

In no time the second bedroom in her apartment was converted into a studio, the bed and other furniture there moved out to make room for Willis Jenkins's huge drawing table and stool, his clothes and the special cabinets he used for his art supplies.

"You're shining like new money," Ursa said to her friend.

"Can't help but."

"I'm jealous." Hugging her.

Five years later Viney was to move the bed and other furniture back into the room. Five years. It took her that long before she could bring herself to tell Willis Jenkins to take his drawing table and stool, his cabinets, his clothes and shoes—especially the shoes: "You can have them! Every last pair of them! Just take them and go!"—and everything else belonging to him out of her apartment, and hand over her keys.

"And come to find out, Ursa, he didn't even have that far to go. Had his next sponsor already lined up down on the second floor. And look who it is. The final kick in the teeth. . . " Then, turning her anger and disgust against herself: "Fool! How blind can you be."

She was in the pool on the top floor of the Parkview while Viney, wearing a bathing suit with an overskirt because of the weight she had put on, was sitting, meditating, on a bench against the wall. The wall of white tiles reached three stories high to the banked lights on the ceiling. Seven o'clock on a Friday evening in late January, and almost a year since Viney had demanded back her keys and Willis Jenkins had moved downstairs. On the streets below the Parkview the blackened remains of a snowstorm from earlier in the month lay piled along the curbs, and the sidewalks were slick underfoot where the snow hadn't been removed and had turned to ice. They had had to hold on to each other to keep from falling on the way over.

Since the breakup Viney had taken to accompanying her nearly everywhere. Sometimes, no matter how late Ursa got in from work she found her waiting. Viney would have let herself in the apartment with her set of keys and would be sitting, waiting, in the dining area off the kitchen, snacking on whatever was to be found there. Or the phone would ring sometimes as soon as she stepped in the door: "Whatcha doing? I'm coming over." Or: "I don't feel like cooking. Let's go out to eat." On Saturdays she neglected her own chores to trail along with Ursa to the shoe repair, the dry cleaners, the bakery; and although she couldn't swim aside from a dog paddle and had never approved of swimming pools—"You can't meet anybody there. The brothers don't swim"—she had even taken to accompanying her to the Parkview.

Eyes closed, legs drawn up in a partial lotus, she sat on the bench set back from the water. Her long hands, the caramel of a Sugar Daddy lollipop, lay on her knees with the thumb and forefinger joined. Wholeness and unity. Inner peace and calm . . . "I'm not going back out there, Ursa," she announced one evening, speaking grimly out of one of the long numbed silences that would come over her from time to time. "I-am-not-going-out-there-again. You hear me?"/"I hear you."/To give her the strength to hold to her vow, she sought out a TM group uptown and began attending meetings and talking about being initiated. "I won't do it, though, unless you do too."/"Oh, come on, Viney, you know I don't go in for all that spirituality stuff."/"Please. Just do it for me."

So that one Saturday afternoon Ursa found herself along with her friend in a stuffy, overfurnished little apartment in the Riverton on 135th Street, not far from the Schomburg. A middle-aged brown-skinned woman whose body, clothes and dyed wavy black hair, "good" hair, gave off the smell of sandalwood, ushered them in and took the gift-offerings they had been instructed to bring: a few pieces of fruit, a small bouquet of flowers and a brand-new white handkerchief. The main part of the initiation took place privately in the adjoining bedroom. Viney went first, and when she was done, Ursa followed the woman into the bedroom, where a large picture of the Maharishi—flowing white beard, a kindly face the same nut brown as the woman's—hung on the wall across from the bed. There, engulfing her in the smell of sandalwood, the woman repeatedly whispered "Ke'ram" in her ear. She was to say it silently with her eyes closed and her spine held straight for fifteen minutes at the beginning and end of each day, and whenever she felt the need. . .

The pool was virtually empty that Friday evening. There was Viney seated like a Buddha against the soaring white wall and herself in the water along with one other swimmer, a white woman about her age whom she saw nearly every time she came to the Parkview. A solitary swimmer like herself. For exactly a half hour each time, the woman did a series of smooth blind laps that scarcely brought her goggled face out of the water. Even when she climbed out at the end of the half hour and disappeared into the locker room she remained hidden behind the goggles and her expressionless face. She never spoke, smiled, or looked at anyone there. What would an inventory of her life turn up, Ursa often wondered, watching her retreating back.

The woman left. She had the huge pool all to herself. Or so she thought, until glancing over as she reached the wall at the deep end and started to make her turn, she saw that Viney had joined her.

Occasionally, when there were only a few people around, Viney would come in the water, paddle briefly back and forth across the shallow end, perhaps do a few scissor kicks holding on to the gutter, then climb out and return to her bench. Tonight, she had entered the pool up near the diving board, and instead of her usual dog paddle she was simply dangling in the water, her back against the gutter, her arms outstretched along the ledge, holding on to it, and her head thrown all the way back.

Ursa was at her side in seconds.

"Viney. . . ?"

The head remained flung back, almost touching the gutter; the eyes were wide open, and there was this river on her face.

"Oh, Viney."

She held her. She reached around, and with her undersize arms gathered in as much of her as she could, this stranger with the thickened waist and fleshy arms and shoulders, and breasts that were twice their normal size. Not even the familiar fragrance of her cologne and the Lustrasilk she used on her hair made her feel and look any less strange. Ursa spoke to her, saying in one breath: "Don't, Viney, please. Don't upset yourself. I thought you had put him behind you. . . " And in the next breath: "Go ahead. Get it out of you. It's about time. You'll feel better. . . " Not knowing what she was saying or what to say. Not that it mattered, because there was no sign that Viney was either listening or could hear her. Was she even aware of the arms around her? It didn't seem so. She simply hung there like a human plumb line that had been dropped over the side of the pool to measure the depth of the water, staring up at the lights in the high ceiling, while the silent river made its way along the ridge of her cheekbones down to her ears and then through the intricate channel of her ears before emptying into the gutter behind.

Ursa held her—as much of her as she could manage—and she felt her own river, which couldn't be blamed on a Willis Jenkins, or on any one person or thing yet, at times, was about everything, all the shit; a river that was simply there, ever present, always threatening to catch her unawares and overrun the levees she had built against it: NCRC, the pool here, the faithful visits to Triunion—she felt it rising in her as well. She tried gently rocking Viney, she kept repeating the words that went unheard, tried comforting her friend, and it was like trying to rock and comfort herself.

Around them the water in the pool was as warm and placid as the sea at her favorite beach in Triunion, the one at Government Lands up-country. "You have to come with me the next time I go home, all right?" She spoke softly. "As often as I've gone with you to Petersburg, you've yet to visit my little island in the sun. That's not fair. You have to come with me the next time I go down. I'll take you to the best beach in all the world. Don't worry, you won't have to go in the water. You can just sit under a palm tree and look glamorous. And have the sagaboys falling all over you. . . "

Silence. The water lapping against the side of the pool and flowing in the gutter was the only sound. The only other movements, aside from the water in the gutter, were the light pumping of her legs below the surface, the rocking motion she kept up, and the river winding through the watercourse of Viney's ear just inches from her.

Nine-forty by the clock on the wall behind the diving platform.

"It's time to get out of the water, Viney. The pool'll be closing soon. Come on."

Still no sign that she was even capable of hearing.

"Let's go eat. I only had a little something when I came in from work and I'm starving. Come on, dinner will be on me. I'll treat you to Chinese on Broadway since it's Friday. . . "

She heard it then: a deep, racking sound that could have come only from the source of the river. Viney's head remained thrown back, her arms rigid along the gutter, her flooded gaze on the banked lights overhead, but her body had begun to heave with a sound like the tearful raging of a mute. "Oh, Viney, don't—" holding her tighter, cradling her all the more, while the racking sound and the heaving went on and on, growing stronger, until soon she could feel it beginning to drain the body dangling like a plumb line over the edge of the pool. She found she had to pump harder to keep herself afloat, and suddenly there was the same rapid kick going on around her heart. "Please, Viney, let's get out. It's time we got out."

The water that had been no higher than the swollen waistline when she first spotted her and came racing over now stood above the bra of the matronly bathing suit. And there was this drag, this pull to her body as if the more than twenty pounds she had piled on in the past year had suddenly settled around her ankles. And the weighted ankles in turn were causing her hands to lose their grip on the ledge. Her outstretched arms were slowly sliding, slipping down.

"Viney!" She was struggling now to keep afloat not only herself but this large slack body that felt as if it had suddenly grown weights around the ankles. The strength in her shoulders and in her arms and legs from all the swimming she had done over the years was suddenly nothing against the growing dead weight in her arms.

"Viney!" Her cry drowned out by the choked raging of the mute.

One limp, fleshy arm slipped from the gutter, broke the skin of the water and disappeared.

"Viney!"—screaming into her ear now at the terrifying thought that the custodian might come to turn off the lights and find both of them up to the game she used to play long ago in the pool at Mile Trees—diving to the bottom of the pool and sitting there to impress, tease and frighten the PM.

"Viney!" This time her scream reached all the way up the acres of white tile to the high ceiling and the bank of lights, and as it came sheering down in what sounded like a hail of shattered glass and splintered light the weighted, near lifeless thing that was bearing her down with it suddenly started as if struck by the raining glass, and the head on the thing, which was arched all the way back, slowly, inch by painful inch, righted itself.

The moment Viney brought her head up, into place again, the river altered its course, and after a millennium it stopped.

"I'm all right now." Said with her face turned away.

Ursa held on. There was still the slackness and the dead weight, and the heaving could still be felt.

"I said I'm all right. You can let go now."

She continued to hold on until Viney finally turned to face her, and then she abruptly dropped her arms. One look at those eyes and she let go. The last of the river had dried to form what looked like a high-gloss, scuff-proof polyurethane finish on a hardwood floor. One glance at it and her arms dropped of their own accord. Seconds later, as Viney turned and started her little primordial crawl over to the nearest ladder, she simply followed behind.

Finishing

AKUA LEZLI HOPE

She slung the rubberbands around the braid
using index and middle as if to snap

in the manner of fingerpopping
where fingers dance
and manipulate in forms
beyond our cousins—
there's no food tool in this
fingers in near scribe or chopstick poise
fingers wending fingers lacing fingers weaving
winding the rubberband
at each braid's edge
as in the crossing of legs
an entwinement of diamonds
the patternback of juncture
sign of interstice and union
funk and form in function
each black edge capped beige
a simple flourish to wrap
solid sap of a tree
to string the circle
and remake intent
to bend the band
and stretch the strap to art.

More Than a Mouthful

FOLISADE

To all the women who swallowed
the lie and see themselves
as less
with
pancakes topped by purple berries
raisins cherries plums and grapes
less than a handful
and barely a bump
to all the women
so gently endowed
you are as lovely
as any

Just Desserts

DEB PARKS-SATTERFIELD

I'm glad you came over 'cuz we got to talk! I was just about to make that chocolate cake I was tellin' you about last week. Anyway, 'member I told you 'bout Charlene? Well, she had that baby . . . and it was ugly. Charlene's baby was ugly. There was just no other way to put it. Nobody in the family pretended that the baby was cute or that it just needed to plump up, *that* would have been too unkind. Pretending is for strangers that don't know how to do anything else. Charlene would take the baby out for a walk and people would stop and stare. Sometimes they'd stammer, cough, then walk away. Other times their faces would commence to workin' tryin' to come up with somethin' to say about that ugly child. Charlene would let them wallow around in their embarrassment for a little bit before she'd say, "I know, I know." Just like that . . . I know, I know.

From the day Charlene's baby arrived we made it our business to get to the bottom of the mystery. It couldn't possibly be our side of the family, so it had to be Charlene's husband's side. He was nice lookin' but we didn't know much about his people. Our side of the family was hearty, good lookin', brown skinned people. We could trace our ancestry back to merchants and traders in the Caribbean. Not one ugly person in the bunch! We could not understand how two beautiful people could produce such an incredibly ugly child.

Mmmm . . . these eggs are a little cold but I think they'll be okay.

We women folk subjected Charlene to an onslaught of questions. Did you eat anything unusual? Were you upset or nervous over long periods of time? Did you wake up with any bad thoughts? Did your husband rub cocoa butter on your stomach like we told him to? I just flat out accused Charlene of goin' to the zoo in the seventh month. Now you all know to stay as far away from the zoo as possible when you're pregnant. We all knew that a trip to the zoo could mark the baby in the womb. You remember what happened to Nonni's child.

Nonni was seven months pregnant and was doin' just fine. She'd consulted me about all the usual things, you know, the sex of the child, how many letters needed in the baby's name to ensure success, and whether the baby would be right or left handed. Nonni told me every single dream that she had, then together we'd match all the symbols in her dream to numbers in the *Mystical Dream Book of Ancient Egypt*. Here's how it works: if you dreamed you was drivin' a car, you'd look up the meanin' of *car* and there'd be a number attached to the symbol. Whatever she dreamt we'd write the numbers on a slip of paper, place a bet with the numbers runner and anything we won we'd put in a little kitty so the baby would have a bankroll when it arrived. Also, we used the same process to come up with a name for the baby. Everything was fine till Nonni's stupid husband convinced her that I was some kind of witch. I wish I was some kind of witch 'cuz I would've zapped him into the jackass that he was! He told her that the herbs, teas and salves that I'd been givin' her were bad for the baby and that if she didn't stop comin' to see me he was gonna leave her! That man had the bodaciousness to call me up on the telephone sayin', "I better not see you nowhere near my house. If you come 'round here again I'll throw hot pee on you from out the window!"

"Oh really!," I said. "Well you best start warmin' it up 'cuz I'm comin' over!"

Then I slammed the phone down. I wasn't goin' over to his house. I had a million other things to do. I wasn't thinkin' about that man. But, not only did Nonni stop comin' to see me, I heard it through the grapevine that she took all the teas, herbs, everything and threw 'em out. Then on the seventh day of the seventh month Nonni's stupid husband told her to meet him at the zoo by the gorilla cage 'cuz he was gonna prove to her once and for all that a baby could not be marked. Nonni went to the zoo, took one look at that gorilla and fainted dead away. For the next two months of her pregnancy she was bedridden. When that baby came out, Nonni and her stupid husband left town in the dead of night and were never seen again. We all knew what had happened.

See, some people don't think fat meat is greasy, you know what I mean?

Oh, this is gonna be a good cake! You can lick the beaters when I'm done.

And speakin' of "some people," guess who showed up at my house the other night? Maurice! That's right, Maurice my ex-husband. I thought Loretta was gonna have a fit, 'cuz, you know, she and me been together for a long time. Loretta had never met Maurice, all she knew was the stories I'd told her about what a horror it was bein' married to that man. So, she was civil to him, then she excused herself to the other room. She didn't dare leave the house and leave me alone with that fool, even though all the fight went out of him fifteen years ago. He claimed he was just in the neighborhood and decided to drop by. Mind you I ain't seen this man in fifteen years and suddenly he's "just in the neighborhood." I knew there was somethin' wrong. He hemmed and hawed then finally admitted that he'd lost his truck drivin' license, again, and that the only job he could get was bustin' suds down there at Nancy's Cafe. I said, "I ain't got no money and you can't stay here, but I will give you some supper."

You can't know somebody half your life and just turn them out. Things must have been really rough for him to show up at my house. But you see, hard times will make a monkey eat red pepper. Last time I saw that man we had the fight of the century! He'd been on the road for three days haulin' stuffed animals for some toy distributor. He was poppin' them little white pills, drinkin' too much coffee and not sleepin' a lick. On the third night he called me from the road convinced that the stuffed animals were tryin' to get him! Can you believe that? A grown man afraid of some stuffed toys. Now I've done my share of drinkin' and smokin' too, if you catch my drift, I know if you high and you stare at somethin' long enough it may start to look a little funny but it ain't gonna get you. I told that fool to get his ass back in that truck, lay off the pills, finish the job and come on home! When he finally got home he looked like ten miles of bad road. See, after he got off the phone with me he popped a couple more of them pills and commenced to drivin' again. At some point during the night he turned around to look through the window and check his cargo and he swore there was a teddy bear mashed up against the window grinnin' at him. He was so unnerved he damn near jackknifed! Maurice skidded that truck over to the side of the road, went back there, opened the door, took out his pistol and shot teddy bears till he could not *see* teddy bears. So, what did he look like deliverin' a bunch of bullet-ridden teddy bears to Toys "R" Us? They fired his butt on the spot. That was fifteen years ago. Now, here he was. I gave him some supper. He looked like a old matted dog so I washed and braided his hair much to

Loretta's dismay. I gave him a little passel of food when he left and that was it.

Oh, but I was tellin' you about Charlene's baby. Mind you we loved that child, but we knew that ugly people have to work harder than as pretty people to get by in this world. Just as women have to work twice as hard and colored people three times that. All the aunts, uncles, cousins everybody decided that we would shower so much love and affection on that baby that there was no way it would feel different. Actually, when you come right down to it, we was just glad the baby was healthy. Oh, well, it'll be all right. Yeah, it'll be all right.

But I know why you came here, you want this recipe.

TRIPLE CHOCOLATE CAKE

4 real eggs, not fake eggs
1 cup of real sour cream, not sour lean
½ cup of water
½ cup of vegetable oil
1 box of chocolate cake mix (*can be generic*)
1 small box of chocolate instant pudding
*12 ounces of semisweet chocolate chips
A tube pan

Preheat oven to 350 degrees. Combine the first four ingredients and mix well. Add cake mix, instant pudding and beat till smooth. Stir in chocolate chips and mix just enough to combine. Pour batter into greased tube pan and bake for one hour. This is a moist rich cake. When the cake is cool place it on a pretty plate and dust with powdered sugar.

*For a variation try mint chocolate chips.

PART FIVE

Is It True What They Say About Colored Pussy?: Sex

The sexual history of Black women in this country is riddled with experiences of cruelty and pleasure, love and hate.

As we move away from a legacy of institutionalized sexual victimization and increase our knowledge of ourselves as sexual beings with our own flavor of erotic power, we lay the foundation for the Black women coming after us to have a much easier time growing comfortable with themselves as whole sexual beings, whether lesbian or straight.

Since Black and Hispanic women now account for too many of the United States AIDS cases, many of us find ourselves discussing masturbation, celibacy, vibrators and other sex toys, and safe sex as we experiment with different ways to express our sexuality in the nineties and beyond.

is it true what they say about colored pussy?

hattie gossett

hey
is it really true what they say about colored pussy?
come on now
dont be trying to act like you dont know what i am talking about
you have heard those stories about colored pussy so stop trying to pre-
    tend like you havent
you have heard how black and latina pussies are hot and uncontrollable
i know you know the one about asian pussies and how they go from
    side to side instead of up and down
and everybody knows about squaw pussies and how once a white-man
    got him some of that he wasnt never no more good

now at first i thought that the logical answer to these stories is that
    they are just ignorant racist myths
but then i thought: what about all the weird colored stories about col-
    ored pussy?
cuz you know colored pussies werent always treated with the highest
    regard we deserve in the various colored worlds prior to our dis-
    covery by the european talentscout/explorers

and we still aint
so now why is it that colored pussies have had to suffer so much
    oppression and bad press from so many divergent sources?
is it cuz we really are evil and nasty and queer looking and smelly and
    ugly like they say?

or
is it cuz we possess some secret strength which we take for granted but
    which is a terrible threat to the various forces that are trying to
    suppress us?

i mean just look at what black pussies have been subjected to starting
        with ancient feudal rape and polygamy and clitoridectomy and
        forced child marriages and continuing right on through colonial
        industrial neocolonial rape and forced sterilization and experimen-
        tal surgery
and when i put all that stuff about black pussies together with the sto-
        ries i hear from the other colored pussies about what they have
        had to go through i am even more convinced
we must have some secret powers!
this must be why so many people have spent so much time vilifying
        abusing hating and fearing colored pussy

and you know that usually the ones who be doing all this vilifying
        abusing hating and fearing of colored pussy are the main ones who
        just cant seem to leave colored pussy alone dont you
they make all kinds of laws and restrictions to apartheidize colored
        pussy and then as soon as the sun goes down guess who is seen
        sneaking out back to the cabins?
and guess who cant do without colored pussy in their kitchens and
        fields and factories and offices?
and then theres the people who use colored pussy as a badge of certifi-
        cation to insure entry into certain circles

finally
when i think about what would happen if all the colored pussies went
        on strike
(especially if the together white pussies staged a same day sympathy
        strike)
look out!
        the pimps say colored pussy is an untapped goldmine
        well they got it wrong
        colored pussies aint goldmines untapped
        colored pussies are yet unnamed energies whose power for
lighting
        up the world is beyond all known measure

Ambrosia

DORIS L. HARRIS

If you were a grape
I
would
pick
YOU
from the bunch
rinse you off in cool water
slowly peel the skin back
baring the luscious fruit
inside,
sucking the juice
savoring
each drop
pure ambrosia
I would lie back
momentarily quenched
so happy
so
happy
you
are
seedless

We Always Were

FOLISADE

I was missing you
remembering hips that used to call to me
lips that stopped my heart
swelled my womanness to overflowing

I was missing you
remembering nights and mornings
when we lay together
planning things we'd do that day
but neither of us moving
except
into
each other's
everything

souls communing
walking
through
our
inner gardens
tasting blossoms   fruit
blooming in our tropics
touching   forests   evergreen
rising from our heat
raining berries   petals   magic leaves
finding pollen
left
on luscious lips
of
sistahs loving sistahs

Piece of Time

JEWELLE GOMEZ

Ella kneeled down to reach behind the toilet. Her pink cotton skirt pulled tight around her brown thighs. Her skin already glistened with sweat from the morning sun and her labor. She moved quickly thru the hotel rooms sanitizing tropical mildew and banishing sand.

Each morning our eyes met in the mirror just as she wiped down the tiles and I raised my arms in a last wake-up stretch. I always imagined that her gaze flickered over my body; enjoying my broad, brown shoulders or catching a glance of my plum brown nipples as the African cloth I wrapped myself in dropped away to the floor. For a moment I imagined the pristine hardness of the bathroom tiles at my back and her damp skin pressed against mine.

"OK, it's finished here," Ella said as she folded the cleaning rag and hung it under the sink. She turned around and, as always, seemed surprised that I was still watching her. Her eyes were light brown and didn't quite hide their smile; her hair was dark and pulled back, tied in a ribbon. It hung lightly on her neck the way that straightened hair does. My own was in short tight braids that brushed my shoulders; a colored bead at the end of each. It was a trendy affectation I'd indulged in for my vacation. I smiled. She smiled back. On a trip filled with so much music, laughter and smiles, hers was the one that my eyes looked for each morning. She gathered the towels from the floor and in the same motion opened the hotel-room door.

"Goodbye."

"See ya," I said feeling about twelve years old instead of thirty. She shut the door softly behind her and I listened to the click of her silver bangle bracelets as she walked around the veranda toward the stairs. My room was the last one on the second level facing the beach. Her bangles brushed the painted wood railing as she went down, then thru the tiny courtyard and into the front office.

I dropped my cloth to the floor and stepped into my bathing suit. I planned to swim for hours and lie in the sun reading and sip margaritas until I could do nothing but sleep and maybe dream of Ella.

One day turned into another. Each was closer to my return to work and the city. I did not miss the city nor did I dread returning. But here, it was as if time did not move. I could prolong any pleasure until I had my fill. The luxury of it was something from a fantasy in my childhood. The island was a tiny neighborhood gone to sea. The music of the language, the fresh smells and deep colors all enveloped me. I clung to the bosom of this place. All else disappeared.

In the morning, too early for her to begin work in the rooms, Ella passed below in the courtyard carrying a bag of laundry. She deposited the bundle in a bin, then returned. I called down to her, my voice whispering in the cool private morning air. She looked up and I raised my cup of tea in invitation. As she turned in from the beach end of the courtyard I prepared another cup.

We stood together at the door, she more out than in. We talked about the fishing and the rainstorm of two days ago and how we'd spent Christmas.

Soon she said, "I better be getting to my rooms."

"I'm going to swim this morning," I said.

"Then I'll be coming in now, alright? I'll do the linen," she said, and began to strip the bed. I went into the bathroom and turned on the shower.

When I stepped out, the bed was fresh and the covers snapped firmly around the corners. The sand was swept from the floor tiles back outside and our teacups put away. I knelt to rinse the tub.

"No, I can do that. I'll do it, please."

She came toward me, a look of alarm on her face. I laughed. She reached for the cleaning rag in my hand as I bent over the suds, then she laughed too. As I kneeled on the edge of the tub, my cloth came unwrapped and fell in. We both tried to retrieve it from the draining. My feet slid on the wet tile and I sat down on the floor with a thud.

"Are you hurt?" she said, holding my cloth in one hand, reaching out to me with the other. She looked only into my eyes. Her hand was soft and firm on my shoulder as she knelt down. I watched the line of the muscles in her forearm, then traced the soft inside with my hand. She exhaled slowly. I felt her warm breath as she bent closer to me. I pulled her down and pressed my mouth to hers. My tongue pushed between her teeth as fiercely as my hand on her skin was gentle.

Her arms encircled my shoulders. We lay back on the tile, her body atop mine, then she removed her cotton T-shirt. Her brown breasts were nestled insistently against me. I raised my leg between hers. The moistness that matted the hair there dampened my leg. Her body moved in a brisk and demanding rhythm.

I wondered quickly if the door was locked. Then was sure it was. I heard Ella call my name for the first time. I stopped her with my lips. Her lips were searching, pushing toward their goal. Ella's mouth on mine was sweet and full with hungers of its own. Her right hand held the back of my neck and her left hand found its way between my thighs, brushing the hair and flesh softly at first, then playing over the outer edges. She found my clit and began moving back and forth. A gasp escaped my mouth and I opened my legs wider. Her middle finger slipped past the soft outer lips and entered me so gently at first I didn't feel it. Then she pushed inside and I felt the dams burst. I opened my mouth and tried to swallow my scream of pleasure. Ella's tongue filled me and sucked up my joy. We lay still for a moment, our breathing and the sea gulls the only sounds. Then she pulled herself up.

"Miss . . . ," she started.

I cut her off again, this time my fingers to her lips. "I think it's OK if you stop calling me miss!"

"Carolyn," she said softly, then covered my mouth with hers again. We kissed for moments that wrapped around us, making time have no meaning. Then she rose. "It gets late, you know," she said with a giggle. Then pulled away, her determination not yielding to my need. "I have my work, girl. Not tonight, I see my boyfriend on Wednesdays. I better go. I'll see you later."

And she was out the door. I lay still on the tile floor and listened to her bangles as she ran down the stairs.

Later on the beach my skin still tingled and the sun pushed my temperature higher. I stretched out on the deck chair with my eyes closed. I felt her mouth, her hands and the sun on me and came again.

Ella arrived each morning. There were only five left. She tapped lightly, then entered. I would look up from the small table where I'd prepared tea. She sat and we sipped slowly, then slipped into the bed. We made love, sometimes gently, other times with a roughness resembling the waves that crashed into the seawall below.

We talked of her boyfriend, who was married and saw her only once or twice a week. She worked at two jobs, saving money to buy land, maybe on this island or her home island. We were the same age, and although my life seemed to already contain the material things she was still striving for, it was I who felt rootless and undirected.

We talked of our families, hers so dependent on her help, mine so estranged from me; of growing up, the path that led us to the same but different place. She loved this island. I did too. She could stay. I could not.

On the third night of the five I said, "You could visit me, come to the city for a vacation or . . . "

"And what I'm goin' to do there?"

I was angry but not sure at whom: at her for refusing to drop everything and take a chance; at myself for not accepting the sea that existed between us, or just at the blindness of the circumstance.

I felt narrow and self-indulgent in my desire for her. An ugly Black American, everything I'd always despised. Yet I wanted her, somehow, somewhere it was right that we should be together.

On the last night after packing I sat up with a bottle of wine listening to the waves beneath my window and the tourist voices from the courtyard. Ella tapped at my door as I was thinking of going to bed. When I opened it she came inside quickly and thrust an envelope and a small gift-wrapped box into my hand.

"Can't stay, you know. He waiting down there. I'll be back in the morning." Then she ran out and down the stairs before I could respond.

Early in the morning she entered with her key. I was awake but lying still. She was out of her clothes and beside me in moments. Our lovemaking began abruptly but built slowly. We touched each part of our bodies, imprinting memories on our fingertips.

"I don't want to leave you," I whispered.

"You not leaving me. My heart go with you, just I must stay here." Then . . . "Maybe you'll write to me. Maybe you'll come back too."

I started to speak but she quieted me.

"Don't make promises now, girl. We make love."

Her hands on me and inside me pushed the city away. My mouth eagerly drew in the flavors of her body. Under my touch the sounds she made were of ocean waves, rhythmic and wild. We slept for only a few moments before it was time for her to dress and go on with her chores.

"I'll come back to ride with you to the airport?" she said with a small question mark at the end.

"Yes," I said, pleased.

In the waiting room she talked lightly as we sat: stories of her mother and sisters; questions about mine. We never mentioned the city or tomorrow morning.

When she kissed my cheek she whispered "sister-love" in my ear, so softly I wasn't sure I'd heard it until I looked in her eyes. I held her close for only a minute, wanting more, knowing this would be enough for the moment. I boarded the plane and time began to move again.

Dildo

TOI DERRICOTTE

She had bought herself a very good-size rubber one, molded from an actual erect penis, with all the raised veins and details of the texture of the skin. It was ten inches long, and her thumb and index finger could barely fit around the circumference. It had balls, reddish dark, kind of pimply thick, with no backs, like a mask.

She had quickly brought in the box, which was waiting on the front steps. Thank God she had beat her husband and children home! She noticed with relief the return address said something innocuous, like Halcyon or Life Streams . . . Whatever it was, no way did it call up the open flood of female jism. She tore into it. Never in her Catholic life had she allowed herself to imagine! True, she had owned a wand once, a long, hard battery-operated thing that she had been afraid to put inside her for fear it would electrocute her. She had tried it a few times, but it soon rusted where the battery went in, probably from washing it! That had been ten years ago. Lately, however, as her sexual encounters with her husband had become less frequent, less exciting, and after she had given up on an affair—scared off by AIDS and Catholic guilt—she had sent for a catalog.

Inside the box there was another box, with a large-as-life astounding picture. Taking the dildo out and handling its rubbery, not too stiff stiffness made her smile—as if she were a goddess looking down on herself from a distance, shaking her head. Of course she rushed upstairs to try it, and she was not disappointed! She was shocked by how quickly she responded, not even needing to be aroused first. She added a lubricant, stuck it in, and reached orgasm—a very deep orgasm—in about a minute, even though she hadn't touched her clitoris!

After, she worried. First, the box it came in was so big she couldn't get it hidden in the trash can. Her husband took out the garbage. The picture of the dildo loomed. The box was too thick to tear. Finally she turned it inside out, strapping it together with a rubber band, then folded it down tightly in the garbage and opened the step-on can several times to make sure the picture wouldn't pop out in his face.

Second, when she left the house shortly after, she noticed that the kitchen blinds were partway open. She had been so excited opening the box she had forgotten to close the blinds. Her neighbor had been out shoveling snow. She went out to check and found that one could see—if one were walking quickly—only a flash of the kitchen. Surely he wouldn't have stopped and stared. Well, maybe if he had, he would have thought it was something she and her husband had sent away for. It seemed less embarrassing if it was for conjugal purposes.

And there were other worries. Would she stretch so that her husband would notice? Would she enjoy sex with him less as a result? Would she go crazy for it, doing it several times a day? What if someone came home? What if the cleaning lady found it, the pet-sitter? What if her mother found it? She hid it in her sweater drawer in the second bedroom. But what if she died? Who would go through her drawers separating out the sweaters to give to friends, the sweaters to Goodwill?

If her husband found it, would he feel hurt, betrayed? If her son found it, would he feel repulsed, horrified? And if it was her mother, would she have a heart attack?

She could see her mother's face—as if the dildo would jump out of the drawer and eat her alive!

She would just *tell* her husband. How would she put it? "I really enjoy sex with you, but I need a little something extra. It's in the second dresser drawer in the guest bedroom. If I die, please get it before my mother."

Maybe, before she died, she'd outgrow the need, confess and throw it out—like Kafka burned his notebooks. But probably she'd have to stand up with it on the last day, before the complete heavenly host—John the Baptist, Peter and Paul, and all the saints, Bartholomew, Linus, and Cletus, the prophets, and even the pure angels, who are no doubt still pissed off after realizing what they *didn't* get in order to be smarter than us and immortal.

Clitoris

TOI DERRICOTTE

This time with your mouth on my clitoris, I will not think
he does not like the taste of me. I lift the purplish hood back
from the pale white berry. It stands alone on its thousand
   branches.
I lift the skin like the layers of taffeta of a lady's skirt.
How shy the clitoris is, like a young girl
who must be coaxed by tenderness.

There's a Window

SAPPHIRE

"IS THIS JUST something to do till you get out? Till you get back to your old man?" she sneered.

I didn't answer her. I just kept pushing her blue denim smock further up her hips. The dress was up to her waist now. I wanted to get one of her watermelon-sized breasts in my mouth. I was having trouble with her bra.

"Take off your bra."

"Oh, you givin' orders now," she said, amused. Her short spiked crew cut and pug nose made her look like a bulldog. Her breath smelled like cigarettes, millions of 'em.

"Yeah," I asserted, "I'm giving orders. Take that mutherfuckin' harness off."

She laughed tough but brittle. The tough didn't scare me, the brittleness did. She nuzzled my ear with her nose, her hot, moist lips on my neck. "Call me Daddy," she whispered.

Oh no, I groaned. She stuck her tongue under my chin. It was like a snake on fire. Fuck it, I'd call her anything.

"O.K., Daddy," I sneered. "Take off your bra." Something went out of her. I felt ashamed. "I'm sorry," I whispered trying to put it back. I had the dress up over her waist now.

"Take it off," I whispered.

"My blues!" she protested, referring to the denim prison smock.

"Yeah, I don't wanna fuck no piece of denim. Take off that ugly ass dress." I was eating up her ear now. My tongue carousing behind her ear and down her neck that smelled like Ivory Soap and cigarette smoke. I was sitting on top of her belly pumping my thighs together sending blood to my clitoris as I pulled the dress over the top of her head. I was riding, like the Lone Ranger on top of Silver. No, take that back. Annie Oakley, I was riding like Annie Oakley. Actually, I should take that back, too, but I can't think of any black cowgirls right off hand. Looking down at her face I wanted to turn away from it, keep my eyes focused on the treasure behind the white cotton harness.

Hawkeyed, crew cut butch, she was old compared to me. How the fuck did she keep her underwear so clean in this dingy hole, I marveled. They acted like showers and changes of clothes were privileges. I leaned down stuck my tongue in her mouth realized in a flash the Ivory Soap clean bra and perspiration breaking out on her forehead was all for me.

She was trying. Trying hard. Probably being flat on her back with me on top of her was one of the hardest things she'd ever done. I admired her for a moment. Shit, she was beautiful! Laying up under me fifty years old, crew cut silver. I'd told her in the day room when she slammed on me, "Hey, baby, I don't want no one putting no bag over my head pulling no train on *me*. Shit, baby, if we get together it's got to be me doing the wild thing, too!"

She'd said, "Anything you want, Momi."

I slid down in the brown country of her body following blue veins like rivers; my tongue, a snake crawling through dark canyons, over strange hills, slowing down at weird markings and moles. I was lost in a world, brown, round, smelling like cigarette smoke, pussy and Ivory Soap. My hands were on her ass pulling her cunt closer to my mouth.

"Here," she said pushing something thin slippery and cool into my hand. I recognized the feel of latex.

"Just to be on the safe side," she said.

My heart swelled up big-time inside my chest. Here we was in death's asshole, two bitches behind bars, hard as nails and twice as ugly—caring. She *cared* about me, she cared about herself. I stretched the latex carefully over her wet opening. "Hold it," I instructed while I pulled her ass down to my mouth. I started to suck; that latex might keep me from tasting but it couldn't keep me from feeling. And I was a river now, overflowing its banks, rushing all over the brown mountains. I was a black cowgirl, my tongue was a six shooter and my fingers were guns. I was headed for the canyon, nobody could catch me. I was wild. I was bad.

"Oh, Momi," she screamed.

Um huh, that's me, keep calling my name. I felt like lightning cutting through the sky. She pulled me up beside her. I stuck my thigh between her legs and we rode till the cold cement walls turned to the midnight sky and stars glowing like the eyes of Isis. The hooves of our horses sped across the desert sand, rattlesnakes took wings and flew by our side. The moon bent down and whispered, "Call me Magdelina, Momi. Magdelina is my name."

Our tongues locked up inside themselves like bitches who were doin' life. No one existed but us. But the whispering moon was a memory that threatened to kill me. She slid down grabbing my thighs with her big calloused hands.

"Yeah, yeah, yeah," the words jumped out my throat like little rabbits. "Go down on me go down on me." Her tongue was in my navel. "Use dat latex shit," I told her.

"Do I have to, mamasita?"

"Yeah," I said, "I like the feel of it." I lied. My heart got big size again. They didn't give nothin' away in this mutherfucker. How many candy bars or cigarettes had she traded for those little sheets of plastic?

"Ow!" Shit, it felt good her tongue jamming against my clitoris. Oh please woman don't stop I begged but at the same time in the middle of my crazy good feeling something was creeping. I tried to ignore it and concentrate on the rivers of pleasure she was sending through my body and the pain good feel of her fingers in latex gloves up my asshole. But the feeling was creeping in my throat threatening to choke me. Nasty and ugly it moved up to my eyes and I started to cry. She looked at me concerned and amazed, "Mira Momi, did I do something wrong?" She glanced around, then at herself as if to assess where evil could have come from. "Not this damn thing?" she says incredulously. Her eyes gleam with the hope of alleviating my pain as she hastily unhooks her bra. I shake my head no no but she has her head down, her hands behind her back pulling the white whale off her brown body.

"I . . . I don' know, you know I have this *thing* about being totally naked—*here* you know. I ain't been naked in front of nobody since I been here, 'cept, you know, doctors and showers and shit," she laughed in her glass voice. "It jus' ain't that kind of place, mamasita. You know you snatch a piece here, there; push somebody's panties to the side in the john so you can finger fuck five minutes before a big voice comes shouting, 'What's takin' you so long in there!' Least that's what it's been like for me. Seven years," she said. The glass broke in her throat, "Seven years."

Her words overwhelmed me. I felt small and ashamed with my pain. But this thing in my throat had snatched my wings. I knew I had to speak my heart even though it felt juvenile and weak. Speak or forever be tied up to the ground.

"I ain't seen the moon or the stars in six months." I felt ashamed—six months next to seven years on the edge of nothing. Silly shit to be tear-jerking about. I started to cry. I had seven years to do yet. She'd be gone by the time I turned around twice. She looked at me thoughtfully, her gray crew cut seemed like a luminous crown on top her forehead creased with lines. "Listen," she said quietly. "In six months or so you'll go from days in the laundry to the midnight to 8 A.M. kitchen shift if your behavior is good. Volunteer to peel the potatoes. There's a window over where they peel the vegetables. You can see the moon from that window."

I felt the nipples of her huge breasts hardening in my fingers. We retrieved two more precious pieces of latex, fitted ourselves in a mean sixty-nine and sucked each other back to the beginning of time. I was a cave girl riding a dinosaur across the steamy paleolithic terrain snatching trees with my teeth, shaking down the moon with my tongue.

Solitude Ain't Loneliness

MICHELLE T. CLINTON

Say for instance you're a girl/   but citified/   a hard sister
like to keep her eyes open when she fucks/   & carries weapons
for the urban night creatures on the prowl/   Say you ain't
got no freudian thing/   but you packing none the less:
   your mucus is acid
   your anger on a leash
& can't no wish from the mouth of a warm eyed boy
make you blink

Before the girl mist can enter you/   before you ever cop
a feminine buss/   & blow the urban rust out your uterus
   you got to clear house
   you got to clean out
all the greasy fuzz/   left behind by the rat pack lot
of ex-lovers

You got to celibate/   in silence
& wait & wait for a red blush to rise up
a sparkling rush as radical as your first blood
as muscular as your momma's hands in soapy water
cold as the shock of the first breath
the earth blew into your lungs

The black sky wants your ass purified
& clear enough to release this city's fear
free enough to close your eyes
go inside & hear her.

The Dream and Lettie Byrd's Charm

IMANI CONSTANCE JOHNSON-BURNETT

In the still purple night of the new moon in Libra when there was not need, nor want, Yasmine stood in front of the mirror. She was clean from a long bath; water sparkled in tiny drops on her forehead. She studied her face and noted the appearance of another brown flesh mole. She was already brown and the little extra dots of color, a common attribute of the women in her family, accentuated the brown even more.

Yasmine thought as years passed her maturing image in the mirror increasingly reflected her mother's face. There, around the nose, and especially around the chin. Yet everyone always said she was her father's child. Her family had even called her Little Sam back when she was growing into her own. She wore the diminutive nickname proudly and thrived in the affection that accompanied it. Being Daddy's girl seemed to mean she was chosen. It also meant she was perceived to be a strong woman-child.

Yasmine yawned in the mirror at her reflection of her mother and her father. She was paying attention to how they were blended in her own identity, a delicately balanced duality. Softness upon strength, strength upon softness. The strength of Little Sam, walking in her father's shoes, coupled with the practical, pliable make-everything-alright softness of her mother. It was all there in her face, inescapable as a signature.

She plucked an itinerant hair from her eyebrow and laughed. The forces that combined to complete her identity had to be rooted in her hair. Neither her father nor her mother had Yasmine's hair. Even if they did, they wouldn't dare let it grow long and loose and wild, like she did. "This is what it is, world," Yasmine thought. "Ready or not, here I come, Lettie Byrd and Sam's child with her own style."

Yasmine flossed her teeth extra for all the times she had forgotten. Then she turned off the bathroom light. With the first part of her nightly ritual complete, she entered her bedroom and from the nightstand she removed her journal filled with poems, unfinished short stories, observations, names, telephone numbers, and things to remember. She mused as she opened to a clean page. "This reflective time to write is as close as it gets to good for me, and as close as I get to God."

With that thought, she began her entry for the night . . .

December 2, 1992

The day was pure energy. In every blink of the eye there was spirit, practice, patience, and forgiveness. Lessons growing in deep silence and trust. Waves of motion danced the aerobic quickstep to be on clock time, and also did electric slide, saa-shay boogaloo, to the bass line beat of the latest diaspora call and recall. Reach out and touch the love there and here, risking vulnerability to become more. Envisioning powerful big picture concepts, captured in doing. Connecting to the collective of hue-man kind stabilizing and bridging over troubled waters. Through the I contact equation, cosmic mathematics is reduced to understanding, yielding enough . . . enough . . . enough. Night comes necessarily, . . . "tenderly, black like me" . . .

Yasmine closed her journal and prayed. She thanked the father-mother god for everything, and released herself to the protective power of the spirits as she climbed into bed.

Her own body heat seemed to melt the cool crispness of the covers patterned with birds of paradise and the need for rest lulled her whole body to sleep: arms, legs, head, feet, toes, breasts, belly, and back. Sleep slowly dragged her out of her body. Behind her closed eyes visions rolled like a movie, then quieted in the shady safe space where the spiral of her femaleness wound down, down, deep.

In sleep, she saw her mother, grandmother, and aunts. They were teaching her a lesson. The eyes of thousands of kind and familiar females were on her as they chanted, "Sistergirl, on any given occasion, you may meet yourself coming and going like the sun, the moon, and the stars. You may grow like the earth, touch the sky, and fly. It's all part of being a woman."

The chanting rose to a fervent rhythm then stopped. Yasmine was laid to rest by the caring arms of the women encircling her. She fell into a state of dream within her dream. Inside there she saw herself witness aloud.

This is my sun. I am enveloped by heat. I am so hot that I feel like I am fire. There is something burning but I do not know what it is. The air is dry. I cannot breathe. There is no air. I am being pushed down a narrow passageway. I am falling head first. I don't want to go. My inner voice is straining. I hear a low growl, a grunt. Wait, wait, please, don't push me anymore. Yes, I am coming.

This is my moon. I am uncomfortable. I am so uncomfortable that it feels like a toothache in my stomach. The taste of my last meal keeps coming back into my mouth. I feel like I am full, so full. I don't want to go out and play. I'm tired and sad for no reason. Something red and brown is coming out of me, down my legs. I am running to find a private place where I can cover myself. Wait, I can't stop the flow. Yes, I am coming.

This is my star. I am wet. I am so wet I think I am water. There is water running from my brow, water between my breasts, water trickling down my stomach, water everywhere. Quick deep breaths are in my ear, a baritone voice is calling my name and saying it is good. I am moving and being moved. My back is arched. I have my thighs spread wide, feet and legs wrapped around a broad smooth back. I hear my own voice in my throat saying, "Yes, yes, please, yes, I am coming."

This is my earth. I am more tired than I have ever been, yet I cannot give up. I am awake and asleep. My body is working without me. When I lapse into a daze I am awakened by a sharp contraction of all the muscles in the middle of my body. I feel like I am on a rowboat in the middle of the ocean without oars. I am rocking with the waves. My mouth is dry. I taste the salt of my sweat when I lick my lips. I must open my body. I feel myself expanding. I feel myself moving. Wait I am working a miracle. I am coming.

This is my sky. I am in a room with no entrances or exits. It is both safe and threatening. I feel like I am waiting for forever to change now. Sometimes nothing is right with everything out of control. Wait, I'm still climbing higher. Wait I am changing and coming.

This is my flight. I am moving on the wings of the wind. I can fly. My grace is like autumn leaves. Spring and summer come in flashes. Memories make me laugh. Some memories make me cry. Sometimes I can't remember anything and the quiet body and mind is peaceful.

Time is on my side, at my front, and in my back. I am a perpetual har-
vest of reaping and sowing, ebbing and flowing. Wait, there is no need
to rush. Wash your hands and watch your mouth. I am a cornucopia
at the center of the table. I am coming, coming, coming, coming.

When Yasmine woke up the clock radio on the nightstand beside her
bed read 5:00 A.M. As she became conscious, she remembered her
dream. She sat up in bed and in the dim gray light of the emerging
dawn reached for her journal again, and wrote a poem.

orgasm

a good girl always says yes
please and thank-you
she never takes chances with her self respect
or the impressions of others
she grows
with freedom of her imagination
as silent partner
she really lives in her head

and while she grows
saying yes to herself
is still not easy
the vocabulary of affirmation
is extraordinary and diverse
we can say yes in so many ways
to the pleasures of life
but the doctrine of emotional protection
coupled with the thought that one's smiling soul
can become a victim of circumstance
establishes a barrier of
significant consequence

a woman of age and time
with a sense of responsibility and empowerment

grown up enough to face effort failure and success
i find
the beginning of coming
a deep soulful release
intense colored tones
that shape and share and
agree with me
yes yes yes
finally
yes

The Liberation of Masturbation

EVELYN JOYCE REINGOLD

Look at these two hands
They are warm, soft, sensitive To Touch,
To Warmth, To Softness, To Wetness
They are mine
   Extensions of myself;
   Expressions of my sexuality
To do with as I please
And that's the way it should be. Yet,
   For much too long, Touching
   Myself was supposed to be wrong

My fingers are slim, long, sensitive,
Agile—they look fragile
But make no mistake, they are strong
And they are mine
   Extensions of myself;
   Expressions of my sexuality
To do with as I please
And that's the way it should be. Yet,
   For much too long, Touching
   Myself was supposed to be wrong

The nipples on my breasts are responsive,
Yielding to the warm softness
Of my sensitive hands and fingers
They too are mine
To Touch, To Feel, To Squeeze,
To do with them what I please. Yet,
   For much too long, Touching
   Myself was supposed to be wrong

My agile fingers run through my curly pubic hair
Exploring each part of the warm, soft, wet place there
It is mine
To do with as I please
And that's the way it should be. Yet,
  For much too long, Touching
  Myself was supposed to be wrong

My warm, soft, sensitive touch feels good to me
My body gives me pleasure
It is mine
To do with as I please
I can share myself with you
If I choose

But, I know what touch feels like
Because I touch myself
I already know what turns me on
Because I explore
With My Hands, My Fingers, My Senses
To fully express My Sexuality
Which is mine
To do with as I please

Encounter and Farewell

PATRICIA SPEARS JONES

It's all foreplay, really—this walk
through the French Quarter exploring souvenir shops,
each of them carefully deranged, as if dust were to settle
only at perfect intervals. Yes, to the vetiver fan
that smells sweeter than sandalwood or cedar.
No to the mammy doll dinner bells.
No to the mammy dolls whose sewn smiles are as fixed
as the lives of too many poor Black women here:
motherhood at twelve, drugged, abandoned by fifteen,
dead by twenty (suicide, murder) so easily in Desire.
And yet, their voices sweeten the snaking air,
providing the transvestites their proper Muses,
all of whom have streets named for them in the Garden District.

A soft heat settles on Terpsichore,
just inside the gay bar where the owner's pink flamingoes
complement silly songs on the rescued Rockola.
Who can dance to that Lorne Greene ballad, "Ringo"?

Dixie beer is the beer of choice; marijuana the cheapest
drug. Relaxation is key, since it's all a matter of waiting
for the right body to stumble towards you. Lust perfumes
parties in the projects, bar stool chatter at the Hyatt,
lazy kissing on the median strip stretching down Tchoupitoulas.

If Professor Longhair were alive, he'd teach a lesson
in perfect motion: the perfect slide of a man's hand
down a woman's back;

a lesson you learned long ago before you met me. We are
making love as we did before in Austin and Manhattan.

But in this room on this costly bed our lovemaking
starts out the slowest grind, then, like this city's weather,
goes from hot to hotter, from moist to rainstorm wet.
You're tall, A., and where there should be tribal markings
there are scars—football, basketball, midsixties grind parties
where something always got out of hand. There's the perfect
amen. You're your own gospel.
And you bring good news to me—the way you enter me
like grace, the way you say my name, a psalm.
No. That's not it. It's the engineer in you that
gets me. Your search for the secret line that goes
straight to the center of the earth. Deeper and deeper
you go until there's no earth left in me. And we
hum and moan a song as old as our selves gone back.

There are too many souvenirs in your eyes.
Gifts given too often, too hastily, never opened.

Outside a city sprawls its heat, seeks out every pore,
licks every moment of sweat as we shiver in this chilly room
taking each other's measure. We say good bye again and again.
As if every kiss, every touch we make, will shadow
all our celebrations.

And, they do.

The Late Mrs. Hadlay

JO ANN HENDERSON

Eartha Mae Hadlay was forty-eight years old when it all started. She was, by anyone's standards, a beautiful woman. Cocoa brown, tall, shapely, and always stylishly dressed. Her body was middle-aged full but tight from her daily walks and visits three times a week to Everybody's Fitness on Jackson Street in the heart of the Central District. Her face was magnificently sculpted and had just the right balance to accentuate her full lips and large doe eyes. When she walked she had a long, slow stride which caused a flirtatious swivel in her hips that other women tried to imitate because it sent men into instant, sweaty fantasies about erotic, sticky interludes. She looked and carried herself with the vain confidence of a woman half her age. That's why she was shocked when Cecil left her for a younger woman.

She didn't know right away that another woman had taken his attentions, nor had she suspected it. He had always told her that her looks meant everything to him. So she tried everything she could to keep them up. She had denied herself most of life's sinful pleasures which could cause a body to age unflatteringly. She had even denied herself the privilege of becoming a mother. Cecil didn't want to see her small waistline thickened or her stomach distended, not even for a day, let alone nine months. Of course, she was quite taken with her own attributes and none of those sacrifices were of any consequence to her.

It was an evening in May when she arrived home after a full day's work and her usual two-hour workout to find that Cecil had removed all of his belongings from the house. Until she had thoroughly searched every room for any sign of him she didn't notice the note he had left for her on the dining room table, next to the vase of red roses. It simply stated: *"Baby, need some space and time to find myself. Stay fine. Cecil."* The cowardly bastard hadn't even given her the satisfaction of a good fight before he left. After she thought about it, she figured she shouldn't have been surprised, the son of a bitch never had any damn class. But the thought was no consolation to her. She could feel a scream well up inside her that exploded in her chest before it found its way to her throat.

Like any other woman who has ever counted on a man who lets her down, Eartha grieved herself half crazy. That is, until she noticed that her grieving and crying had shed her of seventeen pounds. Eartha Mae had melted from a statuesque 155-pound diva to a 138-pound brick house, and it seems the whole neighborhood had taken notice. Especially the members at Everybody's Fitness and the young men on the outdoor basketball court of Leschi Elementary School.

She enjoyed the conversations of the men at the gym. They made her forget her worries over Cecil and what he might be doing with another woman. They had just the right words to make her feel as special as she looked. On almost every visit she could count on someone's "I haven't seen anything as beautiful as you since the exotic flowers of the Caribbean." Or, "Baby, your workout is paying off like the Exacta at Longacres." She ran into Cecil's colleague Cornell Thornton there who asked her out for drinks a couple of times. That was a great boost to her ego, but she decided against it. She had already suffered enough humiliation behind Cecil's leaving her. She didn't need the rest of the world talking about her dating one of their mutual friends.

What the young men at the basketball court lacked in words they more than made up for in looks. She enjoyed passing them during her walks home in Leschi. Their half-naked bodies glistened with perspiration, which clung to them like dew on fresh leaves in early morning. Their physiques were perfect without effort—sinewy, muscular and chiseled like the statues of marble gods in a Roman garden. Even their names were pretty and rolled around the tongue like fine cognac: Shakhir, N'Gai, Jamar, Rashad.

She would often stop and watch them play basketball. The small pleasure eased the pain of her return to a house which no longer accommodated a man. Occasionally one or two of them would speak to her and hold light conversation. Nothing sophisticated or flirtatious, it was just a pretext for them to eye one another's good looks. Eartha delighted at the idea that they thought she was much closer to their age than she actually was.

On a day when she decided to shop a little before walking home, she noticed that the usual game on the outdoor court had broken up by the time she passed the schoolyard. A block from her home, she heard the conversation and bouncing ball of two or three of the boys behind her. As she approached the stairs leading to her front door a voice from behind her said, "Help you with your bag, Ms. Hadlay?" Eartha was startled, but didn't want to show her surprise. There was no telling what these young bloods might do.

When she reached the porch she turned slowly and looked squarely into the face of a Denzel *gonnabe* whose startling good looks shortened her breath. Standing five-nine in her flat shoes Eartha estimated him to be at least six feet. He was a rich sable brown with perfect teeth and deep brown eyes framed with *coverguy* lashes.

"How did you know my name?" she asked.

With his finger he tapped the tin stand. "It's on the mailbox."

There was something about this one that seemed more mature—definitely more handsome. He was just the right thing to jump-start an older woman into a new attitude. Eartha opened her mouth and shocked herself with her response. "Certainly, thank you."

He threw the basketball to one of his playmates, who caught it, gave his pal an understanding nod and kept walking. The youth bounded up the steps, picked up the bag and followed Eartha inside.

"What's your name?" she asked, as they entered the kitchen.

"Jamahl," he said, looking too good for words.

"Well, Jamahl," said Eartha, snapping the ring on a can of Coke. When she turned to face him she held the side of the can marked *Classic* between her breasts and asked, "Can I offer you something to drink?"

Eartha always regarded women who acted this way with disdain. But, her body had been idle for three months, and Jamahl's presence had brought that fact achingly to her attention. A little aggression was what she needed to get where she wanted to go with this young man. She had never tried seduction before but amused herself with just how damned good she was at it.

He said, "Yes, thank you," to her invitation to something to drink, but walked past her to the refrigerator, took out the bottled water and asked, "Can I have a glass, please?"

Eartha was disappointed. In spite of his mature appearance, she had to remind herself he was just a kid. "How old are you, Jamahl?" she asked.

"Nineteen," he responded, gulping down the first glass of water and pouring himself another.

Just a kid, she thought. But this seduction seemed to have taken on an energy of its own and somehow the boundaries created by their age difference seemed to have faded away. Cecil had always said that sex was the most dynamic form of communication between two people and she definitely wanted to *talk* to Jamahl.

"Besides playing basketball, what else do you like to do?" She allowed the sleeve of her warm-up suit to brush his bare arm as she walked past him headed toward the living room. As Eartha passed him, he bent over and kissed her on the cheek. She stepped back, crinkled her nose and looked at him. Jamahl pulled the hem of his tee shirt to his forehead to mop it while taking a quick sniff at his armpits. "Sorry, I'm a little sweaty from playing basketball."

"If you'd like, you can take a shower in the bathroom down the hall," said Eartha. Rather than reciprocate his advance, she continued on her way into the living room. She turned back toward him and said, "You'll find towels in the linen closet just outside the bathroom door."

Their starts and hesitations toward each other displayed that they were both nervous. While Jamahl was in the bathroom Eartha decided to go into the bedroom to change her clothes. She took off her warm-up suit and examined her body in the mirror. Despite a slight sag to her breasts and roundness to her tummy she knew she looked good enough to excite him. But she could tell from his reactions that he probably had not been with anyone over seventeen. And it had certainly been a long time since she had been with a nineteen-year-old. As a matter of fact, the last one was Cecil. She allowed her mind to hang on the thought of Cecil for a moment. He would certainly be disappointed in her if he could witness her antics of this afternoon. He would think she was acting like a sleaze lusting after this young boy.

At that moment she remembered the woman her friend Clarisse had pointed out at the Ebony Fashion Fair last month as Cecil's new roommate. She was a twenty-five-year-old who looked like all the imitation white women she had seen in those popular hip-hop videos on BET. Eartha didn't consider the woman's looks extraordinary, but her youth had startled and bothered Eartha. It was the only area in which she couldn't compete with her rival. Looking again at her image in the mirror she thought about the young stud who was preening for her in the bathroom. She decided, *fuck Cecil,* and snickered at the ridiculousness of the statement at that moment.

Her body was a little ashy from the shower she had taken following her workout. She silkened it with the moisturizing oil she kept in the drawer of the nightstand and took extra care of the rough areas on her feet by massaging them with cocoa butter. She took another look in the mirror and felt satisfied with the results.

To accentuate her body Eartha selected a pair of black spandex pants and a black georgette big-shirt. Except for the double-layer patch pockets which covered her breasts, the shirt was sheer and silhouetted her frame. As she was buttoning the shirt she eyed the can of Coke she had brought with her into the bedroom. She took a cotton ball from her cosmetic box and doused it liberally with the Coke. She then painted the nipple of each breast and drew a line from the center of her breasts to her pubic bone with the syrupy liquid. Eartha cracked a slight side grin at the feeling of naughtiness in her actions and the fantasies which fed them. She decided to remain barefooted, left the pants on the bed and went back into the living room in only the big shirt to wait for Jamahl's return.

She had barely positioned herself on the couch when she heard the bathroom door open. To Eartha's disappointment, Jamahl came out of the bathroom wearing his sweatpants as he clumsily made his reentry. His bare feet and chest told her he was trying to look adult and confident about his conquest. He would have made a striking entrance if he hadn't been rubbing the palms of his hands on his pants along his sides and shifting his eyes from side to side as if he was expecting someone to tap him on his shoulder and tell him he was going in the wrong direction.

Eartha rose to meet him as he approached the couch. She came close enough to feel the warmth radiate from his body. She then slid her hands into the waistband of his pants and pressed down on them. As his pants dropped to the floor she allowed her face to meet his. She rested her hands on his shoulders, let them slide down his arms and clasped his hands as she took a half step back to look at his deep brown body.

He was a perfect size and muscular, but not big. The hair on his arms, legs and chest was as fine and soft as eiderdown. The sensation of his touch caused her nipples to harden and the hair to bristle on her arms.

Jamahl bent to kiss her and this time she reciprocated. After a couple seconds she stopped and said, "Don't do that."

"Huh?" said Jamahl. "But I thought you wanted me to . . . "

"That's not what I mean," said Eartha. "Don't purse your lips and thrust your tongue so quickly. Just hold your mouth the way you normally would and relax your muscles. Here, let me show you."

Eartha craned her neck to reach his face. She pulled a slow, silent breath as she neared him to take in the scent of his skin and breath. She barely brushed his lips with hers using the slightest tip of her tongue to trace the outline of his lips with it before slowly introducing it into his mouth in search of his. As their bodies pressed Eartha felt as if they were swaying to unheard music until she realized that, with one arm around her waist and his hand cradling her head, he was lowering her onto the couch. She considered this quite a bit of finesse for a nineteen-year-old. She didn't know whether it was her imagination or if he actually tasted sweet. In just the faintest audible sound she whispered, "W-o-o-w."

The spell was broken when Jamahl started to squeeze her breast with one hand and grope between her thighs with the other. Eartha needed a lay too badly to accept it this way. She knew he would probably be hurt or offended if she said anything. Instead, she swung one leg over his upper hip and moved her weight forward until they began to rotate and she had assumed prominence in their tangle of limbs. She straddled him in a crouched, sitting position. His body felt taut and supple under hers, like the fine leather of an expensive luxury car.

Jamahl looked at her as if to drink her beauty and slowly began to unbutton her shirt. Eartha kissed his fingers as he did so and began to slowly gyrate against his pelvis. By the time her breasts were exposed, Jamahl had learned by example to be slow and deliberate in his experience with her. He massaged her breasts and ran his hands down her body until they cupped her hips. He raised his head until his mouth met the nipples of her breasts. His eyes bucked at the sweetness of their taste. Eartha had been watching for that moment and had to giggle at the surprise registered on his face. Before he could say anything she slipped his penis into her vagina to distract him.

Eartha was enjoying her role of sexual aggressor and used this encounter to satisfy her body's longing. Twice when Jamahl was on the verge of orgasm she raised her hips high enough to expose the shaft of his penis. With three fingers she squeezed his organ using the pad of her thumb to press the prominent vein on the underside of his penis to delay ejaculation. At the same time she used the knuckle of her index finger to massage her clitoris. The second time her body exploded. Her responsive squirming sent them both the release they had been seeking for the past half hour.

Jamahl fell asleep on the couch and Eartha covered him with the afghan she kept in a basket next to the fireplace. She fixed herself a cup of tea and sat opposite him in the dark and watched his languor. It wasn't until that moment that she began to consider all the reports, stories and conversations she had heard about safe sex. She decided to dismiss it as useless to worry about something after the fact. Instead, she lost herself in thought about what had just happened—*Cecil*—what to say when he awoke—*Cecil*—whether she wanted another sexual encounter with him or any other man, and **Cecil.**

His confused uneasiness and Eartha's mature frankness made it easy for her to dismiss Jamahl after she allowed him to slumber for a couple of hours. She discovered that neither of them had much to say, nor did they feel a need to say much. She invited him back the following week and decided she would work on this safe sex thing in the meantime.

During that week Eartha acquainted herself with a selection of the sex merchandise carried at Fantasies *un*Limited. She was surprised at how much seemed to have changed since she was nineteen. The pimply-faced clerk with orange hair behind the counter ran through all the do's and don'ts of safer sex play. Eartha purchased fifty-two dollars worth of oils, glides, fluffs and latex and only concerned herself about how to introduce them to Jamahl on his next visit. That Tuesday night Eartha knew she wouldn't have anything to worry about when she noticed Jamahl trying to discretely slide a Kiss of Mint condom on the nightstand on Cecil's side of the bed. She invited him back the following week and every week after that for the next two months.

The two of them recognized the liaisons as sexual exploration. Jamahl was grateful for the dependability of regular sex. Eartha was grateful for the opportunity to discover the banquet of sexual pleasures which, to that time, she had only read about or heard of. She discovered that great sex was its own aphrodisiac. In anticipation of Jamahl's visits and while in the throes of passion Eartha surprised herself at just how little she thought about Cecil. For the first time that she could recall, she was enjoying sex for the sake of it and not because of an emotional attachment to a man.

She had returned from a visit with Clarisse one night to find Cecil waiting for her in the dark of her living room. When she turned on the light he startled her by saying, "Have you lost your damn mind?"

"What are you doing here?" asked Eartha.

"Never mind that," said Cecil. "People are talking about you all over town. Fucking that kid and embarrassing me."

"Cecil, I am not going to play this game with you," said Eartha as she walked past him toward the kitchen.

"Don't try to ignore me, woman," Cecil said, grabbing her arm. "A teenager—with his hands all over you."

Eartha yanked her arm away from him and yelled, "Listen, when you were fucking a kid and embarrassing me, people were talking about *me* all over town and you never cared enough to call once, let alone show up. It's not that they're talking about *me* that has you pissed. It's that they're talking about *you*. Don't think I haven't heard that that young, dizzy bitch you've been living with left your pitiful ass." All of the rage, hurt and disappointment Eartha had experienced over Cecil during the past six months was in her voice.

"Don't change the subject," yelled Cecil. "This isn't about me, it's about you."

"It is about you, Cecil," interrupted Eartha. "It's always about you. You are always putting on a front to try to impress people that you're something you're not. We rattled around in this big-ass house because you had to have enough bedrooms to ask your friends to stay over when we gave a party. It wasn't enough to have an expensive car, you had to put a telephone in it to look important. A telephone you only use to call the goddamn restaurant to say we're on the way or to ring up your friends to say we're waiting downstairs. It took me a while to figure it out, but you would never have married me if I couldn't have made *you* look good."

"That's not true and you know it. I loved you. I still love you," said Cecil.

"Of course you love me, Cecil. I've been compliant and accepting," shouted Eartha. "I accepted all your ridiculous exhibitions. I had to remain perfect for you, but I never said shit when you got paunchy and started to lose your hair. How long did it take your playmate to discover you wore a toupee?"

The blow to his vanity crushed Cecil. He plopped back down in the chair. "I'm sorry for that, Eartha. Didn't you hear me say I still love you?" asked Cecil. "I've always loved you."

"Who gives a shit?" said Eartha. "I loved you nonstop for thirty years and when you decided to trade me in for a new model my love didn't matter. You just walked the hell out. And, as for that teenager, he's the best thing that's happened to me in years. He brought out a new woman in me and we're both having a good time. Now, get up and get out."

Eartha turned and went into the bedroom. Cecil followed her and tried to turn on the charm he knew he could always rely on.

"But, baby . . . "

He had no words to finish the sentence, all he could do was look hurt.

Eartha felt from a distance the love she once had for Cecil. But it was masked by the pity she felt for him at that moment. She understood all too well the pain he was experiencing. She froze as she saw him slowly approaching her. Their eyes met and, for the first time she could recall, she saw Cecil cry openly. He laid his head into the curve of her neck and enveloped her with his arms. Slowly she allowed her own arms to creep up his back and embrace him in comfort.

They clung to each other crying for what seemed to Eartha like a lifetime. The release of all the pent-up anxiety of the past six months gave her the pathway to the new self she had started unfolding with Jamahl.

When they finally made love, each of them experienced it as a new encounter. They talked, held each other and had sex until the sun was up. Eartha was pleased to find that Cecil had discovered oral sex. She was disappointed to find that he was as mediocre at that as he had been at everything else sexual they had done together. Cecil was amused at the assortment of fruit-flavored body oils and motion lotions she now kept in the bedside chest. He told her he wanted to continue to come around until he discovered how she used all of them.

At eight-thirty Eartha told Cecil he'd have to go home so she could get ready for work. He didn't want to leave and thought they should continue to talk until they had worked out their problems.

"We have too many problems to work through in a day and a night," said Eartha.

"Our problems are complicated by the other people we've let into our lives," said Cecil.

Eartha cut him a stony side glance which telegraphed her thoughts about his recent living situation. It stopped his aggression on the subject and in a more subdued tone he continued. "If you stop seeing that boy we'll be in a position to start working on our other stuff. I know most of it is me. But I'm willing to try if you are."

"I'm willing to listen to what you have to say," replied Eartha. "But I'll give up Jamahl when it suits me to do so. Right now I don't want to discuss it any further and I don't want to be late for work."

Cecil was hurt, as she knew he would be. She saw him trying to delay her preparation for work by dressing slowly and continuing to talk. When it was time to leave she kissed him on top of his head and told him, "You can let yourself out."

For months Eartha had hoped that Cecil would be in the house when she came home. Now she felt violated and decided that he had invaded her privacy. The day after they made love she had the locks changed.

Eartha discussed Cecil's reappearance in her life with Jamahl on his next visit. He seemed indifferent to the news and didn't see it as a complication. Eartha smiled at the naivete of youth, but delighted in the simplicity of her relationship with him.

For the next three weeks Cecil called every day and asked Eartha if he could come by. She held his visits to two nights a week and continued to see Jamahl once during the week. She decided to keep four days for herself to do as she pleased without anyone's involvement or approval. She was resolved to run her life this way from now on.

In mid-December Eartha found herself in the middle of the holiday season with no desire to be with either man. She decided to make a fresh start in the new year and let both of them be a part of her past. She and Clarisse planned to attend the Seattle Black Firefighters annual New Year's Eve bash at the Sheraton this year in search of new prospects.

Jamahl would be an easy recycle. Divorce was more time consuming and tricky, and she expected Cecil to fight it every step of the way. She surprised herself that she was no longer as broken up about the idea of divorce as she had once been. Her plans would have been easily carried out had it not been for one minor incident. On Christmas Eve

Eartha noticed that, for the first time in her adult life, her period was inordinately late. That morning, with one hand clutching the bathroom door and the other clutching a home pregnancy kit, she uttered the first real prayer she had said in months.

"Lord, please let this be the onset of menopause."

PART SIX

Eclipse:
Black Women in Love
with Men

When Alice Walker defined "womanist" in *In Search of Our Mothers'
Gardens,* she included women who sometimes love individual men
within that definition. Navigating our way through the confines of sexism to negotiate nonsexist, egalitarian relationships with men has been
an ongoing struggle for many a womanist.

The stark reality of verbal and emotional abuse, in addition to battering, has caused many a sister to think twice before entering a poten-
tially volatile relationship.

But the intense feelings of emotional vulnerability, the joy of experiencing connectedness with a kindred spirit, and the potential soul-
sharing available in an intimate relationship with a nonabusive partner
continue to entice those of us who are straight or bisexual to seek
and/or maintain fierce couplings with progressive men.

▲▲▲▲▲▲▲▲▲

revolution starts at 11:50 a.m.//april 2, 1993

karsonya e. wise

for amir

i woke up listening
   to the sound of you sleeping
the rise and fall
   of your breath

lulling me gently back to sleep

. . . and i started thinking
of how revolutionary it really was
to wake up . . .
   in a cold house
   under a warm blanket
   to the sound of a black man at peace

Mama Day

GLORIA NAYLOR

George, I was frightened. Can you understand that? Things were going so well between us that I dreaded the day when it would be over. Grown women aren't supposed to believe in Prince Charmings and happily-ever-afters. Real life isn't about that—so bring on the clouds. And each day that it was exhilarating and wonderful; each time you'd call unexpectedly just to say, I was thinking about you; each little funny card in the mail or moment in a restaurant when you'd reach over for no reason and squeeze my hand—each of those times, George, I'd feel this underlying panic: when will it end? And it was worse when we were in bed. You'd take me in your arms with such a hunger and tenderness, demanding only that I be pleased, that I'd feel a melting away of places in my body I hadn't realized were frozen voids. Your touch was slowly making new and alive openings within me and I would lie there warm and weak, listening to you sleep, thinking, What will I do when he's not here? How will I handle all this space he's creating without him to fill it?

And you—you would be so cheerful the mornings after you slept over. Running down to the deli to get us fresh rolls and orange juice. Circling some announcement in the paper for a show we could catch that weekend. Never understanding that it was three whole days until the weekend and my seeing you again. Three days was time enough to settle into what my girlfriends were saying: "He sounds too good to be true." I'd look around that empty apartment and yes, it had to be that—untrue. You were only part of some vision, or at best a temporary visitor in my life. Too good to be true. Too good to last. I found enough courage to ask you that one night, do you remember? No, men don't remember those things. You thought I was teasing you to prolong the moment when I brought your head up from between my thighs and stroked your lips with my fingers. What will I do when you're not here? I said. It stung me that you took it so lightly: I'm not going anywhere for the next fifteen minutes, I plan to be coming.

The more you began to mean to me, the more I was losing control— and I hated it. I wasn't angry at you for phoning later than you said you would, for ending an evening early because you were genuinely tired—I was angry at myself for allowing it to matter that much. And when I was brooding or sarcastic after you finally called, it never seemed to bother you. You'd laugh it off, and that would make me angrier. It was horrible feeling that I needed you more than I was needed. And so I would push you, making petty demands. If you cared, you'd do X. If you cared, you'd do Y. I was tearing my hair out, and all you had to say was, I'll call you when you're in a better mood. Giving in to me so effortlessly made you all the more unreal. He just wants to glide on through this, he doesn't care. If he cared, he'd . . . What? Fear is unreasonable, and that's what I was being. And it seemed as if I couldn't stop myself from picking up the phone and instead of telling you how I really felt—

"So you're not coming over Monday night *again?*"

"I don't come over any Monday night. You know that's for football."

"And I'm supposed to believe that?"

"I don't see why you shouldn't, I've never lied to you."

"Or I've never caught you."

"Ophelia, if you want to take the train down to South Ferry, get on the boat, and come over to Staten Island tomorrow, you're welcome. But on Monday, I watch the games."

"And you watch them for *six hours* on Sundays, too."

"That's right. And I even have my satellite dish so I can follow the Pats when they're not on network."

"So where is that supposed to leave me? If I want us to go some-where Sunday afternoons or Monday nights, it's tough shit, right? I take second place to some overgrown clowns running around in—"

"Is there something you wanted to do Monday?"

"That's not the point."

"Then I don't know what the point is."

"Well, then clearly there's no point in my trying to explain it to you. When someone doesn't care, they just don't care. Obviously, there are things in your life that matter more than me.'

"Of course there are. My health, my work—to start off the list—*and* the New England Patriots. It's a short season, you'll just have to live with it."

"And if I don't want to?"

"Then you don't."

"You know, George, if you really cared. . . "

"I don't care that much, damn it!"

After making you hang up on me, for a brief moment I'd be satisfied. Just imagine if I'd been a fool enough to tell this man how I really felt about him—see the way he treats me. He's insensitive and selfish. No doubt about it, he'd walk right over me if I ever opened up. Yes, for a brief moment I was comfortable feeling that I was insulating myself from all the damage you were capable of. And then it didn't seem so awful that one day it would be over. Good riddance to bad rubbish, I could handle that version of you. Sounds crazy, doesn't it? Here was a relationship I needed to turn into a catastrophe, out of fear of losing a perfect one. And when I was in that state of mind, I found plenty of support:

What are you so upset about? The truth had to come to light.

A leopard can't hide his spots but for so long.

It's easier to get run over by a flying saucer than to find a decent man in New York.

If he's not married by now, you shoulda figured something was wrong.

I couldn't sleep well those nights. Why should I call you when you had hung up on me? Slammed down the phone, as a matter of fact. Maybe I had gone a little too far, but there was no reason for you to act like that.

"But I do care."

"Huh?"

You had the most disconcerting habit of calling me back and picking up a conversation where we may have left off two hours or even two days before.

"I said, I do care."

"You should tell me that more often."

"Maybe you aren't listening."

I don't think I was. Because I kept picking fights about your football games. It was the only thing that seemed to tick you off—that and being called a son-of-a-bitch. I had a pretty dirty mouth and it often amused you. Southerners can't swear, you'd say with a laugh, you make *bastard* sound like it should be a woodwind instrument. November and December gave me plenty of opportunities to complain; important games were played during the holidays. And it's not as if I cared about Thanksgiving or Christmas, I hadn't grown up celebrating either of those. I was eighteen years old and going to school in Atlanta before I even saw a live Christmas tree. And all of the forced gaiety and noise about the holiday I found unsettling. But Selma was having a huge Thanksgiving dinner party and I wanted to show you off, but you were going out of town for a game. And no, I didn't want to come along. Outside Detroit—where it was probably a million degrees below zero? Besides, I was determined that you were going with me to that dinner.

"I am serious about this, George. Dead serious."

"I'm going to the game."

"Then don't call me when you get back."

"I've heard that one before."

"No, I really mean it—don't call me."

"You mean that—over a stupid party?"

"Yes, I really mean it."

"Okay, Ophelia. I won't call you."

"You mean that?"

"Yes, I really mean it. You mean it, don't you?"

"*Yes.*"

So why didn't he call? This was the end, the absolute end. That dinner party was a total disaster. Selma had gotten drunk and put too much wine in the stuffing, so it looked like her turkey was having diarrhea. And after another half bottle of Johnnie Walker, she got onto one of her favorite subjects—black men dating white women. Later that night I caught a twenty-second news clip about the game, saw a red-headed blur in the crowd, and swore it was Shawn. The bitch. Some women have no pride—they'll go to any lengths to run after a man who doesn't want them. Not me. What did Grandma used to say? She was short on money but long on pride.

My pride had to stretch a long way. November left, December came—no call. I was utterly depressed when I wrote home, and even more depressed when I got my Candle Walk package the next week. What in the hell was I doing in this city? It was cold and unfriendly. I took out the sweet orange rock Grandma had sent me and Mama Day's eternal lavender water. Seven years away from that place and December twenty-second still didn't feel right without my seeing a lighted candle. The same old news from home, but if those letters had ever stopped coming, I don't know what I'd do. I got to the line "The last thing you need is a no-good man," and started to cry. They were so right. Your phone rang twelve times—twelve.

"You know I didn't mean it."

"I didn't know, Ophelia. But I was hoping."

Eclipse

MARY WALLS

Rema tried to muster up the energy. It took a lot of energy to see a counselor. She didn't know why she should have to pay someone to listen to her.

During a session, her therapist, Carol, asked her to talk about her feelings of shame. Rema said, "It stems from my first lover, a man named Lem. We met in college. I wanted to get a degree and make my family proud of me. He said he wanted the same thing. We dated. He was nice to me. It was the first time I fell in love and was sexual. I stayed a virgin by choice until I was twenty-one. I was also very naive about sex. He didn't push me. He wanted me to enjoy myself. He was nice in the beginning." Rema slowed her thoughts and began to feel comfortable opening up.

"For a while I was happy in the relationship. I felt flattered being loved. But after a while he began to ask me for money. I wasn't prepared for this. I didn't have much. He said if you love someone you give them things. I took him out to dinner for his birthday, even bought him a present. On my birthday he didn't even call." Rema felt tears but held them back. She continued, "He asked me to help him whenever he needed something. But when I asked him for things he became impatient. He said he needed a woman who was strong enough to stand on her own two feet, because life was so hard on him. At one point he asked me to marry him, thank God I had the sense to say no." Rema paused, then continued, "After I knew him about three months, he told me about another woman he was seeing. He had dated her before we met. He told me he loved me and that he was with her because she could provide cooking and cleaning. I tried to put her out of my mind, going back and forth between wanting to end the relationship and wanting to continue seeing him."

"Around this time I learned that my mother had cancer, so I guess I needed to be with him sometimes. By this time the relationship was just him coming over to talk, have sex and get money from me. He talked to me about the other woman, how they would get into violent fights. It made me afraid of him."

Carol asked Rema why she had stayed in the relationship and Rema replied, "Sometimes it felt good, sometimes he gave me comfort. I didn't know that he had hurt me so much. It was a time in my life when I felt very afraid. I didn't want to lose two people's love at the same time. I needed to feel loved and Lem had told me he loved me."

Rema took a deep breath and continued, "Then he talked me into having oral sex. I didn't really want to do it. One time he forcibly held my head over his penis." Carol told Rema to let herself feel the pain. She told her it was okay to cry, it was okay to feel the shame. Rema cried and released emotions she'd held inside for years.

Then the healing process began. Carol said, "I see you as a victim. He took advantage when you were under stress. You need not feel responsible for what happened."

That evening Rema watched the moon slowly pass from the shadow of the earth. She felt the strength and power to move forward. She felt sorrow for Lem. He missed the love she could give.

Song Through the Wall

AKUA LEZLI HOPE

you will not punish me
you will not split me in two
you will not knock on my doors
you will not tap on my wall
you will not enter
you will not exit
you will not park your car in my garage
you will not contain your missile in my silo
you will not conjugate me
you will not fiddle faddle or dally with me
you will not find my treasure
you will not lick my pot
you will not fill my refrigerator
you will not butter my roll
you will not toast my bagel
you will not baste my chicken
you will not taste my manna or sip my nectar
you will not fry my egg or lick my bowl
you will not yin my yang, ting my tang, or sniff my yoni
you will not raise my dead my spirits or my hopes
you will not run your trains down my tracks or through my tunnel
you will not rain on me, flood me, thunder me or lance me with your
    lightning rod
you will not be a bee to my flower nor a bear to my honey
you will not move my mountain nor the earth under my feet
you will not look at me and smile with those seducer's eyes
nor will you speak to me with that steel-melting voice
you will not know my next move
you will not guess what I need
you will not you will not you will not make me love you

Dues

MATTIE RICHARDSON

The puffy-faced man with stiff hair asked me how I felt. I told him I felt like the rent was due. And how would he like to be this close to sleeping in a car? So he asked me how I felt about the incident in the store and I told him that I felt like the car was broke down and my baby girl, Nita, had to get to school and I had a job interview that morning.

Then he asked me how I felt when I ruined that poor man's life. I said I felt like I was runnin' late for the first job interview I had in months but I missed the bus and Nita was scared, this being her first day of school and all.

When I finally dropped her off I could see her wave bye in the same clothes her cousin had last year and then look around at all the other kids in their new sneakers and bright new school bags . . .

But, you know, I had to run and catch the uptown No. 7 for this job interview. I had this awful, scratching feeling like the rent was due. When I opened the door to Scoletti's National Brand Outlet I could see Mr. Scoletti himself over by the cash register smiling and staring at my chest. Then I knew what was up. He didn't even look at my application. He just told one of the stringy-haired women to mind the store while I went with him to his office for an "interview." By this time I felt like the car needed to be fixed and the rent was real late and the phone was on disconnect notice. It wasn't that bad. I mean, all he wanted to do was rub me up a little bit, you know. But, after all that he said he would call me *if* a job came through.

By the time I left I was shakin' really hard. Somethin' was scratching at me bad, like I was going to be peeled from the inside out. It hurt a pain that wasn't burning or sharp or dull but like I was peeling and I needed it to stop.

I don't know how long I stood outside that store. Something pulled me back inside. All I know is I looked around to see the old man walking towards me real slow like they do in the movies. He was shaking his head no. All I could see was no. The big no that had been following me around making my insides peel ever since I walked into that place.

Then, it's like something took me away from it all. I could see what I was doing but it was like it wasn't me doing it. I don't remember lighting the first rack of clothes on fire. I could hear them screaming no at me. I remember going to the cash register and opening it up. Everybody must have been caught up in trying to put out the fire because I don't remember anybody trying to stop me. Everything went by real slow like I was in some kind of dream or a movie. Once I had the money, I very calmly walked out to the bus.

By the time I got home Berto was waiting for me. He seemed so concerned about me. He asked where I had been and if I was OK. He said Nita's school called him at work and wanted to know how come nobody came to pick up Nita. He said that he called Carmen, his mother. Carmen picked her up and so she was staying with her grand-mother overnight. He seemed really interested in what happened to me. I obviously wasn't quite myself. I really thought he cared, you know? I didn't want to burden him with all the stuff that happened, what I could remember anyway. I just wanted to sit and think for a while. I never get to just think by myself. Berto always comes in after a bad day, goes into the bedroom with a scowl on his face saying, *"Déjame, eh?"* before I can get in a sentence.

He offered to let me sleep this time. He said, *"Véte a dormir.* Get some rest. *Todo 'stá bien."*

Soon, I drifted off into sleep. A restless, worried sleep. I dreamt of Scoletti's hands only they were huge. He had cold, marble hands. A chill clamped over me, penetrating my insides, activating the peeling again, jolting me awake. There was Berto trying to get me to have sex with him. All I wanted was rest.

"Come on just a little bit. I've had a hard day and I need some understanding."

"Look, Berto, it's late, I'm not in the mood for this."

"Hey, what about me? I'm out there working hard every day all I ask from you is some cooperation. Is that too much to ask? Just a little support."

"Don't you think I'm trying to look for a job? Do you think I like living like this?"

"You don't even take care of your child. I didn't say anything when you come back here four hours late and looking like you been out all night. Another man would have accused you of stepping out. I should go where I'm appreciated. I ought to go and let a real woman give me what I need, not some crazy, spaced out Negrosa bitch like you."

"I take care of Nita."

"Then where were you this afternoon when your child needed you? You forgot about your own child. What kind of mother are you?"

What kind of mother am I? I can't believe he asked me that. He sees how much I love Nita. You know the first thing they asked me when they hauled me in is why I didn't pick her up from school. The cops didn't even ask me about the fire at Scoletti's until it was clear I wasn't going to answer any questions.

This one stubby, strung-out white cop was pacing around, saying I'm going to be charged with neglect and asking me if I beat my kid. So, this time I told *him* no. He looked at me like he knew me. He thought he had seen me before, like all the black women that ever walked into a holding pen belonged there, deserved to be there. My life melted with their lives and all I could do was to say no. Nothing I could say would make a difference in how he judged me. No to what he thought of me. No to anything and everything he could imagine me to be, because he was wrong. So I said "No" real loud, and I said it over and over. Some of the other women in the station saw me going off and they started doing it too. It flipped them out.

The cops put me in the hospital in the first place because they were fucking scared. The doctors there wouldn't even let me have a piece of paper and a pen—said I was a danger to myself and others. That's when I started talking in my head. I figure if I say what happened over and over then I won't need no paper, I'll remember it. At least this way they can't take it away. I'll just remember the whole thing.

They wouldn't give me any paper at the police station either. They had said the only thing I needed to write was a confession. Those cops didn't know what to do. What else had they wanted me to say? How could I have convinced the cops if I couldn't even convince Berto?

All the time we was arguing that night, Berto never took his hand off the inside of my thigh. His grip was solid. So hard the tips of his nails were digging into my flesh. He wasn't yelling, but tiny droplets of blood were forming on my skin. His eyes were as cold as ever. I kept saying wait a minute, let me tell you about what happened today and he said, "No. *Cállate, ya.* You talk too much. All talk and nothing else.

Instead of being out there with who-knows-who, I'll show you what you should have been doing."

He kept moving all over me and the no in his voice clicked in my head. I was sick of his no. His no just got louder and louder till I was burning with it. Ripped up with it. Peeled raw with other people's no. I didn't want to do it. He was trying to get me to hand over my life. I don't do that for anybody, you know? He wouldn't listen. It was like he plugged up his ears and he couldn't hear me. I wasn't there. I had to make the peeling stop. It was going to tear my insides apart. I couldn't take that.

Finally, I grabbed his hands, looked at him and said, "No, let me show you what happened today."

duplication

jonetta rose barras

for abdoulai

Let ten thousand men
be like you
muted saxophone voice
onyx eyes set inside
a face etched
from ageless mahogany
hands that cup
terra cotta dreams
for thirsty women
with rose petal faces
with moonsong voices
with caribbean sunshine eyes
with palm-tree-swaying hips
without men
like you to love
in midday heat
after lunch, during
siesta stillness
before cool cricket-filled
evenings
or to remind them of another time
another land, not arctic cold
without men like you
on lonely sunday mornings
genuflecting at bedsides
singing wordless praises.

In the new day
let ten thousand men

be like you
with stories hidden
in the unending lines
of their faces
of their veined hands
of their angular bodies
of their muted hearts
let them cradle
babies and guide
old cane-holding men
across streets that lay
without movement or
rhythm or ritual
let them know your name
and call it their own
as they rise quietly
facing the east.

Wounded in the House of a Friend

SONIA SANCHEZ

Set no. 1

> *The unspoken word*
> *is born, i see it in our*
> *eyes dancing*

She hadn't found anything. I had been Careful. No lipstick. No matches from a well-known bar. No letters. Cards. Confessing an undying love. Nothing tangible for her to hold on to. But I knew she knew. It had been on her face, in her eyes for the last nine days. It was the way she looked at me sideways from across the restaurant table as she picked at her brown rice sushi. It was the way she paused in profile while inspecting my wolf-dreams. It was the way her mouth took a detour from talk. And then as we exited the restaurant she said it quite casually: I know there's another woman. You must tell me about her when we get home.

Yeah. There was another woman. In fact there were three women. In Florida, California, and North Carolina. Places to replace her cool detachment of these last years. No sex for months. Always tired or sick or off to some conference designed to save the world from racism or extinction. If I had jerked off one more time in bed while lying next to her, it woulda dropped off. Still I wondered how she knew.

> *am i dressed right for the smoke*
> *will it wrinkle if i fall?*

   i had first felt something was wrong at the dinner party. His colleague's house. He was so animated. The first flush of his new job i thought. He spoke staccato style. Two drinks in each hand. His laughter. Wild. Hard. Contagious as shrines. Enveloped the room. He was so wired that i thought he was going to explode. i didn't know the people there. They were all lawyers. Even the wives were lawyers. Glib and self-assured. Discussing cases, and colleagues. Then it happened. A small hesitation on his part. In answer to a question as to how he would be able to get some important document from one place to another, he looked at the host and said: They'll get it to me. Don't worry. And the look passing back and forth between the men told of collusion and omission. Told of dependence on other women for information and confirmation. Told of nights i had stretched out next to him and he was soft. Too soft for my open legs. And i turned my back to him and the nites multiplied out loud. As i drove home from the party i asked him what was wrong? What was bothering him? Were we okay? Would we make love tonite? Would we ever make love again? Did my breath stink? Was i too short? Too tall? Did i talk too much? Should i wear lipstick? Should i cut my hair? Let it grow? What did he want for dinner tomorrow nite? Was i driving too fast? Too slow? What is wrong man? He said: i was always exaggerating. Imagining things. Always looking for trouble.

Do they have children?
one does.

Are they married?
one is.

They're like you then.
yes.

How old are they?
Thirty-two, thirty-three, thirty-four.

What do they do?
An accountant and two lawyers.

They're like you then.
yes.

Do they make better love than i do?
I'm not answering that.

Where did you meet?
when I traveled on the job.

Did you make love in hotels?
yes.

Did you go out together?
yes.

To Bars? To Movies? To restaurants?
yes.

Did you make love to them all nite?
yes.

And then got up to do your company work?
yes.

And you fall asleep on me right after dinner. After work. After walking the dog.
yes.

Did you buy them things?
yes.

Do you talk on the phone with them every day?
yes.

Do you tell them how unhappy you are with me and the children?
yes.

Do you love them? Did you say that you loved them while making love?
I'm not answering that.

*Can i pull my bones
together while skeletons
come out of my head?*

i am preparing for him to come home. i have exercised. Soaked in the tub. Scrubbed my body. Oiled myself down. What a beautiful day it's been. Warmer than usual. The cherry blossoms on the drive are blooming prematurely. The hibiscus are giving off a scent around the house. i have gotten drunk off the smell. So delicate. So sweet. So loving. i have been sleeping, no daydreaming all day. Lounging inside my head. i am walking up this hill. The day is green. All green. Even the sky. i start to run down the hill and i take wing and begin to fly and the currents turn me upside down and i become young again childlike again ready to participate in all children's games.

She's fucking my brains out. I'm so tired I just want to put my head down at my desk. Just for a minute. What is wrong with her? For one whole month she's turned to me every night. Climbed on top of me. Put my dick inside her and become beautiful. Almost birdlike. She seemed to be flying as she rode me. Arms extended. Moving from side to side. But my God. Every night. She's fucking my brains out. I can hardly see the morning and I'm beginning to hate the night.

He's coming up the stairs. i've opened the venetian blinds. i love to see the trees outlined against the night air. Such beauty and space. i have oiled myself down for the night. i slept during the day. He's coming up the stairs. i have been waiting for him all day. i am singing a song i learned years ago. It is pretty like this nite. Like his eyes.

I can hardly keep my eyes open. Time to climb out of bed. Make the 7:20 train. My legs and bones hurt. I'm outta condition. Goddamn it. She's turning my way again. She's smiling. Goddamn it.

What a beautiful morning it is. i've been listening to the birds for the last couple hours. How beautifully they sing. Like sacred music. i got up and exercised while he slept. Made a cup of green tea. Oiled my body down. Climbed back into bed and began to kiss him all over . . .

Ted. Man. I'm so tired I can hardly eat this food. But I'd better eat cuz I'm losing weight. You know what man. I can't even get a hard-on when another bitch comes near me. Look at that one there with that see-through skirt on. Nothing. My dick is so limp only she can bring it up. And she does. Every nite. It ain't normal, is it, for a wife to fuck like she does. Is it man? It ain't normal. Like it ain't normal for a woman you've lived with for twenty years to act like this.

She was Killing him. He knew it. As he approached their porch he wondered what it would be tonite. The special dinner. The erotic movie. The whirlpool. The warm oil massage until his body awakened in spite of himself. In spite of an eighteen-hour day at the office. As he approached the house he hesitated. He had to stay in control tonite. This was getting out of hand.

She waited for him. In the bathroom. She'd be waiting for him when he entered the shower. She'd come in to wash his back. Damn these big walk-in showers. No privacy. No time to wash yourself and dream. She'd come with those hands of hers. Soaking him. On the nipples. Chest. Then she'd travel on down to his thing. His sweet peter jesus. So tired. So forlorn. And she'd begin to tease him. Play with him. Suck him until he rose up like some fucking private first class. Anxious to do battle. And she watched him rise until he became Captain Sweet Peter. And she'd climb on him. Close her eyes.

honey, it's too much you know.
What?

All this sex. It's getting so I can't concentrate.
Where?

At the office. At lunch. On the train. On planes. All I want to do is sleep.
Why?

You know why. Every place I go you're there. Standing there. Smiling. Waiting, touching.
Yes.

In bed. I can't turn over and you're there. Lips open. Smiling, all revved up.
Aren't you horny too?

Yes. But enough's enough. You're my wife. It's not normal to fuck as much as you do.

No?

It's not, well, nice, to have you talk the way you talk when we're making love.

No?

Can't we go back a little, go back to our normal life when you just wanted to sleep at nite and make love every now and then? Like me.

No.

What's wrong with you. Are you having a nervous breakdown or something?

No.

if i become the
other woman will i be
loved like you loved her?

And he says i don't laugh. All this he says while he's away in California for one week. But i've been laughing all day. All week. All year. i know what to do now. i'll go outside and give it away. Since he doesn't really want me. My love. My body. When he makes love his lips swell up. His legs and arms hurt. He coughs. Drinks water. Develops a strain at his butt-hole. Yeah. What to do now. Go outside and give it away. Pussy. Sweet. Black Pussy. For sale. Wholesale pussy. Right here. Sweet black pussy. Hello there Mr. Mailman. What's your name again? Oh yes. Harold. Can i call you Harry? How are you this morning? Would you like some cold water it's so hot out there. You want a doughnut a cookie some cereal some sweet black pussy? Oh God. Man. Don't back away. Don't run down the steps. Oh my God he fell. The mail is all over the sidewalk. hee. hee. hee. Guess i'd better be more subtle with the next one. hee. hee. hee. He's still running down the block. Mr. Federal Express Man. C'mon over here. Let me Fed Ex you and anyone else some Sweet Funky Pure Smelling Black Pussy. hee. hee. hee.
i shall become his collector of small things; become the collector

of his burps, biceps, and smiles. i shall bottle his farts, frowns, and creases. i shall gather up his moans, words, outbursts. Wrap them in blue tissue paper. Get to know them. Watch them grow in importance. File them in their place in their scheme of things. i shall collect his scraps of food. Ferret them among my taste buds. Allow each particle to saunter into my cells. All aboard. Calling all food particles. C'mon board this fucking food express. Climb into these sockets golden with brine. i need to taste him again.

You can't keep his dick in your purse

Preparation for the trip to Dallas. Los Angeles. New Orleans. Baltimore. Washington. Hartford. Brownsville. Orlando. Miami. *Latecheckin. Rush. Limited liability.* That's why you missed me at the airport. Hotel. Bus stop. Train station. Restaurant. *Latecheckin. Rush. Limited liability.* I'm here at the justice in the eighties conference with lawyers and judges and other types advocating abbreviating orchestrating mouthing fucking spilling justice in the bars. Corridors. Bedrooms. Nothing you'd be interested in. *Luggage received damaged. Torn. Broken. Scratched. Dented. Lost.* Preparation for the trip to Chestnut Street. Market Street. Pine Street. Walnut Street. Locust Street. Lombard Street. *Earlycheckin. Slow and easy liability.* That's why you missed me at the office. At the office. At the office. It's a deposition I'm deposing an entire office of women and other types needing my deposing. Nothing of interest to you. A lot of questions no answers. Long lunches. Laughter. Penises. Flirtings. Touches. Drinks. Cunts and Coke. Jazz and Jacuzzis. *Morning. Evening. Received. Damaged. Torn. Broken. Dented. Scratched. Lost.*
I shall become a collector of me.

I shall become a collector of ME.
I SHALL become a collector of ME.
I shall BECOME a collector of ME.
I shall become A COLLECTOR of ME.
I SHALL BECOME a collector OF ME.
I shall become a collector of ME.
And put meat on my soul.

Set no. 2

i've been keeping company, with the layaway man
i say, i've been keeping company, with the layaway man
each time he come by, we do it on the installment plan

every Friday night, he come walking up to my do'
i say, every Friday night he come, walking up to my do'
empty pockets hanging, right on down to the floor

gonna get me a man, who pays for it up front
i say, gonna get me a man, who pays for it up front
cuz when i needs it, can't wait 'til the middle of next month

i been keeping company, with the layaway man
i say, i been keeping company, with the layaway man
each time he come by, we do it on the installment plan
each time he come by, we do it on the installment plan

PART SEVEN

Visitations: Aging

What does aging look like for Black women? Lena Horne, Tina Turner, or the Delany sisters, still independent, strong-minded, and sassy at over one hundred years old?

Are we frightened at the first sign of gray hair on our heads and pubes? Or do we gracefully slide into acceptance of those physical signs of living—the wrinkles in our skin, the sagging of our breasts, the cessation of menses?

And what about sex? Is it a part of our lives after fifty?

The ways in which Black women age are as diverse as we are as a group of women. The aging Black woman must be viewed through a myriad of lenses.

The women in the following stories and poems make the transition into the role of elder-crone–wise woman in the world, with vulnerability, grace, strength, humor, and pride. They are women whose strength of character and belief in their principles grow stronger with each passing year.

Middle-age UFO

COLLEEN McELROY

The aliens have taken over
My body or else how
Could my head become suddenly
Medicine-ball heavy
Their ray-gun zap has left
Me old before my time
My joints so stiff and achy
I could easily teach a course
In robot behavior

Hot flash—night sweat
Is this Uranus or Neptune
There must be aliens
I hear them as they leave their ship
Yelling, "Men'o Pause, Advance!"
They must be males
They make their monthly raids
For female slaves
And what few men they take
Are quickly peeled like wounded
Onions down to their mushy centers
Women require years
First they fatten us in unlikely places
Until stomach and hips sag into gravity
They mean to change our lives
They want our secrets for having babies
But my lips are sealed
I follow a host of sisters and clutching
Passion, bail out
I quit that job—I'm out of here
I'm free to go on living

Oya Mae's General Store

DOROTHY RANDALL GRAY

"I see someone been drinkin' up that fountain of youth. Damn if you ain't changed a lick in twenty years, Miss Oya!"

Miss Oya's round body leaned forward on the cane she kept by her rocking chair. Her eyes strained to see a face on the stocky figure that stood between her and the bright Georgia sun. The visitor stepped onto the porch of her white shuttered house, removed his herringbone cap, and handed her a bouquet of burgundy roses.

"Happy Birthday, Miss Oya. February second, right? See, I didn't forget!"

"That you, Jacob? Come out the sun so I can see what you lookin' like these days." The stooped shoulders sported a worn corduroy jacket with sheepskin collar, and two buttons missing. His gray brows and false-toothed smile threw a familiar look at the unwrinkled skin beneath her brown bandanna.

"Man, I ain't seen you since God left Chicago! Come sit down and tell me how you got so old." Miss Oya held the flowers to her nose while the other hand tucked a wisp of white hair back under her head scarf.

"Your wife dead?"

"She died back in June, 1990. Got a couple of grandkids now. I'm retired."

"That retirin' mess'll kill you. Why quit workin' if you ain't dead?"

"You still got that store? I seen your name on it when I passed through town."

"College boys from Morehouse is workin' for me now, learnin' how to run a business. I'm sixty-nine and never missed a day of work. I still takes Wednesdays for myself though. Told the boys I'd let 'em have the place when I died, but only if they agreed to bury me under that room in the back where you and the mens used to play cards."

Jacob moved his chair closer to hers, and put his hand on the arm of the thick purple cape and crocheted shawl she wrapped herself in.

"You still remember them card games, Miss Oya?"

The towering pines leaned forward to listen. Miss Oya put her hand on top of his with a veiled smile as their minds walked back to another time.

During World War II, Oya Mae Bryant began making dresses and men's clothing for women busy with jobs in factories, and the munitions plant five miles outside of Cachita, Georgia. At eighteen, she sold fried fish and chicken to the Black factory workers, pulling pieces from shoe boxes lined with aluminum foil and paper towels, pedaling her hand-made bicycle cart from building to building, and wondering why her husband, Billy, never wrote or sent any money home from the army.

A year before the war ended, a sargeant knocked on the door hand-ing her a box with Billy's rabbit's foot, a marked deck of cards, a bronze medal, his aluminum spoon, and a brown bandanna. "Blown to bits," explained an army buddy of his who came to visit two weeks later, bringing a letter Billy had never mailed. "They couldn't even find a fin-gernail to send home." Oya Mae refused the army's offer of a military burial. She tied the bandanna around her head, pinned the bronze medal to it, and stuffed the letter into her bra without opening it.

Late one Wednesday afternoon, she put the triangular folded flag, playing cards, and the rabbit's foot into a huge iron caldron, and set them on fire. She placed the ashes in her lacquered jewelry box, and buried them in the backyard under the aluminum spoon, and cup and saucer Billy had used before he left for the war.

Insurance money brought the down payment on a run-down house next to Route 1, and enough chicken and fish dinners to trade for labor to fix up the building. She continued selling handmade cloth-ing, riding fifty miles to Meacon City once a month to buy fabric and thread for women to do their own sewing once the war ended and men came back to claim their jobs.

Eighteen years later, Oya Mae's General Store was a paradise of thick mail-order catalogs from Alden's and Sears, red-handled pick-axes, Gold Medal flour sacks, fertilizer, rakes and shovels, glass bottles of milk, and salted hams hanging from hooks in the overhead beam. Shelves were filled with boxes of roofing nails, penny candies in giant jars, cartons of Old Gold, Chesterfield, and Lucky Strike cigarettes, black cast-iron frying pans, bottles of Alaga syrup, Br'er Rabbit molasses, and Lydia Pinkham tonic for women. Photographs of Joe Louis and Mahalia Jackson, *Life, Look,* and *Hit Parader* magazines, dream books, and Burpee seed catalogs lined the walls.

In back of the store, Jacob McKnight smirked and emptied the bottle with his fourth glass of Miss Oya's homemade whiskey, while Zed Thackeray and Willie Toledo looked at him, at each other, then back at their cards.

"Yo'all just ain't no match for the bid whiss king of Cachita! We done already won two games and now yo'all in the hole. I call that some king card playin', am I right or am I right, Brightman?" McKnight bit off the end of his cigar and struck a match to it.

"Y-you right as rain, partner," echoed Johnny Bright. "We got the keys to this here k-k-kingdom!"

"I'm afraid not, gentlemen. See, me and Zed here thought we'd try losing once in a while just to see how you boys been feelin' for the past two weeks." Toledo slid his cards off the leatherette card table one by one, and fanned them out carefully.

"Bid's on you, Toledo," pushed McKnight. "We ain't got all night!"

"Hold your horses, McKnight, I takes my time. That's why the womens love me." He stroked the slick graying waves in his hair, and picked a piece of lint from his mohair jacket.

"Last goddamn woman you had was probably Aunt Jemima!"

"Well, at least she was willin' to bake my bread. I hear some folks is having trouble gettin' their flame lit!"

McKnight slammed his beefy hand on the table and shot up like a pine tree.

"What the fuck you talkin' about, Toledo! If you feelin' froggy, you better leap!"

"McKnight, don't be starting none of that dumb nigger shit and make Miss Oya have to come back here. Just sit down and shut up!" Zed spoke with a quiet firmness.

"Who the fuck died and made you God, Thackeray? And where you get off tellin' *me* what to do?"

"I bid four no. Ain't nobody love a hole but a mole." Toledo grinned.

"Five," Johnny Bright called nervously.

"Pass. What you comin' in?" Zed pushed the thick glasses back up his nose.

Johnny Bright made a fist and rapped the table with it three times. "Clubs, huh? Sport the kitty, my man."

Johnny Bright turned the six cards over and smiled the gold-tooth smile of a small man. In the midst of a lack of attention being paid to him, McKnight slid back into his seat, his eyebrows still bristling.

"Yo'all better keep it down back there!" Miss Oya shouted through the door. Her copper bracelets jangled into each other as she measured out three yards of checkered wool and frowned. Dreaming about Billy had given her a restless night. She covered a yawn, then turned up the old Emerson radio, and put another piece of wood into the potbellied stove.

Bumble Bee plastic-coated playing cards skidded into each other, punctuating the silence and arranging themselves into books of four on Johnny Bright's corner of the table. Zed stared at the handful of hearts he held. McKnight threw whiskey down his throat and slammed the glass on the table with a glint in his eyes.

"Seen Miss Cicero lately, Thack?"

Zed refused to take the bait.

"I seen her this mornin' in a blue dress and that smile of hers. Man, that's a whole heap of woman. Juniper sure is a lucky man, ain't he, Thack? What I wouldn't give for just one night with Miss Cicero!" Zed tried not to flinch at the mention of his best friend and the woman he had never stopped loving. A halo of intentional cigar smoke surrounded his thinning hair.

Staccato slaps of clubs and spades answered McKnight.

"Damn! You cuttin' hearts already, Brightman?" Zed moaned the loss of his ace of hearts. "You better make goddamn sure you don't renege like you did last week!" His hands shook with a quiet rage.

"Course, that's water under the bridge now, ain't it?" McKnight pressed. "Ancient history, huh, Zed Thackeray?" He threw the name like a curse.

"I like current events myself," Toledo broke in. "Tell me, partner, what you think about them rockets they shooting up in the air?"

"Ridiculous shit!" Zed spat out in disgust. "Spendin' millions of dollars on a goddamn spaceship when niggers can't even buy grits!"

"But they say it's some kind of science b-b-breakthrough gonna benefit mankind," Johnny offered.

"That mankind shit ain't never included us niggers, don't you know that, Brightman?"

"If they can send one white man to the moon, why in the hell can't they send them all?" Toledo smiled.

"They planning to make us extinct anyway," Zed continued. "Soon as they figure out how to get all *their* people out of here, they gonna pick a war with the Russians, spread that radiation shit all over the place, and leave our sorry nigger asses right here to die!"

"Ain't nothin' wrong with war. Men need to fight for their country. How else we gonna stop them foreigners from fuckin' with us? Least I wasn't hidin' behind no goddamn 4-F pair of glasses when it came time for me to stand up and be a man! I ain't afraid of the Japs, the Russians, nobody. I fought the big one in '44 and got me a Purple Heart!"

"McKnight, you wouldn't know a big one if it fucked you up the ass!"

"You ain't got to fight my battle, Toledo. He washing *my* face with this shit!"

"Keep fuckin' with me, Toledo. I'll show you a big one!"

"Show it to your wife. I hear she forgot what it look like!"

McKnight roared and threw his chair across the room. He grabbed the empty bottle by the neck and bashed its bottom against the wall, turning it into a weapon with angry jagged edges.

"Motherfucker, I'll kill you!" He weaved from side to side in his red flannel shirt, slicing the air in front of Toledo while sweat rolled from beneath his herringbone cap.

Johnny Bright trembled over to the doorway, wiry fingers clutching his winning hand like a lifeline. Zed crouched next to Toledo while tightening his hand around the knife in his jacket pocket. His eyes blinked with anger. Willie Toledo sat motionless at the card table. He struck a match, lit another cigarette, and looked McKnight directly in the eye.

"Prove me wrong, nigger, and I'll take that goddamn bottle and cut my own neck. Prove me wrong right now or get the fuck out my face!"

The room stood as still as McKnight glowered at Toledo.

"What the hell yo'all niggers doing back here?" Miss Oya's 275 pounds of luscious fury threw open the door, slamming Johnny Bright against the wall behind it. Her brown bandanna and maroon scoop-neck sweater scowled at the overturned chair halfway across the room, and the broken pieces of glass on her floor.

She clutched the handle of her machete, announcing through dark red lips, "Yo'all prehistoric niggers has got to go! You can't hold your liquor and you can't hold your piss. Get the hell outta my store right now!"

The men stood watching each other.

"Miss Oya don't like to say things twice. Next time be Miss Machete talking to your asses, now move!"

Zed straightened up and took his hand out of his pocket. He slapped on a felt hat, his eyes still fixed on McKnight. Toledo took another puff of his cigarette, then crushed it into the ashtray. He tipped his black Stetson, smiled, "Have a nice night now, Miss Oya," and nudged Zed through the door.

"Where Brightman?"

"I-I'm right here, Miss Oya," Johnny spoke up from behind the door, still holding the playing cards. "Ain't this a cryin' shame? I would've had me a Boston!"

"I don't care if you would've had the whole goddamn state of Massachusetts! Peel your narrow ass outta here!"

Miss Oya slammed the door behind Brightman and filled the room with herself. Billy's bronze medal hung from her bandanna like an earring. Her brown circle skirt gently journeyed the mountains of soft sensuous flesh, coming to rest under a wide elastic belt, and a horizon of curvilinear breasts.

McKnight loosened his grip on the bottle and his anger.

"And you! Grab that broom and sweep every bit of glass off this floor! And pick up that smelly ass cigar. You ain't got to showboat in front of nobody but me now!"

McKnight looked at the hand on her hip, and the machete in her fist. He lay the broken bottle down on the table.

"Yes, Miss Oya." He looker older and shorter than his six-foot-two frame.

Miss Oya watched the heavy mustache peppered with gray, the strong thighs, and powerful shoulders curved around his pain.

"Jacob. . . "

McKnight turned to look at her, trying to stuff defeat into his back pocket.

"Come 'round to the house tonight, about ten."

McKnight stood up and let a smile creep onto his mouth.

"And bring the big one with you!"

The front porch and the smell of pine held their smiles in the warm grip of memories tightening on Miss Oya's arm. Jacob pushed his voice into the quiet.

"I came here to ask your forgiveness, Miss Oya, to apologize for leavin' without saying good-bye or nothin'. My wife had two heart attacks. Said this thing with me and you was killin' her. She turned my own son against me. That boy was my life. I didn't know what to do when I saw hate was making his eyes so narrow at me. I couldn't stand to see that look in your face too."

"That was twenty years ago, Jacob. Why you just comin' to see me?"

"After Lureen died, it took me more than a year just to work up the nerve to come back to Cachita, and see if you was still here. I ain't had one day of peace since I left. Can you please forgive me for what I done?" The plea in his body made him bend close to her cheek.

"You did what you had to do. What else you want from me, Jacob?"

He put his cap on, placing her cool fingers between the rough face of his palms.

"Miss Oya, I know I'm a day late and a dollar short when it comes to you. Time done took some of the edge off me. Missin' you's been like I had arthritis in my heart. I seen you sittin' here just as pretty as you always was, and I almost couldn't walk up to the house. All those years, I never stopped thinkin' about you, Miss Oya. I been goin' over these words again and again in my mind. What I'm tryin' to ask you is, well, I wonder if you might consider takin' me back, you know, marryin' me? Maybe two lonely people can still make each other happy."

A chilling gust of wind blew through the mild winter air. Miss Oya took her hand back. "You come waltzin' in here after twenty years looking like who-shot-John-last-night, with your roses and your memories and your bullshit story? You let somebody buy the dreams out your life, then come here offerin' me what's left over? You ain't even asked me if I got married again, or nothin' about *my* life. Why the hell you think I want some piece of a man with no dreams and no guts?"

"Miss Oya, please. . . "

She turned her rocking chair around, lay the roses on the slatted porch, and faced him with a macheteed stare. "You think I been sittin' on my ass for twenty years just waitin' for you to come back, don't you?

Ain't that some shit! The night you slithered out of town, I was with another man! Always had one, always will. Got a retired professor from the college now sweet on me. If you lonely, that's your cross to bear, not mine. Ain't never married 'cause I didn't need the worriation. Why you think I look so good now? Look what marriage done to you! And Lureen holdin' that son over your head! That's the biggest piece of cow shit!" The sharp edge of her laughter cut straight to his heart.

"What you talkin' about?" Jacob's voice trembled.

"I'm talkin about that boy you been crucifyin' your life for, that's what! He ain't never been no son of yours. That was Billy's boy your wife gave birth to and she knew it!"

"Billy? *Your* husband Billy? Are you crazy, woman?" His body stiffened.

"Him and Lureen was foolin' around while you was overseas and he got her pregnant. That's what Billy wrote in that letter his army buddy brung me back from the war. Fifty years and I ain't never even looked inside that envelope . . . till now." Miss Oya's voice softened. She looked across the red clay road and stared at the trees for a while before she continued.

"Every year the night before my birthday, I'd take the envelope out and put it 'neath my bed under a glass of water with some rosemary in it so's I could talk with him. Thought if I opened it up, I'd be lettin' a piece of him fly away, and I ain't had much left to speak of. Never loved nobody like I loved that man. A big chunk of my heart is still layin' right there in the ground with him. Billy came to me in a dream last night and told me it was time to open the letter. Said I needed to know what was inside. He was askin' me to forgive him. Jacob, I didn't mean to spit in your eye 'bout your son, but you pissed me off presumin' your way in here like that."

Jacob slumped in the chair, the weight of her words pulling his neck down like a yoke. The pine trees whispered behind him. Twenty years of rain came pouring out of his eyes. The herringbone cap fell to the ground, laying bare his naked scalp. Jacob's swollen knuckles gripped his face.

Miss Oya leaned on her cane as she slowly got up and walked around to the back of his chair.

"Still got them big shoulders I see," she said, placing both hands on his jacket.

She leaned forward and kissed the top of his bald head. Billy's medal swung from the brown bandanna like an earring.

"Maybe I missed you every other leap year."

Jacob shook his head and sobbed until he heard Miss Oya's wide hips swish against the satin lining of her purple cape as she walked back into the house.

"Jacob, you come on in here."

He pulled his head from his hands and held his breath.

"And bring the big one with you."

How to Fly Into 50
(Without a Fear of Flying)

SAUNDRA SHARP

Change something: cut your hair, put different art on your walls.

Go dancing to 50's or 60's music, and remember when.

Get Touched! Spend an afternoon at the spa, get a massage, pedicure, manicure, facial.

Make a list of all the obstacles you've survived in 50 years.

List your accomplishments—things that show you've been here on the planet.

Read a poem to someone, have someone read a poem to you.

Dine with Nature—go on a picnic.

Call a friend (who is older than you) just to say "Hi."

Spend an afternoon with someone younger than 12.

Contemplate how your life has changed in the last 20 years, then get rid of everything you no longer need.

Get a complete physical checkup.

Kiss someone at the exact moment that marks your birth.

Buy fresh flowers for your nest.

Enjoy an old-fashioned chocolate malt or root beer float.

Buy an article of clothing that is sassier than the regular you. Wear it with an attitude!

Hug someone every day for 50 days.

Hug yourself twice a day for 50 days.

Plan ahead: create an astounding wish for your birthday cake candle blow-out.

Develop a welcome ritual for new gray hairs.

Learn a current love song.

Make love.

Buy yourself a present.

Set aside time to meditate: think on the glory of 50.

Do something each month of this year to celebrate turning 50. Try to do it on your number day.

Select a PMA ("Positive Mental Attitude") that will help you through the next 364 days. Write it down, paste it on the bathroom mirror or refrigerator, then say it out loud every day.

Seven Women's Blessed Assurance

MAYA ANGELOU

1

One thing about me,
I'm little and low,
find me a man
wherever I go.

2

They call me string bean
'cause I'm so tall.
Men see me,
they ready to fall.

3

I'm young as morning
and fresh as dew.
Everybody loves me
and so do you.

4

I'm fat as butter
and sweet as cake.
Men start to tremble
each time I shake.

5

I'm little and lean,
sweet to the bone.
They like to pick me up
and carry me home.

6
When I passed forty
I dropped pretense,
'cause men like women
who got some sense.

7
Fifty-five is perfect,
so is fifty-nine,
'cause every man needs
to rest sometime.

climbing

LUCILLE CLIFTON

a woman precedes me up the long rope,
her dangling braids the color of rain.
maybe i should have had braids.
maybe i should have kept the body i started,
slim and possible as a boy's bone.
maybe i should have wanted less.
maybe i should have ignored the bowl in me
burning to be filled.
maybe i should have wanted less.
the woman passed the notch in the rope
marked Sixty. i rise toward it, struggling,
hand over hungry hand.

Visitations

BRENDA BANKHEAD

It was summer and school was out. Two girls with dusty legs chased flies in the August air, stalked them through a strip of dirt surrounded by cement. Janetta Reeds walked to a pail of water, her braids swinging like two thick ropes down her back. Her skin had the yellowish tint of the pages of an old book, and the bright darkness of her eyes shone out of her face like green ink. Her nose was sharp and pointed. She squatted by the pail and unscrewed the lid of her jar underwater. Flies buzzed inside, bumping against the sides of glass. Janetta's younger sister, Dora, knelt down beside her. Dora put her head close to the wet jar. Her skin was dark brown. Her hair, freshly washed and unbraided, was a kinky halo around her face. Right now it stuck out in two short braids on her head.

"What you doin', Janetta? What you doin'?" Dora said in a singsong.

"Catching jewels in a bottle, Sis. Jewels in a bottle," Janetta sang back.

"They are like jewels," Dora whispered, "green, buzzing jewels."

Janetta nodded and continued drowning the flies. When they stopped their frantic swimming, their legs curled tight up against their bellies, and Janetta laid them out one by one on the hot cement to dry. When a fly that wasn't dead buzzed sluggishly awake, Janetta, in her omnipotence, smashed it with a flyswatter she held handy. Then she fussily brushed it out of her working space.

Their great-aunt, Ruby Fields, watched them. She stood by the kitchen window waiting for the phone to ring. Her hand held back a frilly blue and white curtain that was starched and ironed to perfection. When she was a little girl her grandmama, a Creole woman from Haiti, had spoken French to her all the time. But that language had been forgotten by her family when the old woman passed away. Ruby was trying to remember the French word for opposites. Now the only words that came to mind were English words for candy. Caramel and fudge. That's what happened when you mixed ingredients the way those girls' mother had. Sometimes caramel, sometimes fudge. Their whole family was light-skinned, all lighter-than-a-brown-paper-bag Creole. The girls' father had definitely not been Creole. His almost black skin had been a matter of discussion for the whole family. When he'd died in a car accident the talk lessened, but his complexion still got tossed around from time to time at Christmas dinners.

The children looked so fiercely alive as they stalked and scurried about the dirt that Ruby pressed her hand harder against the window.

"Why they chatter like little birds!" she exclaimed. "And what they doing?" Ruby looked closer. "Lord! Catching flies in a bottle! Nasty!"

"I seen 'em doing it," John said. "They just like the color and noise of them things beating against the sides of those bottles. Leave 'em be!"

"I don't know about you, John, but Mama raised the rest of us to be clean. Wilma, come see what your daughters are doing out there."

Her niece stood by the stove. She piled chicken bones high on a plate. They were steaming. Chicken salad lay chilled in the refrigerator.

"What?" Wilma said. She set the plate before her uncle and took a seat beside him.

"Flies," Ruby said. "They out there catching flies. In Lord knows what filth. That neighbor's cat uses my yard all the time."

"Oh, Unca John's right. They be alright." Wilma gnawed the remaining meat off a bone. She snapped the bone between her fingers and brought the jagged edges up to her mouth to suck out the marrow but changed her mind and dropped the bones onto the plate.

Ruby's eyes became harder. She looked at her niece. "That's no game for young girls to play. You're not teaching them to be ladies, Wilma."

Wilma's eyes acquired a bit of steel themselves. "It's alright, Aunt Ruby. They be real careful to step around any shit." She continued to break bones between her hands.

Ruby let the dirty word hang between them. She looked out the window again. You just wait, missy. Wait till they're grown and you can't control 'em. You'll come crying then.

Ruby knew it wasn't about control really. It was about being proper. Generations of her family had been raised to be proper. This new generation was going to hell in an egg basket. She would talk to Bea about that when she called but, knowing her friend, they'd probably argue. Bea had been a wild one in her day. Ruby looked at the clock on the wall. Where was that girl?

Bea was Ruby's best friend. She lived in Chicago. Every other week she called Los Angeles. The weeks she didn't call, Ruby called Chicago. The two women had been making these Saturday morning calls for thirty years.

The phone rang. When Ruby picked it up a voice with a Spanish accent asked to speak to Wilma.

"Maria's on the line for you," Ruby yelled.

Wilma wiped her hands on a wet towel in the sink and came to the phone flinging her fingers back and forth to dry them. Ruby cut her eyes at her.

"Alright, alright," Wilma said. She talked into the phone then turned to Ruby. "OK if Maria comes over for a minute?"

"What you asking me for? You live here too."

Wilma hung up and frowned. "She's gonna make her children orphans. She better hurry up and bring them over here." Maria was from Mexico and had left her three children with her mother to come to America to start a new life. Ruby knew she'd left a brutal husband, too, but being a Catholic hadn't divorced him.

"What she doing now?"

"She's cleaning house for a couple on the Westside on weekends." Wilma shook her head. "After she works at the day-care center with me she goes out at night and cleans offices."

Ruby grunted. She understood that kind of drive. It was the only way she had gotten her house.

"The couple Maria works for gave her some stuffed animals they won at a fair," Wilma said, "She wants to give them to Dora and Janetta."

Ruby grunted again. "Knowing those two they'll probably tear all the stuffing out," she said.

When Maria came, Ruby led her to the kitchen and made her sit down.

"I know what it's like to clean houses all day," Ruby said. "I was a maid all my life until my Social Security started coming in." She got a cup and saucer from the cupboard. "You got here so quick. You must of been up the street when you called."

Maria nodded and sat down at the table. "How are you today?"

"We be fine," John said. "Wanna bone?" He pushed the platter towards her.

"John, answer the poor girl in proper English. She's trying to better herself," Ruby scolded.

"Oh I understand," Maria said. "English slang." She surveyed the plate before her and picked out a thigh bone. This she thrust in her mouth.

"Well, not slang really," John said. "Different folks just got different ways of speaking, that's all. Most people don't speak proper English."

"Maybe they do in England," Wilma chirped.

"This ain't England, but for your benefit I will try to speak properly." His eyes twinkled on Maria.

Maria's eyes twinkled back. "You be good, Mr. John," she said. She had an unusually pretty face, heart-shaped with olive skin and thick black eyebrows. Her mouth was wide and full of sound white teeth. She wore her hair pulled back and braided. It brought out her eyes.

Ruby watched them as they looked at each other. Whoa, John! That there woman is married with three children. Well, married enough. You been a loner and a bachelor all your life. It's too late to change now. Ruby was suddenly glad that her brother had never taken her up on her offer to come live with her. He lived way out in Bakersfield. Good. She set the cup on the table and poured coffee.

Maria nudged the white grocery bag at her feet. She raised her eyebrows at Wilma.

"They're outside," Wilma said. "Let 'em stay out there a few more minutes. They'll know you're here soon enough. When it comes to presents it's like they got radar."

The phone rang again. "Thank God," Ruby said. "I was beginning to worry." She rushed to answer it.

"Bea, where you been?"

"Is this Ruby Fields?" It was an unfamiliar voice.

"Yes," Ruby said.

"I'm Bea's cousin," the female voice said. "I'm sorry to be the one to tell you this, honey, but they found Bea sitting bolt upright on the couch in her living room. Dead."

Ruby and Bea had been girls together, jumping with adolescent legs from log to log in the backwaters of Louisiana. Going off to zydeco dances and stomping to that music all day and into the night. Bea had snatched cigarettes sometimes. They had lain in the fields out back of her father's place talking deep into the night about the boys they had danced with, their pursed lips around the cigarettes blowing out a white haze between them and the stars above them.

At seventeen Bea fell in love with a white boy she saw in a Cajun band when she snuck off all by herself to a white dance. Ruby had refused to go. The one place Bea could not drag her was to white dances. Bea crossed the color line all the time with people who didn't know her. Her skin was milky white, her curly hair the color of sand.

"I'm colored," Ruby said. "I ain't gonna pretend I'm anything else."

"I'm colored, too," Bea retorted, "and white, too. I just do it to have some fun. I'm not trying to be passeblanc."

"But you passing just the same. The white world's got more things than we got. You see those things you're gonna want to leave us."

Bea hugged Ruby then and laughed. "I hate them for it," she said. "I hate them all except Clay."

Ruby realized her friend was more innocent than she was. She felt a sudden urge to protect her.

But eventually the world caught up with Bea. Clay had noticed her long legs flashing on the dance floor as he played his guitar. How could he not notice her? When she moved to music she almost set off sparks. He fell in love with her. When his parents found out they looked into Bea's background. Then they paid her parents a visit. Bea told Ruby about the awful scene. Her mother cussed out the boy's father in French. But in the end they sent Bea far up north to Chicago to live with a cousin.

Ruby's heart was broken. She had only been allowed to stay in school until the fourth grade, then she had to drop out to help at home. How could she write to Bea if she couldn't spell that good? She didn't have money for paper anyway. They lost touch with each other. But one Saturday morning after Ruby had been in Los Angeles with her husband for years she got a phone call. It was Bea. She had been back to visit family and had gotten Ruby's number. From then on nothing could keep them from calling every week. When Jack died, Bea came to Los Angeles to comfort Ruby. They cried on each other's shoulders from sorrow and joy.

Ruby learned that Bea had modeled some in Chicago. She had

saved enough money to open her own beauty salon in the middle-class black section of town. Ruby was struggling with three jobs as a maid trying to keep her house payments on time. Owning a beauty salon seemed glamorous to her. On Saturday morning she waited, coffee in hand, until ten o'clock when the phone rang. Talking to Bea was like opening a window and letting some sun into her gray life.

The week before Bea's death, Ruby sat hugging the phone to her ear, listening to the hollow rings.

"Ruby, how you been, girl?"

Bea never answered these calls with "Hello." Ruby could almost smell the smoke curling around Bea's head.

"I'm fine as can be, Bea. How's your week been?"

"It's been a wild week, that's for sure, child. You'll never guess what I done." Bea chortled.

Ruby had to laugh. No, she'd never guess. "Went gambling and won two thousand dollars again?"

"No, better than that."

"You spent your whole Social Security check on a hat you seen in I. Magnin?"

"I been stupid about money but never crazy. Girl, I got me a man."

"You got you a what?"

"A man. Remember those? Man. M-A-N."

Bea was laughing at her. Ruby didn't know what to say.

"Nobody I know?"

"No, no, child. I met him when I was visiting my old shop. He was selling beauty supplies."

"Selling beauty supplies? How old is he?"

"Younger than me . . . by about thirty years!" Bea shouted.

"Oh Bea."

"Oh Bea, what?"

"How much do you know about this man?"

"Enough. His name is Raymond. We love each other."

"In a week?"

"It's been longer than that. A lot longer. I just haven't had the words to tell you. What you saying?"

Ruby switched the phone to her other ear. She lowered her voice. "I'm just saying don't jump in too fast is all I'm saying."

"That's not what you're saying."

"Does he ask you for money?" Ruby blurted.

"What you're saying is that I'm too old and fat and ugly to attract a man. Any man, let alone a young one."

"I'm not saying you're fat, but you have put on weight. 'Specially round the hips, Bea. Now, you know I'll tell you the truth."

"He's moving into my place."

Ruby stood up. Just what she thought. Bea not thinking again. Just blundering along listening to her feelings all the time.

"Bea, if the Lord didn't want us to think he wouldn't have given us brains."

"He give us hearts, too, Ruby. And other things. Raymond makes me feel like a woman again."

Ruby rolled her eyes. She sucked her teeth. "Oh Lord," she exhaled.

"He made me realize I got needs."

"At your age? You better watch that high blood pressure."

"Ruby, I am old. I ain't dead." Bea slammed down the phone.

Ruby did not go to the funeral. She couldn't afford the airfare nor did she want to see Bea in a casket. She talked to Bea's cousin and found out that Bea had been having trouble making rent payments on her apartment. She had sold the beauty salon years ago. She was living off the proceeds, or so Ruby thought. The cousin told Ruby that Bea had been living off her Social Security. The money from the beauty salon had been spent. On what Ruby could guess. She knew Bea could not resist beautiful things. Clothes, furniture, jewelry. Bea had liked expensive things that sparkled and she'd had no qualms about going after what she wanted. What Ruby wanted to know was where had that magnificent man been? Couldn't he have helped Bea with the rent? That's why they were moving in together, the cousin said, to make ends meet.

Ruby slid the coins of her offering into the slot provided for the lighting of candles at St. Timothy's. She drew the long matchstick out of the box and lit it on the flame of a candle already burning. She placed her fingers around the purple glass candleholder as she lit her own. It felt useless, though. Nothing seemed to help her cope with the loss. She'd had a special mass offered up for Bea. She'd been lighting candles for weeks, but each time she walked into the church with its stained-glass windows she felt empty. When she walked out she felt the same. She'd never been like this, not even when Jack died.

"You're a good woman to be lighting so many candles."

Ruby looked up to see Mrs. Wright, a sister member of the Legion of Mary. She was skinny and wore a wig that perched unnaturally on her head. Ruby smiled. Leave me alone, she thought.

"We've missed you at our meetings," Mrs. Wright said. When she smiled her face broke out into a thousand wrinkles. "But we've heard about your loss and I just wanted to say I'm sorry. She was a close friend?"

"Very close," Ruby said. "Like a sister."

Mrs. Wright nodded her head in sympathy. "I know. I know. I've lost all my sisters. That's the problem with getting old. Everybody leaves you."

Ruby's hand trembled on the candle. She put her hand over her mouth.

Mrs. Wright arched her face in surprise. "You got to forgive, darling."

Ruby walked briskly out of the soft light of the church into the bright noonday sun. She almost trotted to her car, blinking her eyes in confusion. It wasn't right that she and Bea had quarreled the last time they spoke. It wasn't right that their last words to each other had been angry ones, missing the target, pushing against each other for understanding. It wasn't right. But what could she do about it now? Guilt and anguish made Ruby grip the steering wheel hard to stay in control of herself.

Ruby parked her car in the parking lot of Jae's Market. She waved to Mr. Jae as he drove out. She'd known him since he opened the market ten years ago. They often chatted about the price of fish and the greenness of the brussels sprouts. Ruby told him when she thought the produce wasn't up to par. He always humored her and even used her as a tester for more exotic items he thought of stocking. They traded dishes once. Ruby's hot gumbo for his dish of pickled cabbage. When Ruby bit into the hot, garlicy cabbage she thought her tongue was going to fall off, but she liked it. The next time she saw Mr. Jae he patted his stomach in satisfaction with one hand and fanned his tongue with the other.

Ruby went into the store. She bought the few things she needed—

coffee, tuna fish, pickles, bread. She walked back out to her car and fumbled with her keys for a minute. Then she got shoved from behind. Her breasts flattened against the windowpane. She could not breath. Someone, a man, was pushing her hard, mashing her against her car door.

"Don't scream, I've got a knife." His voice was raspy in her ear. He grabbed the keys from her hand, opened the car door, and pushed Ruby inside. She hit her knee against the stick shift.

"Aieee!" Ruby began to wail.

"Bitch!" The man grabbed the collar of her coat. "Where your money at? Where it at?" He fumbled around in Ruby's clothes. He pushed his face close to hers and held her with his eyes. They were bloodshot.

Ruby dug in her coat pocket. She threw her change purse at him. "There, there, that's all I got!" Her voice rose higher on each word. She reached her hand behind her and unlocked the passenger door. Ruby jerked her body away from the man. She tumbled out onto the blacktop. She screamed at the top of her lungs, crawling on all fours away from her car, away from the man's greasy face in front of her own, away, away. She didn't hear him escape.

Mr. Jae came from home when he heard about it. He made her sit in his office in the back of the store. He brewed some fresh coffee and made her drink it. When Ruby took the coffee mug, she noticed her hands for the first time. They were torn up, red and scraped, from the parking lot outside. Bits of gravel still clung to her flesh. Ruby brought the warm mug up to her trembling lips. She lifted her eyes and stared at the calendar that was tacked up on the wall. A beautiful woman in traditional Korean dress was serving tea in the picture. The police finally came. When Ruby closed her eyes she still saw the outline of the woman behind her closed eyelids, comforting her.

After the robbery Ruby stopped driving her car. Every time she pushed her key into the car lock, her fingers tingled, her breath came short. She felt that man's breath against her face, felt his hands brush over her breasts. She saw his eyes pinning her to the car door. She had been close enough to see the oil crusted between the folds of his nose. It made her sick to her stomach. For a time she walked to the store but gradually began to feel vulnerable doing even that. The neighborhood was getting worse and worse. Boys gathered, ganglike, on street corners. A woman had had her purse snatched just a month earlier one block over. Ruby began to wait for Wilma to come home. She sat at the dining room table preparing her grocery lists. Mr. Jae asked about her, Wilma said. Ruby told her to tell him she was fine, but more and more she watched the outside world from her living room chair. Or she watched the children play out back of the house through her kitchen window. Sometimes she tilled her garden, but the weather grew cold and her back ached so she stopped.

Bea's cousin called Ruby and told how the landlady took all Bea's clothes for payment of back rent due. The woman went into Bea's apartment while everyone was at the funeral. She took the jewelry, too. Ruby would have gotten a watch of Bea's that she had always loved. Now it was gone. Ruby raved about it when she was alone. She paced from room to room, calling the landlady the dirtiest names she knew.

Medical examination showed that Bea had died of a heart attack, but Ruby knew that wasn't true. Bea's air conditioning was out and that landlady had not bothered to fix it. Ruby knew how hot it got in Chicago. What with Bea's high blood pressure and having relations with that man, the heat must have killed her. Ruby began to call Bea's cousin every day. That landlady and that man ought to be held accountable, she said. Finally, the cousin told Ruby to stop pestering her. She sent Ruby a brooch that Bea had been wearing when she died. Ruby hid it under all the sheets in her bureau. If she couldn't have her watch, she didn't want a damn brooch.

As the year wound back towards summer Ruby felt lighter and lighter as if she didn't have enough weight to keep her on the ground. She felt her arms and legs tingle at night. They seemed to lift on their own volition like balloons filled with helium, rising higher, threatening to take her with them. Other times, as she drifted into sleep she felt a tremendous weight on her chest that seemed to push her down, down, down. When she struggled to scream she found that she couldn't. Her arms and legs and body were paralyzed and would not obey her. These things terrorized her. But she felt too ashamed to tell anyone about them. She began to have fainting spells. The doctor said she was healthy, but by August she had taken to her bed all day. She came out at night to eat supper. Maria came over often, bringing soup. Ruby noticed how close she and the children had become. Maria let the girls loosen her hair, like a carpet down her back, as they sat outside on the steps.

The priest from Ruby's parish made a house call, not to hear her confession or to give her communion like he did every month but for a visit. Ruby curled her hair the night before and put on makeup that morning as if she was expecting a suitor coming to court. Father Paul sipped his coffee in the dim light of her bedroom. Ruby told him about the theft of Bea's things. She couldn't keep the bitterness out of her voice.

"God visits the faithful with afflictions as well as blessings," Father Paul said. "Read the Book of Job. Find strength in that."

"I read it," Ruby commented dryly. "Just goes to show if it's not one thing, it's another." She was in no mood to talk about Job.

After the priest left, Ruby was ashamed of herself. She felt she had failed a test. She slipped down between her sheets and moaned.

It was the morning of the first of November when Wilma informed her that they were going to have a party of their own. Maria was taking care of everything. What for? Ruby wanted to know. Halloween was over.

"This is different," Maria said. "It is to honor the dead. A time to remember. El Día de los Muertos."

"The Day of the Dead," Wilma translated.

"You remember the dead in church as far as I'm concerned," Ruby said. "And you're talking about building an altar and putting dead people's pictures on it? Girl, I know all about that. That's that hoodoo nonsense."

Wilma folded her arms across her chest. "We're doing this. You're invited. But if you don't want to come that's fine."

"Well, I sure can't tell you nothing. Nobody listens to me. But that's pagan worship you're doing there."

That evening Ruby arranged her white comforter more snugly around her body. The spicy smell of chicken and herbs filled the house. Someone in the living room put a record on the stereo. It was in Spanish.

"Don't y'all be bringing any spirits in my house!" Ruby shouted out to them.

There was muffled laughter. Her two nieces appeared at her door.

"How you feeling, Aunt Ruby?" Janetta asked. She held a bunch of orange marigolds in her hands. With her hair and skin tone she was the various colors of a flame. She wore a bright yellow dress.

"Y'all are the only ones that care about me," Ruby said. She patted her bed and beckoned to them. The girls clambered up. Dora wore a white dress so luminescent it threw a glow across her dark brown face. Ruby twined one small tight curl on the girl's head around her finger.

"Who did your hair?"

"Maria," Dora said. She laid her bunch of yellow marigolds on the bedspread.

"Hold those in your hand, Dora. Don't stain my bedspread with them flowers." Ruby fingered the rufflelike petals. "Maria get these too?"

Dora nodded solemnly. Ruby thought how angelic she looked in the white dress. Like she was going to receive her First Communion. All she needed was a veil.

"You look real nice in that dress, honey."

Dora smiled so wide dimples appeared in her cheeks. She hopped down from the bed and twirled on her feet.

"I stand for life," Dora said. Her eyes slid sideways towards Janetta. "Yellow stands for mourning."

Janetta stuck her chin out. "Maria said mourning's important, too. My dress is as nice as Dora's, huh, Aunt Ruby?"

Ruby's eyes traveled down the girl's slim body. Yellow was not a color she would have put on Janetta. It wasn't that it made her skin look sallow. The bright yellow dress, the girl's red hair, the light tinge of orange to her skin competed against each other for attention.

"Janetta, you look as bright as a candle flame. That's what I thought when I saw you standing in that door with them flowers in your hand. Something as bright as you couldn't be in mourning."

"Maria said on the Day of the Dead yellow is for mourning and wearing white means life. Marigolds are the flowers of the dead." She thrust her bouquet out.

Ruby snorted through her nose. She was tired of hearing so much about Maria. "She calls herself a Catholic?"

"That's what Catholics in Mexico *do*, Aunt Ruby." Janetta was impatient. "Know what else? They go sit by the graves all night." She pulled a tiny oblong box out of her pocket. The box had a black string attached to the end of it. When Janetta pulled the string the box opened like a coffin and a skeleton popped out.

The two girls made claws of their fingers. They held them up to each other. "Whenever you see a hearse go by," they chanted. They fell across Ruby's bed, laughing uproariously, thrashing their arms and legs.

"Now y'all! Stop acting so silly!" Ruby felt sick to her stomach. She wanted to shake both the girls at once but felt too weak and small to do it. She pinched their arms instead. "Have some respect for the dead," she hissed. "This is All Saints' Day. You should both be in church lighting candles to them. Or praying for the poor souls in purgatory. When I was a girl . . . Oh, take your flowers and go."

The girls rubbed the bruises on their plump arms. They looked at her with wounded eyes.

"Come see the altar, Aunt Ruby," Janetta pleaded. "There's candles on it for everybody, not just saints. It is like being in church, except not as sad."

"Mama put a picture of Bea on it," Dora added.

Ruby threw back the covers of her bed. She drew the drawstring of her robe so tight around her middle that if it had been a wire it would have cut her in half. She shoved her feet into her house shoes and pushed the children aside as she strode before them.

The room was in hushed light. Candles flickered on windowsills and end tables. Ruby smelled incense. The strains of Mexican folk songs wavered softly across the room to her. It *was* like being in church. Ruby felt her anger leave her like water draining off her body. She shuddered, shifting from one foot to the other.

Maria approached. She wore a black dress and low-heeled black shoes. The candlelight reflected out of her eyes. She lifted her hands in welcome to Ruby, and the silver bracelets covering her arms tinkled like bells.

"So glad you came, Ruby," Maria said. She guided her to a chair. "Let me get food for you."

Wilma, who sat with a forkful of food poised midway between her mouth and plate, plopped the fork down and followed Maria to the kitchen. She grabbed her daughters by the elbows and dragged them with her.

John winked across the room at his sister. "You feeling better?"

"Some," Ruby said. She stared at her fireplace. The mantel was covered down to the floor with one swath of material of black and cream-white. Multicolored fish swam across its design. Whole baskets of flowers were arranged on the floor. Marigolds lay between candles and photographs and little toy skeletons on the mantelpiece. There was food, too. A whole pumpkin pie, tamales, chiles, and small bottles of liquor. A huge platter held rounded, flat pieces of bread.

"What's the food for?" Ruby asked, but she could guess. She hadn't grown up in Louisiana for nothing.

"The dead come and eat with us in spirit," John said. "On their annual visit." He forked browned meat into his mouth. "November first and second."

"How come you know so much about it?"

"Keep my ears open." He winked at her again.

"Bea's picture up there?"

"Yeah. Wilma thought it'd be nice to think of her here with us."

Ruby walked to the altar. She scanned it until she came to a black-and-white snapshot. It was a picture of the young Bea. Her eyes were direct and open as she stared at the camera. Her hair was short in a smart, small hat snug on her head, her long body dressed to kill in a well-cut suit. She looked poised to throw her head back and laugh. A part of Ruby wanted to snatch the picture down and stuff it into her pocket. Another part of her made her reach for the bread instead. She tore off a piece and popped it into her mouth. She looked at the face of the friend whose laughter she kept losing over and over again.

"Hi, Bea," Ruby said. "How you been?"

The Rag Man's New Clothes

GABRIELLE DANIELS

> To some people
> Love is given,
> To others
> Only heaven.
> —Langston Hughes, "Luck"

New Orleans, Louisiana, and San Francisco, California, 1961

Miss Rutha's body sank deeper into Mr. Man's stuffed easy chair in front of the Muntz television that talked on and on despite her increasing inattention. She had been drifting in and out of sleep, between release from and vigilance over the house, as when she swept dust gathered like gray cotton on the porch while looking up now and again to see the old man sitting quietly there. Her eyelids quivered. She hadn't heard the scraping of tricycle wheels . . . ne'mind about the child, don't worry about Ella: she gone, she thought. The front door gaped wide for the screen door to filter in a mild October afternoon. Her lap, almost always covered with an apron, was finally empty. The aroma of the pork chops and onions stewing on the back burner on low in the kitchen had reached the Front Room. Her blue head of hair bobbed, then stilled: behind her lids she saw herself in the new headdress, veil and robe she wore on Saturday night for Black Hawk service with the Sisters at the Israelite Divine Spiritual Church. The robe was all dark navy with a wood-beaded rosary around her waist. Now the rosary seemed to grow as long as living vine. She dragged the little silver cross as she walked, as if it were heavy . . .

Her eyelids lifted; she blinked and stared. Mr. Man was struggling up from the broken and rusty metal slider one more time that day, as the announcer was signing off *The Edge of Night*. She saw his back stiffen. "Oh, Lord," Miss Rutha muttered, rousing herself reluctantly, "he's doin it again."

Mr. Man left the porch, framed with pots of ferns and flowers in varying stages of bloom and decay. Two small green lizards from the garden on the side of the house eyed him carefully as he passed. His limbs were tenuously held together by the union suit buttoned close to his shriveled throat. Usually, he shambled to Mr. Joe's. "Where you at, Charlie?" he croaked to one of his buddies. Then he sat down at one of the chairs outside the bar to talk loudly over the pounding jukebox inside, play checkers and consider the world passing by three or four times a day. Then he'd get up and walk back and then start all over again. This routine did not bother Miss Rutha. But somewhere, since Cassie and little Ella left for California, he had learned a new trick. It scared her. She began to study each wobbly saunter until she could tell when he was going to wander. Instead of going to the left towards Mr. Joe's, he would walk the opposite way a little bit, towards Freret Street, his head cocked like an old dog trying to hear some secret language, and then double back to worry her. Because then he would be in a fog so thick, so quiet, she'd have to lead him by the hand inside. He wouldn't eat. Even Wire Paladin on TV wouldn't bring him awake.

When Ella was still here, Miss Rutha thought, she would wave at Mr. Man as she was skipping or ripping and running all the way to Manalie's to get some candy or some potato chips. She would play with her dolls and dishes on the other side of the porch, or after Miss Rutha had filled up the old washtub for her, sail toy boats into makeshift stormy seas. Her fingers would kick behind the plastic cabin cruiser "like a Ebben-rude," she said. Then Ella would scrunch onto Mr. Man's lap as if she were still a baby and hug him, kiss him until he would tell her, gently, how heavy she was getting, and to get off her tired old grandpa. Mr. Tejeau would have dropped Ella and the Newcomb boys off from Catholic school at about 3 o'clock during the school year.

Cassie would come home from separating laundry and suits and picking pockets at Marquise's pressing shop about 5 o'clock, Monday through Saturday. In summer, the cicadas would sing out just as she arrived. He would touch her arm as she greeted and passed him in his chair, and he would smile his valuable smile of filled and capped gold teeth. Later, Cassie would sit down with him and watch wrestling or *Gillette Cavalcade of Sports*. Cassie and Ella. Cassie and Ella gone. He had been so used to them. We both got too used to that, she thought, gazing at the little wooden rocking chair where Ella would sit and argue with Mr. Man over watching *The Flintstones* versus one of his Westerns. Grown man argin with that li'l girl, she thought, smiling to herself. Too used to that. She squeezed her wedding ring hand. Done got too used to that.

Now she had to remind him to put on a sweater as it turned cool. The union suit he wore was a compromise, but soon it wouldn't be enough. When they first got a letter from Cassie, and she read it to Mr. Man, he had forgotten they had a daughter, a granddaughter, and one somebody on the way. The deep lines in his forehead puckered into one gash. "Who's that? We know this girl, Rutha?" The next couple of hours, she had to shush him, because he was talking so loud. "Sister, Sister," he called through the screen.

"Yass, Yass," she said, "Yass. Em-Manuel, hush yourself up. Please." It seemed to Miss Rutha that the whole neighborhood was waiting for a response. Actually there was no one in view. "What you want, Mr. Man?"

"When little Ella come home from school? Everybody look like they home." He opened the screen door, and she backed up to allow him into the living room.

"Now you know betta. Ella and them gone to California. Been gone a couple of months." She stared at him as if to pierce the mist in his eyes.

"Why Ella and them left, Sister, without telling me good-bye or nothin?" He blinked and groped for the pack of Kents hidden, he thought, in his shirt pocket.

"What you smoking for again, old man? Know you ain't supposed to be smoking that much. That done got you all woolgathered." He pushed her hand away, but she took it again, firmly. Come on, she thought, come on. Almost like I gotta hit him on the head to make him remember.

"Where Ella at, Sister? *Toin* me loose!" he commanded.

"She not here, Em-Manuel!" she said loudly and carefully in his face, the acrid smell of the garlic he chewed for his high blood pressure full on his breath. "She not here. She gone. She gone to California with Cassie. She ain't coming home from school today."

He paused, trying for the shirt pocket over and over, the yellowed nails of his fingers unable to clip the pack or even a cigarette. This was the claw hand, withered from the stroke.

Emmanuel blinked again. "She not coming home today?"

"No . . . ," she answered. This was a sign. She did not dare say more; it might have confused him.

"Oh," he said, lowering his head, the light flickering in his rheumy eyes. Quietly, he allowed her to bring him back to the porch, to sit down on the slider. Then he seemed to get another idea.

"She coming home tomorrah, Sister? Is she?"

Today, Mr. Man brought along some company from his strange walk. Two policemen crept up behind him. "Hold it, Boy," one of them said. "Where you goin?" asked the other in a soft, triumphant squeak. They held him upright between them on the sidewalk. From what she saw, Mr. Man seemed dazed, fragile. They had snapped on one cuff when Miss Rutha pulled on her sweater and rushed out of the house.

"Lord have mercy! Just what, what you think you doin?" she shouted, her glasses flashing with anger in the sunlight.

"Well . . . ah." The first policeman looked doubtful.

The other policeman jumped in, quickly. "You don't need to worry, Girl. Ain't none of your business. We been looking at this man all day and the way he was acting he looked like he was doing numbers. We taking him in."

"Numbers?" Rutha didn't see the people peeking, coming out of their houses from across the street, upstairs, next door watching and waiting, didn't notice how the breeze had stopped ruffling through her blue hair. "Sit him on down over there." She pointed. The other policeman sidled a look at his partner.

"He your husband?"

"I said, sit him down there," Rutha said. Her finger looked more threatening than the guns in their holsters. Sheepishly, they brought the old man back to the slider.

"Take them cuffs offa him," she said shortly. "Now look. Look. Look at his hands. See anything looking like books round here? Look at this hand," and she lifted the withered wrist to show it, deep brown, hardened with infirmity, sandpaper dry. Limp. Em-Manuel! now they done done it! Poor Mr. Man, he was too quiet! "He can't even pick up a pencil, much less smoke a cigarette, and what would he be doing numbers for?"

The second policeman wasn't going to give up so easily. "Well, he was looking and walking up and down the street like he checking for business."

"As quiet as this street is? Look around. I said, *look around*. The man been walking like that cause he got nowhere else to go."

"Well," said the first policeman, who did look around and saw the waiting Negroes for the first time. "He sure looked. . . ."

"Get on outta here," she ground out stiffly. "You hear me? Get on outta here." Slowly, they turned away; reluctant to surrender the field, they looked back. "I said," Miss Rutha repeated with more heat, "get . . . on . . . outta . . . here." They retreated. She bent close to the old man. "Em-Manuel. Em-Manuel." She tapped him. "Man. Em-Manuel." She heard the doors open, slam; the squad car revving, then taking its time leaving the curb.

"What been happenin here?" asked a voice. "Miss Rutha! What the po-lice doin here?" A couple of the folks from across the street. The Wilsons. "Get Dr. Goldberg from across the street," said someone, motioning to the pharmacy on the corner. "Is Mr. Emmanuel all right?" asked another.

He's dying, she thought.

Cassie took out the platter of watermelon, now down to less than a quarter of its original size, and set it on the kitchen table. Her mind had fixed on the melon, one of the last of the season, with each passing step up the first hill on Sacramento, when she and Ella had set out to get a card at the nearby branch library. She hated San Francisco the most when she had to carry that few months load of baby up a hill, almost out of breath at the top. She wanted to tell the little girl to just go and get the card herself and be back by a certain time—she just didn't feel like it. But a sense of do-rightness had overtaken her. Ella could have forgotten her street address, also she might have to sign for Ella's card and the child didn't have her school tags to hang about her neck yet. She might wander about the library in one of her pretend-ings, causing consternation in the well-sculpted brows of the librari-ans. Just like when they visited the City of Paris—or was it the Empo-rium?—downtown for the first time. It was nothing like D. H. Holmes, Maison Blanche, or Godchaux in downtown Nawlins. Ella, in the pull and tug of the shopping throng, just slipped away. Cassie had been frantic looking for the little girl until she found her, oblivious to the crowd of shoppers, in the middle of the store awestruck at the domed ceiling displaying a gigantic map of the world. She almost whipped her right there.

Not looking, she felt for tines in the tableware drawer. Miss Yvonne, Nathan's aunt, would be back from her housekeeping job by about 4 o'clock, so the house was quiet except for Ella's pretend voices coaxing her paper dolls to life in their bedroom down the hall. Miss Yvonne came from Louisiana to San Francisco with her brothers and sisters during the War. They got jobs in Hunters Point, in Oakland, in Marin City building endless fleets of ships. They took over plenty of jobs when white folks went into the service. Then they moved into the Victorians, like this one. All the houses around here, she observed, were too close together hugging the hills, what about fire? They took over the houses where the Japanese disappeared overnight in the Fillmore, even packed into the barracks above the Point.

Cassie sat down, salted the watermelon and tried to pick out as many seeds as she could before she forked the first juicy, sticky bite in her mouth. She closed her eyes with a contentment bordering on afterglow. She grimaced; a slit formed from her mouth. Still, she had to spit seeds.

And Nathan. Ummmm. . . . Soon he would be here. Soon. She married Nathan, she told herself, to give Ella a father, but she hated to admit it: she had missed sex. It took her a while, however, to get used to its new, stronger smell; their juices hitting the air and commingling like a mad doctor's potion. She would be eager for his first touch. Then she would grow distant—a carryover, she knew, from being with Wade. Quietly, she would become unreasoningly furious, barely suppressing an urge to push him off her body.

Sometimes she felt a power akin to looking in the mirror too long. Sometimes she felt undefinable tingling in her thighs. Cassie didn't think Nathan had climaxed after he stopped doing it to her. She thought he had finished.

She would moan and talk with her eyes closed as she dried off the sweat on his back and buttocks with her fingers because it did feel good. It pressed down those layers of loneliness. Especially, of being that sad-faced, sickly little girl photographed in sepia on the traveling photographer's pony long, long ago. She hated being alone with herself even then. Alone in the house on Clara Street in Nawlins all day long and part of the night, waiting for Mama and Daddy to come home from work. She had long run out of pretending games. There hadn't been even an echo to answer her in the house. She didn't know what to do with herself. Loneliness seemed insatiable and pitiless, like little Ella's imagined boogeyman. Little Ella lying beside her, taking the place of her father, did not stay because there wasn't enough room in the house or even the boogeyman. Cassie thought the boogeyman would come for her too, and swallow her up. It roared in her ears when she heard Wade had married again. That his new wife had a little boy with him.

She had stood up during one Sunday dinner, the Queen Anne chair pushed aside and teetering, her hands pressing her ears trying to silence the devilish cacophony which seemed not one voice but several pealing out of her mind, about to push their cries out of her mouth like vomit. She had to run, get away before they—it—ate her up! She ran through the kitchen, odorous with chicken and gravy, through the Back Room with the altar and Ella's playroom, into the backyard. Her galloping mashed figs, which had fallen off the tree, into the ground. Mixed with soil and grass and stuck to her sandal, the fruit made her slip and fall. She lay in the grass in ninety-degree weather, trembling, hiccuping and sobbing, bewildered or angry insects buzzing about her. Inevitably, her mother stood over her blocking out the sun. Miss Rutha's hand rested tentatively on the young woman's shoulder. Later, her head down, walking slowly back to the house behind her mother (she shunned Rutha's arm), Cassie failed to see her daughter leaning outside against the screen door, her young Wade face tight: for the first time, she'd heard her mother crying.

Cassie's jumping up from the table and running away had startled little Ella, but the sight of her mother sobbing and talking through her tears frightened her. It was bigger than her own wails after she fell off the sliding board or fought with Meemsy Newcomb, who pushed her down. Her mother had warned her not to make so much noise, not to yell so loud as she played with the boys. She must be a little lady. But this sound, coming from someone who was so much bigger than her, this sound that was raw, deep and seemed to hurt from a boo-boo she could not see, made Ella scared to come outside. The little girl fled to the room she shared with her mother and slammed the door. She climbed over into the narrow space between the bed and the wall and hid her face on the lid of the box containing her Annie Oakley costume with the two six-guns. Much later, Cassie found her there, asleep.

After the divorce from Wade, Cassie had followed Mama's instructions. No trouble. No out and around the town "'fore day in the morning," warned Mama. Cassie became treasurer of the Women's Auxiliary of St. Peter the Missionary Episcopal Church. She was named secretary of the SocialLights of New Orleans. She was usually home by eleven-thirty. But she could never forget that her Mama had written that letter to Wade. The letter that brought her home to stay. If it was a letter—or maybe a telegram? The letter must have told him the truth: that Cassie had flunked school twice, that she never held a job while Wade was gone, that she had begun to see that boy down the street, Jacy, again. Jacy. That J.C. . . . It was none of Mama's business anyway, she sniffed. I think she was just jealous, mindin my business. She had never found it in Wade's things in New Mexico. Cassie half-believed she'd stay home forever, because of that letter.

At first, she had hated to see Mama watching her at times as if snakes would slide out of her mouth. But no more. She thought of how the gold-filled gleam of Nathan's teeth fascinated her, warmed her. Did she still want six children? She imagined his arms tightening about her. She slurped loudly over the plate of watermelon, her eyes closed to Miss Yvonne's kitchen. Then her mother's words came to her not long after she married Nathan:

"So. How many seeds you done swallowed?"

Pride curled her lips as she remembered. She was sure it was a boy. So very sure. He was growing so nice and round, so sweet and new in her stomach like that other watermelon, the one she bought off the fruit and vegetable wagon, the last summer in Nawlins. And it wasn't just a truck, but a horse and wagon, something one hardly saw anymore, except at the French Market for the tourists. It was good luck to see it, to smell the fresh fruit, to take the change pressed into her hand by the vendor, a red-boned man in a top hat with nappy hair sticking out on the sides who smiled openly despite his missing teeth. She spit out more seeds. She remembered his left front tooth had been capped in gold, the gold framing the ivory into a star.

She opened her eyes. Soon Ella would come over for some of the watermelon. Cassie debated whether she would give her any. No. She can't always have her wants, she thought. She was seven now, and she would have to understand that. I'm finished with her, I've done all I can, and the baby's going to be more important than looking in Ella's face. She chewed into a seed, felt her mistake, spit. Ugh, she thought. Don't look at that part of the plate.

Ella gotta take care of herself now. Didn't I have to learn from Mama and Daddy? When they had to lock me in the house all day so they could work at the laundry? I kept quiet and stayed inside the house. I played in the backyard. The police nevah came to take me away. They nevah was in trouble. Yes. Time to cut the cord. Ella too old to be a child. She gettin big and tall. One of these days, she gotta help me mind this child when I got to go to work or when I got to go out. . . . Let her know how it is to be a mamma. She ain nothing like me. Nothing. When she smiles, laughs, walks and talks, she's like *him*. And I'm tired of looking in her face. She's *his*, not mine. Girl babies—the face of failure. Make it work, I'm going to make it work, this baby's going to make it work. And it's going to be a *boy*. Cassie shifted in her seat, forked, chewed and fired, the platter *ding*ing and *ping*ing sharply as each seed landed in it or ricocheted on the floor. I'll get those later, she mused. This baby gonna be mine. She had dug to the rind. Her face grew warm. I had to learn who was fighting on the radio—Rocky Marciano, Joe Louis—so Daddy would love me, but this baby's gonna love me for me!

"Mamma! Mamma!" It was Ella. Cassie didn't want to answer. She hurried; she was almost finished with the watermelon.

"Mamma!" The first note of panic at the possibility of being alone. Cassie heard Ella scramble to her feet and run to the kitchen.

"No, you can't have none!" warned Cassie.

Ella was taken aback. She stuck her finger in her mouth. "None of what?" asked Ella.

"Water—" and Cassie gulped, her mouth too full to say more. Oh, my—she'd swallowed some seeds after all. Didn't Mama say that meant two babies, or another on the way after this one? Ella looked in the platter, at the scraped rind.

"It's too cold for watermelon, Mamma," Ella observed, "the fog is coming in." One by one, Cassie spit out the last seeds and took a breath.

"Mamma," said Ella, putting her arms about her mother's neck and hugging her. "Pick me up."

"No," answered Cassie, rising with the platter. "You too old for that. You too heavy. You see this," said Cassie, pointing to her belly. "If I pick you up the baby may not like it."

Ella looked dejected. "I'm not too heavy, Mamma," she answered softly.

"Yes, you are." She took a knife out of the utensil drawer to break up the rind into smaller pieces in the sink. Then she threw the pieces in the garbage, and soaped and rinsed the platter.

"And I'm not old!" the little girl burst out. "You're old!"

Cassie laughed. Well, she had to give the child credit. Twenty-six *was* old to Ella. She wiped her hands on a dishtowel. The seeds on the floor could wait. "Okay. But this is the last time, because you're a big girl now. And big girls don't need to be picked up."

Ella grinned. "Okay!" She's not listening, Cassie thought.

"From the den to the top of the stairs."

"Okay, okay!"

"Now, stand on that chair," said Cassie.

Carefully, she lifted Ella. But it was true, Ella was manageable. She giggled with delight and had a good grip around her shoulders, but Cassie let her slip farther and farther down, so that by the bathroom, Ella's feet touched the floor.

"Mamma!" Ella insisted, waving her arms in protest. "You said to the top of the stairs! Pick me up!"

"I told you, you were too heavy," said Cassie, roughly pulling her arms down. "I said you were a big girl. You're not a baby!"

"I'm not a big girl, Mamma! You cheated! I'm not a big girl!" cried Ella.

Ulysses come, thought Rutha as Sister Josephine drove the both of them in her little blue Rambler from the hospital. Ulysses come. He and Ida May, both finally come. I know he didn't wanna come. He didn't wanna come and 'member all that. Looking down at the only daddy he ever know after his real daddy up and left. Mr. Man his only daddy; me his only mamma. Siftin through junk piles to find a pair of shoes before Mr. Man come. It hurt a lot. It hurt almost too much. No account Alphonso Court. 'Fonzo. The ice cream man. I picked the ice cream man. And ice cream melts in the sun.

But he come, Ulysses come. Rutha bowed her head wearily. Not sayin nothin. Just lookin.

"Rutha, we here," announced Sister Josephine quietly. They had arrived only a few minutes before. They sat in the Rambler until Sister Josephine could see Ulysses slide next to the curb in back of them. Rutha began to collect herself. "You need some help out the car?" Sister Josephine asked.

The phone rang as soon as Rutha opened the door. Ulysses and Ida May decided to go home to see about the other grandchildren and return later. Cassie was on the phone. Cassie had had a son. But Nathan was absent for the birth.

"The ship couldn't let him go," explained Cassie. "I can't understand it . . . even if he had waited until the last minute to sign the papers, they should have let him go."

"Don't worry yourself, child." Rutha knew that was a bad sign. A daddy not around for his first child? Why was he in Japan? Hadn't he been there dozens of other times? What was so important there? And there was more she could not say.

"Mama, you okay? You sound so down in the dumps."

"Oh, I'm just tired." Sister Josephine, sitting next to her in the dining room, stroked her hand.

"Where's Daddy, then? I want to talk to him, too."

"Oh," Rutha said quickly, "he's asleep now, Cassie. He's all right. I'll tell him he's got a new grandson. He's got to rest. You just worry about yourself."

"Sleep? Is he sick?"

"No, child. He's not sick."

Cassie paused, because it all sounded so strange. And she had dreamt of her father the night before going to the hospital. There was a field of tall, man-high, golden grain. The stalks bowed and parted as her father walked through the field to meet her, his clothes inexplicably ripped to shreds and tatters. In his wake were rags and strings, which had floated to the ground. Even half-naked, his bearing had been regal and dignified. He asked her about the baby, and she woke up before she could answer. She almost told Rutha about the dream like she used to do in quiet moments, like shelling shrimp for gumbo or Creole. But she shrugged, thought of Rutha's fatigue and the second-by-second expense of long distance. It wasn't the same. "Now I want you all to come to San Francisco."

"We will, child, we will. You take care of yourself, now."

She hung up. Mr. Man was asleep. He was all right. He was now safe in the arms of the Lord. The week before Cassie's water broke walking down a hill, Emmanuel had finally collapsed and was brought to the hospital. He lingered, in and out of consciousness, as if waiting for something to happen. Rutha and Sister Josephine, who was a nurse, and Mimi Newcomb, Rutha's upstairs neighbor, took turns watching over him. Sometimes, they prayed and sang clearly and softly, Rutha taking Man's withered hand in her right, and Sister Josephine's in her left. Sister Josephine's free hand held a Bible.

One night, Mr. Man woke up.

"Sister?"

"Yass. Em-Manuel."

He licked his lips. "I been . . . so much trouble to you."

"No, Em-Man. You ain been no—"

"Sister." He licked his lips. "Forget me." She shook her head, her eyes puddling and spilling. "When I'm daid, and buried, just let me go . . . just forget me. Don't even . . . come back to visit me . . . don't tell anybody where I am . . . just . . . go . . . on . . . with your life." A finger lifted. "It's OK . . . OK. Just turn . . . your back . . . go on." He gazed at her long after he could no longer see.

He must have known, Rutha thought dully, as close as he was to dying, he must have seen the baby being born. Maybe that's why he was waiting, why he was staying so long to make sure the baby was all right. But I didn't want to upset Cassie, with that no-good husband not being there, or tell her how sick Man was. The shock could have killed her or killed the baby, or left her in worse shape.

Mimi Newcomb came from the kitchen with a cup of tea, and set it before her. Rutha hardly blinked. And yet the baby came. Two months premature, waiting for the old soul to depart from Man's body . . . "Sister Rutha?" said Sister Josephine. "Sister Rutha?" Sister Josephine peered into Rutha's face. The eyes were still, as if she were in a trance. "Her mind gone?" whispered Mimi.

They lifted her under the arms into the bedroom. "Oh, oh," said Mimi. "You got her, you got her? There!" answered Sister Josephine. They propped her against the headboard, stuffed the pillows behind her back. Sister Josephine had finished unlacing her shoes, Mimi unbuttoned Rutha's dress when she seemed to come to. Her white, expansive brassiere jingled with protective medals pinned to the right cup, as if she were a soldier decorated for life experience. There was St. Jude, the Sacred Heart, Mother Mary of Perpetual Help, St. Joseph, St. Michael the Archangel, St. Martin de Porres, St. Matthew and St. Theresa. Before Ella was born, Cassie had told her she dreamed about a smiling woman who wore a nun's habit and carried red roses. "That was St. Theresa," Rutha said. A patron saint of childbirth.

"Who. . . ?"

"Rutha? Rutha, you all right?" It was Sister Josephine.

"Who . . . who protect me now?"

"It's all right, Miss Rutha, we here with you," said Mimi Newcomb, who quickly sat on the bed beside her.

"He taken care of . . . " Rutha burst into tears, her breasts heaving, the medals fluttering in musical concert. "Mr. Man, he taken . . . he taken care of. I . . . I done buried two of them. Two mens. They . . . they taken care of."

Without warning, she tried to rip the medals off.

"No!" Mimi and Sister Josephine exclaimed, horrified. They tried to hold her arms. "No, Miss Rutha, no!" "You gonna hurt yourself, Miss Rutha!" shouted Mimi.

"*Medals!* Just medals!" Rutha shrieked. "Who's gonna hug me now!"

After the funeral, it was a long time before the house resumed a kind of routine. Rutha hardly went out. Old Miss Montgomery whined to her niece that her house wasn't as clean as when Rutha was doing it. Mimi Newcomb came downstairs every week or sent one of her boys to ask whether Rutha needed something from Manalie's or from Roosevelt's. She would weep silently in bed at night as the house creaked and moaned. Ulysses offered to get her a dog, but she shook her head. She read her Bible because she couldn't pray, and watched all the Westerns Man had liked. After the second month, she began to box up Mr. Man's clothes. First, his underwear: boxers, union suits, the undershirts like Clark Gable's. Rutha swallowed hard. It seemed like centuries since they last ran the laundry. It was a dim moment only thirteen years old. Man would strip down to this undershirt in the steam heat upon summer heat of that old place. Sweating every day, winter or summer. The steam pressers hissing like a nest of snakes. A fan which simply blew the heat back at them. The scalding water, the harsh soap, and the starch, especially the lye, ate at his arms and hands. Once Man scratched and scratched until blood came. When she would rub his tender arms and hands with cocoa butter or Crisco, he would laugh and say, "Smelling like a Hershey bar," as she despaired of his roughened skin. They all worked together, she in the front, he and Ulysses and two other men in the back. Each night little Cassie, wearing Rutha's apron, which dwarfed her size and made her trip, sat on the wood floor in the hall, big-eyed, waiting for the key in the lock, and then put her arms around her mother's waist or to hold tightly on to her dress even as she took off her coat. Sometimes Cassie would toddle to bed or Em-Manuel would carry her there after she would fall asleep between them. Then in '48, Man had his first stroke. Eventually they had to sell the laundry and she had to go to work for that General MacArthur–lovin Miss Montgomery . . .

Now the socks, the handkerchiefs except for the ones which were all white, including the monogram. She would keep his jewelry. Some of them might go to Ulysses: the cuff links, tie clasps and pins, his watches ticking or dead, with an old wooden box filled with rusting and corroding old coins. And then his suits and ties and shirts out of the closet and the chifforobe, all bought during the '40s, even the pinstripes subdued: all well made, and pressed to correctness. There had been fewer and fewer occasions after his first stroke when he could dress, so they were almost new. She couldn't help it one day: she danced with a couple of the suits, pinstripes against her chest, to an old tune in her head, inhaling his smell tinged with the odor of mothballs. That night, she even laid one of them next to her in bed. She slept with it for a few weeks, making the bed carefully, as if the suit still had a living body in it.

But Rutha could not bring herself to call the Salvation Army or St. Vincent de Paul's. Not yet, and not because it was just after Christmas. So the boxes lay around the footboard and to the other side of the bed, six in all, for weeks on end. The only bother occurred when she had to look for Em-Manuel's insurance policy in the safe; the boxes blocked the door. She saw the tidy little stacks of money, each bound double thick with a rubber band. They had always kept a little something in the safe with the wills and the insurance policies. They never trusted a bank completely. Old Huey had taught them.

She ignored Mardi Gras except for watching the young colored men, some with shirts off in the early morning cold, some with head rags preserving their conks, some showing off plumes and beaded aprons from this year's Indian costumes, practice their chants and dancing down Magnolia Street through a measured slit in the venetian blinds. Their dark, sometimes muscular, ashy arms and legs disturbed her, she suppressed the urge to rush out and yell they needed greasing before coming out in public! Sister Josephine knew her well enough not to pressure her come to Israelite Church with the other Sisters. But Sister Josephine would visit once a month and they would go to the Back Room. There was a fresh white cloth at the feet of the figures of saints while the accompanying candles burned in colored glasses. Sister Josephine did not fail to bring a new spray of flowers each time she came. Rutha would light some incense, and as the thin, gray fingers reached for the holy pictures against the wall, they sat down on the last chairs Rutha had from her Mama Matilda and prayed and sang for an hour or so. Sometimes Sister Josephine would bless her, anoint her forehead and breasts with perfumed oil and pass her hands over her arms ("may your servant Sister Rutha continue the work she was called for") and legs and feet ("may she continue to walk the beautiful pathway of happiness") while tears rained down Rutha's face. Then Sister Josephine would give her the sacrament. Afterwards, Rutha would cook, frying some catfish and okra for Sister Josephine and herself, and call one of the Newcomb boys to bring the leftovers to Mimi.

Still, she felt she could not call and tell Cassie Mr. Man was dead. She knew Cassie was too busy with feedings and shots and changings to be too concerned. But that would not last. Cassie asked about her and Mr. Man, and had sent a photograph of the newborn, who was named Nathan after his father. That too was a bad sign, she thought, and she went immediately to the Back Room to light a white candle for the baby. Then she wrote Cassie that she and Man would come during the summer, and sighed heavily when she gave the letter to the mailman.

Finally it was March, at the rim of springtime. For the first time, Rutha opened the front door wide to let the house breathe. Ulysses had kept the lawn cut but weeds had nearly choked the poppies, the geraniums and the Easter lilies on the side of the house facing Magnolia Street. The roses were hardly but wayward; they needed to be clipped and tied back. Most of the potted plants had finally died, except for the cacti and succulents.

She retied her hair net and found her gloves, the trowel and clippers wrapped in an old rug under the broken slider. She spread the rug, pulled on her gloves and knelt. She tore at the long grass as lizards watched and doodlebugs rolled into frightened balls, then skittered away as fast as they could. Dragonflies captured mosquitoes who hovered close to her meaty arms.

At first, she mumbled to herself. Why didn't Ulysses come and tell her about how bad the garden was? Then she hummed and sang to herself:

He never has failed me yet
Failed me yet
Faith and grace
Gave me courage
And His goodness
I can't forget
Oh. . . .
My nights and my days
He's with me
All the way
He never has failed me yet . . .

"Afternoon, Miss Rutha."

Startled, she turned and looked up. "Oh, afternoon, Mr. Reynard."

His broad smile seemed to take in all of her. Rutha managed to return a wince instead of a smile, and decided to stand up. Mr. Reynard seemed to lean over the fence in a wish to assist her. But she had no trouble getting up. Like he could walk through the fence, she noted. Or walk on water.

He was the Magnolia Street barber. He had three chairs outside his shop where at turns old men smoked and drawled softly in the afternoon shade. This was a more sedate group than the one outside Mr. Joe's. There they were, "sharp as tacks," dressed up with well-buffed shoes and shiny watches. Some wore hats. Mr. Reynard's shop closed on Sunday while Mr. Joe's kept rolling on seven days and nights.

Mr. Reynard cut Mr. Man's hair and occasionally shaved him deftly with a straight edge when Mr. Man grew scared of cutting himself. Sometimes she had let Ella walk over to bring Mr. Man back if he stayed too long, and the Newcomb boys might bring up the rear, the soft wool buzzed neatly to their scalps; their necks dusted with talc.

Mr. Reynard was as stout as she was, with his hair lightly conked and his cheeks slapped with bay rum. His long-sleeved shirt was open at the neck, and he was carrying a heavy sweater over an arm.

"I'm glad to see you're out again after your trouble." When she did not respond, he continued, "I hope I can see more of you as time goes by. We all"—and he indicated the neighborhood—"miss Mr. Man." His voice dipped. "I'd hate to see you shut yourself up."

Stunned, she did not answer beyond a "Well . . . ," but shyly shook her head.

"Well, I'll see you later, Miss Rutha." He walked up the broken pavement past Mr. Joe's, Manalie's on the corner of General Taylor Street and then beyond.

Rutha pursed her lips and then sighed. Oh, no . . . All that working in the garden makes you stop thinking, I want some ice tea, she thought. Then, she looked down Magnolia in the opposite direction, towards Roosevelt's store and Louisiane Avenue, and saw it—yes—another horse-drawn wagon. The fruit wagon man again?

Closer and closer it came at a steady gait, until Rutha pulled off her gloves and rushed to the corner as if yelling for beads from a parade float. "Say, Mister! Say, Mister! Over here, Mister!"

The red-boned man with the strange tooth, his top hat in his hand, stood respectfully on the porch as she huffed the boxes of Mr. Man's clothes outside. Then she pulled out a jacket, the one she had slept with and helped him into it. It fit almost perfectly.

"I know you could use it," she said.

She watched him haul the boxes up to rest on a mountain of rags. The horse scraped the asphalt with his right hoof a few times, the animal equivalent, it seemed, of tapping one's foot. She wanted to ask him what happened to his fruit franchise, thought the better of it, then waved him away in the direction of the departed Mr. Reynard. There must be a lotta rags in that wagon, she marveled. More than a hunnerd, a thousand even. Strings and remnants floated through the air, landing on the street, trees, bushes, telephone poles and humming wires. Look at the colors! Old cotton, stained silk, faded, torn, frayed, burned, part of a sleeve. Quilts! One could make a thousand quilts of things that will never again be completely whole.

PART EIGHT

Sapphire as Artist in the World: Black Women as Creators

I have spent most of my life fascinated by "normal" people and artists. No one in my immediate family was an artist, and though several family members have definite artistic sensibilities, the goal of my working-class family was economic stability.

When I was in high school and told my parents I wanted to be a poet, my father responded that poets were the poorest people on earth. That statement has echoed inside my mind for twenty years. I learned to keep my writing to myself.

After graduating from college, I was fortunate enough to meet colored girl writers, musicians, and visual artists. One of them had the audacity to believe that the entire life she had created for herself was art.

Other than writers I had read about in college, these women were the first living African-American female artists I had come into contact with. Sometimes now, I zealously chant their names and art forms aloud in memory of the emptiness and longing I had felt all the years I had known no Black women artists.

I have discovered that my artist friends are lifelines and mirrors. We affirm the righteousness of the artistic life for each other. We are each other's touchstone, springboard, and lightning rod, when it appears as if the world is unconcerned about our creations.

We rejoice now that Marcia Ann Gillespie is the executive editor of *Ms.*, Maya Angelou the inaugural poet for President Clinton, Rita Dove the first African-American United States poet laureate, and Toni Morrison the recipient of the 1993 Nobel Prize in literature.

And though we have seen many images of the singing Black woman, we have seen too few of the Black woman as sculptor, painter, filmmaker, photographer, musician.

Where are the models of the Black woman as artist, as creator? How do we struggle to create and define ourselves in a world often indifferent to the uniqueness and beauty of our multitudinous visions?

The following section is an exploration of images of Black women artists struggling against silence and invisibility to believe, as Wanda Coleman urges, in the absolute importance of our vision.

If You Lose Your Pen

RUTH FORMAN

and all you find is a broken pencil on the floor
and the pencil has no sharpener
and the sharpener is in the store
and your pocket has no money

and if you look again
and all you find is a black Bic
and the Bic you need is green

and if it appears beneath the mattress of your couch
but the couch is dirty and you suddenly want to clean
beneath the pillows
but you have no vacuum and the vacuum is in the store
and your pocket has no money

it is not your pen you are looking for

it is your tongue and those who speak with it
your grandmothers and doves and ebony spiders
hovering the corners of your throat

it is your tongue
and if you cannot find your tongue
do not go looking for the cat
you know you will not find her
she is in the neighbor's kitchen eating Friskies
she is in the neighbor's yard making love

if you cannot find your tongue do not look for it
for you are so busy looking it cannot find you

the doves are getting dizzy and your grandmothers annoyed
be still and let them find you
they will come when they are ready

and when they are
it will not matter if your pockets are empty
if you write with a green Bic or a black Bic
or the blood of your finger
you will write
you will write

Sister Outsider

OPAL PALMER ADISA

for Audre Lorde

we
women   black
are always
outside
even when
we believe
we're in
but being
out   side
ain't so bad
cause
we be
learning
to love
each other better
we be
learning
to listen
more closely
to one another
we be
learning
to allow
all of us
our humanity

sisters
are too often
out   side

fronting
trying
to get   over
but
we be coming
to   gether
coming
together
ending our silence
transforming
space and pace
searching
and finding
the most valuable
is often
that which is
overlooked   us

rent

gale jackson

the artist brought dirt home in bags. she brought home dirt and sticks and stones. she carried it all in her hands until, when that seemed too slow, she bought a shopping cart. then, bent with the weight of pulling her cart laden with earth, she looked like an old woman. she looked like a crazy old new york city bag lady carrying castaways and dirt and history. if you didn't look carefully you might not see the vision in her eyes. vision or not her son was a little embarrassed. he had been taught to respect his mother's art so he did not say much. her lover, on the other hand, definitively raised her brow. but the artist thought:

> something made them all shave their hair and go to a warrior
> stomp and dance like that and talk like that and probably think love
> was an act of the same brutality to the music they made grinding
> itself, scratching itself into a continuous on and on and on. some-
> thing made them mad. not high. not reefa or crack. them's symp-
> toms. those kids is angry. and rightfully so.

so. she took to filling a pan with water. actually it was a refrigera-tor fresh keeper drawer. she'd dip the canvas into the water then sprin-kle it with earth to stiffen into mud, like god almighty she made skin from mud. she planned to use branches of trees for hair. tree branches, grass, cord, ropes, whatever she could find in the concrete park near her home. she'd be picking between the bottles and the men whose minds were gone. she'd be picking for whatever she could find. to sculpt. first she made a woman. a woman with an ancient face, crying like all those grandmothers be crying now a days. a woman, like porgy, who thrust her broken body from a cart. the woman came first. she was followed by a tribe. the boy looked askance as this population grew and developed. the lover again, without one word, respecting still the art of it but afraid because so many folks be losing their minds, raised her brow. but the artist thought:

seem like the world turning off its axis. boys with uzis. just out
having fun. raping their mamas. killing their brothers. set up.
unhinged. needing to feel. looking for all the world like they
needing to *feel*. flesh. the axis. a hug.

it costs, the artist thought. so then she made one hundred babies
out of the mud stiffened cloth. the flesh of mud and cloth. the stuffing
of newspapers. the whole world inside of them. sculpt. the whole world
out. her studio became the cypress swamp or a doll maker's magical
shop. she thought:

they was in the news. our boys. faces full of defiance and naked fear.
eyes. lips. like an animal with a bit in his mouth. like a boy with a
bit in his mouth. one of my boys. fell off the edge. or was pushed.
holding his head down in perfect mimicry of a tv criminal pose. our
boys. guilty until. they was in the newspapers. they was on tv. it was
bad news. old folks say it always is.

she didn't know them but she knew them. it hurt her. it hurt them
all. the whole household cried real tears for the told and the untold. on
the rims of the bathtub. on the kitchen table. on the john. sometimes,
cause they had each other, they cooked and ate and laughed. but history weighed them down hard. it hurt. and her hands were caked with
mud. she wondered, she thought:

and where are my girls? faceless in the photos. seldom seen. never
heard. their dream swim silent, triumphant or drown. "the unprece-
dented rise of female substance abuse . . . " "the feminization of
poverty . . . " victims of. victims of. where are my girls? "thrown
naked from the roof . . . " found "floating naked in the tub . . . "
where are their names and the aspirations we poured like sugar into
dey mouths? could we have forgotten their mouths?

she dipped the canvas in the mud. she sculpt. she thought about
atlanta. she thought about lubie geter. cause his name stood out. why
did it seem like they were all, all those children killed in atlanta, floating in the river when they was found? murdered. had she gotten all the
stories mixed up? she dipped the canvas in the mud. it's dangerous, she
thought, to be a black child in the world.

something made them all shave their hair close and dub and dub
and grind the words back and forth and in and out. something
made them *feel* like that.

she dipped the canvas in the mud. she was crying. she was in mud
up to her elbows but she hugged her son anyway when he passed her
on the way to the refrigerator and he laughed the way the young can
laugh cause the world is rightfully theirs. then she picked up the stiff
brown cloth again. and she stared at that cloth skin. she stared at it, a
sculptor, looking to trace out what the wood offer. she looked at it looking to trace, to hue, to sculpt the imagination of a tribe.

Sapphire as Artist in the World

WANDA COLEMAN

after William H. Gass

The work such woman does in the world works on her . . . her movements her perceptions her loves. Life is intolerable in a society that
does not value/want her gift; especially when it does not want the
vision she must espouse in the act of putting herself in the world thru
art. What does Sapphire envision? Her innate loveliness of which she
may be defensive or insecure. But if she seeds her self-doubt in a nurturing self-love she may harvest the rapture of creation. Otherwise she
may fill herself with hate, but will her skin contain it? Hate blurs. Certainly she cannot create when her vision is blurred/out-of-sync/arhyth-
mic. Rhythm is a state of concentration so complete it leaves her
defenseless, opens to all in tune with it. Intonation is her other
means/meaning into sensation by which her faculties embrace/subvert.
To achieve satiation upon embracing she must *see* the world she
enlarges (with her art) clearly if not without fear. She is its lover and
she must excite it until its richness rises in response to her Afro-cen-
tric beauty perceived at last. To openly hate and fear her lover is to
invite rape. She must see the hardness in the blood, yet recognize the
hardness as required for effective penetration/dialogue. Therefore she
is the natural enemy of social oppression/impotence. She resists the
aesthetic softness of a society that would sublimate/smother her spirit.
In this context her subversion is catholic, but given sufficient direc-
tion/education her willfulness undermines everything false with exact-
ing precision. In the end her society will reject or even destroy her.
History is clear on this point. To insure her place in the world Sapphire
must make her art her revolution. And in so making she must remain
undaunted, without compromise. She must be aware of the power
which extends thru her bones, the profound stubborn belief in the
absolute importance of her vision.

My Muse Relentless

AKUA LEZLI HOPE

my muse is upon me relentless
he is the shover
he pushes and pushes me
and twists my body
with demanding caresses
my juice is not enough
nor is my sweat nor my fear nor my longing
my muse is upon me
and won't let me rest
we are coupled and gasping
he is the elephant in sky
he is the gray whale
i see the many teeth in his mouth
his full lips are parted
he does not bite but thrusts
me in another direction
turns me around and then around
applies me to his largesse
and wipes me with his generosity
he is what i asked for
he does not kiss but clutches me
i think i want to sleep
his tongue is in my ear
he fills my nostrils
his scent stronger than incense
i cannot shout him out
he flicks his tongue across my nipples
i can only sing him in
my muse is upon me
he is what i asked for
but he doesn't always visit

i have learned to make do in his absence
i keep a good kitchen
i have appliances
my muse is upon me
he is bigger than i thought
he drives me through pleasure and discomfort
he stretches me
i am dazed
he wakes me
my head reels with this insistence
i want to scream but others are listening
the silence drives the passion deeper
my mouth is open
my ears stuffed with the roar of his many voices
he is here
he is here
i try to accommodate him
i wrap my thighs around him
arch my back and
type

Bianca

BRIDGETT M. DAVIS

Bianca slowly pushes a needle into her black chenille sweater, then pulls it through, arcing her arm high above as the heavy black thread follows. Tiny gold sequins cling feebly to the sweater, waiting to be sewn back in place. They jiggle, then sparkle in the dim light of her little room. She pauses to puff her cigarette.

Nighttime is easing atop the daylight. In two hours, Bianca will be singing at the Nuits Blanches Club. She isn't ready. Her throat feels rough, scratchy, rebellious. She wishes she had honey and lemon to sip, to soothe. *I talked too much today in French class,* she thinks, *All that silliness about Thomas and his car. "Thomas, votre voiture est très rapide, n'est-ce pas?" Who cares? Who ever asks men named Thomas if their cars are fast? French classes should teach practical phrases, like, Of course it's yours. There's been no one else.*

This thought tickles Bianca and she laughs, causing the sweater in her lap to shake as two glittery sequins float to the floor, twirling and twirling before they land. The sight of their slow-motion fall makes her angry, robs the moment of its humor.

"Shit!" she says, tossing the sweater aside. Bianca rises, stands before the long mirror nailed to the closet door. She poses, bare chest brazen, hands on her hips. She picks up her sweater, slips it on over black stretch pants and pulls two sequins off the right flower design to match the one on the left. She likes this sweater, a real find at a vintage shop in L.A. She enjoys wearing a garment with some stranger's past woven in its cloth. She reaches for her cigarette, puffs hard, stubs it out in an I LOVE NEW YORK ashtray. She doesn't love New York. She loves Paris.

She has loved Paris since she visited the city for a week's vacation two years ago. One look at the Eiffel Tower jutting into the skyline and she was determined to save her money, sell her few possessions and move to the City of Light. Her goal was to be aboard an airplane, en route to France, on her birthday. She made it.

This is good, she thinks, studying herself in the mirror.

Strong, dark, 30-year-old face . . .

She was never cute. Her eyes are set far apart, her lips big and her long, slightly tilted nose out of sync with her face. Growing up, boys chose her to play first base, saved their love taps for the other, smaller, delicate-faced girls. She never learned that a flutter of the eyelashes or a coy glance could lure the opposite sex. Unaware, she courted herself instead of men.

Long fingers, square dignified hands . . .

Her mother had wanted her to learn the piano with those long fingers, but her father had taught her to garden instead. He'd been a landscaper for rich people living along the Florida Keys. By the time Bianca was 10, he was 65 and retired. She helped him cultivate the little gardens on his own two-acre property. In silence, they would plant, weed and prune rows and rows of vegetables in one plot, flowers in another. Her father didn't talk much. He let her wear overalls, taught her how to plant seeds beneath a full moon and water them at dawn, making the earth damp and ready for the sun. She used to imitate him, cracking her knuckles, then pulling the fingers until the joint popped—creating a pair of female hands still long, yet big-boned and strong.

Short, sculpted afro . . .

She doesn't like her hair when it grows longer than this, gets independent of her. Bianca spent seven years as a hairdresser once, in her other life. She worked her way through perky salons where circular light bulbs blazed around mirrors and everyone called everyone else Babe. Her clients were all white women. She loved their hair, thin and silky like horse tails or full and cottony like French poodles. Washed in two minutes, blown dry in five. Straight-forward, honest hair. Easy work. Nothing like the hair salon—beauty parlor—in St. Petersburg, Florida, where her mother stood on her feet, working for 10 hours a day for 20 years. Where permanent calluses grew on her mother's index and middle fingers from years of clicking smooth, blue-handled hot curlers between them. Sometimes burning her forefinger as she placed a hot pressing comb against a young girl's scalp.

The smell Bianca hated most. Hair frying. Cooked like catfish in melted grease or burned like a wayward lover in pungent lye. Hot curlers, hot dryers and hot combs used to whip those women's hair into shape, into submission.

"Sit still, Beatrice," her mother would say whenever she sat her down in that salon chair and came after her with the straightening comb. Her mother was business-like, curt and impatient with her, wasting no jokes or easy conversation on Beatrice the way she did paying customers. Fast was her mother, efficient and merciless—pulling the child's coarse hair back in a marble-topped rubber band so tight the neighborhood children called her Chinese Eyes.

She stopped sitting in her mother's parlor chair on a Tuesday when she was 14. That was the day her mother swung her around in that swivel seat and made her look at herself in the stark, bulb-less mirror.

"There's some things a girl ought to know about herself," said her mother, eyes staring hard into the reflection of Beatrice's smooth face. "You just listen to what I got to say. Don't you say nothing till I'm through."

Her mother parted a section of her hair, combed it, oiled it, sliced a hot comb through it, making it sizzle. Then she slipped the curlers with blue handles into their open-ended oven, leaned back, took a breath.

"Your daddy, he's not really your daddy."

Beatrice didn't move, didn't blink. Her mother kept clicking, clicking, clicking the curlers giving her daughter Shirley Temple curls she was already too old to believe in.

"It was just something that happened, before I found the Lord. I don't want you fretting over it. Your daddy, he don't know, praise the Lord. But you, you're a young woman now and you need this here information to keep you clear on who you are. No need for somebody out there in the streets to think they can tell you more about yourself than you can."

Beatrice stared back unblinking at her mother's reflection. "That's not true."

"Look at yourself." Her mother nodded her head at the mirrored reflection. "Do you look like him?"

"My nose," she said, touching a nostril with the tip of her finger. "Daddy always said I had his nose. He always told me that."

Her mother shook her head. "I did that, gave you that there nose. Do you know what hell this here household woulda been in if you'da come out with a pug nose? Praise the Lord! Lowery Jr., that was your real daddy's name, he's dead now. Now he had him a broad, wide nose. And I could see right off, you was gonna have my color, my eyes and his nose. So I rubbed it long. From the time you was a baby, I rubbed it every night. Sometimes before you fell asleep, sometimes after. Molding things on a baby is easy to do, what with their bones still soft-like and changeable. Why, Bruce Walker's got two little dents in his head today because his daddy gripped onto him the wrong way when he was a baby. Praise the Lord."

Her mother dipped one finger into a can of Royal Crown pomade, rubbed the grease between her hands, then smoothed it on her daughter's hair, pressing down so it made Beatrice's head go back, chin cutting the air and lumpy throat facing the ceiling. Finally, the mother placed a rough, greased palm against each of Beatrice's soft cheeks and whispered to the mirror. "Child, don't think too much on it. Talked it over with your Aunt Ethel and she agreed with me. Figured life would be easier for you all the way round with a nice, long nose. Just thank me, thank God and go on 'bout your business. The Bible say, 'My God will supply all your needs according to his riches in glory by Christ Jesus.' Praise the Lord." Then her mother patted Beatrice's shoulder three times, the way she did her customers before she said, "That'll be six dollars. You have a good day now. Keep that hair oiled and I'll see you in two weeks."

That was a long time ago. The last time she sat in her mother's parlor chair. She was relieved when the Black Power movement came to Florida, freeing her from her mother's hostile hot comb. She wore an afro, big and bushy at first. As she grew older, the hair got shorter. She kept it natural and it kept her free. Free like the white girls. Free to walk into the shower with shampoo instead of a shower cap and free to go swimming without concerns about her hair going back.

At 16, Beatrice left home. She took nothing with her, not even her name. Left it in the beauty parlor mirror, in her mother's creased face, in those rough hands that had rubbed her father away.

She ran off to a university in Arizona, the one that sent a nice letter to the house saying they were looking for Negro girls to train to be nurses. That didn't last. She attended two classes, then never returned. The maxim "Doctor Knows Best" irritated her. She decided to do hair instead. What Phoenix did teach Bianca was the sex appeal of a sunrise. For the ten months she lived there, enrolled in beauty school, she often stayed up through the night—forgetting to sleep just to watch the way the sun slipped out of the flat earth, rich and orange and runny as an egg yolk naked from its shell. But a sunrise isn't everything.

Her next stop had been Atlanta. "Southern comfort is what I know," she told a manicurist friend the night before she left Arizona.

Then came New York. "The Big Apple has so many people, nobody will have time to pay me any attention," she said to Joel, her Georgian roommate. "You can have my bicycle. I won't be needing it."

Los Angeles was next. She liked L.A.: Working at a salon in Beverly Hills, catching famous and beautiful women with water dripping down their faces, shampoo stinging their eyes. Still, flawless women can be boring too.

"I don't think I could live in another country, always feeling like an outsider," said her Californian girlfriend, Wendy, as she helped Bianca pack for her move to France.

"Paris is the only place I feel like an insider," Bianca said, rolling a pair of leggings and stuffing them into the corner of her khaki duffel bag. "It's like finding your soul mate. I just know I'll fit in there."

"Yeah, maybe. But I've seen those movies about American expatriates who never really feel accepted." Wendy frowned. "You know, they're not French, so they get snubbed, then they come back here and they don't feel right in America because they've been gone too long. They don't fit in *anywhere*. I mean, look at poor Rick in *Casablanca*. That's no real life, if you ask me."

"You watch too many movies, Wendy. Besides, I'm not going to be an ex-whatever-the-word-is. I'm finally going to belong somewhere, live someplace that feels like home for a change."

"You'll get bored, Bianca. You're a drifter. Face it. Wherever you lay your hat is your home."

"So I'm laying my hat in Paris, okay? Now, help me zip up this bag, honey, before I miss my plane."

Now she is here. Singing. A year she has been in Paris, first washing the hair of French women in a salon near the Champs-Elysées. Traveling across the border to Amsterdam every two months to renew her visitor's stamp in her passport. Shocking the salon owner when he asked her to do the hair of the models from Martinique, Ivory Coast and Haiti who came in for quick wash, blow dry and curls. "I don't know how to do black women's hair," she told him. He fired her right then, said "he needed a more versatile American girl working for him."

"Ahhh, your voice, it's so, how do you say, sultry." The French men said that to her. They found her voice husky, its masculine sound making it ever more arresting and inviting.

"You are a singer, no?" They asked that question again and again. One day she walked into a tiny bistro near Montparnasse and announced: "Je suis une chanteuse. I am a singer." They hired her.

Now she is a singer—with Rolland's band. Rolland knows she grew up listening to no music in her mother's strict, Pentecostal house. Nothing except an Aretha Franklin album slipped to her by a next-door neighbor. She played it very low on a record player she kept hidden under her bed. She'd have to lie on the floor to listen. To Bianca, the gospel-tinged soul singer sounded like what music magazines said she was—a "fast" preacher's daughter. In the world and of it. Bianca thought of her as a kindred spirit. So that, the day she decided to start singing, she had only Aretha as a guide. Not to sound like her, but to sing like her—without faking. So Bianca opened her mouth and let whatever come out, to hear what her own life sounded like. Every time she sang, she was as eager as the audience to discover what that sound was. Based on how one phrase came out, she'd adjust the next. So Bianca seldom sang the same way twice. In fact, she didn't think of it as singing. She thought of it as exploring herself while people watched. It excited her.

"The most erotic place in the world to be," she told Rolland, "is on stage. I mean, where else?"

Bianca wants a residence permit. She needs a permanent job, which means she needs Rolland. Or she needs citizenship, which means she needs a husband. A husband who will be too full of himself to notice the absence of domestic detail. A husband who will give her a Yorkshire terrier and a house. She'll give him foot massages and occasionally sex. Then Paris will truly be home.

In the hall, she can hear the girls' laughter. They are waiting for her outside the door. They knock, two small fists with pink knuckles rapping in unison. Bianca swings open the door.

"We are so long waiting for you," says the long-haired blond one.

They are French girls, sisters, young, giggly. Virginie and Magdeleine. They want Bianca to call them Ginnie and Maggie. "We will walk with you to the club," says Magdeleine, the short-haired brunette. Bianca hugs them both. The girls enjoy speaking English with her, to improve their own textbook knowledge of American talk. Bianca's fragmented French barely gets the same workout when she is with them.

She met them near the university. Magdeleine was carrying three books: one by Camus, another by Anaïs Nin and her own hardcover diary. Virginie's hands were free. They have become useful friends, these giggly girls. They usher Bianca through the real Paris, the Paris kept tucked away from tourists behind affected French snobbery. Bianca has sat in the window seat of their parents' summer chateau and secretly watched their *maman* crying on the lawn. She has slept overnight, three abreast in the giant, soft featherbed of the girls' sprawling apartment with its view of Notre-Dame. There they curl up on either side and feed her stories of quiet, French childhoods, of times when they brought home good grades from boarding school and their mother let them crawl into her bed and sleep beside her. "It is a very big treat for French children to sleep with their mamans," explained Magdeleine. "It is very much a honor."

And too, she has drunk champagne from crystal glasses while listening to the girls' uncle play French nursery rhymes on the grand piano while everyone drank too much and sang and laughed. The uncle Bianca thinks of often. His blue eyes smiling at her over the piano keys as he sings. He speaks little English. She speaks less French. They have seen each other twice. They smile across rooms.

"Let's hurry, I want to get to the club early tonight," says Bianca, grabbing both girls' hands as they head out of her room at the student residence and onto the crowded streets of Boulevard St. Michel.

An American dance movie is playing at the St. Michel Cinema. Bianca stares into the eyes of the girl looming over them on the billboard above, her long legs gapped, a ripped t-shirt dropping from a shoulder blade. Bianca likes her. She read that this girl auditioned for the leading part in the movie without knowing how to dance. And she got the part. Someone else, someone unknown, someone with hair like hers filmed the dance scenes. But this girl, the one staring down from the billboard, got the part. "She's flawless," says Bianca as they pass under the Flashdancing girl's stare. "Flawless."

Ten blocks they walk to the club and once there, Jean Claude, the owner, jokes with her about her portable fan club. The French girls enjoy being groupies. They plop down at a front table, happy to sit for an hour before the show begins. Jean Claude prepares hot water and lemon for Bianca's throat. She carries the drink to the empty stage, stands spread eagle and sips.

"Mademoiselle, I have a message for you," says Jean Claude, approaching the stage. "It is a caller from London. A Jasmine Bridges. She has left for you a number." He hands her a piece of paper.

"Jasmine?" Bianca pauses. *Oh,* she thinks. *That doe-eyed girl who came dancing with us at Le Place a while ago. The one Rolland brings around the club sometimes.* Bianca stares at the paper in her hand. *What does she want with me? She wears skirts and high heels. She's one of them.*

For years, Bianca has stayed away from other black women. She believes they talk about black men as if their penises are jewel-encrusted. "My man this" and "My man that." And when they're not talking about their men and how to keep them, they're talking about other women.

"Girl, did you see what that child had on? Now you know she ain't had no business wearing a dress that tight. Must be a leftover from the old days when she was two sizes smaller."

She used to listen to them talking on and on in her mother's beauty parlor. She doesn't understand them, their conversations, their preoccupations. So obsessed with holding on to their lover-men. Lover-men with whom they eat big, home-cooked meals, only to go on crash diets. Lover-men with whom they sit lethargically in front of ball games they don't understand, only to frantically join aerobics classes later. Lover-men for whom they spend their money on silk dresses with matching pumps to show off big behinds and big legs, only to pay their rents ten days late. And lover-men for whom they get their hair fixed on Saturday mornings, only to sweat out the edges in Saturday night beds. She doesn't understand them.

The only black women she ever knew were the ones who came through her mother's shop and the ones who went to school with her at St. Petersburg Grammar and High. They were all the same. You mention the way the sun comes up over the horizon at dawn and makes the dew glisten on magnolia leaves, they want to tell you how white women are taking their men. As if that somehow changes the beauty of a sunrise. Black women, she thinks, don't notice the blues and oranges and greens of the world. They know only two colors. Absorbing life the way her mother watched *The Wizard of Oz*—on the old black & white TV. By the time she and Toto landed in Oz, for all Bianca's mother knew, Dorothy hadn't gone anywhere. She was still in Kansas.

Here in Paris, Bianca can experience every color Oz has to offer. She can meet people, people who accept her and can help her. People like the French girls. The giggly sisters are fascinated by her, without judgment and without expectation. They could never say, "Who she think she is, Miss Thing, walking around like she don't recognize the black on her?" the way girls whispered when she walked by back in St. Petersburg.

She wants to get to know the French girls' uncle. He could be the answer to her residency dilemma. Or Rolland. He could help too. She thinks of this as she walks into Jean Claude's office, closes the door, grabs his private telephone and dials the London number.

"Hello?" says Jasmine.

"It's Bianca, honey. I heard you called?"

"Yes . . . yes I did," says Jasmine. Her voice is breathy. "I'll be in Paris for the day. To shop. And, well, I wanted to talk to you about . . . I have a favor to ask of you. I wanted to know if you'd have time to meet me for lunch tomorrow?"

"A favor?" Bianca raises her eyebrows. "You want a favor from me?"

"Yes I do. But I have to talk to you about it in person, okay?"

"All right, I suppose we could meet. If you like."

Jasmine lets go of a fat sigh. "Good. Is noon all right?"

"Fine. You could meet me here at the club." Bianca says goodbye, then shakes her head.

Why would she want a favor from me? she thinks. *"I don't have anything she could use."*

The soft strains of Rolland's sax drift back into the office. Bianca clears her throat, then strolls quickly out of the room, moving toward another night of what she's come to crave—anonymous applause.

PART NINE

A New Kinda Woman: Twenty-First-Century Black Women

One of the main characters in the first feature-length film in theatrical distribution by an African-American woman, Julie Dash's *Daughters of the Dust,* is described as a "new kind of woman." A woman who makes independent sexual choices, Yellow Mary is financially independent, bold, mobile, and ripe with the wisdom of life, as well as respectful of nourishing aspects of tradition and family. She is a powerful model for African-American women of any century.

Now, as we stand at the cusp of the twenty-first century and look into the knowing eyes of our sisters, we see mirrored there hope, courage, and an undying flame of resistance.

We learn from the determination and grace of our mothers' lives and prepare stronger emotional lives for ourselves and our daughters.

We celebrate our bountiful, indestructible Blackwomenselves and in the words of Ruth Forman, touch, in our deepest darkest places, our power.

Raised by Women

KELLY NORMAN ELLIS

I was raised by
Chitterling eating
Vegetarian cooking
Cornbread so good you want to lay
down and die baking
"Go on baby, get yo'self a plate"
Kind of Women.

Some thick haired
Angela Davis afro styling
"Girl, lay back
and let me scratch yo head"
Sorta Women.

Some big legged
High yellow, mocha brown
Hip shaking
Miniskirt wearing
Hip huggers hugging
Daring debutantes
Groovin
"I know I look good"
Type of Women.

Some tea sipping
White glove wearing
Got married too soon
Divorced
in just the nick of time
"Better say yes ma'am to me"
Type of Sisters.

Some fingerpopping
Boogaloo dancing
Say it loud
I'm black and I'm proud
James Brown listening
"Go on girl shake that thing"
Kind of Sisters.

Some face slapping
Hands on hips
Don't mess with me
"Pack your bags
And get the hell out of my house"
Sort of Women.

Some Ph.D. toting
Poetry writing
Portrait painting
"I'll see you in court"
World traveling
"Stand back, I'm creating"
Type of Queens.

I was raised by
Women.

the corner is not a place for hiding

jonetta rose barras

I cannot be held
to past peace offerings
old jambalaya recipes
I am
losing me
who followed Father Kenny
at the way of the cross
reading Latin
wondering
what does all this mean
why can't I shout
run up the aisle
why do I persecute myself
mea culpa, mea culpa, mea
maxima culpa
traditions sometime
slow
my
pace
I want to move faster
lose all control
be unrestricted
dance from the corner
stand
in the middle of the room
naked
exposed

Prayer for the Nineties Woman and the Natural Woman Too

TAMARA MADISON-SHAW

These iron-pumping, track-jogging, Jazzercise-stepping, food-starved, anorexia-nervous, bulimia-bitten, thyroid-thumped, lipo-sucked, cosmetically-cut, electrolycized, bikini-clad women with their cropped-shoulders, propped balloon-breasts and stiffly-starched spines can kiss my cafe au lait, never-girdled, swivel-hipped, untamed behind that rumbles with its own rhythm, five foot eight, 200 pound, stretch mark–strumming, AAA grade, no artificial flavors, sweeteners, or preservatives, 100% natural woman entire ass.

Amen

Matchmaker, Matchmaker

COLLEEN McELROY

Cassie's hair was cut like a whisper and barely covered her scalp. Her knee-high boots extended the length of her slender legs, and the Tuareg shawl she'd draped around her driver's jacket merely confused the old men who turned to watch her pass. She had no sooner stepped into the metallic light of the entry-level vestibule when one leaned forward and in a hoarse voice, wet with the rattles of age, called to her: "Hey girl." Cassie pretended not to notice the men. On her routes, she had seen groups like this in terminal buildings of every city—old men who had been transit workers or veterans of the last war or those who simply loved the notion of travel, but now were confined to watching others come and go while they basked in the fake solar light of an atrium preserve. There were six of them sitting on the benches in front of the Kalava Station atrium. Two at the end of the bench were dressed in old-style Army uniforms, fatigue greens the military hadn't used for over a decade. Those two concentrated on a fast-shuffle card game, but the other four chewed on random subjects like goats put out to pasture. It was one of those four who had yelled at Cassie.

The culprit was at the periphery of her vision, but Cassie could see his buddies were egging him on. They were the type who made daily visits to the terminal, and after years of watching women walk away from them, they had fixed notions of what they were willing to accept as female. Cassie did not fit those notions. Not that she knew, nor would have cared to know exactly what those old men were whispering. As she walked down the aluminum sweep of the hallway, past the benches where the men squandered a great deal of their remaining days, she had only one thought on her mind: She was late, and her lateness would limit the amount of time she'd have to relax before her next client. Fran would already be in the lounge, ready to chide her for being late, although Fran had never been known for her punctuality. But more importantly, Willow would also be waiting, her electric chair locked against a table, her agenda set, her mind impatient to get on with the day. Cassie wasn't quite sure she was ready to deal with another one of Willow's lectures, and she certainly wasn't willing to be the brunt of a discussion of how time was running out for everyone. She pressed the button on her watch, but almost before the sequence appeared, one of the old men yelled: "Hey what time it is?"

She looked at him and shook her head. It was the same old man who had called to her before. She recognized him by his dark skin, creased and more leathery than the man-made fabric she was wearing. He was grinning, so she extended the movement of her hand from her watch into some gesture that might have passed for a greeting—partly out of deference to his age, and partly to acknowledge that his color, like hers, set him apart from those around him. But even as she wiggled her fingers in his direction, her inner voice told her to ignore him. *You'll never get rid of him,* the voice said, and as if to confirm her suspicions, the old man shouted: "Hey, com'here. I got some talk for you."

Cassie walked a bit faster. Not that the old men could tell the difference. From the way she walked, they would not have known she was hurrying. She timed her stride, using the muscles of her hip and leg to extend the width of her next step. Her shoulders turned into each footfall so that her body moved in a coordinated measure of shoulder, torso, and leg. With this pace, she could have walked for hours, if she were allowed hours of walking time. She was not. In fact, as a licensed driver, Cassie rarely walked, and when she did, like today, she had to make the most of it. So she walked in a way that loosened all of her muscles, the echoes of her boots spilling into triangular patterns of sound—floor to wall and then to bench, where the old men's bodies blunted the reverberations of acrylic tiles and metal wall panels. Cassie moved past the men, her head held high, her footsteps propelling her forward in long lithe movements like those of a soldier or a pole vaulter. And the old men shook their heads and muttered about the decay of the young generation.

These old men had seen their share of generations. They had lived through births, deaths, the country's wars, the surprise of a new century. Now life had left them with the leisure time of occupying a hallway bench outside the transportation terminal's atrium. There, they watched people rush back and forth to vehicles they had only dreamed about as young men. In those days of watching, they saw travelers, like Cassie, who could make a trip from one continent to another, indeed one space station to another, in as much time as it took them to remember the names for all the modes of travel. Watching filled the time of their days, and travelers, like Cassie, occupied their minds for comfortable stretches of that time. While she was in view, several of the men would consider the earth tones of clay, sky, and feather painted onto Cassie's loosely woven shawl, or the glimmer of her light brown scalp showing through the dark smudges she passed off as hair. Fewer still would recall the leathery gleam of her polymar boots and jacket emblazoned with the insignia of an independent driver, her long fingers clustered with rings, or her eyes, bright with the relief of indoor light after so many hours of driving across the midland states. But most would enjoy the conspiracy of watching that allowed them to exchange comments about Cassie or any other hapless passerby. And when she reached the bend in the corridor, they would let Cassie's image disappear from their minds as easily as if that turn in the hallway had led her into deep space or another dimension. But all of them would follow the pattern old men had followed for millennia: As she walked away, they would look at Cassie's hips swaying and try to remember how it was to feel a woman's body next to theirs.

It was just as well they could not let Cassie know what they were thinking. In her world, she gave little time to any man who examined a woman in terms of how well she fit some imagined form. And unlike those old men, she was well aware of how a body's shape could be altered, how liposuction or diapliation or molecular surgery could bend the body into new configurations. Cassie knew how to operate the many components of a complicated transportation unit, and for her, the body was a muscular unit that could be tended with the same detachment as any machine. Fifty years earlier, she would have been labeled athletic. Twenty-five years earlier, that label would have changed to naturalist. But in her world, the line between the natural and the artificial was a mere convenience marked by survival and degrees of efficiency. No, it would not have been a compliment for the old men to suggest that it was simply a pleasure to watch the youthfulness of her body. "Sometimes you have to download all that efficiency crap," Fran would say. And Willow, who years ago had run out of patience with sex, would add, "What are you going to do when you're sixty? Look back at nothing?"

Cassie may have had a vague second of wondering what those old men were thinking, but she stuck to her primary objective of placing one foot firmly in front of the other, and high-stepping to the terminal lounge. As she covered the distance of the entry-level hallway, she barely acknowledged the sight of the atrium—its dingy palm fronds leaking color onto plaster-cast statues, set there to represent the new century's celebration of natural life. Three dwarf deer and the handful of birds managing to survive in the terminal's preserve drooped from the midday heat of solar lamps turned too high for a northwestern climate. Cassie remembered her parent's description of early atriums planted throughout the city—"so dense with vegetation, leaves rustled like running water, and flocks of birds mated and squabbled all the time," her father had told her. Cassie moved faster, urged not only by her lateness, but by the desultory sight of animals too drowsy to move out of the direct rays of the solar lamps. As a result, she was almost overpowered by the aquarium's green darkness when she turned the corner at the end of the corridor.

The sea pool marked the shaded area leading into the lounge, and unlike the vestibule entry, where the old men were soaking up the atrium's artificial sunlight, the shadowed hallway was slightly damp and rank with the odors of salt water oxidizing on the retaining walls. Cassie could see a few bottom fish scouting the depths of the aquarium, but she was not close enough to the wall to view the upper levels of sea life. Not that she needed to. There were thirty or forty such atrium–sea pool preserves in the city, and down the coast, near the space portal, nearly twice as many. More than once, she had picked up a client who wanted to tour a city's preserve. When she was first licensed, those tours were a respite from the hard driving of open road. Later, they became an excuse to park at the landing ramp and stay inside her vehicle while her clients marveled at how nature could be incorporated into commune living. Now, all she recognized was the integrated stench of chemical solvents and algae. That, and the absence of sound.

"Silence. That's the way it is up there," one of her clients had told her when she picked him up at the launch base. "It's so damn quiet that sometimes all you can monitor is your own sweat building. Then you start to hallucinate and think it's some kind of ship coming after you." As soon as the car had left the launch site, that client had ordered Cassie to take him to the nearest public place—"anything with human noise," he'd said. She'd taken him to Kalava. In less than an hour, he was ready to go home to Ocean Six. "My ears hurt," he'd told her. When he'd left, the silence was deafening.

Now, she pushed her way into the lounge through three sets of automatic doors, and walked smack into the noise that had made her client's ears ring. After that silver tube of a hallway, with its ooze of mold and old men dozing on the benches, the mass of bodies crammed into the main room of the lounge made her stop for a moment. She was always surprised when she entered those places where throngs of people crammed into such a small space, as if, somehow, the planet had shrunk into one room. On this visit, she slammed into a knot of bathers heading toward the steam rooms. A few steps farther led her into the middle of another group bound for an intercity shuttle about to leave one of the eight loading platforms. A tour guide counted bodies while a cart, heavy with luggage, squeezed the group out of position for the next lift. The guide's job was not made any easier by people yelling at each other, or stepping out of line to talk with friends waiting for another outbound shuttle. Cassie elbowed her way through the group and into the main chamber of the lounge.

There, it was impossible to tell who was doing what to whom, or going where and how. On the viewscreen, a dot matrix printout flowed red with the usual schedule of arrivals and departures of various craft, while the intercom continuously corrected those announcements. The computerized voice intoned destinations in an asexual whine that garbled the messages every time. Travelers cringed as they tried to unscramble the noise. Tour guides hurried groups to loading ramps at either end of the room. Land cars waited at the docks. Cassie saw a few cars bearing the insignia of the same dispatch office she used, but this was her R-and-R time, so she plunged toward the escalator, and headed for an upper level. Looking back at the horde clamoring for space aboard transporters, she could understand the government's ban of private cars, and the restriction on the number of licensed vehicles used in any form of travel.

"But Francine, I can't understand why everybody has to be on the move all the time," she said. "It's like go-go-go before the cosmos catches up with us."

"It's a living." Fran laughed.

They were sitting in a juice bar on the upper level of the lounge.

For Cassie, the room's only saving grace was the comfort of its seats. Like most drivers, the molded curves of transporter seats had left her with lower back problems, and she welcomed a chair built for comfort rather than efficiency. But the room had its drawbacks also. On one side, it was bracketed by a nursery, with the squeals of young children sliding into a multicolored cloud of small plastic balls occasionally overriding the soundproof glass wall that separated the bar from the nursery. The wall allowed mothers to observe their children in the act of "safe swimming," as it was called. Cassie had yet to realize her dream of watching one of the little brats disappear forever into Ping-Pong heaven, or remain suspended against the ceiling of an adjacent room that had been designed to keep them weightless. When she grew tired of joyous toddlers, she could turn in the opposite direction and watch their older siblings tune out the world. In that room, sixty or so pubbies were slouched in transporter chairs, receivers in place as they subjected their fourteen- and fifteen-year-old brains to the concentrated stimuli of cathode lights. The room was pitch dark, except for a big screen above their heads, where the flicker of light rays changed as the pubbies thought-provoked low input beams into simulated attack patterns, their eyes riveted on this neon light show.

Cassie sighed. "And there it is, folks. Pubescent training for space wars. But at least it's quiet up here. Where's Willow?"

"In the W.C.." Fran nodded. "They've plugged a new delf tube into her gut. This one's mega-duty. It's got her in the W.C. every few hours."

Cassie grinned. "Hey, it spared me a lecture on being late."

"That is provided I keep *my* mouth shut," Fran said. "Look, go easy on Willow. She and Elise just had a fight. Willow's really having a rough time with this round of treatment."

"Yeah, she always is," Cassie muttered.

Then she swiveled her chair toward the view windows. The entire upper level of the lounge was designed to revolve on a 360-degree orbit. When Cassie turned to the window, the orbit was just moving past the sector where the new proton generators had been built. It was no coincidence that the generators had been erected on the clinic site of the old Clearwater Eco-balance Project. Tearing down the Project's clinic facilities and building a new power source on the site was the government's attempt to erase the Clearwater fiasco. But Willow was a product of that fiasco, and there was no way to erase Willow.

"I didn't mean that the way it sounded," Cassie said. She unwrapped her shawl and began loosening the multitude of zippers on her uniform jacket. "I just warp-out sometimes."

"You get warp-out? Nooo. . . . Don't tell me. Not my little sister," Willow said as her electric chair hummed into position at the end of the table.

Her raspy laughter drew the attention of several lounge patrons, and when Cassie stood up to greet her, those who had tried to follow decorum by not looking at Willow and her chair turned to stare at Cassie, who had discarded her uniform jacket and left her six-foot frame covered only by a second-skin undergarment of shiny latex. When Cassie leaned over to kiss her sister, her tall, muscular figure, so perfectly shaped she could have been sculpted out of the red-brown clay of Tuscany, made Willow's stick-thin body seem unmistakably pathetic. From the waist up, Willow was as wiry as her name indicated, and with the light sparkling against the pale green corneal implants, her eyes, in contrast to the darkness of her skin, seemed as bright as moon-fire. That look gave strength to her friends, and put her enemies on guard, but that look only held true from the waist up. From the waist down, she was dependent on the by-products of the very technological systems that set the fire in her eyes: her modular chair, the blood transfer units, the colonic apertures, and the hours of clinical treatments. After more than a decade of medical attention, Willow carried the scars of the Clearwater Eco-balance Project, and it did not take much to trigger her most recent treatise against genetic experimentation. Cassie always stepped lightly around the subject, but Willow did not make it easy for her.

"So . . . how's the taxi service? You ferry any late-great scientists we should know about?"

"A simple hello would suffice." Cassie laughed.

"I said hello," Fran offered.

Willow grunted. "You'd say hello to a penguin if it appeared."

"Only if he were pushing your chair, sweetie. I draw the line somewhere. Speaking of drawing the line, where're our drinks?"

"I canceled them," Willow said. Her expression was deadpan, and at first, Francine wasn't sure she hadn't done just that. Then Willow added, "I don't think this is a bar. I think they're running some kind of twenty-first-century beauty contest back there. All those pusses are

▼ 341 ▼

leaning into the comp panel like the light discs can measure their bustlines." She pointed a skinny finger toward the service cubicle as if she were about to zap a waitress. "Twelve years old and they can't punch in a drink order."

"They're sixteen, and probably it's not their fault," Cassie said. "Maybe the system's just down. Hang on to your remote, Willow. They'll be here."

"I knew more than all of them put together when I was sixteen."

Fran laughed. "When you were sixteen, you knew more than everybody, put together or not."

They all laughed. Cassie reached over and patted Fran's shoulder. "Get her, Fran. Don't worry about that chair. It can't be more than a hundred or so volts."

"Un-un, sister dear. Mega-volts." Willow giggled. "Mama made sure I got the best."

"That's our mama. Looking out for her own." Cassie had pulled off her boots, and was scratching the soles of her feet against the bottom rung of the table.

Willow caught the motion, and frowned. "Getting naked, are we? Putting on a little show for the people, princess?"

Cassie stuck out her tongue. "Doesn't that chair have an orbital pattern I can set for your skinny ass? Willow-in-space. Has a nice ring to it."

"*Drinks* . . . ," Fran announced, as they were interrupted by a waitress. They were quiet as the glasses were set in place and Willow counted out the correct number of tokens to pay the waitress.

Cassie took that opportunity to begin massaging her feet. The pressure of the rung against the insteps of her feet pulled all the tension from her body. She could imagine herself at home with Willow and Famein, their younger brother—the three of them waiting at the table for her mother to serve them tall thin glasses of her special drinks, usually made more palatable by the color than the taste. Cassie smiled to herself. It was so convenient to think of three of them, but actually, only she and Famein were related. Willow had been adopted at the age of sixteen. She had come to live with them after Cassie's mother had treated her for injuries sustained while working on the Clearwater Project—"hard labor in the laser fields," as Willow put it. But now it seemed Willow had always been with them, a snappy little voice whipping Cassie and Famein out of childhood and into the mine-fields of adulthood. "Well . . . puss-puss, look at the little pubbie," Willow had sneered when she'd met Cassie. They'd fought for the first six months, and later, that uneasy peace had ripened into friendship. Willow never gave an inch on her appraisal of Cassie's privileged life, and Cassie never allowed Willow to use her physical limitations as leverage in their battles. In some ways, this had bonded them closer than many blood relatives were bound to families.

But as Willow had said the day Cassie brought Francine home from school with her, "Sometimes you get sisters where you can find them."

The three women silently toasted each other, then savored the first swallow of their drinks. Willow had ordered Cassie's usual thick red drink, so deeply colored it made natural beets look pale by comparison but, as Cassie swore, was potent enough to hype her adrenaline and leave her road-ready. For herself, Willow had ordered an equally thick green, gooey mess full of protein supplements, while Francine had a frothy cream something laced with calcium and iron. When Willow questioned her concoction, Fran shrugged. "Who knows? Maybe Gil and I made a baby by mistake. This girl's got to be prepared."

"If I believed in something other than the Great-oneness, I'd say: Lord help us. You're not seriously considering adding another life to this dreadful misfortune we're in, are you? Look around you. Do we need any more?"

Obediently, Fran and Cassie looked. Obviously, the departure time for a few transporters had been called. The population in the room had shifted to afternoon arrivals. Their faces held the jumpy expressions of travelers trying to track their body clocks. A group of official types—"captains of industry," Willow liked to call them—were occupying one of the booths. They had plugged their equipment into the lounge's main computer terminals, and were readying themselves for an impromptu meeting. At another table, a woman was engrossed in cross-checking data, her fingers moving across a keyboard like black-birds pecking for bait in a small patch of ground. In the booth next to her, a pale man of uncertain ethnicity spoke directly into a micro-corder. He was so involved in this task, he did not notice the old man leaning over the edge of the booth, watching him. But Cassie recog-nized the man as the one who had spoken to her when she'd entered the building. Usually, the guards chased the bench warmers back to the corridors, but this one seemed to have evaded detection. It wasn't that he was harming anyone, but his obvious wealth of leisure time was likely to set people on edge. Cassie, aware of how little R-and-R time she was allowed, began to grow nervous watching him. Her mother had said: "Time is like the sea—always moving vast and restless." Cassie was forever at the restless end and on her way to somewhere. It was difficult for her to remember idle time, time to do nothing, time to play as the children were playing in the nursery, or space out like the pubbies in the video room.

"I don't know if I can imagine myself being a mother," Fran said. "But it could happen with me and Gil, you know."

"Oh, not the *L* word! Not *love!*" Willow sneered. "What fantasy!"

"OK," Fran said. "I'm having an out-of-body experience. OK with you, Willow? Make you feel better?"

"Speaking of fantasy, how's Elise?" Cassie asked.

Willow laughed. "She's fine. And don't get me wrong. I'm not condemning fantasy. Each of us must have fantasies. Even I . . . " Fran rolled her eyes and hooted. "Go ahead," Willow continued. "Laugh. But you know I speak the truth. I'm talking about the difference between instinctive and learned acts. By allowing your fantasies full rein, you do what you've learned. With that man . . . " She fiddled with the buttons on her modular panel as if she were going to push back from the table, then she added, "Well, you act it out, that's all."

Fran held up her glass and saluted. "Sex, the final frontier!"

But Cassie wiped red foam from her mouth and said, "Hush Fran. You too, Willow. Remember: We're not all anti-anti-male."

Willow rolled her eyes. "Really? Aren't we all bedeviled by the same moon, a luminescent force drawing us to our deaths? We are all half-wives, clocked and checked by the same cursed cycle of events, and male or female, we are strapped by the tides of this moon."

"I told you," Fran whispered. "She's been fighting with Elise."

Willow ignored her, and gestured toward the viewing windows. "A poem: Behold the moon on a summer's night. It swaddles us in afterbirth, and dancing in its eerie light, we scream and feed the fire. We. . . "

"Too much medication," Francine added.

"So . . . How's the research coming?" Cassie interrupted.

Willow grinned. "Not bad. I've got a couple of Woebe's on the run. Got their white butts trembling. With luck, I'll get this shit licked before I die."

"You're not going to die." Fran laughed. "You're too evil."

Willow pretended to growl. "So Fran, how's the hubby?"

Fran arched one eyebrow. "You're asking about Gil?"

"Yeah. . . . And I didn't choke on it either," she added when she saw Cassie and Fran exchange looks. "Hey, I didn't marry the man-child. Although it is beyond me why you would want to marry someone who is playing around in the same sandbox your father played in. Job-wise, that is. Weather! What could be more Pavolian? I guess that comes from having your plumbing hang outside. That's the problem with men. Makes them worry about performance. Gil has a one-track mind. Every night, he lays you across that track and screws you silly."

"As long as I'm the only woman on that track," Fran said, "just pull in your probe, Miz Talking Head. And my father was a damn good weatherman. He spotted the Clearwater effect before anyone else."

Cassie shook her head. "Willow, you amaze me. You can go from moon cycles to weather to Gil and sex without dropping one megabyte."

Willow grunted. "Speaking of sex, dear sister, you getting any? Who's beating down your door? Are you still turning them away because they're not quite right? You know what's wrong with that business you spout about people-of-color . . . ," Willow began.

"Oops, here comes another jump." Cassie laughed.

"And it calls for another drink," Fran said, and signaled the order.

"For your information, it's all connected," Willow told them. "The idea of cosmic order is pre-Babylonian, even discounting the unification of world science, it's still a matter of chance. Weather is a matter of chance, but Gil is still caught up in stimulus-response. Positively medieval. Think of how simple our lives would be if we depended on such preliterate ideas as: Thunder makes it rain, or trees make the wind blow? A one-track mind thinking somebody is going to make something happen to you. That's why the world wasn't ready to cope with 'people-of-color' when this century turned up. Take it into account, Cassie. Look at all the books written back when about how things were going to be now. We'd invent this and this would happen. We'd invent that and that would happen. The future would be pristine and white like Orwell's world. Something was supposed to happen to all people-of-color by the last day of 1999. Otherwise, would I be in this chair?" She held up her hands to salute with a "Voilà," and almost upset the incoming tray of drinks.

Cassie waited until the new drinks were set in place, then pointed to the window. "Fran, does anything look different to you out there?"

Fran shook her head. "Un-un. Looks like the same old burnt-off piece of ground to me. Little patches of stubbly trees trying to take hold. The ocean. A couple of proton generators setting out there on the mudflats. A new road between here and Clearwater, but otherwise, half the town here and half the town gone. Looks the same to me."

"I thought so, but damn if it didn't seem like we'd hit a Möbius somewhere between Babylon and 1999. I've got to stop looking out of a window when Willow flags that chair into high gear."

Willow smiled. "The window is always there, Cassie, my sweet. It is solid glass, albeit composed of tiny molecules in constant motion giving us the illusion of solid matter."

Cassie reached over and pinched her. As she yelped, Cassie laughed. "She's right. All that illusion shit is solid matter."

"Why do I put up with you?" Willow groaned.

"Cause we're all you've got." Cassie winked. "So, you and Gil are going to try for a baby, huh?" she asked Fran.

Fran nearly choked on her drink. "Whoa . . . Slow down. Who's talking baby? I said: maybe. Maybe! Get it? I know it sounds the same but keep your hands in your lap. This girl isn't leaning into anybody's nursery yet."

"One of us has to, and you're the only one married."

Willow cleared her throat. "Excuse me. Have we overlooked an important clue here? I was out of that race from day one, and that was before I ever knew about lesbian births. Now thanks to the government's sweet little experiments, even that alternative doesn't matter. So what is this one-of-us crap? From where I'm sitting, strapped in I might add, looks like it's up to you two."

Fran leaned forward. "You know, I had this dream. In the dream, Gil and I did have a baby, but we also had this big dog. Kind of like an old man of a dog. . . . Wait, before you jump on me, Willow, it could have been an old woman of a dog, OK? I don't know how to describe it. But what happened was we left the baby and the dog in the room, and when we came back, we couldn't find the baby. The dog was sitting there grinning at us. Then I noticed the dog was sitting on top of the baby. The baby was perfectly naked. . . . Yeah! Perfect. Except it had this blue belt tied around it. And the dog was all furry and covering up the baby so the thing couldn't breathe. When I yelled at the dog, it moved back and looked down at the baby as if it didn't know it had been sitting on top of it. What do you think?"

Cassie looked at the metallic sensory band circling Willow's chair, and shrugged. "I don't know. What do you think, Willow?"

Willow grinned, "Beats me."

"You two are full of it," Fran said, and went back to her drink.

"Now there you go with two again," Willow protested. "I told you to count me out. We just need to get this one paired up." She nodded toward Cassie. "Look, I've got this new thing the lab developed. . . "

Both Fran and Cassie groaned.

"No, no. It's great," Willow said. She pulled her microcorder from its pocket, and hooked it up to something that looked like an oblong box with a panel opening at the top. When she peeled back the panel, a sticky residue, like soft Velcro, clung to both sides. Willow smiled. "Cassie, this will give you a perfect match of genetic type. I just need a specimen."

Cassie frowned. "Excuse me? I beg your pardon?"

"That does it." Fran laughed. "She's gone totally nova. She wants you to pee in the panel."

Willow said, "I can do without the derision, Francine. This is a simple scientific experiment. Cassie, give me some skin. Just let me scratch a little dermal tissue. The panel runs a bio compute for your mate. Totally scientific."

"Oh, like the scratch-and-sniff litmus for allergies," Fran said.

"More like a litmus for black-enough," Cassie snapped. "You can nuke that box, Miz Matchmaker. It's chance meeting or nothing. Like weather. Get it?" She began pulling on her boots.

She had one leg in the air, the boot halfway up her calf, when she felt a slight movement on the seat next to her. A sharp nudge at her elbow tipped her drink, causing some of the ruby red liquid to splatter. Fran and Willow both gave startled intakes of breath as Cassie grabbed the glass before it fell. Then Cassie turned. The old man was about three inches away from her.

"Hi," he said. His face was small, heavily wrinkled around the corners of his eyes and mouth. His mustache was wispy and frail, a pencil line of hair under his nose, but most of the creases around his mouth were hidden by the stubbles of a gray beard. Even without his wrinkled skin, just the presence of facial hair marked him as a throwback to another generation. His eyes, once brown and now rummy gray with cataracts, attested to the fact that he had not attempted corneal implants, and confirmed the generational difference.

"What-cha-want?" he asked.

Cassie sighed. "Nothing." She swirled her drink, mixing the foam with the liquid.

"I said: Wha-cha-want?" he repeated. When he signaled the waitress, Cassie could see his knuckles were oversized and as gnarled as tree bark. "See those men over there?" he asked. "They my friends." He squinted at the corporate types sitting at the window booths. When the old man waved at them, they did not wave back. "Yeah, they my friends," he added. "Years ago, I could relate to them, but now they cut me off. Think they too busy for an old man. Hey—Bert, Bertie!" The businessmen whispered to each other, but never acknowledged the old man's greeting.

"Maybe I can get a sample from our friend here." Willow laughed.

Cassie glared at her. "Don't you dare."

"I get you anything you want," the old man said. "Just ask. I get it."

Willow put her gadget on the table. "Let me try it, Cassie. It won't hurt."

"Put that away," Fran snapped. When she grabbed the box, she inadvertently touched the test panel. It was only a slight touch, but she drew back her hand as if she had been stung. "That hurts. Like getting stuck on a cactus."

But apparently, the contact carried directly to Willow's microcorder. As the input signal beeped, she said, "It's a take," and watched the computations appear on the screen.

"That one of them fancy phones?" the old man asked.

Willow halted the printout, and showed him the instrument. The old man touched it, then jerked his hand the way Francine had.

He was sucking the pain from his finger when Cassie asked him, "Don't you have something to do?"

"I do whatever you do," the man said. "Where you going? You over up there?"

He gestured toward the window. The sky had gone from a stone gray flatness to clouds as hopeful as pillows. Cassie did not know if the old man meant over, as in the booth with the businessmen, or up, as in the sky where the exhaust trail of a transporter was still visible. "Look. See that little tail? They waving from the sky. They got life on Mars?" the old man asked. "You been on Mars? Why they go up there if they got no people? All the ships always going and coming everywhichway. Like Johnny-jump-up-here-I-go. Like somebody throwed them up in the air. Green lights flashing. Like all the stars gone wild. I got to ask: You think Johnny-jump-up throwed down stardust so we know he still there?" The old man gave a squishy giggle—part air, part spit. "Say: twinkle twinkle winkle star . . . ," he sang.

Fran and Willow started laughing, but Cassie shoved her way to the end of the seat. "I've got to go," she snapped, and began pulling on her jacket.

Willow checked her computations. "Not a bad match," she said. "However, Fran's chart skews a bit more than the one on our friend here. Your turn, Cassie."

"Forget it," she muttered.

"The sky and stars, they too far away," the old man said. "They been swallowed. The sky is a great big church whirling right off in space. You seen it?" he asked Cassie.

Cassie stopped midzipper. "Look. Why are you picking on me?"

He was going to answer, but the waitress arrived with his order, a watery drink, pale colored like the skin of an oyster. A tube of lemon extract was on the plate beside it. Cassie curled her lip at the sight of the glass. Fran said, "Yum-yum," then winked at Willow.

The old man pulled a pile of payment tokens from his pocket. "Count 'em," he said to the waitress, "but don't cheat me."

The waitress looked at Cassie and Cassie turned away. "Count 'em, and take what you need," he added, then took a loud slurp of the drink. The waitress picked up some tokens and shuffied away, shaking her head.

Cassie was remembering her route schedule when she felt another sharp nudge. Sighing slightly, she turned to face the old man again.

"You married?" he asked.

"Right question," Willow said. "This is working out better than I'd imagined."

"You'll pay for this," Cassie told her.

"You married?" the old man repeated. "You cute. I like to talk to women."

That was obvious, but Cassie said nothing. She reached for her drink. It was weaker now, more foamy. Just as the glass reached her mouth, he nudged her again. Cassie sighed more deeply this time. "You two could help me," she told Fran and Willow. They merely grinned.

"You sure you don't want anything?" the man asked.

"No," she said.

He was persistent. "You got kids?"

"Whamo! He's sure full of the right questions." Willow laughed.

"What is this?" Cassie snapped. "A get-Cassie virus infecting everybody? If I wanted to be married, I'd plant myself in some commune and pretend I couldn't breathe without help. Maybe I could find me somebody like Gil."

"Whoa. . . . Do I look like that's what I did?" Fran protested. "Do I look like I'm helpless? You better check your data banks, sweetie."

Willow waved away her protests. "We're not talking about you, Francine. We talking about Cassie. Now you say you're straight, Cassie, but you keep letting these men get away from you, girl. Check the ratio. Three in the last five years. And you let that woman from Ocean Six take the last one. Come on . . . give me a dermal specimen."

Cassie shook her head. "I just have to go on losing them, Willow. Sometimes all you can do is fatten the frog so the snake can have a nicer meal."

"I get you something to eat," the old man said.

The three of them turned, startled to find him still sitting there. As Fran and Willow finished their drinks, Cassie deliberately thought of the exact route she'd take to get to her next client. She was halfway there when she noticed the old man duck his head beneath the shadow of his arm. Quickly, he removed his teeth and put them in a napkin. She hid her quick smile behind the sleeve of her jacket as she hooked the side zipper to her waistband. He nudged her again.

"Squeeze my lemon." He grinned.

Cassie looked at him. He smiled and wrinkled his nose. Even his eyes held laughter. Cassie had no idea of how to tell an old man she didn't want to squeeze his lemon, so she shrugged and picked up the citrus tube. Carefully, she let the juice dribble into his drink. "There," she said.

Fran and Willow applauded. The old man looked pleased. "I asked if you had kids."

Cassie finished her ruby red in one long, determined sip. "And I told you: *No!*" she shouted. Her obvious anger startled Fran and Willow.

"You don't have to get so smart," the old man said. He eyed her as he gummed the end of the citrus tube.

With his head cocked to one side, he reminded Cassie of her own father—just a little tired but still working with a sense of humor. That humor walked a thin line between hurt and anger. Over the years, she'd watched her mother channel anger into her work. Finding an outlet had been more difficult for her father, especially after he'd been injured in the riots that followed the war. These days, he could not talk about the difference between whites and blacks without making a wry joke. These days, he was liable to keep some insignificant injury hidden for weeks until even he had trouble pinpointing the cause. At those times, her father could almost convince her that the world had grown past its old battles with race. Almost. "Open your eyes," her mother would say. "That stuff didn't die just because it's a new century, a new day. We're still dealing with the same old wrecks called humans." As the old man's gnarled hands reached for his wallet, Cassie remembered she had not called home in over a month.

He held out his wallet. "I got kids, you know. I was alright when I was young. You want to see my kids?"

Fran said, "Yes," and Willow added, "Sure. I'd love to."

It took him a while to get to the pictures. They were sealed in plastic like old-fashioned ID cards, the plastic scratched and slightly yellowed. Those worn pieces of paper were his identity, his family. He squinted at each of them before putting them on the table. His face was close to Cassie's, but she didn't turn away from the sour smell of lemon on his breath.

"This is my youngest, Benjamin," he said. "I call him Ben, but when he turned eighteen, he said call him Benjamin. He's in the military. Up there in the sky, they tell me." The face of a young boy, five or six years old, smiled at them from the yellowed print.

"That's Eddie. He's a devil. Smart as a whip," the old man said.

They nodded at Eddie's picture.

"And this is my girl." As his grin spread, he didn't try to hide his bare gums. "She's ready to go into high school in this here picture. She was so smart, they put her to work on the Projects."

Cassie handed Willow the picture of an eighth-grade girl. Willow shook her head. That face could have belonged to any one of the thousands who worked the Clearwater. Cassie cross-checked the district pin, the gold locket hanging around her neck, the chipped front tooth and pressed hair done up in pigtails. Maybe she'd seen other pictures like this among the ones her mother had studied at the clinic. She wondered what her mother would say, how she'd react to her only daughter, the girl who'd left home vowing never to return, but was now sitting in a dingy terminal lounge looking dreamy eyed at a faded picture held by an old toothless man. Then laughing at the kind of joke her father might have made, she wondered what her mother would have to say about her daughter squeezing an old man's lemon in public.

"I can't stay here forever standing between you and daddy," she had screamed at her mother. "I can't stay here proving you saved kids like Willow for a reason. There's more to me than that. I'm not just the good side of whatever went wrong with Willow. You can't keep trying to make me into something I'm not."

"Whatever you are is right here," her mother had said.

The old man interrupted her thoughts. "They cute, huh?"

"Just look at their father." Willow grinned. "They had a good start. See, this is what I mean about hanging in there."

"Quite a family," Fran added.

Cassie smiled, "I've got to go now," she said and checked her watch.

"What time it is?" the old man asked.

Cassie told him, but she was thinking of the client she'd picked up at the launch site, the one with tender ears and heart. "Time stands still out there," Cassie's client had complained. "It's quiet and it doesn't move. Dawn is no more than dusk. Days are the same without weather. Down here, we put tags on life—a golden age, the faded past, the dark ages, a velvet night, a bright future, light years, pretty soon. Time in assorted colors. But up there, it's all the same. Never changes. We still try to make time, try to jam 4000 years into a matter of hours. The sky is littered with our wrecks."

She double-wrapped the Tuareg shawl around her jacket and stood up. "See you later, Fran. You too, Willow," She leaned over and kissed her sister. "Tell the folks I'll call them real soon. And give my love to Elise."

Willow patted her hand. "Come by and see us. Elise doesn't bite. I've trained her."

"Come back and see me again," the old man said. "I get lonesome sometimes. Even with all these fine ladies around here." He smiled at Fran and Willow.

"Yeah," Willow added. "And bring some dermal slides. I'll have this scanner set for a perfect match next time I see you."

Cassie waved and kept walking.

"Don't take but a little time," the old man called out.

"Yeah, I know," Cassie said.

"And say hello to that guy from Ocean Six if you see him." Fran giggled. The others giggled along with her.

Cassie answered without breaking her stride. "Say hello yourself. I'm not speaking to that space-jockey."

Their laughter trickled out the door and followed her into her vehicle, where it settled into the seat beside her. Or was it their laughter she saw trailing a red streak across the horizon where the sun was racing toward Japan, New Guinea, Australia ... ending another day there as it promised the beginning of a new one here?

At Least Once a Week

RUTH FORMAN

dedicated to Smell This

sisters
light one stick of jasmine incense
and seven mulberry candles
in the bathroom
with the lights out

sing
magenta to yourself
as you step into the bathtub
create new verses
to scrub the pain out of your hair

soak in your letters
just ten more minutes
til your exhausted fingers
wrinkle

then
completely cleansed
step out
dry yourself off
to withstand the cold air

don't
wash the tub
let the magic linger
into a ring
of unified voices

blow out the candles
the incense glows
and smell
in the darkness
our power

Uterus Root

MICHELLE T. CLINTON

"this class i took in santa cruz
in women's studies
was my first real woman identified experience
my first long straight look
at the big & wonderful & historically relevant
vagina, the pussy, the mother cunt
& how every body comes through the womb
& how the white boy existentialists
a dying breed say:
you are born alone
& we know better
we know your momma was right there
right from between her legs
your first home
the sound of your first heart beat
set your ass up for the drum
& dancing & fucking & everything that is a natural rhythm

it was the feminists first
hipped me to the root
the uterus root
see boys make their seed
they just mix it up on a regular basis
on a day to day basis
on a minute to minute basis
& discharge it
their bodies expel those seeds
into the indifferent night
nocturnal ejaculation
when they can't find nothing
to catch that nut

for them straight girls
& they boyfriends
honey, he's probably fixing some up
right now, something hot & sweet
he want to let loose in you
someplace, tonight

but girls, see
we was born w/ every egg we'll ever have
we made every one while we was growing
inside the womb of the mother
so my momma made the first molecule of me
inside the belly of the grandmother
& the grandmother held the first
biochemical trace of my ass
& pass me inside the belly of my mother
& my mother walked around close to twenty years
w/ me inside her ovaries
& she guarded me against venereal disease
& technology
& i set up inside her
w/ all the other eggs
floating in the blood of her emotion
& the father came along & touched her
& i commenced to grow"

masks, trumpets, gris gris and us

jonetta rose barras

what of women like us
undefinable
women taught to
love men feverishly
be August humidity and
fried fish smell on them
taught to be
Bourbon Street
Saint Charles elegant
Desire Project
broken bottle
sharp, dangerous?
what of women like us
haunting
lullaby, hurricane
tornado
women
taught to wear chapel veils
to play Bach with our eyes
secondline with our hips
to carry razors, bibles
bouquets of thorny roses
to sweeten the air with
desire, death or
us women
dancing
laveau dancing women
taught to play
blackjack, roll die
shoot pool bet on
us women

taught to ride
the Mississippi's crest
kiss the sun and name
our unborn children
after undiscovered planets?
what of women like us
who are strange enough
to be desired but
too untamed
to ever be possessed?

Legacy/Repeat After Me

AKASHA (GLORIA T.) HULL

My great-grandmother
compacted all her grief
until it festered as a life sore
in her side
She huddled it close
changed her pus-stained rags
in secret
Nobody in the family
knew about her shame
until they smelled the cancer
which ate her breath away

My grandmother
never found her proper nourishment
They said she ate "too much cornmeal"
Pellagra, we call it today—
a deficiency disease
which killed my grandmother
little, quick woman
who never stopped moving
until she died

My mother lives out
their lives of lack and limitation
old pains, old wounds, old angers,
resentment, grief, fear, and shame
Her milk soured in the mouth
of my baby brother
Thirty-eight years later
they cut the whole breast off
Lack of self-love, love—criticism

hardening her joints
she still holds on
holds on

All this they willed to me
this freighted legacy
I want
to cast away

I say—to myself—
repeat after me:

Throw out those old clothes
    (Let the latest and hottest fashions
    take their place)

Give the leftover spoonsful to the dog
    (God will set a fresh dish
    on the table)

Do not hoard pieces of string, clean rags,
or colored ribbons
    (Say: What I need will be at hand
    when I need it)

Give up extreme gratefulness for pennies
    (so that thanks for thousands
    can be made)

Give away love
    (then love, and then more love
    will fill the place)

Let go fear
    (Come power
    and possibility)

Expel anger
  (Welcome joy)

Let go of children
  (who will then embrace you happily
  at every turn)

Release pain and dis-ease,
  (Spirit pushes
  the healing through)

And now
I say:
repeat after me
▾

21st century black warrior wimmins chant for strengthening the nerves & getting yourself together

hattie gossett

for edwina, donna, joan, debbie, roberta

sisters   mothers   cousins   girlfriends
aunties   lovers   grandmothers   daughters

we honor yo bad wimmins selves

we pour libation to you

sisters   mothers   cousins   girlfriends
aunties   lovers   grandmothers   daughters

you who sing the original break(out) songs: steal away/steal away/steal away/cuz we aint got long to stay here

you who wont bow down to no father or husband or lover or boss or government

you who are the womanlover or the manlover

you who waylay rapists and child abusers and absentee landlords in alleyways and on rooftops

you who resist the dopedealer and outslick the pimp

you who keep mr executives hands in their place

you who plan and carry out the work slowdown and the strike

you who outmaneuver the overseer in the fields under the hot sun or
    in the factory on the airconditioned assemblyline

you who break up all madames fine china and sprinkle rust on her
    imported linens

you who mix dried blood and powdered glass into mastas quiche&salad

you who raise children to love themselves and create solutions

you who dream and plan and work with us for the future

                with

                yo

                bad

                wimmins

                selves

                        we honor you

                with yo bad wimmins selves

                        we pour libation to you

                with yo bad wimmins selves

                        we wear your colors

                with yo bad wimmins selves

                        we eat your foods

with yo bad wimmins selves

we dance your dances

with yo bad wimmins selves

cuz you give us something

with yo bad wimmins selves

that is carrying us through this world

with yo bad wimmins selves

we honor you

with yo bad wimmins selves

we call on you

with yo bad wimmins selves

witness us in our battles

with yo bad wimmins selves

witness us in our battles

with yo bad wimmins selves

witness us in our battles

with yo bad wimmins selves

with

yo

bad

wimmins

selves

Biographies

Opal Palmer Adisa, Jamaica born, is a writer and storyteller. Her latest book is *Tamarind and Mango Woman* (SisterVision Press, 1992), which won the PEN Oakland/Josephine Miles Award. She is an associate professor at California College of Arts and Crafts.

Ai is the author of *Cruelty* (Houghton Mifflin, 1973), *Killing Floor* (Houghton Mifflin, 1978), *Sin* (Houghton Mifflin, 1986), and *Fate* (Houghton Mifflin, 1991). Her latest book is *Greed* (W. W. Norton, 1993). She lives in Arizona.

Maya Angelou is the author of several autobiographical works and collections of poetry. Her latest book is *Wouldn't Take Nothing for My Journey Now* (Random House, 1993). She is Z. Smith Reynolds Professor at Wake Forest University.

Viki Akiwumi is a poet at work on her M.F.A. in creative writing at Brooklyn College.

Brenda Bankhead is a Black woman writer born and raised in Los Angeles. Her work has appeared in *Obsidian II, Black Literature in Review,* and the anthologies *The World Between Women* (Herbooks), *The Time of Our Lives, Women Write on Sex* (Crossing Press), and *Love's Shadow* (Crossing Press). She has work in *Catholic Girls and Boys,* to be published by Penguin in fall 1994.

jonetta rose barras is a native of New Orleans, and the mother of Umoja Shanu and Afrika Midnight. She has been published in *The Black Scholar, Callaloo, Main Trend, Race Today, Obsidian,* and the anthology *The Poet and the Poem.* A journalist by trade, she currently is a reporter for the *Washington Times* newspaper in Washington, DC.

Lucille Clifton's latest book of poetry is *The Book of Light* (Copper Canyon Press, 1993).

Michelle T. Clinton, recipient of an NEA fellowship and an American Book Award, writes, teaches, and struggles for her health in Los Angeles. Her most recent volume of poetry, *Good Sense & the Faithless,* is published by West End Press, and her spoken word recording *Blood as a Bright Color* is on Alliance Records. She has a black belt in Okinawan karate.

Wanda Coleman is a poet and short story writer as well as a recording artist. She cohosts "The Poetry Connection" for Southern California's Pacifica radio. Her latest book of poetry is *Hand Dance* (Black Sparrow Press, 1993).

J. California Cooper's latest collection of short stories is *The Matter Is Life* (Doubleday, 1991).

Gabrielle Daniels was born in New Orleans in 1954 and since the age of seven has lived in California. Her grandmother the late Rev. Ruth Matthews Taylor was a Spiritualist minister. Gabrielle spent 1993 working on her novel in progress at the Headlands Center for the Arts in Sausalito, California.

Bridgett M. Davis is an assistant professor at Baruch College (CUNY) in Manhattan, where she teaches journalism and literature. She is a contributor to *The Black Women's Health Book* and is currently at work on her first novel, *Nights Without Color*.

Toi Derricotte's latest collection of poems is *Captivity*. She received the Distinguished Pioneering of the Arts Award, United Black Artists, in May 1993. She teaches poetry at the University of Pittsburgh.

Kim Jenice Dillon was born and raised in Seoul, Korea, and at age five moved to the United States. She earned an M.A. in creative writing from San Diego State University and is currently pursuing a Ph.D. in literature from the University of California, San Diego.

Rita Dove has published a collection of stories and five books of poetry, among them *Thomas and Beulah*, which was awarded the Pulitzer Prize in 1987, and *Selected Poems*, published in 1993. In 1993, she was named poet laureate of the United States.

Kelly Norman Ellis is an instructor of English at Kentucky State University and a doctoral candidate at the University of Kentucky. She is a founding member of Affrilachian Poets, a writing ensemble with roots in Kentucky and the rural South. She is a Jackson, Mississippi, native.

Fatisha is a poet-astrologer now residing in Seattle patiently waiting to win the lottery. Her chapbooks include *Sapphire Longing in the Blue Dust* and *Love Tongue & Mother Wit*. Her son, Tabala, is also a poet.

Folisade is a fifty-something African-American poet and writer who finds writing more soul satisfying than teaching English ever was. She recently completed her first novel and is working on a book of metaphysical principles for women.

Ruth Forman's first book of poetry, *We Are the Young Magicians* (Beacon Press, 1993), won the 1992 Barnard New Women Poets Prize.

Marilyn Fullen-Collins strives to bring the uniqueness of the African-American experience to her work. Her first book was *Pathblazers, Eight People Who Have Made a Difference* (Open Hand Publishing, 1992). Her short stories have appeared in *Morena: A Journal for Women of Color, Seattle Arts Review,* and *Earth's Daughters*. She is an educator on multicultural issues and works as a case manager with the Homelessness Project, endeavoring to empower homeless women and their children.

Marita Golden edited the best-selling collection *Wild Women Don't Wear No Blues: Black Women on Love, Men and Sex* (Doubleday, 1993). Her latest novel is *and do remember me* (Doubleday, 1992).

Jewelle Gomez is the author of two collections of poetry and a novel, *The Gilda Stories* (Firebrand Books).

hattie gossett's work has appeared in numerous anthologies. Her latest book is *presenting . . . Sister No Blues* (Firebrand Books, 1988).

Dorothy Randall Gray is a writer, performance artist, and jewelry designer. She founded the Heartland Transformational Institute and developed a creative writing method based on over twenty years of study in African, Christian, Eastern, and Native American spirituality. Her collections include *Muse Blues, The Passion Collection,* and *A Taste of Tamarindo.*

Joy Gray has been trying to capture the world in words for nearly as long as she has been able to speak. After working as a print journalist for years, she has turned to writing fiction, which she believes is "the sweetest obsession."

Doris L. Harris received the 1993 Astrea Foundation Award. She has also received the Nikki Giovanni Poetry Award. Born in Pittsburgh, she now lives in Seattle. She is the author of the chapbook *Refreshments.*

Jo Ann Henderson is a sexuality educator who makes her home in Seattle with her two children and husband of twenty-three years. A graduate of the University of Washington in speech communication, she often speaks and writes on African-American and female sexual issues. *The Late Mrs. Hadlay* is her first published work in a series of short stories she has written.

bell hooks's latest books include *A Woman's Mourning Song* (Harlem River Press, 1993) and *Sisters of the Yam: Black Women and Self-recovery* (South End Press, 1993).

Akua Lezli Hope is a 1993 winner of the U.S.–Africa Fellowship at Ragdale and a 1990 winner of a National Endowment for the Arts fellowship. Her manuscript "Fuel for Beginners" was a finalist in the 1990 Barnard New Women Poets Series.

Akasha (Gloria T.) Hull's first collection of poetry, *Healing Heart,* was published by Kitchen Table: Women of Color Press. She is director of the Women's Program at the University of California, Santa Cruz.

gale jackson is a poet, writer, storyteller, librarian, student of history, and worker in cultural education. Her work has appeared in numerous journals, including *IKON, Callaloo, Ploughshares,* and *The Kenyon Review.* Her publications include a collaborative anthology with two other women poets, Kimiko Hahn and Susan Sherman, entitled *We Stand Our Ground* (*IKON,* 1988) and a forthcoming folktale adaptation, *Rattlesnake's Tale.* She is currently working on two collections, *the precision of the embrace* and *Seduction.*

A. Yemisi Jimoh is a mother, wife, writer, and teacher living in Houston. She has published articles in the *Birmingham Times* and the *Western Journal of Black Studies.* She teaches at the University of Houston.

Imani Constance Johnson-Burnett is the founder of Sisters in Divine Order, a spiritual self-help collective for women, and their Word of Mouth Band (WOMB). Born in Philadelphia and schooled at Howard University and the University of Massachusetts, Amherst, she currently chooses to live in Los Angeles with her daughter, Janinah. Imani also directs a foundation fellowship program for community leaders, attends First A.M.E. Church, and published her own collection of short stories and poems entitled *Soul Kiss* in 1993.

Patricia Spears Jones is an award-winning poet. She grew up in Arkansas and now lives in New York City. Her poetry and arts reviews have appeared in *The Kenyon Review, The American Voice, The Village Voice, Essence,* and anthologies such as *Ordinary Women* and *Homegirls.* She recently completed a Mabou Mines Commission for a new theater work loosely based on Gorky's novel *Mother.* She received a 1994 NEA grant for poetry.

Colleen McElroy is a professor of English and creative writing at the University of Washington, Seattle. She has published a textbook on speech and language development, six books of poetry, and two collections of short stories, *Jesus and Fat Tuesday* (Creative Arts Book Company, 1987) and *Driving Under the Cardboard Pines* (Creative Arts Book Company, 1990).

Terry McMillan is the author of the best-sellers *Waiting to Exhale* (Penguin, 1992), *Disappearing Acts* (Penguin, 1989), and *Mama* (Houghton Mifflin, 1987), as well as the anthology *Breaking Ice* (Penguin, 1990).

Tamara Madison-Shaw is a performance artist, poet, and fiction writer. Her work has appeared in *Raven Chronicles, Pleiades, Portland Review, The Black American Literature Forum,* and *Literati Chicago.* She is the author of *Sistuh's Sermon on the Mount* (Open Hand Publishing, 1993).

Paule Marshall's latest novel is *Daughters* (Atheneum, 1991).

Laini Mataka lives in Washington, DC. She is the author of *Restoring the Queen* (Black Classics Press, 1994).

Thylias Moss's latest work includes the poetry book *Rainbow Remnants in Rock Bottom Ghetto Sky* (Persea Books, 1991) and the children's book *I Want to Be* (Dial Books for Young Readers, 1993).

Gloria Naylor's latest work of fiction is *Bailey's Cafe* (Harcourt Brace Jovanovich, 1992).

Deb Parks-Satterfield is an actress, playwright, and comic monologist. She is also a founding member of the African-American, lesbian comedy group 4 BIG GIRLS. She lives in Seattle with Risa, her partner of eleven years, and Zanny, the 2000-year-old cat.

Viki Radden was born in Germany and has lived in New Zealand and Japan. She is the recipient of a Hawthornden International Fellowship for Writers.

Evelyn Joyce Reingold, the eldest of five sisters, was transferred from the San Francisco Bay Area to Washington State in 1977 and has lived in Seattle since 1980. She has traveled extensively through Africa, the Caribbean, Asia, Europe, Israel, Mexico, and the United States.

Mattie Richardson is an African-American and Caribbean, lesbian, feminist writer, and activist. She currently lives in Albany, New York, where she is the Associate Publisher of Kitchen Table: Women of Color Press.

Sonia Sanchez is a poet, mother, activist, and professor. She is the author of thirteen books, the latest of which is *Under a Soprano Sky*. She teaches at Temple University.

Sapphire's work has appeared in *Women on Women, High Risk 2, Critical Condition: Women on the Edge of Violence, Queer City: The Portable Lower East Side*, and *War After War*. Her latest book of poetry is *American Dreams* (High Risk Books/Serpent's Tail). She lives in New York City.

Kesho Scott teaches American studies and sociology at Grinnell College in Iowa. She is a coauthor of *Tight Spaces* (Aunt Lute Books) and the author of *The Habit of Surviving: Black Women's Strategies for Life*.

Tiye Milan Selah is a native of Deptford, New Jersey, and currently resides in Seattle. Her early interest in writing was cultivated through parental support and extended family roots in the A.M.E. Church, her first audiences for creative expression. She is interested in story-telling about life themes including ethnic family medicine and folklore, autochthonous history, spirituality, and music.

ntozake shange is the author of the highly acclaimed choreopoem *For Colored Girls Who Have Considered Suicide When the Rainbow Is Enuf*, as well as *The Love Space Demands, Ridin' the Moon in Texas, Three Pieces, Nappy Edges, Sassafrass, Cypress & Indigo, A Daughter's Geography*, and *Betsey Brown*.

Saundra Sharp is a writer, filmmaker, and actress. She is the author of *Black Women for Beginners* (Writers and Readers Press, 1993) and four volumes of poetry. She is producing a health video for women and volunteers with a homeless support agency, Chrysalis Center, and the ecology group Tree People, in Los Angeles.

Charlotte Watson Sherman is the author of the short story collection *Killing Color* (Calyx Books, 1992) and the novel *One Dark Body* (HarperCollins, 1993).

Alice Walker co-wrote her latest book, *Warrior Marks* (Harcourt Brace, 1993), with Pratibha Parmar.

Lillien Waller is currently working on her M.F.A. in poetry at Sarah Lawrence College.

Mary Walls is a health educator living in Seattle. She works with GIRLS, Inc., of Puget Sound, directing special projects to meet the needs of girls and young women.

Jackie Warren-Moore is a poet-playwright–newspaper columnist. She lives in Syracuse, New York, with her husband, four daughters, and grandson. She believes in the power of the word.

Sherley Anne Williams's works include the widely acclaimed novel *Dessa Rose* (William Morrow) and the award-winning children's story *Working Cotton* (Harcourt Brace). She lives in California.

karsonya e. wise is a twenty-five-year-old afrikan-amerikan wummon poet currently completing her graduate work at the american university. she recently completed her first chapbook, *red zinger love/starved blues: notes of a wummon/child.* she is editing her second documentary *. . . through the eyes of the beholder,* and is in preproduction for the shooting of her first independent feature film *sapphire blakness.*

Permissions

Index